BIOFIRE

BY RAY GARTON

McNolte felt sweat trickle from his armpit down his side beneath his shirt, and his hands were beginning to feel tremulous, partly out of fear, and partly because it had been about an hour since he'd had a hit.

"Like I said, Mr. Trafficante, I'm not buying this for me. It's as good as sold as we speak." That part was true. "Then, things are going to change for me, I promise you. Once I get back into advertising, I can pay off this loan in no time at all."

Trafficante nodded slowly, and a little sadly. "I sure hope so, McNolte. You get back into advertising, I'll be your first client. You're a fucking genius." He lifted his right arm, holding the thick envelope out over the desk. "I'm only going to ask one thing of you, McNolte. That you don't fuck up this loan the way you fucked up a great career."

McNolte chuckled and shrugged. "I don't see that happening, Mr. Trafficante, I really don't. I wouldn't have come to you if I didn't have this whole thing worked out. Really."

Trafficante nodded again, then gestured with his hand. McNolte took the envelope.

"Thank you, Mr. Trafficante. Thank you very much. You won't be sorry you did this, I promise. In fact, I'll pay it back so fast, you'll forget the whole thing happened."

"You do that, kid. Just remember. You got the loan because I like you a lot. But I never let liking somebody get in the way of my business. Understood?"

McNolte nodded once, sharply. "Understood."

He could not get out of there fast enough.

ACKNOWLEDGMENTS

Even though *Biofire* was published more than twenty years ago, it took some effort to prepare it for publication this time, and I had help from some supportive friends. I'm grateful to Becky Narron, Scott Connors, Randy Eberle, Rhonda Blackmon Walton, Sam W. Anderson, Mickie Caparilli-McGowan, Geoffrey Bergeron, and Erinn Kemper.

My Patreon supporters, who have generously pledged their support to my work on the upcoming novel *Foreverblood*, were good enough not to mind when I took a break from that book to prepare *Biofire* for publication. For their kind support, I owe my heartfelt thanks to them:

Andy McCorkle, Angela Exum, Barry Simiana, Becky Narron, Chuck Hartsell, Derrick Woodruffe, Ed Kurtz, Geoffrey Bergeron, Graham Thornton, James Matthew Neeland, John Bender, John F. D. Taff, Kellie Stacey, Ken King, Larry Kinney, Latrice Innes, Laurel Steven, Michael Sauers, Robert S. Wilson, Noel Scott Badger, Wendy Marie Muir, Randy Eberle, Robin Trischmann, Ron Knoblock, Ryan Lieske, Tim Feely, Todd Clark, and Webberly Rattenkraft

DEDICATION

*As always,
for Dawn, my love*

INTRODUCTION

*B*iofire was published in a limited edition by Cemetery Dance Publications in 1998, and until now it had not been published again. It was written at a time when I was between agents and there was no one to shop it around. I moved on to the next book, returned to my former agent Richard Curtis, who then represented the next book, and somehow *Biofire* slipped between the cracks. I decided it was high time the book had a shot at a wider audience more than twenty years after its original publication.

I'm sure *Biofire* would not have fared well with New York publishers. It's one of those books that seems to repel them because it defies categorization (the same problem I had with *Sex and Violence in Hollywood*). While it has elements of horror, it's not quite a horror novel. It's not science fiction, but it features some mad scientists. It has some of the sensibilities of noir, but it's not a noir novel. The book is full of criminals, but it doesn't really qualify as crime fiction. It is probably best described as a thriller, although some might object to that label, as well. It is an amalgam of genres, which is the kind of book that drives marketing departments crazy.

Biofire contains gangsters, mad scientists, an abused wife who finally rebels, a man who has messed up his life possibly beyond repair, a lot of homeless people, a friendly iguana, and an affectionate nod to noir writer Jim Thompson. None of these things are necessarily grounded in any time period. I considered moving the novel twenty years ahead and having it take place in 2019 and even began the process of updating it. I decided, however, to leave it right where it is, partly because I realized it worked perfectly well in 1998 and there was no reason to change it, and partly because I have a lazy streak. I did some tightening and polishing, but the story has not changed in any way.

I read a lot of noir fiction in the 1990s, more than horror. I fell in love with it. David Goodis, Cornell Woolrich, Jim Thompson, James M. Cain, Gil Brewer, John D. MacDonald, and others—I spent a lot of time with those guys and soaked up their work.

I think I needed a break from the supernatural. That's mostly what sets horror apart from something like noir. Both are dark and full of dread; one involves otherworldly forces and non-human creatures that we sometimes use to interpret the ugly aspects of being human, while the other focuses quietly on that ugliness and uses it to interpret us. I think I turned to noir to remove the buffer of the supernatural. I began experimenting with the genre in my own writing. One of the results was *Biofire*.

If you've read any noir—and if you haven't, I recommend the genre and all of the writers mentioned above—you know that the city in which the action takes place is itself often a character in the story. Cornell Woolrich used this especially well in novels like *Deadline at Dawn*, in which the city is a dark, oppressive presence throughout, impossible to escape. I like that particular trope because it rings true to me; every big city I've ever been in has felt like a character with its own personality. I ended up marrying that to an idea I had been kicking around for a horror novel about a secret, government-funded project that's turning people into weapons. The city in which *Biofire* takes place is big, unnamed, brooding, and, I hope, ominous.

Secret government projects pop up occasionally in my work. I keep returning to the subject because it's real. It feels like horror fiction, we've always associated that sort of thing with horror and science fiction, but far too many times in American history, the United States government has treated this country like a big lab full of rats. It's happened often enough to go beyond being a pattern; it's a routine practice. And yet there are still so many people unaware of it. They still see it in movies and TV shows—sometimes even movies and TV shows attempting to expose the fact that it goes on—and it still feels like precisely that: something from a movie or TV show. But it's quite real and it does occur. We've learned of horrific unethical experimentation by the government—Operation Top Hat, Operation Bluebird, which later became Operation Artichoke, MK-Ultra, and others—that took place throughout the 20th century. And decades from now, we'll learn about the experiments that occurred in the opening decade of the 21st century. This delay of disclosure helps to keep it all from seeming real to us. It's something that happened in another time. Surely we don't do things like that *today*.

Wrong.

Let's travel back a couple of decades to 1998.

That was the year White House page Monica Lewinsky claimed to have had sex with President Bill Clinton nine times from 1995 to 1997, launching a scandal that hungrily consumed countless hours of TV airtime and seemed unwilling to die. Every newspaper published editorials on the subject, every comedian did bits on it, and parents expressed outrage that they would have to explain to their children what a blowjob was and why the president was getting them from a woman who was not his wife. It was a different time. A time when the behavior of a United States president actually mattered. A time when parents still believed their kids didn't know what a blowjob was.

I seem to remember turning the news *off* more often than turning it on back then, which is something I'm still doing today. The signal-to-noise ratio is all messed up, especially now, when the noise is deafening.

Hit movies playing in theaters that year included *Saving Private Ryan, Armageddon, There's Something About Mary, Mulan, Fear and Loathing in Las Vegas, Rush Hour,* and a movie that would later achieve cult status, *The Big Lebowski.* James Cameron's 1997 blockbuster *Titanic* won a record eleven Oscars in March at the 70th Annual Academy Awards.

Dawn and I still went to the movies pretty regularly in the 1990s. These days, it's rare that a movie comes along that we want to see enough to pay the exorbitant theater prices and endure crowds of people who seem to think they're sitting in their living rooms. The experience has decomposed into something that's more often unpleasant than enjoyable, so we just don't do it very often.

Among the bestselling books in 1998 were *Cold Mountain* by Charles Frazier, *The Long Road Home* by Danielle Steele, *You Belong to Me* by Mary Higgins Clark, and *The Street Lawyer* by John Grisham. I was too immersed in noir to have time for current bestsellers.

It was the year Kasey Casem returned as host of *American Top 40* after a decade-long absence. The Top 40 of 1998 list included songs by LeAnn Rimes, Savage Garden, Boyz II Men, Chumbawamba, Metallica, Mariah Carey, Will Smith, and Sara McLachlan.

I think I stopped paying attention to Top 40 songs sometime around 1990. An occasional song still got through, but mostly I listened to other music. While I was writing *Biofire*, I was starting to get into jazz. Oscar Peterson, Erroll Garner, Miles Davis, Dave Brubeck, Vince Guaraldi and others made up the soundtrack as I wrote.

The year 1998 saw the launch of new TV shows like *Dawson's Creek*, *Celebrity Deathmatch*, *Sex and the City*, *Whose Line is it, Anyway?*, *The King of Queens*, *That '70s Show*, and *Charmed*.

I was a TV kid growing up; I told time by what was on TV. I memorized the *TV Guide* at the beginning of every week. We only had three networks, so the shows were much easier to keep up with than they are now, with the galaxy of TV stations and networks we live in today. I think it was in the '90s that I started to lose interest in TV. Oh, I still watched, don't get me wrong— *Seinfeld*, *Buffy the Vampire Slayer*, *The X-Files*, *Frasier*, and *Law & Order* were among my favorites. But TV lost its importance in my life and I no longer felt the need to schedule my time around what it had to offer. If I missed something, I missed it; I could catch it during the summer reruns, if at all. These days, I watch little broadcast TV. Like everyone else, most of our home entertainment comes from Amazon, Netflix, and other streaming services. But to be honest, I'd rather be reading a book.

As of January of 2019, according to Wikipedia, there were 4.39 billion internet users. But in 1998, the internet had been in the general public's awareness for about seven years and people did not yet understand it, therefore they didn't trust it. The biggest complaint by users at the time was slow connections. The obnoxious screech of a dial-up connection being made was always followed by excruciatingly long waits for a single webpage to open. Search engines were in their infancy, and social networks simply did not exist as we know them today. According to Pew Research, 57 percent of non-users in 1998 never worried about what they might be missing online. Can you imagine that today? People don't stay off their phones long enough to wonder what they might be missing on the internet. It seems to drive everything today, but back then, the worldwide web had not yet become a big part of American life.

I approached it all with caution and slowly made my way to the internet. I'm not happy about it. The internet has devalued everything, and we have made ourselves so dependent on it and on computers that when the lights go out—and they will someday, for whatever reason—people will be eating each other in the streets within twenty-four hours.

While cell phones existed in 1998, they were not nearly as prevalent as they are now and were prohibitively expensive, with some costing thousands of dollars. No one had ever heard of a "smart phone" yet, and the idea of a phone having intelligence probably would seem creepy—as it should. Today, cell phones have become an extension of human beings in a decidedly Cronenbergian way; it's unlikely that you'll find anyone *without* his or her cell phone at any given time. But if, say, you found yourself in imminent danger and were being pursued by people who want to kill you in 1998, then you probably didn't have a cell phone on you to call for help. For situations like that, people still relied on pay phones—if you could find one that worked. While they were commonly in poor repair, they were pretty easy to find back then, on most street corners, in most businesses, and in metropolitan areas they could be found in long banks on the sides of buildings.

Dawn and I each have a small flip phone and our provider is

the pay-as-you-go TracFone. We've both watched people walking around with their heads down, eyes on their phones—alone even in a group, isolated even while surrounded by people—and decided we did not want that to be us. Cell phones have created a pretty creepy transformation in people. They cannot be without their phone nearby so they can check it regularly, again and again, to make sure they're not missing anything. The way we see it, they're missing a whole lot—but not on their phones.

I hope you enjoy your time spent in 1998. And while you're there, beware the Laughing Man.

1.

PILLOW TALK

Emma watched as he floated slowly down from the peak of his pleasure. It always took him a while, because she made sure his orgasm did not come easily. She made him teeter on the edge for what must have seemed to him forever, just as she used to do to her husband, Landon, in those early months of their marriage. Back when they had sex and spoke to one another, even showed affection on occasion, back before they took separate vacations, and separate bedrooms. Now, she straddled her lover, not her husband, watching as he lay exhausted beneath her, drained, even stunned, still inside her but small and shriveled, used up.

Beneath her, Leo sparkled with sweat, as usual, and it wasn't very flattering, because somehow it made him look even fatter. It didn't bother her, really; it was simply an observation she had made during their numerous assignations, always in that same enormous penthouse suite at the Olympus Towers. The room was held for him alone. Normally, that would not be an easy thing to acquire at such an enormous and exclusive hotel as the Olympus, in the middle of one of the biggest and busiest cities in the country, the world. But it was easier for him because he owned the hotel. It was one of the two places where they regularly met; the other was an intimate restaurant on the marina near Greyton. Leo did not own that particular establishment, but the owners treated him as if he did.

Emma reached down and ran a hand over Leo's enormous, sweat-slicked barrel chest, passed her fingers through the glistening, curly patch of black-and-silver hair that formed a perfect V before it ran down his belly and then spread out again.

She was still wearing her blouse. It was always the same. When she entered the suite, he was waiting for her, in bed, naked, and he could never wait for her to get all of her clothes off. So Emma always ended up having sex with something still on, whether it was her stockings, her bra, or, as today, her cream-colored silk blouse. She did not mind in the least. She knew that in the end, which would be today, it would work in her favor. It would serve her purposes perfectly.

The blouse clung to her perspiring skin and was unbuttoned and open wide in front. Minutes after they had started, he had begged her, quite breathlessly, to unbutton it herself because he wanted to fondle her breasts while they had sex, but he was too much of a gentleman to rip it open in front and send buttons skittering in every direction.

That was what Emma liked about him: he was a gentleman. There was little else to like about the man but, unlike her husband, he was a gentleman.

He was somewhere in his fifties, and judging from those broad shoulders, strong thighs, and that deep, powerful chest, he probably had an impressive body once. She understood that he had worked his way up from the streets, like so many of his kind, and she could imagine him as a young man, cocky and strikingly handsome, with aggressive strength in every movement, even the smallest gesture. But years of inactivity, rich foods, and too much liquor had made it all run to fat. His belly was big, but with that chest it was not as noticeable as it would be on a slighter, narrower frame. He still had a head of thick, wavy hair, all of it a glorious, shining silver, like finely spun steel. And his large, square jaw kept his face from looking round and pudgy, as would have been the case for other men at his weight. In spite of all he had going against him, he was a man whom many might still considered quite handsome in spite of his girth. And those who did not certainly could not deny that he carried about him an air of wealth, power, and raw strength that kept them from saying so out loud.

But none of that mattered to Emma in the end. It was just a way of passing the time, this examination of him as he slowly rose from the depths of his sweaty stupor. Neither his looks nor his body were important to her. In fact, the sex meant nothing, either. Although she was quite proud of the convincing performances she had given during their time together, she had not experienced a single orgasm. She had felt nothing, except for the need to make it all work so she could achieve the desired result.

His eyes opened slightly and he raised his right arm slowly, as if it were made of lead, touching the tips of his round, beefy fingers to her left breast, stroking it downward until all four fingertips came to rest on her nipple.

"You...are...wonderful, you know that?" he said in a moist, throaty whisper. "I'm not the marrying kind, but if I was..."

She smiled down at him. "Thank you. It's nice to hear things like that."

He cupped his big hand beneath her breast and pushed upward, squeezing gently. "Aw, come on. You keep telling me that husband of yours doesn't appreciate you. I don't know how he couldn't. I mean, he's a cold and shrewd businessman, and I admire him for it. But to have you to go home to every night...I mean it, Emma, I've had 'em all, if you don't mind my saying. I've had an active sex life since I was twelve. But the things you do for me...the things you do *to* me...I've never had sex like this. Ever. With anyone. And if you don't mind my saying, I've not only had 'em all, I've had the *best*." He turned his head slowly back and forth on the pillow. "But you've wiped 'em all out. You've ruined me for other women." He shrugged his shoulders clumsily against the pillow and said, "So, tell me. How can a man as smart as your husband not appreciate what he's got... when he's got *you*?" He lowered his hand from her breast and began stroking her thigh.

Still smiling, Emma said, "Mr. Lizard has more important things on his mind than me."

He smiled a lopsided smile, which was rather disconcerting because his teeth were so small, like the tiny, bright deciduous teeth in the mouth of a little boy. His sweaty, hairy belly shook as he laughed, and he slapped her thigh playfully. "Mr. Lizard. You call him that all the time. What does that mean, that Mr. Lizard?"

"Remember the know-it-all guy on TV who used to teach kids about science? Mr. Wizard? Well, that's my husband. He thinks he knows it all, thinks he's Mr. Wizard. But the truth is, he doesn't know anything. About life, about love, about... anything at all. And in reality, he's a reptile. So—" She leaned forward. "—he's Mr. Lizard. Plus he's got that damned pet lizard of his."

He nodded. "Ah, yeah, Rupert. He's very proud of that lizard."

"Yes, proud the way an artist is proud of his creation. But he didn't create that lizard. He doesn't create anything. Except money."

"Yeah, well, in this world, that's all anybody cares about."

Lying on top of him, she gave him a long, slow kiss. Her open blouse bunched up on him and he pushed it away.

"Take that thing off and curl up with me," he said, patting the space of mattress right next to him with his right hand and pulling the blouse off her shoulder with the other.

Perfect, Emma thought. *Absolutely perfect.*

She slipped the blouse off, grinning now, and tossed it onto the floor. Then she got off of him and onto the bed, knowing his eyes were on her the entire time, so she knew he would see it. But just in case, she turned her left shoulder to him for a moment as she settled in beside him on the bed.

"Holy shit," he said, sitting up.

"What's the matter?"

"That thing on your back!" he curled his fingers around her arm and tugged, making her sit up with her back to him so he could see it again. "What the hell is that?"

She bowed her head a moment, not wanting to sound eager to tell him. "A bruise," she said quietly after an appropriate pause.

"Yeah, that's a bruise, all right." There were distant rumblings of anger in his voice. "What the hell hit you, a train?"

She pulled away from him, then turned to face him, giving him a weak smile as she ran her fingernails lightly through his chest hair and toyed with his nipples. But she did not meet his eyes.,

Finally, in a whisper, she said, "I told you Mr. Lizard doesn't appreciate me."

Then she looked at him with heavy-lidded eyes and an expressionless face. She wanted to see his reaction, wanted to know if, after all these weeks of the best sex he'd ever had, his reaction would be as she had hoped.

She was not disappointed.

His eyes widened slowly as his thick eyebrows curled downward in the middle. His lips tightened and his upper body stiffened. "You mean...*he* did this to you?"

She bowed her head and said quietly, "It's nothing, really. I'd rather not talk about it." She smiled then. "Are you hungry?"

"We *are* going to talk about it," he barked, chin jutting, small lower teeth exposed like the lower fangs of a bulldog. He swung his legs around, got off the bed, and began pacing, naked and sweaty. As he spoke, he swung his arms about animatedly and clenched his teeth again and again. "You mean your husband *beats* you? Like some kind of *slave*? I mean, I can take a lot from somebody I do business with. I've done business with the worst of 'em, believe me. But there are two things I cannot and will not tolerate in the men I deal with: cocksucking and wife beating. Especially..." He stopped and faced her. "Especially when that wife is you."

"Please, Leo, don't worry about it. Really. I'm sorry it even came up in the—"

"Don't worry about it?" He sat on the edge of the bed and pulled her toward him she could face her. "How could I not worry about it? Why didn't you tell me before? How...*why* do you put up with it? Why don't you divorce the son of a bitch?"

Once again, she averted her eyes and shrugged.

"Well, why don't you? It's not like divorces are hard to come by these days."

"Let's not talk about it, all right?" she said, turning away and getting off the bed on the other side. She picked up her blouse and put it on, but did not button it, then started looking around for her panties.

"We will talk about it, Emma." He stood and his voice grew louder as he said, "You're not leaving this room until we've finished talking about it. Has he threatened you? Is that it? A man who will beat his wife is liable to do anything. So, tell me. Are you afraid to divorce him? Is that the problem?"

After a long silence, she sat on the foot of the bed and covered her face with both hands as she began to cry softly, nodding. Finally, she said into her palms, "He said...that he'd kill me if I tried to leave him."

"Hey, hey, baby, come on, now," Leo whispered soothingly, "let me get you a drink, okay?" He hurried over to the liquor cabinet. Ice cubes jingled against glass and liquor sloshed.

She lowered her trembling hands from her face as Leo handed her a scotch. She sipped it once, then again. She was quite proud of herself so far, and more than a little surprised. She was no actress, and she knew her performance would be pathetic if it were not for the fact that everything she said was true.

She could hear his little teeth grinding together as he moved toward her, sat beside her, and put an arm across her shoulders.

"Jesus," he muttered through his teeth, "how long has this been going on? I mean, you two've been married, what...eight, nine years?"

"Nine years in May," she whispered, taking another sip.

"Well, I'm guessing he hasn't been doing this that whole time, or you'd have left him right away. Right?"

She shook her head slowly against his chest. She had gone over the line somewhere along the way. All the thinking she had done, all the remembering, to prepare herself for this particular moment on this particular night had pushed her a bit too far. She could not stop crying. They were real tears and real sobs, and what she felt in her guts was real pain for the years that might have been happy and content with someone else. She tried to get her sobs under control so she could speak.

"It's been going on the whole time," she said, sniffling. "From the beginning."

Emma Donelly had been wealthy since birth, so she had not married Landon Shaw for his money. Her father, who had also been born into wealth, had successfully followed his father into the real estate business. When Emma was seven years old, her parents had been killed when their private plane had gone down in Mexico. After that, she had lived with her grandparents. They were good people, well-meaning and careful to see that she had everything she could possibly need or want. But she missed her parents. They had doted on her so, their only child, and the luxuries their wealth provided had paled in comparison to their attention, affection, and almost tangible love for her.

She had gone to a boarding school, then college. Her grades had cuddled up to perfect and she had passed through her education smoothly, but without a single idea of what she wanted to do with her life. It was not necessary for her to do *anything* with it if she did not want to; she had more than enough money to live in high comfort to her dying day. But Emma *did* want to do something with it, she simply could not figure out what that might be.

From the day her parents had died, she had carried with her a distracting feeling of frustration, a sense that something was not, and never would be, resolved. But she did not know what that was, either.

It was in that state of mind, two years after she had graduated from college, that Landon had found her. By then, her grandparents were gone; they had died within six months of one another during her junior year in college. She was truly alone in the world, then, with no family and few friends, just a lot of servants in her grandparents' sprawling mansion in New England, and lots of lawyers and accountants who stopped just short of bowing to her whenever she entered a room. She felt like a fine sprig of down back then, at the mercy of the wind, floating through her life with no direction.

Landon had been very different back then, attentive and loving. Now, in hindsight, she knew he had not been different at all, just clever and calculating.

They had met at a dinner party, and he had pursued her without restraint after that evening, Flowers, gifts, phone calls, cards with beautifully written notes in them—and all of that had come before their first date.

Emma no longer found Landon handsome because now

she could see nothing but the glistening black rot that made up his personality, his very being, beneath the handsome exterior. But back then, before she really knew him, he had taken her breath away. Tall, with a firm, athletic, nicely sculpted body. A face that was almost too long but saved by a beautiful smile, a straight, regal nose, and full lips that were just short of being pouty. Hair that was fine, but dark and wavy, and he let it grow a bit longer than one might expect of a man who wore almost nothing but flagrantly expensive and impeccably tailored suits. But his strongest feature by far were his eyes. They were more eloquent than his words, and their touch was every bit as firm as that of his hands, or even his lips.

Emma cringed whenever she heard the phrase "she was swept off her feet," but that was precisely what happened to her. Added to his constant shower of gifts was the way he treated her in bed. He had been so gentle at first, so slow and considerate; he seemed to enjoy her body like no other man she had ever known. Back then, she had been charmed by the fact that his hands trembled during foreplay, while he was touching her so gently, fondling her lovingly, building her pleasure slowly.

Now, of course, she knew his hands had trembled because he had been fighting his real desires, keeping his hands from doing what he had *really* wanted to do with them—the things he did not hesitate to do so freely once they were married. The things that *really* got him hot.

They had an epic wedding, every second of which was planned by Landon's people, and because he was a public figure—his methods of doing business, like Landon himself, were rather extravagant and showy and the press loved him for it—the wedding was highly publicized.

It took six months for Emma to start feeling regret. It came to her in much the same way consciousness comes to a patient who has undergone a long and major surgery. Later, Emma realized that it was not regret that had come to her, it was reality.

Landon had married her not out of love, but out of need. He needed a wife, an attractive, smiling woman on his arm when the cameras flashed and the microphones were placed before him, a lovely face at parties to soften up potential business associates or possible business targets who might otherwise be uninterested, or even hostile.

The truth had come the first time she had gone to one of those parties in an unsocial mood and had not smiled, had not been as friendly as he had wanted her to be; the truth had come in the form of Landon's fist. That first time, as it was happening, as he was beating her and telling her what she had done wrong—not shouting at her, but speaking in a low, throaty tone—she was horrified, but told herself that it was an isolated incident, a freak occurrence, even as he pounded her back with his fist. She was sure it had something to do with the pressure he was under, and she had only exacerbated it with her petulant behavior at the party. Those weak, silent reassurances crumbled into insignificance, however, when she felt his erection against her hip and realized what was happening to him, that beating her was turning him on, he was getting off on it.

His fist was not his only weapon. Sometimes, he could do far more damage with words and actions. But physically, he had a number of methods of punishing her, the worst of which was The Towel. That's how she thought of it, simply as The Towel. She hated the feel of terrycloth against her flesh now, and only dried herself with Egyptian cotton towels after showering. Terrycloth made her physically ill.

She had thought often of simply helping herself rather than trying to find someone to help her, someone like Leo, but she had always been too afraid to try. She certainly had the ability, the ammunition. But not the guts. And even if she did, there was no one she could take that ammunition to, no one would believe her, or who was not already on Landon's payroll.

Landon's business was far more secretive than most people realized. Most of the people at those dinner and cocktail parties and charity functions thought that Landon was simply President and CEO of OdysseyCorp Labs. They thought his job involved nothing more than overseeing a lab that existed only to cure the ills of mankind.

But Emma knew better. After all, she had helped Landon entertain many of his business associates at the house. She had played hostess to plenty of their own parties, dinner and cocktail and otherwise. And she had overheard a lot of hushed conversations between Landon and one client after another.

Emma was neither blind nor deaf, and she certainly was not dumb. She knew what went on at OdysseyCorp Labs, and Landon knew that she knew.

He had told her only once that everything she saw and heard in the house was not to be repeated to anyone under any circumstances. And because he had driven the point home with The Towel, and threatened her with worse, she had never considered violating his rule.

But still, she knew a lot. She could go to the police and tell them everything she knew about her husband and his business, and he probably would be in big trouble. But that would only work if he did not own the police department, or the entire city government. And his ownership extended far beyond those two entities to county, state, and federal government. Landon was quite generous with his ownership.

And he owned her. There was no way to escape the fact that he owned her free and clear, just as he owned all those antique cars in his many garages, just as he owned his big, ugly house and his company. He owned Emma. And she knew she could not break free of him alone, not without help.

That was why she had turned to Leo.

"Sweetheart, baby," Leo whispered, tucking a finger beneath her chin and lifting her face to him, "why didn't you tell me?"

"I haven't told anyone. It's just not something I talk about. He said if I told anyone, he…he'd do something worse than just…kill me."

Suddenly, he slid from the bed and knelt before her, naked, sweaty, fat. If her sobs had not been real ones, if she had been faking the whole thing, the sight of him kneeling there would have made her burst into uncontrollable laughter, not out of cruelty, but simply because it was such a comical sight.

He clutched her small hands between his meaty, hairy-knuckled mitts and stared into her eyes with such intensity that, for a moment, she thought he was going to start crying as well.

"What do you want me to do?" he said. "I'll do anything

you want. I'll tell him you want a divorce. And believe me, if *I* tell him, he'll go along with it. I'll *make* him."

She shook her head. "He'd find me later. That's what he's always said he would do. Find me. No matter what." It was the truth. And it almost started her crying again, but she fought it. She had to be in control now. This was the moment toward which she'd been working so hard. Tears and sobbing would only muddy things up. She had to be in control.

"All right, then, fuck that," he muttered. His head turned this way and that and his eyes darted all over the room, as if looking for the solution, perhaps the right words written on the ceiling or on a wall. Finally, he locked his eyes onto hers again and his face stiffened, became intensely serious, almost threatening. "Do you want him dead?" he asked quietly.

Just as she had planned, just as she had rehearsed, she looked at him with a mixture of shock and surprise—shock that he would even suggest such a thing, then surprise that she had not thought of it herself. Slowly, her face relaxed and looked at him lovingly.

"You would do that for me?" she said.

"Anything. Anything for you. Especially now that I know about *this*. If that's what you want, it's done." He squeezed her hands tighter between his. "Look, I've known your husband a long time. We've done a lot of business together. Good business. He's always been a hard bargainer, but fair. He's good at what he does, and he's a very powerful man. But sweetheart, for all his power, he's just a blip on my radar screen. I've had nothing but respect for the son of a bitch...until now. See, I live by a very strict code. To a lot of people, that code may be pretty lopsided, but it works for me, and for me, it's the law. All things considered, I think it's fair and just. What your husband has been doing to you...well, for all the things people might say about my code, that son of a bitch has been violating it six ways to Sunday. And my code says that guys like him should be dealt with in ways that most people wouldn't even consider. So, I'm asking you now, sweetheart, and I want an answer. Do you want him dead? Because if you do, you just have to say the word. I'll have it done, no mess, no trouble with the law, done and over with, he's outta your life. Is that what you want? Do you want him dead?"

Inside, she wanted to let out a cheer, to shriek with joy, jump up and down and flail her fists in the air. But that could wait. For now, she simply looked into his eyes and answered the question she had been waiting so long to hear.

"Yes, please."

2.

TAP DANCING

"I can't tell you how much I appreciate this, Mr. Trafficante," McNolte said. He faced the man across a massive desk, both of them standing, smiling.

In his right hand, Mr. Trafficante held a plain white business-size envelope which bulged with its contents.

McNolte, who knew that the envelope contained a great deal of cash, darted his eyes back and forth between Trafficante's face and the envelope in his hand as an uncomfortable silence grew between them.

"Before I give this to you, McNolte," Trafficante said quietly, still smiling, "I want to say something."

McNolte's eyebrows rose slowly. "Yes?"

"You know, you were a fantastic ad man. Before that, I'm sure you were quite a journalist, as well, but I'm only familiar with your work in advertising. Your campaign for my casinos was brilliant. And your work on my chain of video game arcades? Well, what's a video game arcade but a room full of video games, right? But you, hell, you turned my chain into a fucking nationwide sensation. You were great. I'm a big admirer of your work, your mind. Not only that, McNolte. I like *you*. I really do. I like you a lot. You're a good guy, a smart guy. But I want to remind you of one thing. The only reason you aren't in advertising anymore is that fucking white powder you're gonna buy with this money I'm loaning you."

McNolte responded quickly, starting with a smooth lie. "But I-I'm not doing that anymore, Mr. Trafficante. The only reason

I want to buy the cocaine is that I know I can sell it. In fact, I've got people waiting for it right now. I mean, you're right, everything you said, it's true. My habit was why I lost my job. It's why I'm in the position I'm in now. But once I sell this coke, I'll have enough money to pay off all my debts, then I can get a decent job and pay you back."

Trafficante's shoulders shook as he chuckled. "Even at my rate of interest?"

"Well, yeah, it's pretty steep. But I'll pay it off. And then, well, if I could get the last job I had, I can get another. Right?"

Trafficante nodded slowly. "That's the only reason I'm giving you this loan, McNolte. Because I know you've got a hell of a brain in your head. The only thing that worries me is this. You say you've kicked your habit, but you say it awfully fast for somebody who's off the nose candy. If you don't happen to sell that coke, maybe you'll use it yourself. And in that quantity... well, maybe you won't have much of a brain left. That means you won't be able to get a job. Or pay back this loan. That wouldn't be good, McNolte. Because the interest is one thing, but not paying off the loan is another thing entirely. In that case, I usually start with fingers. Then I move on to kneecaps. This is usually over a period of weeks. If you're lucky, I'll have only one of your eyes gouged out. That'll slow things down a little, hold off the inevitable. But no matter what, if you can't pay off this loan, McNolte, I'll have you killed."

McNolte felt nauseated all of a sudden. He tried to keep smiling, but it wasn't easy. He wiped a hand over his mouth and cleared his throat.

"I understand, Mr. Trafficante. But even if all that were to happen—and I swear to God it won't, because I'm buying the coke tonight and I'll have the whole thing sold within three days, no kidding—I wouldn't be able to pay off the debt if I was, you know, dead. Don't you think?"

Trafficante smiled. "If all that were to happen, I wouldn't care that the debt was unpaid. My concern would be the message sent to others by an unpaid debt that I didn't address. I'm not a church charity, McNolte. I'm a businessman. If you can't pay off this loan, then I'll have to collect. Something would have to be collected. If not money, then your life. That way, prospective customers will know that I take my business very seriously."

Everything Trafficante said was spoken as casually as if he were discussing sports or the weather.

McNolte felt sweat trickle from his armpit down his side beneath his shirt, and his hands were beginning to feel tremulous, partly out of fear, and partly because it had been about an hour since he'd had a hit.

"Like I said, Mr. Trafficante, I'm not buying this for me. It's as good as sold as we speak." That part was true. "Then, things are going to change for me, I promise you. Once I get back into advertising, I can pay off this loan in no time at all."

Trafficante nodded slowly, and a little sadly. "I sure hope so, McNolte. You get back into advertising, I'll be your first client. You're a fucking genius." He lifted his right arm, holding the thick envelope out over the desk. "I'm only going to ask one thing of you, McNolte. That you don't fuck up this loan the way you fucked up a great career."

McNolte chuckled and shrugged. "I don't see that happening, Mr. Trafficante, I really don't. I wouldn't have come to you if I didn't have this whole thing worked out. Really."

Trafficante nodded again, then gestured with his hand. McNolte took the envelope.

"Thank you, Mr. Trafficante. Thank you very much. You won't be sorry you did this, I promise. In fact, I'll pay it back so fast, you'll forget the whole thing happened."

"You do that, kid. Just remember. You got the loan because I like you a lot. But I never let liking somebody get in the way of my business. Understood?"

McNolte nodded once, sharply. "Understood."

He could not get out of there fast enough.

Once in the car, McNolte decided against dipping into what little coke was left in the baggy in the glove compartment. He just wanted to get the hell away from Trafficante's building, away from Trafficante himself. The man had scared him nearly to the point of speechlessness.

That was a threat, McNolte thought frantically as he sat at the wheel of his car a moment to calm himself. *The whole fucking conversation was a threat. He could've just said pay it back or I'll kill you and it would've saved a lot of time, but no, he had to smile and be nice and compliment me and offer me a job while he was talking about fingers and kneecaps and eye-gouging, and* then *he said to pay it back or he'll kill me. My God!*

Rain fell endlessly from the black sky. An occasional bolt of lightning shot through the night, illuminating bloating storm clouds for a shuddering instant, after which the rumble of thunder rose briefly above the throb of the city.

There had been a concert that night at the City Center, some over-hyped band on a limited four-city tour. By the time McNolte tried to make his way across town to Miklos's apartment, the Center's massive parking lot was vomiting up a steady stream of cars that brought traffic to a halt. He found himself stuck in the gridlock for a while, jittery, impatient. He shot down a side street at the first opportunity, deciding to take a less direct—and considerably less safe—route rather than wait for the traffic to move.

Instead of creeping through traffic, McNolte drove through the narrow streets of the city's dark, brooding Old Town. He was already nervous enough, but the thought of driving through the deadliest part of town with all that money in the car—Trafficante's money, no less—made his nerves sing like cicadas on a summer night in the country.

He drove past once-grand hotels that now looked like amusement park haunted houses, hotels that once offered caviar on room service menus but now charged hourly rates and probably had stopped bothering to clean the bloodstains on the carpets. The old Stratford Theater, where expensively dressed crowds had once gone to see the finest new plays, was now the Viper X-Plex, a run-down porn theater; men lingered furtively in the shadows of doorways and awnings all around it. Directly across the street—where once stood Ricardo's, the city's most elegant restaurant in a time-dimmed day gone by—cadaverous drug addicts and fearful homeless people lurked among the rubble of the now-empty lot. He drove around a couple of buses idling in front of the filthy, cavernous bus station, which hunkered in an eternal cloud of exhaust fumes and hungrily swallowed up travelers day and night. He knew he was home free as he began to pass rows of tenement buildings, all of which looked ready to collapse under their own weight, but each of which teemed with hungry, screaming, desperate life.

A few minutes later, he was driving along the old red-brick wall that ran along the edge of half of the city's sprawling park. Whatever quaint charm the old wall once had was now buried beneath cryptic messages scrawled in spray paint of all colors. The wall opened abruptly at the entrance to the park's zoo, and just beyond it stood the towering concrete elephant which every mayor for the past twenty years or more had vowed to tear down, but which remained from one administration to the next. The elephant's trunk rose high between two long tusks with dulled points. The once-gray paint job was now a sludgy brown, and graffiti marred the thick, tree-trunk legs. It was slowly falling apart; bits of the ears were gone and the edges of the yawning mouth appeared to be rotting away. It had once delighted children on their way into and out of the zoo and had even adorned postcards and souvenir posters; now it resembled a great prehistoric mastodon discovered frozen in glacial ice, which had been allowed to thaw and was now decomposing.

McNolte, who seldom passed the zoo's entrance, flinched slightly at the sudden sight of it and his breath caught sharply in his throat, as if the hulking concrete beast were bounding forward, about to stomp thunderously on his car, sandwiching McNolte and Trafficante's precious money between two slices of crushed metal.

Once the elephant was behind him, McNolte found himself giggling ridiculously, high on the adrenaline rushing through him like shining mercury. His giggle became a throaty laugh, and he muttered to himself, "Stupid elephant. Stupid fucking concrete elephant."

But as he said those words to soothe his nerves, to smooth over the fact that he was behaving irrationally, another voice spoke inside him, deep inside, asking the same questions over and over again.

How did this happen to me? How did I get here? My God, how did I get here?

In a once-upon-a-time-ago life, Neil McNolte had been a journalist. As a boy, he had cut his reading teeth on newspapers with his dad's help, and had left the other students in the dust by the first day of his first grade year. He had an almost dream-like fascination with the transformation of actual real-life events into stark black letters on folded sheets of paper that came to his house every day, letters that formed words that formed sentences, and paragraphs, and finally stories of real people doing real things.

Once he was finished studying journalism in college, he got a job at the *News and Review,* a struggling free press paper in the city that collapsed only seven months after he had come aboard. But he had gained some confidence during those months, and afterward had a series of jobs at small to mid-sized papers. He spent a few years at the *Tribune,* a daily that seemed on the verge of folding all the time, but which was, even now, still around. After that, he wrote many of the stories that appeared beneath the screaming headlines of the *Searchlight,* the city's weekly tabloid.

It was during his stay at the *Searchlight* that he met Trisha Beddo, a petite, perky young woman with honey-colored hair and a chirping voice who worked in the advertising department. He spent months avoiding her because he found her *too* perky. The smile on her face seemed frozen there, as if pulled back with tape that was hidden beneath her shining, perfectly-coifed hair, and that chirping voice of hers—especially in the early hours of the day—affected him like a garden rake being dragged over a chalkboard. One afternoon, as he was pouring himself a cup of coffee in the lounge, he fell instantly in love with her when she approached him, held out her mug, and said through her smile, in a low, throaty, and incredibly sexy voice, "Next time I have to have a meeting with some bitch who insists that her psychic telephone network be advertised specifically on our astrological page or not at all, I swear to God I'm gonna staple her labia to her forehead." He laughed so hard, he spilled coffee on the floor as he filled her mug, and by the end of the conversation, they had agreed to meet for drinks after work.

He found that she was not that smiling, chirping, perky automaton at all. Trisha, like McNolte, hated working for the tabloid, but knew a good thing when she had it. She was a completely different person outside of work and gleefully mocked her office persona. Everything about her changed when she was not on the job; her body was looser, more relaxed and animated, her voice exhibited a range it did not have from nine to five. But most of all, her eyes were alive as they talked in the back booth of a bar down the block from the *Searchlight* building, their faces lit by a squat candle in a red bowl. After hours, Trisha's eyes were playful as she joked with him, and quite soft when she asked personal questions about him.

They went to bed without dinner that evening and made love late into the night, wonderful, laughing, shouting love with occasional pauses filled with whispered questions as to why they had not found one another much sooner. They had been so close, but at the same time, so far apart until that night.

Afterward, somewhere in the neighborhood of three in the morning, as they ate scrambled eggs and Pop Tarts in bed, they agreed to remedy that. But it would be their secret. The gossip vultures at work would never know, would never be able to discuss them in whispers in the break room.

They kept their secret well. They had been living together for nearly three months by the time anyone found out they even spoke to one another during working hours, let alone after work. That was only because McNolte was the first one Trisha rushed to when she was fired from her job. She had been fired after having an ugly confrontation with a longtime client, a prominent psychic who promised wealth and happiness to all who called her team of psychics at her 1-900 number, and who made demands of Trisha that were unreasonable. The argument had ended when Trisha told her, in not so chirping tones, and while brandishing a stapler, that if she were *really* psychic, she would know exactly how much danger she was in at that particular moment.

That evening, McNolte learned that Trisha's outburst had

not been simply the result of frustration, or even job burn-out. She was pregnant. She had known for days and was afraid that when she finally told him, he would leave her, or insist she have an abortion, or perhaps even both. His reaction was instantaneous. He proposed on the spot, and she accepted.

McNolte's newly expanded relationship with Trisha tainted him at work. Her boss, the stern, fiftyish woman who headed up the advertising department and looked like her face would be broken by a single smile, was having an affair with McNolte's boss, the editor-in-chief, a rather prissy, pursed-lip Australian man who looked as if his face were slowly being sucked inward by way of his rectum. McNolte had known nothing of their relationship because he ignored, even actively avoided, all the gossip in the building; he dealt with enough of that in his assignments and had no interest in hearing more during his lunch break. He was not fired outright; instead, his work was criticized with growing frequency, and the stories he was assigned became more demeaning. He could smell the coffee, so he started looking around for work elsewhere.

That was when everything became too good to be true. Everything was so wonderful that he could not help wondering when the other shoe would drop—it was his nature. He got a job at the *Journal*, the biggest paper in the city, and one of the more respected papers in the country. On the basis of his work prior to the *Searchlight*, he was asked to start work immediately. During his farewell handshake with his boss at the *Searchlight*, McNolte smilingly told the man, "I wouldn't want to be your dick," and left his office chuckling.

He and Trisha were married a month later in a small ceremony, with only a few friends in attendance.

Seven months later, Trisha went into labor prematurely. She gave birth to a perfectly sound baby girl who was stillborn only because of a rare mishap: a knot in her umbilical cord. Unable to stay the night in the maternity ward, Trisha went home the same day. They left the hospital with the assurance from the doctor that they would have no trouble having another child, none at all. They listened to her words, but paid them little attention. They were already grieving the baby they would never have and would be too busy with that for a while to even consider trying again.

Trisha found a managerial job in the advertising department at the city's most popular talk radio station while McNolte took his job at the *Journal* and ran with it. His articles quickly began to get serious attention, some getting picked up by Associated Press and United Press International, and he was frequently invited to join discussion panels on CNN.

Seven years, a lot of attention, and a few journalism awards into his job at the *Journal*, McNolte was surprised when Trisha brought up the subject of having another baby. He knew it had to be hard for her to do. He could see the wound opening in her eyes as she spoke of it one night in a low, whispery voice. They discussed it now and then over a period of weeks, then months, neither rejecting nor accepting the idea, but approaching it with caution.

Then something happened that completely changed their life together. McNolte was approached by an advertising agency that admired his work, his ability to use the language and turn a clever phrase. The agency had its headquarters there in the city but it was a multinational company. And it wanted to hire him. He discussed it with Trisha, but they did not need to discuss it long. While they were not hurting financially, the advertising job paid three times their combined incomes, with benefits which, on their own, made the mere idea of rejecting the offer ludicrous. He accepted the job, and Trish happily walked away from hers to devote her full attention to their new nest on First Bay Avenue in Wakehurst, an upscale neighborhood that was sort of a suburb within the city.

It was that change in their lives, that abrupt elevation of status and security, that made them decide it was time to have a baby. Everything was going so well that it suddenly seemed as if they could do no wrong, as if no harm could possibly come to them or the child they hoped to have.

Looking back on that time, McNolte wondered if things would have been different if he had not taken the job at the advertising firm. But it was ridiculous to ponder such things, of course. Worse, it was self-torture. What had happened had happened. What had been done was done.

After parking across the street from Miklos's building, McNolte snatched the baggy from the glove compartment, reached into it for the small spoon that rested among the remaining power, and took a couple of quick snorts. Then a couple more. Then he finished off the baggy.

McNolte leaned his head back and closed his eyes, enjoying the sudden jolt of happiness, then the steady buzz that began to work its way through his body. It made his fingers feel like fingers and his toes like toes, made his lips feel like they were incapable of letting anything inane pass between them, and made his eyes feel like they could see just beyond what was visible.

He took an empty suitcase from the back seat, got out of the car, and went into the building with the envelope of cash in the inside breast pocket of his sport coat, hoping that Miklos had some beer.

It was an elegant building in the city's Bancroft district, a neighborhood much farther from Old Town in its wealth and security than in miles.

The doorman, Phil, opened the door and smiled as he said, "Evening, Mr. McNolte."

"Hey, Phil," McNolte said, returning the smile.

He got out of the elevator on the fourteenth floor and walked into Miklos's apartment without knocking. It was bare except for the sofa, coffee table, a couple of torchiere lamps, and several cardboard boxes of varying sizes with their lids taped closed.

He found Miklos sitting on the edge of the sofa, hunched forward, cutting some coke on the glass-topped coffee table. Standing a few inches away from his busy hands was an unopened bottle of Chivas Regal.

"Hey, McNolte," Miklos said without looking up, his words darkened slightly by his faint Greek accent, "you're just in time. This is a momentous occasion."

McNolte went to the sofa, put the suitcase on the floor and sat down beside Miklos, watching as he continued to work with the coke on the table.

"What's the momentous occasion, Miklos?"

"This is the last of my personal stash of coke, and my last bottle of Chivas." He dropped the razor blade on the glass tabletop with a gentle clank, then leaned back with a sigh. "If you've got the money I think you've got, I can pay off some bills and keep the new apartment for about five, maybe six months." He paused a moment, frowned, made a raspberry sound with his tongue protruding between his lips. "What am I saying, that's not a fucking apartment. Ventriloquist dummies have better digs. Anyway, after that, unless things change, I'm a dead man. It would have been one thing if I'd just been fired from the magazine. But they practically threw me out the door physically. Then they spread all those stories about me. He's unreliable, he's volatile...and now he's poison. Ah, well, I suppose I was. Am. I don't know."

"Don't worry, Miklos, you'll come back before long. A photographer like you? A bad rep can't bury your talent. I mean, look at me. I'm down, but not out. This coke'll take care of my bills, get me back on my feet. I'll have another job in no time."

"I'd sell it all myself, but I don't have the time. I need the money now, even if it's not as much as it would be if I'd sold it on the street myself." He chuckled coldly. "I'm doing you a big favor, my friend, remember that. But it's out of necessity only, not out of any generosity." He scrubbed both hands up and down over his face. "Getting a job isn't my only worry. The IRS has drilled me a new asshole. This is my third, by the way." His hands slapped down on his thighs. "Those sons of bitches are worse than the mob. You owe the mob money you can't pay off, they just kill you and get it over with. The IRS, on the other hand, likes to torture you slowly, pull your life apart a bit at a time."

The skin on the back of McNolte's neck tightened at the mention of owing money to the mob. He tried to ignore it as he reached into his coat, took out the envelope, and dropped it into Miklos's lap. "Well, you're not dead yet," he said. "Here's the money. You can count if you want. Just use it well."

Miklos laughed as he opened the envelope and looked at the money. "I'm not gonna count it, I trust you. Jeez, what do you think I am, anyway. C'mon, McNolte, help me out. I don't want to do the last of my coke alone."

"Well, I won't say no to a hit. Got any beer?"

Miklos nodded toward the bottle on the table. "That's all I've got. Wanna buy it?"

"What?"

He laughed as he picked up the bottle of Chivas and handed it to McNolte. "Just kidding. Go ahead, open it. We'll have to drink from the bottle, though. I've packed all my glasses."

"No problem," McNolte said, opening the bottle. "I'm not proud."

As Miklos took the first hit of coke, McNolte took the first swallow of Chivas, then another, and another. He handed the bottle to Miklos, then turned his attention to the coke on the glass tabletop.

Each hit led to a few more swallows, which led to another hit, and the momentous occasion lasted longer than McNolte had planned.

When McNolte finally left the apartment and returned to his car, the large suitcase he carried was packed full of cocaine, and he was feeling the effects of Miklos's momentous occasion. He chided himself silently for staying so long, for drinking and snorting so much, but the coke had been damned good. Miklos had always had the best.

The rain was still falling steadily and the night's chill had grown more biting. McNolte had planned on making three stops with his full suitcase before going home, but in his present condition, he decided to make only one. His rent was overdue and he could not go home empty-handed. The rest could be done tomorrow, and more the day after that.

With the suitcase on the back seat, McNolte folded his arms on the steering wheel and leaned his head on them. He stayed there for a moment, taking a few slow, deep breaths. Then he sat up, started the engine, and drove away from the curb.

Mixed with the chemicals that were coursing through his system was a warm and soothing sense of relief. He got the money. He got the coke. His profit margin would be a healthy one. His worries would finally be over.

That thought made his flesh crawl. It was a comfortable thought, the idea that his problems were finally over, one he was familiar with. It was a thought he'd had before. Back when he had taken that advertising job.

He decided it was dangerous to think that way because it would never be true. Not as long as he was alive. Life was full of problems.

Back then, though, he was not worried about paying off debts created by his habit, or getting a job, or paying back the loan from Mr. Trafficante. Back then, the problems that he thought would be over were problems he did not even have yet. He did not know what he was thinking at the time.

With the salary he would get from his new advertising job— wherever that might be—he and Trisha could live comfortably and not worry about any expenses brought about by having a child. Trisha enjoyed the idea of being a full-time housewife and mother, and McNolte no longer would have to work under the same around-the-clock pressures he'd had at the *Journal*; there would be no more late-night calls to cover something happening in the wee hours, no more impossible deadlines looming over him menacingly. They could live in a neighborhood that was safe and suitable for children, a neighborhood with a good school. They would not have to worry all the time. They could enjoy their life together.

Again, he cringed at the thought. It was so full of certainty, but nothing in the world was certain. He had thought it before, back when he and Trisha had lived comfortably on his salary at Cutley-McCormick. He'd had a small but comfortable office there with his name on the door, his own secretary, and because of the reputation he had built, people there treated him like a visiting dignitary.

Although they kept trying on a delightfully regular basis, Trisha did not get pregnant again. Her doctor assured them it meant nothing, that getting pregnant always seemed easier to do when one did not *want* to than when one did. He suggested that her subconscious fear of losing another baby might be creating more stress than she realized and he gave her the name of a therapist if Trisha thought that might help.

It was the happiest time McNolte could remember, the best time of his life. Bits and pieces of it fluttered through his mind as he drove through the rain and out of the city, almost to the rhythm of the clumping windshield wipers.

That time in his life was not so long ago, but now when he thought back on it, the memories were fuzzy. It was almost as if he were standing in the icy-cold night looking through a frosted window at vaguely familiar people warming themselves by a fire inside, but the closer he got to the pane, the more his breath fogged up the glass, and the more ghostly those people became. McNolte hoped those memories would become clear again one day. But for now, he knew it was for his own good that they remain vague, not because they were distant but because he knew that to dwell on what he'd had, on what he had lost, and probably would never have again, was to kill himself.

McNolte had been trying to kill himself long enough. That was why he had lost the life he'd had, and he knew it. He did not deny that he was at fault; he had at first, but not anymore. That was why he had borrowed the money from Mr. Trafficante, why he had used it to buy all that cocaine from Miklos, and why he wanted to sell the cocaine now, *needed* to sell it. One last brief bit of dealing. The money he would make from that would be the life preserver that would keep him from going under for a third and final time. It would allow him to focus on bringing himself back from the near-dead.

It was during that happiest time of McNolte's life that the rot and decay first began to set in, hidden away, spreading rapidly, but invisibly, undetected, like a secret cancer. It had happened on a night like any other, at a dinner party being thrown by McNolte and Trisha at their house. Cocktail and dinner parties quickly became a regular part of their life once McNolte started working for Cutley-McCormick. Through his work, McNolte and Trisha suddenly found themselves with a social life they had never imagined they would have. But it was not all social; there was always work to be done while the drinks were poured and the hors d'oeuvres served. There were new clients to make love to and potential clients to seduce. And it was for just such a seduction that McNolte had thrown that particular party.

The potential client had been a young man, about ten years younger than McNolte, named Griffin Schultz, whose already popular nationwide chain of computer stores was about to launch a nationwide internet provider, which Griffin wanted to make sure was just as popular as his stores. He was young but savvy, charismatic and vital, and McNolte, whose job it was to work into the chit-chat a pitch for his campaign for the new venture, was impressed, even a bit intimidated although he was on his own turf. They danced a dance of words and laughter for the first part of the evening, McNolte and Griffin, and the young man began to show what appeared to be a sincere interest in McNolte's ideas. So when Griffin asked McNolte to accompany him to the bathroom—quite casually and without causing the slightest hitch in their energetic, momentum-building conversation—McNolte followed immediately and took no time to think the request an odd one.

Their dance went on as Griffin removed from his pocket a small vial of white powder and a tiny, delicate spoon. As they continued to talk, the rhythm of their conversation uninterrupted, one responding to the other without pause, Griffin dipped the spoon into the vial, held it beneath a nostril, and sucked it in sharply. Then he repeated the process with the other nostril, never disrupting the cadence of their verbal waltz, behaving as if they were still out there among the wandering, well-dressed drinkers and nibblers. They kept talking as Griffin held out the vial and spoon to McNolte, who shook his head once, only slightly, waving a hand dismissively, and Griffin shrugged one shoulder and said, oh, c'mon, go ahead, it's really good stuff, and the rhythm was interrupted for a moment, the dance stumbled for a heartbeat, as McNolte, not wanting to lose step or interrupt the flow, took the vial and spoon, dipped the spoon and, still talking, took one strong sniff of the powder between sentences, then handed the vial and spoon back.

Simple as that. Perfectly innocent. No harm intended.

The sublime dance going on between them picked up speed after that one hit of cocaine, and they stayed there in the bathroom talking, laughing, their steps precise, always with the beat, and McNolte knew he had the account, knew the campaign for the whole chain of stores was his, knew Griffin was sold, and while they bantered, as if in the afterglow of consummated relationship, Griffin pulled out the vial again— was it only minutes later? A half hour? An hour, perhaps?—and took a couple more hits, then offered it to McNolte, who did not hesitate this time, took the vial, the spoon, and took two hits, one in each nostril. It was not bad at all, snorting that stuff up his nose, not like he had imagined. It felt kind of good, in fact, and his smile grew bigger. So did Griffin's, as if they shared a secret, a knowledge that they were the holders of some great and powerful gift, the Holy Grail, the Ark of the Covenant, eat your fucking heart out, Indiana Jones.

And that was the beginning.

McNolte did not know it at the time, of course. He thought he had simply snagged a plum account for Cutler-McCormick, a feather in his own cap. He had told Trisha about it on the way home, after she asked why he was so jumpy, why he was talking so fast, and she had laughed at first, a nervous sort of laugh, then said maybe it was not such a good idea to be doing stuff like that if they were trying to get pregnant, and he had laughed then, not nervous at all, but a little too loud, maybe, and he said not to worry about it, really, it was just the way this guy worked, after all, she saw what he was wearing, the tinted glasses, and he pulled out that little vial, and McNolte had simply gone along with it, that was all, nothing to worry about, nothing at all.

Famous last words, he knew that now. But not then. He had been totally ignorant of the dark cloud that was already rolling in over him, blanketing him in its shadow.

After that, when people were doing cocaine around him, McNolte noticed in a way he never had before, and when it was offered, he accepted, until one afternoon, pressed for time, up against a presentation deadline with very little to present, swamped with work and knowing he would have to stay late, he bought some of his own from a fellow worker, just a little, enough to keep him going until he was caught up, until the work was out of the way, and sure enough, McNolte was at his desk long after everyone else had left, long after the sun had gone down, but he was too immersed in his work to notice, aflame with creativity, productivity, burning through his work like a comet through the sky, and when he got home late that night to find that Trisha had already gone to bed, he was still so full of fire that he went to work in the nursery, finished up the crib he had started weeks ago, and when Trisha shuffled in, sleepy-eyed and wondering what he was doing at such an hour, he took her in his arms, led her back to bed and made powerful, sweaty love to her once, then again, and by the time he wanted to try once more, the sun was coming up outside and Trisha was wide awake, asking with a combination of amusement and annoyance exactly what the hell had gotten into him, and McNolte realized that in a few hours he would have to give the presentation he had spent so much of the night before preparing, and it was not until that moment that he realized he was starting to come down again and needed another hit. But the little bit of coke he had bought was all gone, so he would have to get some more, maybe leave for work a little early, after a cold shower and some strong coffee. He could find the guy he had bought the coke from yesterday and get some more, pump himself up for that presentation. Get the juices flowing again. As he took his shower, McNolte tried to remember the name of the guy he had bought the coke from, but could not. Over coffee, Trisha scolded him for staying up all night when he knew he had something so important to do the next morning. He told her he was fine, though he sounded exhausted, looked drawn. She kept at it, and he finally snapped at her, told her not to worry about him. Then he left for work, still trying to remember that guy's name.

In the following weeks and months, McNolte was not even aware of the fact that he was repeating the same process over and over, until he was buying enough cocaine at one time to make sure he would not run out again right away, enough so he would always have some on hand for those nights of marathon work, or some for those mornings after such nights when even a bitterly cold shower was not enough to get him out the front door, or just when he *wanted* to do some, just wanted the kick it gave, on the weekends, maybe, when he did not have to worry about work and could just enjoy it, hell, he worked hard enough, he had a little something of his own coming, right? A little pleasure that was his alone, shared with no one else and enjoyed in the privacy of his own grinning, humming mind.

Whenever he thought of that time, of his trip down that dark tunnel—first walking, then jogging, then running as he put more and more distance between himself and the light that was his life—he thought more of Trisha than anything else. Of that first time she had approached the subject, so cautious and uncertain, asking him if he had been doing more cocaine, like he had that night a few months ago at one of his boss's dinner parties. Of the sparkling mixture of fear and sadness in her eyes when he smiled and said to her, "Oh, yeah, but that's nothing to worry about, honey, really, I mean, it's not like it's gonna be a regular thing, nothing like that, it's no different than having a cocktail while talking business, that's all." Of the second time she brought it up, with anger in her eyes then, her voice trembling to maintain a civil tone as she listed off the things she saw happening to him: he was always sniffling as if he had a cold, he could not sleep unless he polished off a bottle of wine at night, sometimes more, and even then his sleep was fitful, and he was having uncharacteristic mood swings, snapping at her, often getting angry over the pettiest little things.

McNolte could not remember how he had talked his way past that, but he had then, and a few times after that, as well. But as he changed, so did Trisha. She withdrew from him, would not speak to him for long stretches. And finally, she left. It was not sudden. She had spent a few weekends with her parents and had threatened several times to leave for good if he refused to get help, and at first, he had promised her he would, but later insisted that he did not need it. He had tried to fool her into thinking he was cutting back, staying away from the nose candy, but no amount of surreptitiousness helped. She always knew. Until finally, she said she could not bear the thought of having his baby, of him being the father of her child. Then she left.

And that was only his cloudy, unfocused version of what had happened, with the ugly fights, the screaming, the crying, all of that carefully edited out. The softer version. The one that didn't hurt quite so much. Didn't make him want to step in front of a speeding train.

Work had been something else entirely. While his marriage was falling apart at home, McNolte was soaring at Cutler-McCormick, becoming a shining star in the advertising firmament. Everything he touched turned to gold. He could do no wrong, he was incapable of stumbling. But when things changed there, they changed quickly.

It happened right after Trish left him. He had kept it to himself for a while, certain she would be back, but so terrified she would not that he froze inside, as if his soul had seized up with rigor mortis. To fight that, he turned to the cocaine, and to relax the effects of it, he turned to alcohol, but he did not sleep at all, just rolled and thrashed in his bed until it was time to get up and have another hit. His fall occurred so suddenly, he did not have time to notice he had stumbled.

First a friend who worked in the graphics department suggested to McNolte that he lay off the coke because it was starting to show and could become a problem, people were talking, and that was how problems started. But McNolte had reassured him, confided in him, told him that Trisha had left and he was just going through a bad time, that was all, would be fine, really.

But McNolte could not ignore the stares from others, nor deny his own nagging fear that he was doing something wrong of which he was unaware, the suspicions being whispered behind his back.

Then, suddenly, everything was so different that even the cocaine was not the same, did not do for him, to him, the wonderful things it had always done. Before, it had always made him move through life with such speed and ease, such flawless agility. But then, as if all that had been a glorious dream, McNolte opened his eyes one day to find himself in a waking nightmare in which he did not move at all, but the world and everyone and everything in it, life itself, roared past him, around him, thundering straight into his face and then passing by with a hollow, mocking, and horrible silent shriek.

One day, he arrived at work, even later than usual, to find he no longer had an office, or a job.

He told himself at first that everything would be okay, he could control the damage if he applied himself. He had made quite a bit of money at Cutler-McCormick and had saved up enough to get by for a while. But a letter from Trisha's attorney reminded him that the money belonged to her, too, and she would be getting half of it in the divorce. Still, he told himself he had enough to live on while he found a new job.

But there was no new job. And he quickly realized he did not have enough money to live on *and* maintain a steady supply of cocaine for the sleepless, snorting creature that lived inside his head, screaming whenever it was not fed the white powder it constantly craved.

He had been tap dancing ever since, robbing Peter to pay the piper.

But things were going to change now. Finally. He was determined to make them change. There was light at the end of the tunnel, he knew there was, and he only needed to round that dark curve just ahead to see it. He would use the money he was going to make off the coke to get himself into a rehab program. He would look for work, maybe start making friends again. Real friends, not the low-lifes he had been hanging around with to feed his habit.

There was a time when he told himself he would go to Trisha, and when she saw that he was a new man, damaged but under repair, she would forget all that had happened before and they could reconcile. But he eventually admitted to himself that was not going to happen. McNolte was damaged, yes, but Trisha had been deeply wounded. By him. By simply showing up in her life, clean and sober, he would only be opening those old wounds, and he did not want to do that. He still loved her too much. He always would. But he knew he would never have her again.

Once he was on the freeway, McNolte eased into traffic and left the rain-blurred glow of the city behind him. After a few miles, he cut off the freeway and drove along an old cracked road that took him east into the dark, hilly countryside that spread out between the city and its suburbs.

He was on his way to make his first sale to Trevor Beckett, the aging art critic for the *Journal*, as well as the author of a number of successful books on art and artists, and one bestselling potboiler novel set in the art world. McNolte knew Beckett from his days at the paper. They ran into each other occasionally in the city, at fundraisers and cocktail parties, and always took time to chat. Beckett ribbed McNolte about his success, jokingly accusing him of selling out for the big bucks. McNolte did not know him well, but he knew him well enough to ask during one of those chats if he would be interested in some quality cocaine at reasonable prices, well enough to know what his answer would be. At sixty-six, Beckett's looks, charm, and wit were not what they once had been and he was having much less success attracting to his bed the hot young men to whom he had grown accustomed over the years. It was no secret that cocaine was his preferred remedy.

McNolte had an appointment at Beckett's large alpine-style house in the hills at eight that evening; unfortunately, it was eight forty-five already and it was a lengthy drive. McNolte hoped Beckett was not too angry at him.

It was not a pleasant drive. McNolte was jittery and never quite sure if he was driving too fast or too slow. Each shard of reflected light that shimmered over the windshield or his mirror made him jump because he was terrified of being pulled over by a cop and found with all that coke in his possession. He turned on the radio; FM was out of commission because the antenna had been broken off of his car, but AM reception was poor in that area and stations only bled over one another and staticky, blurred-together voices scraped against his nerves until he reached down and turned it off again. The wipers were on high-speed but still did not move fast enough to keep up with the torrential rain, and as he put more distance between himself and the headlight-clogged freeway, everything beyond his own headlights became a black abyss.

He missed a turn and had to double back once, then got onto the narrow, winding road that led up the hill to Beckett's house, craning his head forward and squinting to see through the rain.

Intensely jumpy, his hands trembled as he clumsily lit a cigarette while driving, then cracked the window, taking one deep drag after another, first on the cigarette, then on the cold night air that rushed into the cab. The farther up the hill he drove, the narrower the road became. Muddy embankments arose on both sides of him, the right taller than the left, making him feel claustrophobic and even more nervous.

The windows began to fog up and McNolte felt a jolt of panic in his chest because the defroster had not worked in weeks. With his cigarette dangling from his lips, he rolled the window down all the way, wincing at the raindrops that spattered him.

When he saw the flash of movement to his right, his first thought was, *My God, a mudslide!* He spat the cigarette from his lips as he made a blabbering sound of fear and slammed his foot down on the accelerator, hoping to race past it before the mud could block his way or, even worse, bury his car and swallow him up.

Even though he smashed the pedal beneath his foot, everything—the car, the rain, time itself—slowed down to a torturous crawl.

His next thought was nebulous and inarticulate, but had something to do with too much booze and coke, because the mudslide appeared to have eyes. And horns.

McNolte understood that it was a deer only a fraction of a second after the right front corner of his car hit it with a nauseating crunch.

McNolte screamed.

The buck tumbled over the hood of the car and its head slammed through the right side of the windshield. Silver webs of cracks shot across the safety glass instantly, making it impossible to see what was ahead of him.

McNolte continued to scream, no longer aware of his foot on the accelerator. His elbows locked, arms stiff between him and the wheel, shoulder blades digging into the back of the seat. He could not stop turning to look at the twisted face of the animal, its antlers clacking against the passenger-side window as its head jerked spastically, wide eyes rolling, legs kicking frantically and making a horrible clatter against the hood. The buck's mouth opened and emitted a shrill, pinched sound, like an infant being tortured.

The buck's wail and McNolte's scream intertwined and drilled into his skull with a hot, barbed bit.

McNolte did not stop screaming until he realized that the car was rolling and he was rolling with it, slamming around in the cab like a pinball because he had not fastened his seatbelt. Shortly before losing consciousness, he vomited explosively and began to cough and choke.

He had no way of knowing how long his blackout had lasted and did not take the time to wonder as he opened his bleary eyes and peered through the murky darkness.

The gawking buck jerked its head, mewling pathetically in its final bleeding moments.

McNolte heard the sounds of dripping and hissing...and the crackle of flames. He gagged on the smell of smoke and the cloying odor of gasoline.

Still blinking in and out of consciousness, he moved to get out of the car, then found himself crawling through the rolled-down window, then dragging himself over the muddy ground through the rain, away from the car, retching as he crawled, head exploding with a shattering pain that made him groan. He stopped for a moment to turn his head painfully and look over his shoulder.

The car was completely upside down and on fire. Something was in his eyes. At first, he thought it was smoke, but when he rubbed the back of his hand over his eyes, he realized it was thick and warm and wet, and there was a lot of it. And it was not rain.

He crawled on through the mud, trying to cry out, make some sound that might serve as a release for the pain that continued to build in his head, but he could not. His throat was paralyzed.

There was a thick *whump!* sound behind him and a rush of hot air swept over him. He would have looked over his shoulder again to see what had happened but saw no point because the blood had blinded him completely.

He continued to crawl and retch until the pain slammed his face into the mud. Once again, consciousness left him, but the steel needles of pain somehow remained in the blackness.

3.

AFTER HOURS

Although his secretary had left nearly two hours ago, Landon Shaw was still in his office in the city, finishing up some business, dictating a few letters into a microcassette recorder.

It was an enormous office, impossibly clean, right down to the four small wastebaskets scattered throughout. They, along with the ashtrays, were emptied every hour on the hour from nine to five. It was decorated in dark earth tones, with a lot of shiny oak surfaces. The many shelves held books on every aspect of business, reference books on medicine and various sciences, biographies of inventors and scientists. One wall of shelves displayed neat rows of detailed models of antique cars, each one handmade and worth thousands of dollars, each in its own rectangular glass case. Outside of his work, cars were Shaw's passion, old and new, and he had another collection of them in his garages at home that was far more impressive than the one on his office shelves. He was, in fact, in the process of acquiring a Rolls Royce Silver Cloud. The mere thought of it made his mouth water.

His desktop was a vast kidney-shaped oak field that spread before him like a continent that he controlled with godlike autonomy. It was never less than impeccably appointed, with everything in order, no papers stacked without razor-even edges, no book or file opened before him that was not properly centered and never so much as a pen or paperclip out of place.

The wall behind him was mostly glass; six large rectangular windows gave him a sprawling view of the city. At the moment, the blinds were drawn on all but the two windows directly behind him. Dusk had melted away and the city was a blanket of glitter beneath the stormy night sky. Now and then, a flash of lightning illuminated the bloated clouds and thunder rolled over the city lazily.

Shaw loved his office, even though he spent only half his time there. He liked the great space it gave him, and especially the bird's eye view of the city. It was a room that reeked of order and power and wealth, and he saw it as a microcosm of his entire business, his entire life.

Landon Shaw was President and CEO of OdysseyCorp Labs, which he had started from scratch eleven years ago. Before that, he had made a sizable fortune in the computer business. He knew little about computers, but he had a gift for noticing the direction in which the wind was blowing , and he had made a fortune off them by filling his company with people who were the best in their field. Com-Tech was a big success, but there came a time when it was obvious that everyone was going to be making a fortune off of computers, and Landon Shaw did not want to be part of a trend, even if it was one he had virtually started himself. He had left that business and spent a couple of years looking for his next frontier.

Before he made a fortune from computers, he had dreamed up a clever business for which he had received no credit whatsoever.

A brilliant student, Shaw had skipped the third grade and graduated high school just shy of his sixteenth birthday. By then he had already obtained a scholarship to Harvard, which was a big leap from his tiny hometown of Dilly, Wisconsin. His major was business, which was his goal, his strength. But it was not his talent. That was something else.

Shaw realized early on that his true talent lay in reading people. Reading them quickly, finding their strengths and, most importantly to him, their weaknesses. He could size up a person after a short time of watching closely, observing silently. He could quickly determine what made that person tick, what made the ticking slow down or speed up, or stop. It was that talent, not his sense for business, that was responsible for his success.

His favorite class during his first year at Harvard was Macroeconomics and Psychology, taught by Professor Jerrold Kehoe, who, in fact, hardly taught at all. He made a big impression on students in the first week, then turned everything over to his graduate student assistants, only to return at the end of the semester to make a grand exit.

Professor Kehoe was one of Harvard's stars. He appeared regularly on news networks and financial talk shows, wrote a column for the *Wall Street Journal*, and was a favorite on the lucrative lecture circuit. He had written three bestselling books on economics and had been the most quoted economist in the country for at least a decade. Shaw admired him a great deal and was thrilled to take his class. But what thrilled him even more was Kehoe's graduate student, Tom Rubie, who actually taught the class, did all the work, and who could not take his eyes off Shaw.

By then, Shaw had had sex with three women, two of them his age, fellow students, and one of them his high school English teacher. He'd had no interest in men, but his interest in women was minimal; he knew the incredible power of sex, the control it offered—or denied, depending upon one's position—and that was what appealed to him, not the actual sex itself. He preferred the position of control, and he knew that, with Tom Rubie, he could have it if he wanted.

Shaw allowed himself to be seduced by Rubie, not because he was attracted to him but because he saw a potential he wanted to realize. It appeared on the surface that Rubie was the seducer, but Shaw was in control every step of the way.

His scholarship took care of his tuition, but beyond that, he was struggling, eating a lot of popcorn and ramen. Shaw knew that Rubie had access to Kehoe's exams, the answers to their questions, and if he played his cards right, he knew both he and Rubie could benefit from that. Rubie's attraction to him, his complete sexual captivation, helped make that happen.

When Shaw presented the idea—in bed, in quiet, lover's whispers—Rubie smiled and agreed even more readily than Shaw had expected. In fact, it was at that moment that Rubie made a remark Shaw remembered and filed away for future use:

"And if he finds out," Rubie had said with a laugh, his breath hot on Shaw's neck, "we can always threaten to tell everyone that he's a flagrant plagiarist."

Shaw and Rubie made a lot of money selling the answers to Kehoe's exams—and Shaw made a lot more than Rubie ever knew because he did business behind Rubie's back—but all the while, Shaw's mind chewed on that one careless, quiet remark made by Rubie. He wondered how much truth there was to it, and how he might profit from it. He brought it up casually in a conversation with Rubie one evening, again after sex, when Rubie was always smiling and most vulnerable, and Shaw learned that Kehoe was, indeed, a plagiarist. He had a secret file made up of papers written by his finest students, papers filled with cutting-edge ideas, theories, and even brilliant forecasts about the future of the American and global economies, all of which received mediocre grades and were stopped in their tracks so Kehoe could integrate them into his already established theories and use them in his column, books, and lectures, expound on them in his television appearances. One night, Shaw playfully suggested that they have sex in Kehoe's office, on his desk and his sofa, and was surprised when Rubie immediately agreed. While they were there, Shaw subtly convinced Rubie to show him that secret file, and he did. It was one of Shaw's fondest memories because it was such a victory for him.

Shaw invested the money made from Kehoe's exam answers, nurtured and cultivated it. At the same time, he was cultivating an idea in his mind, letting it grow, keeping it to himself. He knew it was a good idea, maybe even brilliant, and he knew that somehow he would be able to marry it to Kehoe's plagiarism. He was not sure how yet, but he was patient. Besides, he had an education to absorb, a reputation to make as a brilliant student and an innovative thinker in the field of business. The time would come.

That time came in his senior year, after his useful but brief relationship with Tom Rubie was a vague memory, having been succeeded by many other relationships which had been useful in other ways. Shaw made an appointment with Professor Kehoe. Actually, he made several of them, because Kehoe was a popular man and had little time for a mere student, so the appointment was postponed again and again. But when it finally happened, Shaw greeted the man with the proper amount of respect and admiration, fawning over his accomplishments, expressing his gratitude for Kehoe's classes, telling him how fortunate he felt to have been a student of his. And then, once Kehoe had been kneaded to the appropriate softness, Shaw began to share his idea. But rather than presenting it as an idea—

I've been very impressed with your assistants, as well, Professor Kehoe. You've surrounded yourself with some brilliant young people.

—he approached it as nothing more than a change of topic in the conversation—

You have a great eye for talent. In fact, I'm rather surprised you haven't used that eye outside of Harvard. I suspect you would be just as brilliant spotting talent for others.

—a simple thought that had just occurred to him as he sat there chatting with Kehoe over his old, scuffed, messy desk—

In fact...come to think of it, Professor...I bet you could make quite a success out of your eye for talent, your organizational sense. I mean, well, think about it. Consider this. With your talent for picking the cream, you could put together a staff of your own, then use that staff to do for other companies—new, young companies just starting out, or maybe failing companies in need of revitalization—what you've been doing for yourself. Picking the best of the best, bringing them together, organizing them in such a way that allows them to meet their full potential.

—but one which captured his imagination, fired him up enough to embellish on it, play with it—

Yes, I can see that causing quite a stir, Professor. Kehoe Concepts, that's a good name. You and the hand-picked employees of Kehoe Concepts offer your services, which are based on your tried and true strategies, your finely honed methods of placement, organization. I don't think it could lose, Professor.

—a simple, spontaneous idea which he presented as a possibility, in which he stirred the professor's interest, made him lean forward and rest his elbows on his desktop as he listened intently—

But I guess it wouldn't really work if you did that now, would it, Professor? I mean, if you actually did it. As if it were your idea. Because, after all, it wasn't. It was mine. And if you claimed it as yours, that would make you...well, a sort of plagiarist, wouldn't it? And it wouldn't do, I mean, it simply wouldn't do for someone of your standing to be perceived as a plagiarist, would it, Professor Kehoe? That could destroy you. Wipe you out.

—an idea which made the professor's eyes narrow, made the jaw of his long, narrow face set, made his head nod ever so slightly as he stared at Shaw, studied him.

Seven months after Shaw graduated, Kehoe announced a new venture, Kehoe Concepts, a business consulting firm made up of brilliant young minds that would breathe new life into the business world, revolutionize the way American businesses were structured and executed. And to head up this venture, Kehoe appointed one of his own former students, one of his best, someone who would set the very tone for Kehoe Concepts, a young man for such a position but no younger than any of the other brilliant members of the team: Landon Shaw.

A few years later, Shaw realized that others were beginning to do what he was doing and in the way he was doing it, so he had moved on to computers. And once Com-Tech was old news, he had walked away from that, too, in search of something else, taking his time, patiently looking for a soft spot, a vulnerability, something he could control.

The field of medical and genetic research had become interesting. Aside from incurable diseases that already existed—arthritis, muscular dystrophy, multiple sclerosis, and of course the Big C, among so many others—there were new ones crawling out of the woodwork, not the least of which was AIDS. But in his careful and laborious research, he discovered another field ready to explode, one that was closely related but quite different.

Medicine and genetics formed a burgeoning field of research in which the government had gotten involved. DNA testing was still in its infancy then but was being spoken of nonetheless, and it was beginning to show up in the business of solving crimes, among other things. Shaw was certain there was more to all that than met the eye, and with a little more research, a few discreet questions of high-level contacts, and some clever extrapolation—the sort of thing in which he excelled—he became certain that he could be on the ground floor of what would soon become an explosion. The general public would be ignorant of it. Even the stockholders and administrators and employees of the company he planned to create would, without effort, be kept completely blind to this new field he expected to blossom in the near future, and blind as well to the true purpose of the company.

That company was OdysseyCorp. It was presented as a medical and genetic research lab, the purpose of which was to discover new and more effective ways of preventing, treating, and curing disease, including new diseases facing medical science, and treating recently discovered biological causes of mental illness and chemical addictions.

OdysseyCorp was a success from the beginning because Shaw acquired the best people in every field covered by the company, and he used every means available to him to do so. Absolutely every means. The stockholders were happy. Even the press was happy, because Shaw employed a top-flight, sharp-edged team of publicists to make sure that the tiniest discoveries and developments were handed to the press as major breakthroughs. The name OdysseyCorp repeatedly made headlines in every major newspaper and was covered by every major newscast in the world because of those tiny, overblown breakthroughs.

In the meantime, through the network of connections Shaw had developed, some of the right people were notified that OdysseyCorp was capable of doing so much more. The company had one hundred separate departments. Ninety-nine of them dealt exclusively with various diseases, contagious and otherwise, and genetic causes of mental illness and chemical addiction. One department lay dormant, waiting to be used. Department #100 was, for a long time, nothing more than letters and numbers typed on paperwork passed through many hands and seen by many eyes, but it served no purpose and was therefore either ignored or completely unknown by virtually everyone at OdysseyCorp. It showed up on paper so often and meant so little that, in no time at all, it was dismissed by all who saw it, long before it actually began to function as an operating part of the company. Its actual purpose would have been a mystery to anyone who noticed it, but by the time it began to function, people had long since stopped noticing it.

Department #100 was—although the official title appeared on no paperwork and was never mentioned aloud by anyone, thus unknown even in the highest offices of OdysseyCorp— Weapons Research. That was the explosion Shaw was expecting and on which he planned to capitalize—biological and genetic weapons.

Everything else was overused and out of date. Guns, tanks, missiles, and bombs would one day be overtaken by weapons that were silent, invisible, and deadlier than a dozen minefields. With the field of genetics opening up, he had no doubt the military was already working on weaponizing it. Shaw had no idea what, precisely, a genetic weapon would be, but he hired people to handle that kind of stuff. He specialized in the *big* ideas. And he was certain this was one of them.

The next battlefield would be the human body, whether it was the weapon or the target.

Landon Shaw was right again. The government was happy to call on him. The Pentagon was OdysseyCorp's biggest customer, although that fact was not publicized in any way. It was a secret relationship. Like an affair with a married woman.

Department #100 was responsible for seventy-nine percent of OdysseyCorp's revenue. Of course, it took a little book juggling to keep the stockholders ignorant of that truth; the profits were spread smoothly over all the other departments. While OdysseyCorp Labs was seen by stockholders, the public, and even the pyramid of workers who made it what it was, as a corporation devoted to relieving humanity of disease and suffering, the Pentagon was pouring hundreds of millions of dollars into OdysseyCorp to find new ways of dispatching enemies in great numbers, as well as new ways of controlling allies, including the very public that saw the company as some kind of good Samaritan. All of that money was being spent on a tiny handful of people who worked on projects so secret that they did not exist. People who, for the most part, knew only what they absolutely had to know in order to effectively contribute to the project to which they had been assigned.

But the government was not the only entity with enemies to dispatch. There were other organizations and individuals who had people they wanted to get rid of and people they wanted to control. Most of them preferred to remain anonymous and dealt with Shaw through a representative. He often had little to no idea with whom he was doing business. Shaw referred to them as his shadow clients. They were people who had nothing to do with the United States government. They had no government front to legitimize their activities, all of which were illegal.

Whenever Department #100 was commissioned to do research and develop a product that Shaw thought might interest one or more of his shadow clients, he notified them through channels. The money he made from them was his own, of course, and he tucked it away in offshore accounts.

There was a project under way at Department #100 that he knew would interest more than a few of his shadow clients. He would spread the word soon, and the results of the project would be passed quietly and invisibly to the highest bidder.

Landon Shaw controlled his company the way he controlled his office, the way he controlled his life. Everything in place, all surfaces clean, and nothing unpleasant in sight.

Even now, with his secretary gone, and two glass rectangles of city-sprinkled night behind him, Shaw's office was in perfect order. Although he leaned back in his chair as he spoke quietly into the microcassette recorder, he did not put his feet up on his desk, as many men would. In the last two hours, he had emptied his ashtray into the wastebasket twice, although he had smoked only two cigarettes and one cigar, and before leaving, he would empty that wastebasket himself rather than leaving it for the hired help. He knew that sleep would not come as easily that night if he left behind a mess at work.

He spent the other half of his time in his office in the OdysseyCorp building just outside the city, but this was where he met his clients. This was where he felt most in control because there were no doctors, no scientists, and none of their assistants walking around in their white coats with their clipboards, looking preoccupied with their work (which was really *his* work, because the whole company was *his* work), and looking as if, in spite of their smiles and pleasant words, they knew how much smarter they were than Shaw, how far ahead of him they were intellectually, how much more they knew. How much better they were than he. None of those smug people were around when he was in his city office. He was in total control and there was nothing in sight to suggest otherwise.

While speaking into the recorder, he stopped mid-sentence when the large, oak double doors of his office burst open suddenly and a large man stalked into the room without knocking. He smiled as he closed the doors behind him. It was an aggressive smile that seemed to have some darkness around the edges.

"Leo!" Shaw said, leaning forward to set the recorder on his desk and standing with a grin. "Believe it or not, I was just thinking of you," he lied. Among his many shadow clients, Leo had been a regular from the beginning. He was not afraid of dealing with Shaw face to face. Leo Trafficante was not afraid of anything.

Shaw knew Leo considered him a friend because they socialized together and had been to each other's homes multiple times, and anything he might say to remind Leo of that right now seemed like a good idea, because that was not a happy smile on his face. He offered his hand to shake as Leo approached, and said, "What brings you here at this hour?"

Leo ignored his hand and, still smiling, glared down at the tiny recorder. "Your little machine still on?"

Shaw chuckled. "Of course not." He picked up the recorder, popped the tape out, and placed it on the desk.

Shaw was still smiling, but he felt a knot in his gut. Something was not right. It was not like Leo to walk into his office—*any* office, for that matter—without knocking, without making an appointment. It simply was not his way. He had old-fashioned good manners. Leo did not hesitate to have his enemies, or anyone who got in his way, shot in the face, but the man had impeccable manners. And he was alone, which was also unusual. Normally, he was accompanied by his personal secretary, Ollie, and one or two bodyguards who were larger, younger, and harder than himself. Something was up, and Shaw's sensitive stomach was already starting to react.

"Would you like a drink, Leo?" he said, starting to walk out from behind his desk toward the bar.

Leo leaned forward, clutched Shaw's elbow tightly, and said in his quiet, moist way, "I don't want a drink, Shaw. This isn't a social call. Just stay right where you are, okay? We're gonna talk."

Shaw let his smile melt away and frowned slightly. "Sounds important, Leo. Is there a problem? Something I can do for you?"

Leo's smile grew a bit, showing both rows of his small, square teeth and the much larger gums into which they were fastened.

"Yes, there is something you can do for me, Shaw. You can die. Right now. Just drop dead and save me the trouble of having to kill you."

The shrimp salad sandwich Shaw had eaten an hour ago began to threaten a sudden and violent reappearance. As good as he was with people, as confident as he was in his manipulations of him, Leo made him nervous because he knew what the man was capable of. He maintained his composure, smiled again, and cocked his head as if trying to understand the joke.

"What's the punchline, Leo?"

Still smiling, and with a low, quiet chuckle, Leo said, "The punchline is that I came here to kill you."

Shaw's eyes narrowed a bit, but he said nothing.

"Yeah, you heard me right, Landon. I came here to kill you."

The smile disappeared again as Shaw's arms folded slowly across his chest. "I...I don't understand, Leo. Have I done something to upset you?"

"Upset me?" The big man leaned forward and flattened his beefy palms on the desktop. "If you'd upset me, I'd give you a call on the phone. If you'd upset me, we'd get together and have a little talk." His smile became a sneer as he shouted, "If you'd just *upset* me, I wouldn't wanna fucking *kill* you, would I?"

Raising his eyebrows high, Shaw reached down, opened a small wooden box on his desk, removed a cigarette from it, and lit up. "I take it I've done...what?" He took a long drag, then exhaled smoke slowly through his nose and mouth as he smiled again. "I don't understand, Leo. We're friends, right? I mean, hell, we vacationed together once, remember? And aside from that, I've got something I think you'll be very interested"—

"You're a fucking wife-beater."

Shaw stumbled over his words and his smile became crippled. "I beg your pardon?"

"I said, you're a fucking wife-beater. I saw the bruise. She told me. She told me everything."

"Emma?"

"How many wives you got?"

"I-I-I...I don't understand, Leo. You say Emma told you something about...well, see, I'm trying to figure out what kind of conversation you could possibly have with my wife that would lead to such a spurious—"

"We've been having an affair, Landon. For months now."

Wearing a curious frown, Shaw lowered himself back into his chair. The fact that his wife had been fucking Leo bothered him not in the least. The fact that she had so effectively turned Leo against him was unbelievably infuriating, and even though he did not like to admit it, not even to himself, it was terrifying. He would have to handle this situation with extraordinary care. Later, he could decide how to deal with Emma. But she would be dealt with, and severely.

Shaw said, "You mean to tell me you're going to allow my private and personal life with my wife come between our business relationship? Our friendship? Is that it?"

Leo leaned forward even further, until it looked like he was going to fall flat on the desk. Saliva glistened in the corners of his mouth as he said in his wet, muttering way, "You're a cancer, Landon Shaw, a fucking cancer. Men like you, you're a disease that your fucking lab couldn't even begin to cure. Even if curing diseases was what your fucking lab did in the first place, which we both know is bullshit."

"So, you've...come here to kill me. I'm curious, Leo. How are you doing to do it?"

Leo slid his big hands off the desktop, stood up straight, and glared down at Shaw. "Normally, I wouldn't even be here. I pay people to do this sort of thing for me while I'm someplace else. But I wanted to be here for this because see, Shaw, just like they say in the movies...it's personal. See, I...well, this sounds crazy, even to me, because I'm just not the type, but...I love your wife, Landon. I swear to God, I love her like I was...a kid in school having his first crush. She's made me feel like a young man. I've never met a woman like her in my life. And I've had the best of 'em, let me tell ya."

Shaw smirked while his stomach burned. "Leo, are you going to stand there and write a love letter to my wife, or are you going to tell me how you plan to kill me?"

"You're gonna write a short little note. Then you're going out the window."

"Out the *window*?" Shaw glanced over his shoulder at the glass. "These windows don't even open. Do you know how thick the glass is? What, you expect me to just write a note and then throw myself through the glass to die on the street below just because you say so? You're crazy, Leo," Shaw said with a laugh.

"I've got two gigantic fellows outside that door who will come in here and prove I'm not crazy by throwing your smug ass through the fucking window after you write your little note."

Leo was not alone after all. It was no surprise.

Shaw leaned back in his chair, trying to relax, while his mind screamed with activity, searching for an out, a foothold, for some way to—

"Wouldn't it be nice if you didn't have to do it this way, Leo?" he said.

Leo frowned. "Had to do what? What way? What the hell're you talking about?"

Shaw leaned forward and folded his arms on the desk, looking up at the big man. "I wasn't lying, Leo, when I said I was thinking of you when you came through that door," he lied again. "I've got a new project. It's already underway. Project Biofire, Leo. You like the sound of that?" He allowed his eyes to smile, but his mouth remained expressionless. He did not want to go too far too fast.

Leo's eyes narrowed to black, bloodless slits in his fat face, but he said nothing.

Shaw found his silence encouraging. "I'm talking about something completely unlike anything OdysseyCorp has ever done before, Leo. Something ground-breaking. And something I think would be especially suited to you. Perfect for you and your work. How would you like it, Leo, if you didn't have to—"

"Shut the fuck up before I start slappin' the shit outta you like the bitch you are," Leo said. He spoke quietly, but the words carried the weight of a shout, and Shaw's mouth snapped shut with an audible clacking of teeth.

As hard as he tried to control it, Shaw felt his rage burning in his face for Leo to see. He took a drag on his cigarette, placed it on the edge of the large ashtray, then exhaled smoke as he leaned back in his chair, away from the desk, from Leo, his body relaxed, his insides bubbling with anger. And cold with fear.

"I'm surprised at you, Leo. Even disappointed. This isn't like you at all."

A grin peeled back slowly over Leo's disturbing teeth. "I can almost hear your thoughts," he said. "You're so cocky, so fucking confident you're gonna get by me on this, you're already thinking ahead to what you're gonna do to her for telling me this, aren't you? Yeah." He nodded once. "You're already punishing her in your head. Bet you got a fuckin' hard-on right now, don't you? Just thinking about it probably charms your snake, you sick fuck."

"It's not like you to let something like this interfere with business, Leo."

"I told you, it's *personal*, this's got nothing to do with business."

"That's where you're wrong." Shaw spoke more quickly now, but still quietly, with a hint of urgency, importance, but not even a shade of fear. "Killing me now, for whatever reason, would set you and your business so far back in the Stone Age, you'd be wiped out before the wheel was discovered. You'd be left wide open to your competitors, Leo. You'd probably be dead within a year after this new item goes up for auction. And no one would ever suspect you'd been murdered."

Leo's right eye narrowed. "The fuck're you talking about?"

Inside, Shaw smiled.

"As long as I'm alive," he continued, "this project will proceed exactly as I've planned, and the product will be made available to you, Leo. You're getting first heads-up on this. But if I'm killed...well, then it will be out of my hands."

"What project?" Leo's tone was low, but impatient.

"It's already underway, and it will be completed. But who knows what will be done with it? It'll go to the government because they commissioned it. But who else? Maybe you, of course. Maybe. But if not, then you would be in big trouble. Out in the cold. You wouldn't know what hit you. And neither would anyone else."

Leo came around the desk quickly, his intense stare never for a moment loosening its iron grip on Shaw's eyes. He slapped a big hand onto Shaw's chest, closed it tightly on his shirt, tie, and one lapel, jerked him with ease from his seat, and pressed his back against the thick glass pane of one of the windows behind the desk.

"You're pissing me off, Landon," Leo growled wetly through his small, clenched teeth. "I'm startin' to think maybe I oughtta kill you right now, myself, with my bare hands. If you know something I should know, you'd better tell me now, goddammit, or you're gonna wish you *had* gone out the fucking window."

Shaw fought for control of the storm raging inside him, tried not to think thoughts of lashing out at Leo, roaring in his fleshy face, pushing his thumbs into the man's pig-like eyes until they punched through bone and sunk into gelatinous brain tissue. But Shaw's voice was completely level when he spoke.

"If you're going to kill me, Leo, then do it. I'm not especially afraid of dying, and I'm not afraid of you at all. But. If you want to hear what I have to say, remove your hand from my chest and take a step back."

The moment froze then and stretched out interminably,

and Shaw became vividly aware of everything around him: his office—where he was most powerful and confident—the night outside the windows, the city lights, the smell of cigar smoke, and of Leo's garlicky breath.

There was indecision in Leo's eyes. Shaw could tell that he wanted very much to know what he had been talking about, and under normal circumstances, he knew Leo would have let go of him by now. But those eyes also told Shaw that Leo wanted very much to kill him as well. The man was agonizing over his situation, and that meant, to Shaw, that Leo had been quite serious earlier; he really *was* in love with Emma. As far as Shaw was concerned, that made Leo the human equivalent of a rabid dog.

Then, when it seemed neither of them would never move again, Leo slowly released his hold and stepped back, gradually lowering his arm to the side, never taking his eyes from Shaw's.

"What did you mean?" Leo said. "Earlier. About me being out in the cold. Not knowing what hit me."

Shaw smiled just a little and started to step around Leo, saying, "Let me make you a drink and we can—"

Leo slapped a hand to Shaw's shoulder and stopped him cold. "I'll make my own fucking drink, thanks. You stay in your chair."

Shaw nodded once, turned and lowered himself back into the chair.

"You bought yourself a little time, but you're not off the hook," Leo said as he walked crab-like to the liquor cabinet, keeping an eye on Shaw. He smirked as he poured scotch into a glass and said, "I'm still looking forward to seeing what color your insides are when you hit the sidewalk." He pushed a leather-upholstered chair closer to Shaw's desk and made himself comfortable in it with a long, breathy sigh. "I just think it's sad you won't be feeling it," he went on. "You sure as hell deserve to. Beating up on a woman. Threatening to kill her if she tries to defend herself or leave you. That's pretty low. Low as you can get in my book. Hell, even *cocksuckers* don't bite off each other's cocks, if you know what I mean. Beating your wife. That's *low*." He removed a cigar from beneath his coat, unwrapped it, and lit up, all with his right hand while holding the drink in his left. "Now. What's this project you were talking about, Landon? And don't jerk me off, here, okay? I don't have all night."

Shaw eyed his cigarette. It had burned down to the filter and a long tube of ash curved downward into the bowl like a skeletal finger.

"Mind if I have a cigar?" Shaw said.

"Long as you don't make any quick moves doing it." Leo smiled, cigar clutched between his teeth. He reached into his coat, removed another, and handed it to Shaw. "Have one of mine. They're better." He leaned back in the chair, plucked the cigar from his mouth and gestured with it toward the dead cigarette. "You know, you really oughtta knock off those things. They'll kill ya." Then his eyes squinted and his hillock of a belly rocked with quiet laughter.

Shaw took his time lighting his cigar, puffing it, watching the smoke rise slowly. But inside, his mind was racing. He had no doubt Leo was serious about killing him. He could make no mistakes. He would have only one chance to change Leo's mind by convincing him that he, Shaw, was more valuable alive. It meant spilling the beans about the project much sooner than he had planned, but he had no choice. If he could not convince Leo that Project Biofire was more important than his feelings for Emma, there would be no Project Biofire, contrary to what he had just told Leo.

"About eight months ago," Shaw began, "I was commissioned by the Pentagon to revive a project they'd killed about six years back. Actually, the project wasn't killed, it simply wasn't going anywhere. We were attempting to isolate the specific source of telekinesis in the human brain so we could"—

"Tele *what*?"

"Telekinesis. The ability to move objects with nothing more than the mind, the power of thought."

Leo took a thoughtful sip of his drink, then smirked. "Like that horror movie with the teenage girl?"

The rapid activity in Shaw's mind stumbled a moment as he tried to figure out what Leo was referring to. An instant later, he had to fight the urge to roll his eyes. "You mean *Carrie*. Yes. Like that. We were trying to learn exactly what caused it so we could control it. Even instigate it in people. But it never quite got off the ground. From the very beginning, nothing clicked and we ran into one dead end after another. It was finally abandoned by the Pentagon. With a little more time to re-staff the project, we might've gotten somewhere, but they wanted something from nothing and they wanted it yesterday. So far, that's the only time a project was not carried out successfully by OdysseyCorp, and I intend it to be the last. Anyway..."

Shaw leaned back in his chair, choosing his words carefully, controlling the level of his voice, relaxing as he watched Leo closely, noticing the most minute changes in his eyes, the smallest twitch of his lips, anything that might give him a sense of what was going on behind that fat face.

"After the Berlin Wall went down and the exchange of information began between America and the former Soviet Union," Shaw continued, "the Pentagon was stunned by the amount of work the Soviets had been doing not only in the field of telekinesis, but in telepathy, pyrokinesis, precognition, all forms of psychic warfare. Even spiritualism, for God's sake. Communicating with the dead, can you believe that? U.S. intelligence always knew they had an interest, but we had no idea just how extensive it was, or how much money and time they were willing to spend on it. They did a good job of concealing that."

Still wearing the shadow of a smirk, just a slight curl of the left end of his mouth, Leo narrowed his eyes. "Like I said earlier, Landon. I don't have all night."

"The Russians had made much more progress in telekinesis than we had, but just like we did, they hit a dead end. They reached a sort of plateau, couldn't get any further. The government shut them down. But the woman heading up the project, Antonina Barikov, tried to talk them out of it. She claimed the work they'd done in telekinesis had opened some very interesting doors in a related but different field, and she tried to convince them to keep the project open, rename it, redefine its goals. They suffered from tunnel vision, though. They weren't interested in any tangential discoveries she might have made. Her records were

filed, though. Her writings were kept, put away. Apparently, so
was she. She...*retired* from government service in 1990 and was
killed in a car accident a few months later. Even if the Soviet
government *had* been interested in pursuing her findings, the
wall fell and everything changed before they had the chance."

Leo smiled. "And your Pentagon friends got hold of her
work later, right? Liked what they saw?"

"About ten months ago, yes. Once they looked over her
writings, they suddenly lost all interest in telekinesis. They'd
found something more useful, more powerful. Of course, they
feigned disinterest, agreed with the Soviets that it was a good
try, but a failed project. And then they brought it to me."

"Okay, Landon, I'll bite," Leo said quietly, still smirking.
"What was it? What'd this woman stumble on?"

After a long moment of staring directly into Leo's eyes,
Shaw smiled and tilted his head in a friendly, curious way.

"Tell me, Leo. How many people do you employ to do the
kind of work you came here to do tonight?"

"That's none of your fucking business, Landon, you know
that."

Shaw nodded, almost apologetically. "Okay, okay, don't
answer. But we're friends, right, Leo? We've known each other
for how many years? So let's not pretend. I know what you do,
you know what I do. I'm just being up front, that's all. Okay,
forget I asked the question. Let's just use a hypothetical number.
Let's say you've got, oh, ten employees to do your wet work for
you. Of course, I'm sure it's more than that. After all, you're a
very powerful businessman with connections all over the world,
Leo, you probably have *many* more killers than that working for
you." He saw Leo's face darken a bit, saw the man's chest puff
up as he took in a breath to speak, and Shaw's words began to
come faster so Leo would not have a chance to interrupt. "But
let's settle on ten for now, and let's say that every time one of
those ten assassins does a job, he has to spread a little money
around, grease some palms, maybe call in some favors from a
few people in your debt in order to pull off the hit, to make sure
nobody's in his way and the target's where he's supposed to
be when he's supposed to be there. Now, all of those expenses

come out of your pocket. And all the risks, too, you could call those expenses, as well. And on top of all that, you have to pay the killer his fee, am I right, Leo? All that money, all that trouble, the potential exposure, the danger of your man being caught, of the hit being traced back to you—how would you like to get rid of all that? How would you like it, Leo, if you could trade in those ten killers for one and eliminate all that risk? *All* of it, Leo."

Shaw could almost hear the nasty, wet sound of the hook lodging in Leo's throat. The man was leaning forward in the chair now, clenching his cigar tightly between his teeth, rubbing the tip of his thumb hard against the edge of the glass he held.

"There would be no chance of a competitor's fatal *accident* ever being uncovered as a murder. No chance, I mean no chance in *hell* of your name ever being involved. Wouldn't that be nice, Leo? Wouldn't that save you a lot of money and put your mind at ease?"

When Leo spoke, his words were slurred around the cigar in his mouth, his lips hardly moved, and his voice was a throaty rasp. "The *hell* you talking about, Landon?"

Still smiling, Shaw placed both hands flat on the desktop, speaking in a tone that was almost warm, the tone of someone sharing a happy, intimate secret with a friend.

"By the time Antonina Barikov's project was shut down in Russia," he said, "she had a subject who, from a distance of ten feet, could move light objects over a table. Things like cups and plates, toy cars and dolls. But every time he did it, everyone within *twenty* feet of him became violently ill. There were nosebleeds, heart palpitations, elevated body temperatures, dizzy spells, fainting. One assistant suffered a mild stroke. While the subject's telekinesis was being carefully controlled and improved upon gradually, this particular side effect was a wild card. Nothing they tried succeeded in stopping or controlling the harmful effects the subject's telekinesis had on anyone nearby. That was what Barikov stumbled upon. While the subject was moving objects with his mind, he was actually affecting the *bodies* of the people around him, creating physical changes in them. While they were trying to perfect parlor tricks, they stumbled upon a psychic doomsday weapon. But no matter how hard Barikov tried to convince her government that this was far more important than their deadlocked telekinesis project, they wouldn't listen. They wanted the parlor tricks. So, we've taken Barikov's work to places they wouldn't. And so far, Leo...so far, we've succeeded. We've improved on it. And we're going to improve on it some more."

The leather upholstery on Leo's chair chattered softly as he shifted his position, took the cigar from his mouth so he could take a swallow of scotch, then put the cigar between his teeth again. But he said nothing.

"Right now, Leo, I have a monkey that speaks sign language in one of my labs," Shaw whispered. "That monkey can do at will what Barikov's subject did accidentally. We don't have complete control over it yet, but we will. Soon. And when we do, that's going to be the deadliest fucking monkey on the face of this earth. It's gonna make an Ebola monkey look like Curious George."

Leo stood slowly, walked around his chair, then turned to face Shaw from behind it. "I still don't understand. This monkey...what can it do?"

Inside, Shaw was overcome with relief. He was not sure until that moment, but now he knew Leo was sold. From his facial expression, tone of voice, body language, he could tell— Leo was *his*. The relief welled up in him until it came out in a joyous laugh, and without missing a beat, Shaw leaned back and made that laugh work for him.

"Leo! Haven't you been listening? If that monkey were here right now, it could kill you with a heart attack. An embolism. A stroke. Respiratory failure, for Christ's sake. Leo, this monkey could have you on the floor dead in a second, and it would be entirely of natural causes."

Leo said nothing. A strip of perspiration glowed above his upper lip.

Shaw said, "The project head is about to try out an idea of his, see how it works. He's pretty certain he's located the part of the brain that controls this ability, and he's convinced that if he surgically fuses that part of the brain with the, uh...the, uh..."

He sighed and shrugged one shoulder. "You'll have to forgive me, Leo, I'm not a scientist. I just know how to pick 'em, I don't speak their language."

Leo looked mildly annoyed. "I didn't come here for a fucking science lesson. Just give me the gist."

"My man is convinced he's close to a breakthrough and will soon have the flaming under control."

"Flaming?"

"That's what we call it. The monkey gives you a heart attack, you're flamed." Shaw laughed again as he stood, watching Leo carefully, waiting for him to respond with angry disbelief. But he did not, just as Shaw had suspected. He was deep in his own thoughts. Shaw walked over to the liquor cabinet, trailing blue-gray smoke from his cigar, and sloshed some scotch into a glass, then took a sip. He turned to face Leo again. "I'm telling you, Leo, this is the most incredible thing I've ever dealt with, the most amazing thing I've ever seen. Maybe it will make war obsolete. Maybe wars will be fought quietly all around us. I don't know, Leo, but I know this: before long, we'll have a *person* who can do what that monkey can do, and after that...well, it'll be a whole new ball game. After that, the hit man will be obsolete. The assassin a quaint artifact. No more sharpshooters, no more poisons. Hell, chemical warfare will be old news, and we haven't really had a chance to *use* it yet, have we?" He began to walk toward Leo slowly. "And if this were to fall into the hands of one of your competitors...maybe one who would like very much to get you out of the way...that competitor could have you killed, knowing that it could never be traced back to him. And even while you were dying, Leo, you wouldn't know you were being murdered." He planted the cigar in his mouth again, stepped up to Leo and put a hand on his shoulder. "And here you are, Leo, being given a chance to get in on the ground floor. But—" He released a long, regretful sigh. "—You're going to kill me."

Leo stood behind the chair staring straight ahead at one of the windows behind Shaw's desk. He did not even acknowledge Shaw's hand on his shoulder.

Shaw's heart skipped a beat as he looked closely at Leo's face in profile. He thought he'd snagged him, but he still saw struggle and uncertainty there. He was convinced he had Leo wrapped around his little finger, but the man clearly was agonizing over his interest in what Shaw had told him. He looked, for a moment, as if he might weep.

It was a mystery to Shaw. What could the man see in Emma? What was it about her that could stand in the way of Leo embracing what he had just heard? After years of marriage to her, Shaw knew Emma was not worth it, and he found himself feeling a bit sorry for the man.

After a long, deadly silence, Leo turned his head slowly until his eyes were on Shaw's, and said, "And now you're thinking I won't kill you because of this, right?"

Shaw puffed on the cigar. "All I'm thinking, Leo, is that it would be a mistake. A big mistake over something so silly."

Leo took the cigar from his mouth and clenched his teeth hard for a moment, flexing his jaws as his eyes bored hotly into Shaw's. "It's not over something so silly, Landon." Then he bent his head down to glare at Shaw's hand on his shoulder. He kept staring until Shaw pulled it away, then he turned and began to pace slowly. "Who else knows?"

"I thought you were going to kill me."

Without looking at him, Leo barked, "Don't *fuck* with me, goddammit, who else knows?"

Shaw sat on the arm of the chair. "Maybe nobody. Maybe a lot of people. Look, Leo, what I'm saying is this. If you kill me now, you'll never know. The project will be finished, the Pentagon will get what they're paying for, and…maybe someone else will, too."

Leo stopped pacing and glared hatefully, murderously at Shaw, nostrils flaring. "You've already given this to somebody else? You little shit? Is that what you've done?"

Shaw smiled. "I guess if you really wanted to find out, you could torture me, but that wouldn't be very practical, would it, Leo? So, let's say you kill me. Once Project Biofire's finished, what would you do then? Who would you talk to? I mean, who else is there here at OdysseyCorp for you to deal with? My secretary? Poor cute little Carmen?" He chuckled. "What would you do, demand that she hand the records over to you? You think that would work? Who would give you want you want if I were gone?"

They stared at one another silently for a moment, Shaw relaxed and smiling, Leo looking as if he wanted to rip Shaw's throat out with his bare, meaty fingers.

"On the *other* hand," Shaw went on quietly, "let's say I haven't told anyone. Let's say the only one who knows is you, okay? You mean to tell me, Leo, that you'd rather kill me than have a chance at this?"

Leo's face changed suddenly. His head pulled back, eyebrows rose, mouth opened in a bitter smile and he laughed. "A *chance*? Oh, that's funny. There's no chance involved here, Landon. You win. I'm not gonna kill you. Not tonight, anyway. But I'm telling you right now, chance isn't gonna be involved in this. *No* auction. You hear me?"

Leo waited silently for an answer, but none came.

"No auction, Landon. I'm not bidding with anybody over this." His face changed again. The smile remained, but the rest of his face became a mask of murderous hatred and his fleshy cheeks trembled slightly. "None of your usual customers— no towel-headed sand-niggers, no fuckin' neo-Nazis, no little psycho countries on the come with money to burn. *Nobody*. Don't have any doubts, Landon, this is *mine*. Nobody else even hears about it. And one more thing."

Leo lunged forward suddenly and Shaw felt his body stiffen, his heart speed up, and his smile slip off his face like a painting dropping off a wall in an earthquake, because the enormous man was bearing down on him like a truck, suddenly holding his cigar in his hand like a dart ready to throw at a board on the wall, and he shoved the cigar in Shaw's face, held the glowing red and gray ember so close that Shaw could feel its heat on his face and in his eyes. When Leo spoke again, his voice was a breath and his eyes were deadly weapons.

"You leave Emma alone. You understand me? *Alone*. You let her go on her way. You let her find some happiness. And if you try to stop her, if I find out you've touched her or threatened to touch her, if I think you've even *thought* about so much as plucking a hair off her head, I swear to God, Landon, all bets will be off. You'll die the slowest, most painful death in the history of human existence. You'll beg me to kill you."

As he spoke, Leo moved the hot end of the cigar closer to Shaw's face, and Shaw began to perspire and clench his teeth as he resisted the urge to pull away.

Leo went on. "I don't care if I *never* get your fucking product, that's what'll happen to you if I find out you've tried to hurt her or keep her from leaving you. Understand, Landon? Have I made myself clear? We either do it this way or I kill you right now."

Slowly, carefully, Landon nodded.

Without pulling the cigar away, Leo nodded, too. "Okay," he said, "I'm gonna be watching your wife-beating ass. Real close. Don't piss me off. Don't make the mistake of thinking you're in control this time, as usual, because you're not. Don't fuck up, Landon. I mean it."

And then, as if he were late for an appointment, Leo pulled the cigar away, smacked his drink down on Shaw's desk, turned, and stalked out of the office, pulling the door closed hard behind him.

Shaw remained were he stood for a long time, frozen in place. He finally allowed himself to ooze over the leather-upholstered arm and into the chair, exhausted, drained, and trembling.

His success with Leo was no comfort as he recovered from the adrenaline-charged fear he had been hiding so well. He had talked his way through a dangerous situation, but the truth of the matter was that, for all Shaw knew, Project Biofire would never be more than a monkey who could talk to deaf people and kill anyone with its eyes.

All that really mattered, though, was that he, Shaw, was still in his office and not on the sidewalk below. He was still alive to take care of the problems at hand. One of those problems was Emma.

4.

A CHANGE OF PLANS

The traffic on Lincoln had slowed to a halt half an hour ago and Emma had been sitting in the car ever since, feeling progressively more anxious, even a bit claustrophobic. She was tempted to get out of the Mercedes, which was the only car her husband would allow her to drive, and abandon it to walk through the rain a block or so and catch a cab.

As soon as it had become apparent that she was going to be there awhile, Emma had called ahead to Shades, the restaurant where she and Leo always met, to leave word that she would be a little late. But that had been thirty minutes ago.

She rolled down the window and leaned her head out into the rain, needing to feel it cold and wet on her face, needing a few gulps of night air, even if it was thick with car exhaust.

On each side of the city's main thoroughfare, walls of steel and glass swept sharply upward, forming a canyon that gave only a slender view of the black night sky high above. Milky light glowed from many of the windows and formed a kind of pale, ghostly mist in the rain high above the street.

Ever since she had married Landon, Emma had come to hate the city a little more every year until she thought she would go insane if she did not get and stay out of it, away from it. Everything about it reminded her of him. She could not separate the two in her mind.

The city was a great, hunkering beast that breathed black smoke and spat sewage, and like some fairytale monster, it was cruel and oppressive and enslaved every living creature within its reach.

Landon was like that. Sometimes it was difficult to tell which of the two was worse.

But that was going to change soon. At least, she hoped it would. As she looked up into the falling rain, she prayed it would, as soon as possible, so she could breathe again.

Emma pulled her head back in and rolled up the window because her hair was getting wet and she wanted to look nice for Leo. She checked her watch to see that ten more minutes had passed; she considered calling the restaurant again. Leo did not like to be kept waiting, and it would take her another twenty minutes once she had gotten out of the belly of this beast of a city. She was reaching for the phone again when the cars in front of and beside her began to move. Putting the car in gear, she sighed with relief. But her sigh was a hollow sound because she felt no relief at all.

It had begun that morning. A feeling of unrest, an inability to concentrate, a vaguely nagging sense that something was not right. That something was quite wrong.

It had been two days since she had seen Leo, since she had finally heard him ask the question she had been dreaming about for so many months. Two days gave her more than enough time to start worrying, to begin to doubt that it would really happen.

Leo had given her no details. She did not know when or how it would happen, and she did not want to. She wanted to be able to express genuine surprise when she got the news. But, at the same time, she could not stop wondering *if* it would happen. It seemed too good to be true.

As the traffic picked up its pace, she saw the cause of the delay. At the intersection of Lincoln and Sixth Avenue, what appeared to be two cars were mangled together in a nightmarish sculpture of shattered glass and wrinkled metal. A line of flares shimmered on the wet pavement and police officers directed traffic around the wreckage.

In minutes, she was outside the city and ignoring the speed limit, unable to wait any longer.

For what? she thought

Emma was filled with a dark sense of great anticipation, but she was not sure why. After all, it was just another dinner with

Leo, another evening of food and drinks and fondling in their private booth in a back corner of the restaurant, separated from the other patrons by a curtain of deep maroon velvet.

What do I think is going to happen? she asked herself silently.

Then: *Quit playing dumb. You're afraid he's going to tell you he won't do it. For one reason or another, he isn't going to have Landon killed. You've become a real pessimist over the years, Emma; things have been so bad for so long, you can't imagine anything good happening.*

She tried to put it out of her mind and think of other things. Anything. She kept an eye out for patrol cars, popped an old Eurhythmics album into the CD player, lit a cigarette. Anything to keep her mind off of...everything.

When she arrived at Shades, Emma parked behind the restaurant in her usual space, hidden from the road and from other patrons parked in front. Leo's car was nowhere in sight, which was not unusual; most likely he'd had Ollie drop him off with a couple of his bodyguards.

She hurried through the rain, cold in spite of her long, heavy coat because she wore no stockings or underwear. She never did when she met Leo at Shades; that way, he could reach beneath her skirt, stroke her thighs, and reach between them to fondle her as they ate and drank, staring at one another with heat and longing.

Emma went in through the service entrance and followed a winding path through the steamy, busy kitchen, alive with the sounds of voices and cooking, redolent of steaks and seafood and seasonings. Leaving the kitchen, she went down a short hall and ended up behind the maître d's station.

Everett, the maître d', turned and smiled when he saw her, reaching into his coat.

"Good evening, Miss," he said. He never called her anything but Miss, and referred to Leo as "the gentleman" or "Sir."

Everett removed a small white envelope from inside his coat and proffered it. "The gentleman said I was to give this to you."

Emma stared at the envelope, her lips parted and drying rapidly as she breathed through her mouth.

"Miss? Is anything wrong?"

"Isn't...isn't he here?"

"I'm afraid not. He had another gentleman deliver this to me."

With effort, she reached out and took the envelope. Her heart was thundering in her chest. Something was wrong, she knew it.

Emma stared down at the blank, sealed envelope as if it were some unidentifiable alien artifact.

"Your table is ready if you'd care to eat," Everett said.

"Um…just give me a moment."

"Of course."

He turned away and left her standing there alone as he tended customers.

The envelope would not open. It was a living creature trying to hide something from her, keep from her a vital piece of information that would have a monumental effect on her life. She clawed at the sealed flap with growing frustration, plucked and scratched and—finally, she ripped the envelope apart and let it fall from her fingers as she unfolded the note. Lines of Leo's clumsy script crawled across the page in black ink.

Emma dearest—

I'm not much with words. You know that. I'm even worse with the kind of words I need for this. I'm trying to find them.

I want you to know that I love you. I've never loved anyone before. Not anyone. I didn't think I was capable of it. But I am very much in love with you. I'm also in love with a thing. My work. My business. It's my life. And I'm afraid it still comes first and always will. Which is why I'm no good for you.

I'm afraid the plans we discussed will have to be canceled. You know what I mean. And I think it would be best if we didn't see each other anymore. This decision is final.

But if he tries to hurt you or prevent you from leaving him if you want, you must call me immediately and leave a message to let me know. Call only the number below.

You have changed my life, and I will love you for as long as I live. Maybe longer.

Leo

A sharp, dry sound caught in Emma's throat as she stared open-mouthed at the words, one hand rising slowly to touch four fingertips to her lower lip. Her heart, which had been hammering just a moment ago, seemed to have stopped, like her breathing.

"No," she said. It squeaked out of her constricted throat, a rusty metal sound. "No. God. Please. No. He got him. Landon got him. Even *him*."

"Miss?"

Startled by Everett's voice, she jerked away from him.

"Are you sure you're all right?"

"Yes, Everett, I'm fine. Just...fine."

"Would you like to sit down?" He snapped his fingers at a passing waiter and said, "A glass of water, quickly." Then he turned to Emma again, reached out and took her elbow and said, "Come over here and take a seat, Miss."

"No," she said, more firmly than she had intended. She pulled her arm from him. "Thank you, Everett, but...I'm just going to...go."

Emma spun around so fast, she nearly collided with the waiter bringing her a glass of water. She stepped around him, hurried down the hall, pushed through the swinging door into the kitchen, and hurried outside to the car.

She sat behind the wheel staring through the windshield at the back wall of the restaurant, the letter crumpled in her fist. Eventually, she smoothed out the small sheet of paper, turned on the dome light, and read it again.

"How?" she whispered to herself when she finished. "How? How?"

She sat there for a long time, asking the same question over and over.

On her way home from Shades, Emma did not drive as fast as she had before; she was in no hurry to get there. She had so many questions, and they were tumbling all over one another in her mind, a great avalanche of unanswered questions.

How had this happened? What had changed Leo's mind?

He had made reference to his love for his business—was that it? Could his business be *that* important? More important than she?

Emma had one good answer to that question. The only way Leo's business could get in the way of having Landon killed would be if his business was with Landon. If that was the case, then Leo was not choosing his business over her, he was choosing *Landon* over her. And if that were the case, what were the chances that Landon might know about what she had attempted? Did he already know she had tried to have him killed?

"No," she muttered to herself, shaking her head as she drove. "Leo wouldn't do that to me. He...he'd never tell. No."

She believed that Leo truly loved her. She had not expected it; her only intention had been to give him the fuck of his life and get him on a leash. His confession of love, though perhaps not the most eloquent, was flattering, moving. She could not help feeling proud of the job she had done. She felt no guilt for manipulating the man's feelings with such calculation. He was a gentleman and had been good to her, but when it came right down to it, Leo was a monster. That was why he and Landon got along so well.

What would Landon do if he had found out?

Emma knew what Landon did when she had a little too much to drink at a party or did not smile enough at a press conference. She chose not to think about how he might react to something like this. She hoped never to find out.

Now that Leo had turned his back on her, anything could happen.

Emma drove on through the rain, heading for home and whatever awaited her there.

The Shaw residence was located almost thirty miles outside the city, and seven miles from the nearest neighbor, which was OdysseyCorp Labs.

The house had been designed by an architect friend of Landon's and looked like something out of one of those architectural magazines in which it most likely would be described with phrases like, "audaciously unconventional" and "stunningly original" or "brimming with character" and "distinct in its individuality."

Emma thought it looked like a giant, white, two-story maxipad with silver trim, and she despised it. It was every bit as cold and sterile as the massive structure seven miles away; the mansion's electronic security system, along with the guards who patrolled the area at all times, made it almost as secure as the labs at OdysseyCorp. It was surrounded by acres of green, wooded land, and within walking distance of the back door was a small man-made lake stocked with fish for Landon and his cronies.

She parked in the circular drive, not bothering to put the Mercedes in one of the eight hangar-like garages attached to the side of the house. It was impossible to tell if Landon was home, but she hoped he was not. Before getting out of the car, she glanced at her watch. Ten minutes to eleven. Typically, the only time of day Emma saw him, if at all, was in the morning, unless he had a party or some other function to attend, in which case she had to accompany him and give her lovely-happy-wife performance. In the evenings, if he was home at all, he spent most of his time in his home office, then went straight to bed.

Still sitting behind the wheel, Emma took a few deep, slow breaths and let them out tremulously. Praying that Landon was not home, she got out of the car and hurried through the rain and up the white marble steps. In the shelter of the portico, she stopped at the front door and punched four numbers into the small, rectangular keypad on the wall, then said, "The sheep are safe." A dull, metallic click sounded in the double doors and she turned the black knob, pushed one door open, went inside, and flicked on the foyer light.

Emma knew the servants had already gone to bed. She stood in the foyer and listened for any sounds that might give away Landon's presence. All she heard was the ticking of a clock and the rain falling softly outside.

She went upstairs without turning the light off in the foyer, peeling her coat off as she walked wearily down the hall to her bedroom. Once inside, she kicked her high-heeled shoes off her feet, nudged the door shut behind her with her right elbow as she hit the light switch with her left hand, all in one smooth motion.

The overhead light did not come on.

"Shit," she muttered, tossing her coat in the general direction of the chair positioned at her vanity. She heard the change and keys in her pockets jangle as the coat slid from the chair to the floor with a whisper.

Emma walked through the darkness with ease, knowing every inch of the room. She was reaching for the lamp on the nightstand when the match was struck. Its flame hissed to life and wavered slightly, casting a soft, orange glow over Landon's face. He touched the flame to the end of the long, dark cigar clutched between his teeth and began to puff, making the tip grow an angry red with each draw.

She froze in place, arm outstretched, fingers poised to switch on the lamp, jaw suddenly slack. She was too frightened to make a sound, even the smallest whimper of fear. Even her breath had caught in her throat like a prickly thistle the instant she had heard the rasping of the match because she knew, before the thought could take cohesive form in her mind, what it was and who had done it, and she knew that she had walked into a trap.

The cigar came to life and its smoke began to curl around Landon's head, his face bathed in the flickering glow of the match flame. Scissoring it between the knuckles of two fingers, he plucked the cigar from his mouth and extinguished the match with a short, sharp exhalation of odious smoke.

The room was dark again except for the watchful eye that glared at the end of the cigar.

Run, she heard her own voice say in some deep, dark dungeon of her mind, faint and echoing.

She could, she knew she could. It would only take a quick spin, three strides, and she would be out of the bedroom and running down the hall. But she was barefoot and the keys were in her coat pocket on the floor; she would need the car to get away. But she knew she would not have tried that even if she'd had the keys on her. The thought of flight always crossed her mind in times like this, when she knew what was coming.

She even saw herself doing it in her mind, imagined it vividly. But in the end, she was unable to break through the numbing paralysis that overcame her, and she did not run, did not move, did not even speak. She simply surrendered herself to her fate.

Quiet breaths of movement came from the bed and the lamp on the other side clicked on. Emma flinched.

Landon's eyes were on her as he lowered his left hand from the lamp. He had two pillows behind his back propped against the headboard, and he was stretched out on the bed, ankles crossed. He wore his forest-green cotton-velvet robe with black satin lapels, gray silk pajama bottoms, and black leather flannel-lined slippers. Beside him on the bed were the three light bulbs he had removed from the overhead light. He looked so relaxed, as always, so content, without a care in his life.

But Emma knew that was not the case. She recognized the tightness at the corners of his mouth and around his eyes, the slightly crooked set of his jaw, things that only she would notice that made it clear he was not at all content.

"Hello, Emma," he said. His voice was quiet, level and completely empty.

Her lips quivered as she worked the words out of her mouth with effort. "Hel…hello, Landon." Her voice was a rasp.

He drew on the cigar, then let the smoke out of his mouth and nose slowly, let it flow like milk from his nostrils and between his lips as he rolled the cigar between thumb and forefinger.

"You're later than I expected," he said, still quiet. "I thought you'd come right home as soon as you found out you'd lost your boyfriend. Drove around a little, did you? Maybe stopped for a drink to drown your sorrows?"

Emma did not reply. She realized she was still standing in the same frozen position she had been in when Landon had lit his match. Letting her arm drop to her side, she stood up straight.

His eyes did not waver from hers. He did not even blink.

"I hope you didn't try to call him, or something like that," he went on. "That would be a pathetic thing to do. And it would be embarrassing to me. So I hope you didn't do that, Emma. Did you?"

"No. No, I didn't do that. I just...drove for a while. That's all."

He swung his legs over the edge of the bed and stood with his back to her for a moment. Leaning forward, he picked something up off the floor but kept it out of sight for the time being as he walked slowly along the side of the bed.

"I hope you've got that out of your system," he said as he turned and walked along the foot of the bed, left arm curled behind his back, hiding whatever he held.

Emma's heart began to beat faster as she stared at his left elbow, looking for a glimpse of whatever was behind his back. She knew, of course, what it was, but she hoped for something else, anyway. It had been a while since he had been angry enough to use The Towel, but she supposed finding out about Leo did the trick.

But how much more did he know? Did he know only about her affair with Leo? Did he know the real reason for it? Did he suspect?

"I don't want to see you moping or pouting because you've lost your playmate, Emma," Landon said as he came closer slowly, steadily. "Because..." He bowed his head slightly, cocked it to one side, and chuckled coldly through a smirk. "...God knows..." Another chuckle as he moved closer, his breathing a little heavier now, as if something were building in him, and when he spoke again, it was in a growl. "...I'm angry enough as it is, you cunt!"

He struck with the flashing speed of a snake. His arm swung out from behind him in an underhanded arc, and the oranges wrapped in the damp towel slammed into Emma's midsection with hardly a sound.

Emma doubled over and the pain screamed for her, silently, bursting in her gut and slicing upward into her chest, downward into her pelvis and thighs, exploding, spreading. She gagged as she stumbled a few steps, then fell forward onto the bed, her arms clutched tightly over her abdomen.

Emma heard the rustle of Landon's slippers on the carpet as he walked behind her, but she was in too much pain to protect herself in any way. She lay face-down on the bed, clutching her stomach, teeth clenched, small grunting sounds of pain squeezing from her throat.

The Towel came down on her lower back, just over her right kidney, and struck again and again in the same area.

In too much agony to scream, she opened her mouth in a yawning, silent cry, pressing the side of her head into the bed, eyes tightly shut one moment, then open wide the next. In spite of her pain, she was able to conjure a foggy thought, a silent plea to no one, to nothing, that Landon would not damage her internally.

The pain so distorted her perceptions that she was still reacting to being struck even after Landon had stopped. Her convulsive jerks slowed gradually to a stop until she lay flat on the bed, breathing in short spurts, arms folded beneath her, shoulders hunched up around her neck. Tears glimmered on her cheeks and spittle ran from a corner of her mouth.

In spite of all the pain, those oranges wrapped in the bath towel would leave no marks.

The Towel landed just inches from her face and fell open; the oranges rolled over the bed, some thumping to the floor. She could smell their sharp, tangy fragrance, and she hated it. She had not been able to eat an orange in years.

"The fact that you had an affair doesn't bother me," Landon said behind her. As he spoke, his voice went from a quiet and civilized tone to a high, maddened shriek, and back down to quiet and civilized again, without warning. "I expected it. I decided that, as long as you were discreet, it wouldn't be a problem. God knows we haven't had sex in a long time. And people like us, people of our station, we have affairs, it's just a fact of life. It's even expected of us, I think. It's not a big deal. But. When you decide to have an affair with someone you *know* is a business associate of mine! When you do *that*! Well…that's a different situation. That's not a harmless affair, it's…an affront. An assault. On me."

Emma slid her arms out from under her slowly, her body still weak with pain, and closed her fists around clumps of the bedspread, trying to hold in the sounds of pain that fought their way up to her throat and tried to claw their way out.

"You have abused the privileges I've given you," Landon said, sounding perfectly under control now, almost pleasant. "I've allowed you a great deal of freedom in spite of your obvious hatred of me. I've let you have your own car, your own activities. Your own life. And I've done that knowing that you possess more knowledge of my work than any of my clients and nearly all the people who work for me. I've come to trust you because I know that you know what will happen to you if you stray from the path."

She heard him puff on the cigar, smelled its rank smoke as his slippers *shooshed* over the carpet.

"But apparently none of that is enough. Because not only have you chosen to seduce one of my clients, you have the fucking gall to—and I-I-I really find this shocking because you must have *known* what would happen!" His voice was getting crazy again. "You actually tried to get him...*to kill me*!"

Landon stopped moving, stopped breathing, and there was a stretch of silence before he started breaking things. Objects thumped against the wall. A loud shattering of glass made her jump and she knew he had broken her vanity mirror, but it was nothing more than a vague thought floating through her fog of pain.

But her pain had not kept her from hearing him. And now she knew how much he knew. He knew everything. Once she knew that, she resigned herself to death. She fully expected him to kill her.

"That was pretty unwise, Emma. Pretty unwise." He laughed and it was the sound of an icepick rapidly stabbing into a block of ice. "If you were smart, you would have tried to kill me yourself. But to have someone else do it...and someone like Leo, a fucking *client* of mine. Don't you realize, Emma, that Leo is *mine*? Leo and so many others like him—they *belong* to me! I *own* them! In fact, I own them in much the same way that I own *you*. Leo couldn't kill me. He would *never* kill me. I'm too fucking important to him. But you..." That laugh again, that spiky, stabbing laugh. "...you were nothing to him but a piece of ass. A cunt. A warm, squirmy place to put his cock. You thought *that* was enough to get him to kill me? Oh, God, you are such a stupid woman, Emma. A man like Leo...you know, he's a powerful man, very powerful. He can have anything he wants, whenever he wants it. You were just a diversion, that's all. Now, *I*, on the other hand, am also very powerful. But much more so than Leo because I have the things that Leo and his kind want. And in order to get them, they have to dance to my tune. *My* tune, do you understand, Emma? You can't play this game. You're a fucking spectator, do you hear me? And when you step in and try to take part, you just make an ass of yourself. And because you're my wife, you make an ass of me, too. And I won't have that."

Behind her, more pacing. Slippers shuffling over the carpet. Breathing. Puffing. Cigar stench.

"I'm not sure how to handle this, Emma, I'm really not," he said, calm again. "But I'm going to do my best for the time being. See, I just can't trust you anymore. You know things about my work, about OdysseyCorp, things that simply cannot get out. Over the years, you've overheard conversations over dinner, over drinks, when I'm on the phone. You've picked up a lot of information, I'm sure, during the years we've been married. And now that you've done *this*, I cannot trust you in any way whatsoever. Not even a little. So I think the first way to address this problem is to withdraw your privileges," he said again.

Privileges...what privileges? she thought in her murky stupor of pain.

"I don't think it's a good idea for you to have access to the car, so you won't. From now on. I think it would be a good idea to assign some of the servants to keep a very close eye on you at all times. Especially Mrs. Babcock. So I'm going to do that. But that won't be all, Emma. Like I said, I still haven't decided how to handle this. You've stepped so far out of line I don't even know where to begin, but I assure you, I will not let this go. Things will change, Emma. Drastically. And soon. For you, I mean. Not for me. Because you're the one in trouble. Big, bad trouble. But I think...for starters..."

Emma felt his hand grasp her left ankle hard and squeeze tightly. The idea of struggling occurred to her, but she ignored it. There was no point.

"...this might be a good idea."

She heard the wet smacking of his lips as he puffed on his cigar several times, rapidly.

He pressed something to the middle of the sole of her foot. At first, she felt nothing and did not know what it was.

Then the pain began, burning into and through her skin like a fat, round laser beam. It was the lit end of Landon's cigar pressing into her foot.

Emma began to scream, but it quickly melted into a ragged, hoarse bellow that collapsed into a fit of coughs. She kicked her leg, but at first she could not wrest it from his grip. Then he let go and her leg kicked freely as she screamed and screamed.

The pain continued, grew worse, and she thought he was still holding the cigar to her foot somehow. Then she realized he was pressing it to the bottom of her other foot.

Her screams became louder for a moment, then became so intense that they were nothing more than a single, high-pitched note, like a test for the Emergency Broadcasting System. And then...they faded into nothing more than raspy exhalations.

Through the blood-thick fog of pain that filled her mind, she heard his voice, sharp and clear and, again, even a little pleasant.

"I'll have someone from the lab come in tomorrow morning to make sure they don't get infected. But I don't want them to get better. Not for a while. You're going to be staying inside for a time, Emma. And I hope you understand that you brought this on yourself."

A moment later, she heard the bedroom door close.

Emma did not move from the bed. She lay face-down, her fists clutching the bedspread, mouth biting it, chewing it viciously as she continued to make small whimpering sounds of misery.

5.

RECOVERY

McNolte did not feel like himself the day he was to leave the hospital. He was not sure *what* he felt like, but he knew it was not himself.

He sat on the edge of his bed in a pair of jeans and an old blue flannel shirt that one of the hospital volunteers had rustled up for him, left arm in a sling, feet in the dirty old sneakers that had survived the accident, waiting for the nurse to come with the wheelchair so he could be pushed out of the hospital. But he was not particularly anxious for her to arrive.

Richard, a friend from the ad agency where he had worked, had invited McNolte to stay with him until he decided what to do with himself, and McNolte planned to use what little cash he'd had in his pocket when he had wrecked the car to catch a cab over there. He was not fond of the idea of camping on someone's sofa, but he had nowhere else to go.

His apartment was no longer his apartment, and all of its contents were being kept by the landlord until McNolte paid up; if he did not pay the balance owed within the next six weeks, his belongings would be sold. His car, of course, had been burned to a crackling crisp in the accident. Along with the suitcase full of cocaine.

The thought of that one particular loss made him feel vaguely ill, but little more. He knew it should terrify him, chill him to his bone marrow, but it simply did not. He decided he was still numb; the enormity of his situation had not yet settled in. His hair had not even grown back completely from the surgery, and he was woozy from all the medication they had been pumping into him. It simply had not soaked in yet, that was all.

He had sustained severe head injuries, along with a broken arm and several cracked ribs. Surgery was required to remove chips of bone from his brain. He still wore a bandage over the incision on the left side, and all the hair had been shaved off that side for surgery.

McNolte stared out the window beside his bed at the city, watching the rain fall from the dirty steel sky, looking down at the small people skittering over the sidewalks, their cars stopping and going on the streets below. But it no longer felt like the city in which he had grown up, worked, and succeeded... then failed. Now he was an unwelcome stranger within its limits. Not only did he have nowhere to go, but he had no money to spend once he got there.

A blood test after the accident had revealed him to be under the influence of alcohol and cocaine; his license had been revoked and once out of the hospital he was to go to court for sentencing. He faced a heavy fine, maybe jail time, or both. On top of that, he now had hospital and doctor bills that would be with him for a small eternity. He was glad the deer had not survived; it probably would have sued him for damages.

The more he thought about it, the more McNolte began to think the buck had been the luckier of the two of them.

The best thing about his stay in the hospital—probably the only good thing about it—was that it had made quitting cocaine a lot easier than it would have been otherwise. Between the anesthesia and the pain medication, he had been too doped up to notice any withdrawal symptoms.

That was another thing he did not feel yet: the urge to snort some coke. He did not even feel the absence of that urge yet, an urge that had been with him every passing minute for so long, controlling his every thought, decision, and act. He was sure it would come back sooner or later, but at the moment, as he looked through the slightly tinted window pane, the only thing he really felt, aside from a dreary, slightly blurred grogginess, was the need for a cigarette. That urge had not gone away.

"Ready to leave, are you, Mr. McNolte?"

He turned, sliding one knee up onto the bed, to see Dr. Liu walking toward him, looking over his chart on a clipboard.

"All dressed up and no place to go," McNolte said, half-smiling.

"Well, I told you I had an idea where you might be able to go from here. I made a call this morning, and it's all set if you're interested."

"Interested...in what?"

"Are you familiar with the South Street Mission?"

"Sure."

"They're ready to take you there. Unless, of course, you have some objection. But you led me to believe you preferred not to impose on your friend from work. Someone is waiting to come pick you up if you want to go."

"A mission? Is it going to cost extra?"

"It won't cost a thing." Dr. Liu was around fifty, shortish, stout, with a head of thick black hair. "This isn't just a regular mission. They have a clinic there. The facilities are pretty impressive. The place used to be a department store. I do some work there occasionally on a volunteer basis, and I know the man who runs it quite well. I called, told him of your situation, and he said to send you over. They'll take care of you until you get back on your feet. And by the way, they've had a lot of experience helping people with drug problems. Once you leave here, you'll need some help. I don't want you to pick up your old habit again. I don't think you want that, either."

"Even if I did, I couldn't afford it."

"Maybe there's some truth in the old saying that it's God's way of telling you that you make too much money."

"Or that you're an idiot."

"I suppose. Of course, it's up to you, but I would strongly urge you to take advantage of the opportunity. You won't have to impose on your friend, and it'll take a lot of pressure off your situation. And it'll be better for you in the end, I think."

McNolte nodded slowly as he thought it over. "I guess you're right."

Dr. Liu wrote on the chart, then slipped his pen in his breast pocket and tucked the chart under his arm. "I've indicated on the chart that South Street will be your temporary location, so if it doesn't work out there, call my office and leave word of where you'll be. But as long as you're going to be there, I might as well check up on you when I come in for the clinic. That way, we don't have to add anything to your bill. It's big enough already, don't you think?"

McNolte turned away from the doctor and looked out the window again, giving a ghost of a shrug. "That's very thoughtful of you, Dr. Liu, but it hardly makes any difference at this point. I really can't see myself ever paying off that bill."

The doctor walked around the foot of the bed and turned to face McNolte. He leaned his back against the wall beside the window and folded his arms, pressing the chart to his chest.

"It's natural for you to feel depressed," he said. "Anyone who goes through a car accident, then surgery, an extended hospital stay...well, depression is a common side effect. I just don't want you to let it get too strong a hold on you, do you understand?"

McNolte turned his head slowly to look up at the doctor. "I don't think I feel depressed. In fact, I'm not sure what I feel. If anything."

"Depression hardly ever *feels* like depression. That's one of the reasons I'm sending you to South Street. You'll be in good hands there, better off than if you were to go stay with a friend. Later, if you haven't snapped out of it, I'll consider treating it with medication. But I'm not too quick to hand out happy pills. The whole damned country's Prozacked out of its mind, and I don't want to add to it. Just...try not to be too hard on yourself for the predicament you're in now. Don't kick yourself too hard."

"When I go to this mission, what am I going to do there?"

Dr. Liu smiled. "Recover. You've got a lot of thinking to do. As long as you do the right kind of thinking, make the right choices. You can start your life all over again. Do whatever you want with it. Do you see what I'm saying?"

McNolte blinked once, slowly. "Is this what you give out instead of Prozac? Pep talks?"

The doctor laughed, reached down and patted McNolte's shoulder gently. "I guess it is. But look at it this way. They're free."

Several minutes after Dr. Liu left McNolte's room, an enormous man walked through the open door grinning like a lunatic.

Still sitting on the edge of the bed staring out the window, McNolte looked over his shoulder at the man, then stood apprehensively.

He stood a couple of inches over six feet and had long, bushy white hair that fell past his collar. The features of his face were located between the wiry, white caterpillars of his eyebrows and the bushy, white Santa Claus beard and mustache that bore the faint yellow stains of nicotine around the mouth, and although the sun was nowhere to be seen in the sky that day, his eyes were hidden behind dark lenses that were clipped to his wire-rimmed glasses. He wore a purple shirt beneath a bulky green down jacket with a fur-lined hood hanging behind his head, and a pair of jeans. He appeared to be rather rotund, but it was difficult to tell if his size was solid or flabby while he was wearing that puffy jacket. He kept grinning endlessly, as if someone had just told him a joke that he was not yet ready to share with anyone else.

For a moment, McNolte wondered if the man had wandered out of the psych ward, but then realized that made no sense because he was wearing street clothes.

"Mornin'," the man said with a slight wave of his right hand. "You McNolte?"

"Yes. Who...are you?"

"I'm P.W." He pronounced the second initial "dubbayuh." There was in his voice the residue of a southern accent. "Come to pick you up. You're goin' to South Street, right?"

"Yes, I am."

"You ready? Or am I early?"

"I'm waiting for the nurse. She's coming with the wheelchair."

"Yeah, they're picky about things like that, ain't they?" He gestured toward the orange plastic chair against the wall beside the closet and said, "You mind?"

"No, please, sit down."

McNolte sat on the bed again as P.W. scooted the chair over by the window and seated himself with a sigh. "I bet you're glad to be gettin' outta here, huh?"

"I'm not so sure. I don't really know what I'm going to do with myself now that they're through with me here."

"Oh, you got nothin' to worry about, babe. Willy and Mama Charity'll have you back on your feet in no time."

"Willy and Mama Charity? Who are they?" McNolte was not sure he wanted to know. They sounded like a folk singing act.

"Willy runs South Street. Well, I guess they both run it. Come to think of it, it's hard to tell *which* of 'em runs it. Anyway, Willy's a preacher, see. The Reverend Wilton Childs. But he doesn't like to be called reverend, or anything like that. Just Willy. About twenty, twenty-five years ago, see, he started this nondenominational charity organization called Project Samaritan, then ended up with that old department store building on the corner of South and Beacham. Not the best part of town, but, hey, what's a mission for, huh? Mama Charity, now, she's..." P.W. frowned, worked his jaw back and forth a few times beneath his beard, as if he were chewing on his thoughts. "Well, nobody really knows *who* she is or where she came from. She's just there. Always has been. She's Willy's right hand. Pretty flamboyant lady, she is. Hell of a lot of fun. I wouldn't mind gettin' to know her a lot better, if you know what I mean. But I'm afraid she'd beat the livin' shit outta me if I tried."

McNolte did not know what to say, so he just turned and looked out the window.

"You musta been in a hell of an accident, huh?" P.W. said. "But you look like you came out all right. You got lucky, gettin' Doc Liu. He's good people. I overheard him tellin' Willy about you. We get all kinds down at South Street, y'know? Willy and Mama Charity'll take good care of you. And they're damned good at helping people get the monkey off their backs. Hell, they helped me. Dragged me in off the street a drunken mess. Good thing, too. I think if I'd had another drink, my liver would've crawled up through my insides and strangled me to death, y'know?" He grinned at McNolte. "They'll work with you hard, as long as you work with them. And they can work wonders if you'll just let 'em."

McNolte frowned. "Look, I don't mean to be rude, or anything, but...did somebody publish a pamphlet on my troubles, or something?"

P.W.'s shoulders bounced with silent laughter. "It's pretty hard to keep secrets down at South Street. It's big and clean and they got good food, but it's an awful loud and crowded place. Not much room for privacy. Everybody pretty much knows everybody else and what they're doin'. Or what they're tryin' to *stop* doin', if you know what I mean."

McNolte's frown melted and his eyebrows rose slowly. He wondered if maybe he should catch that cab to his friend's apartment after all. But then, how long could he stay with Richard? A week? Maybe two? Then what?

"Hey, don't sweat it, pardner," P.W. said. "It's a good place to be and you're gonna do fine there. You'll be with good people. And you're lucky to be goin' in conscious. I woke up there days after they brought me in. Mama Charity was floatin' over me like an angel, lookin' down at me with that big smile of hers. Thought I'd died and gone to hog heaven." He shook with more silent laughter, then winked at McNolte. "When you meet Mama Charity, you'll know why that's funny."

By the time the nurse arrived with the wheelchair, McNolte found it even harder than before to decide whether or not he was glad to be leaving the hospital.

6.

PROBLEMS AND SOLUTIONS

Landon Shaw paced his office at OdysseyCorp Labs headquarters as he carried on a conversation over the speaker phone. He smoked a cigar as he moved around leisurely, straightening a wall hanging here, adjusting a book on a shelf there. Shaw glanced now and then at a small, round, unlit light on the bottom right corner of the sleek, white phone; if it began to blink, he would know the conversation was being tapped from the other end, most likely recorded, as well.

"I don't know what to say, Maxwell," he said pleasantly. "I consider your stockholders *my* stockholders. Your company is far too valuable to OdysseyCorp. You're our biggest and most important supplier, and I simply refuse to lose you, so I'm not going to—"

"I told you, Shaw, you've already *lost* the services of this company, dammit," an angry voice interrupted. "I refuse to deal with you and your filthy lab. And it's got nothing to do with the stockholders. Until now, I've handled this in a very professional, businesslike manner. But you've gone too far, going to the stockholders yourself like this. Who the hell do you think you *are?*"

"I think I'm your biggest customer, Maxwell. I think we're good for each other, and I went to the stockholders because I couldn't let you go through with this. It's a bad idea."

"What the hell is it your fucking business what I do with *my* company? You're way out of line, Shaw. Now, like I said, I've been very professional about this so far, but I want you to remember that I know enough about you to sink your fucking lab and get you into a hell of a lot of trouble. I'd prefer not to handle this situation that way. I'd prefer to take the high road and just sever our relationship here and now. But if you keep this shit up, I'm prepared to do whatever I have to do to get you off my fucking back."

Shaw went behind his desk and sat in the chair, leaned

back, and took a drag on the cigar, let the smoke out slowly. "I'm well aware of what you know about me, Maxwell, and I'm confident we can settle this without any ugliness on either end. See, Maxwell, I have a great deal of admiration for you and your company. I admire anyone who carries on the family business. Believe it or not, I'm quite fond of tradition, of the family bond, and the idea of a man filling his father's shoes. Or, in your case, your father's *and* grandfather's shoes, because your grandfather was the beginning of it, wasn't he? With his interest in minerals, I mean? The only problem is...I don't think your father and grandfather would approve of what *you've* been up to."

A few frustrated, sputtering sounds came over the speaker, then: "What the fuck are you talking about, Shaw?"

There was a muted beep and Shaw's secretary, Carmen, spoke over the intercom. "Dr. Jorgan is waiting to see you, Mr. Shaw."

He leaned forward, hit a button on the intercom, and said, "Tell him to wait." He leaned back, relaxed, and continued. "I carefully research every company, every person I deal with, Maxwell, and you and your company are no exception. I've learned a lot about your father and grandfather. They were good men. Family men. Respectable. Admirable. They worked hard and earned their success. But at the same time, they kept their families at the top of their lists of priorities. From what I can tell, they were more faithful to their wives than most, and they adored their children. But you, Maxwell...I don't think you're cut from the same cloth as those men. In all the research my people did, there was no evidence that your father or grandfather had a taste for young boys. Unlike you, Maxwell."

A brief gagging sound on the other end of the line was followed by silence.

"I don't think your father and grandfather would approve of your habit of ignoring your family to seek out smooth-skinned teenage boys with whom to perform ugly, nasty acts. Of course, they're dead. Your father and grandfather, I mean." He paused to draw on the cigar again, savoring its flavor as well as the thick silence that continued on the speaker. "But your wife and children are not dead. I'm sure they would be horrified to learn the truth about you. I'm quite certain your stockholders would, too. To say nothing of the law, which tends to frown on such relations between adults and minors. Even borderline minors. You wouldn't want any of that to happen. Would you, Maxwell?"

He waited, rolling the cigar slowly between thumb and forefinger. It took a long time, but the response finally came. It was spoken in a hoarse whisper, with the slightest hint of sniffles and tears mixed in.

"You son...of a bitch." Then, after a deep breath: "I could...I could be recording this conversation, Shaw."

"Don't be an idiot," Shaw said, glancing again at the still-dead light. "I know you're not recording anything. It's illegal without permission in this state, anyway, and would only get you into trouble. Do you think I'm stupid, Maxwell?"

Silence.

"Now," Shaw continued, speaking casually, "there's always the chance that you don't care if anyone finds out about your, uh...behavior. That would be unwise, but I've considered the possibility, and I've come up with another way of convincing you to maintain your business relationship with OdysseyCorp. Considering your other activities, you seem to have no use for your family. So, if we can't come to an understanding about this, I'll have your family killed. Depending on my mood, I might even have it done in such a way as to suggest that you are the killer. *That* might cramp your style with the boys, don't you think? Of course, you'd have plenty of company in prison, but I'm not sure those fellows would be up to your standards."

Shaw waited again, but no response came. Nothing more than a quiet, strangled sob.

"If all else fails, Maxwell, I may decide to have you killed so that your company can carry on without you in the manner to which I've become accustomed. After all, that's the only thing I'm concerned about, really. Your company. You're unnecessary. Besides, I've really hit it off with your stockholders. I think they like me. So...why don't you think on these things a while. In the meantime, I expect the next order to arrive punctually, as usual. If you have any questions, you can always call me. Have a nice day, Maxwell."

Shaw leaned forward and severed the connection with the push of a button. Then he hit the intercom and said, "Send Jorgan in, Carmen."

A moment later, Dr. Alan Jorgan shuffled into the office.

He was short, about five six, and was shaped like a pear. Atop his round head were just a few rust-colored tufts, surrounded by a wreath of thick hair that grew past his collar and looked like it had never been combed or brushed. His forehead was creased even when he was not frowning, and it was always covered with a thin, glistening sheen of perspiration. His beak of a nose hooked over a poorly trimmed mustache, and the lenses of his horn-rimmed glasses were smudged and so thick that they magnified the puffy half-moons of flesh beneath his eyes.

He wore a gray sport coat over a plain white shirt that sported a couple of food stains and was buttoned all the way up to his fleshy throat. His baggy, black Dockers bunched up around his raggedy black sneakers, one of which was untied.

Jorgan closed the door behind him and went straight to the chair in front of Shaw's desk. As always, he turned the chair slightly to his right, leaned his left elbow on the armrest and faced Shaw with his chin on his fist, right ankle resting on his left knee, foot dangling.

"So, Alan," Shaw said, "to what do I owe this visit."

"Well, things aren't turning out quite as we'd expected, Mr. Shaw."

"Ah. Well, I'm not entirely surprised, but I'm not worried, either. It's been my experience that nothing ever goes quite as planned. That's why I like to remain flexible."

As Shaw spoke, Jorgan's eyes wandered to a bank of shelves, one shelf in particular. On that shelf, in an antique gold frame, stood an eight-by-ten portrait of Emma.

Jorgan gazed at the photograph every time he came into the office. It was quite obvious that Alan Jorgan was enamored of Emma's face. It was, indeed, a lovely face. The picture had been taken shortly before they had married and Shaw could not remember ever seeing her look more beautiful, more glowing. Jorgan contemplated the photograph wistfully—at least, as wistful as Jorgan ever got—each time he entered the office. Shaw remembered inviting Jorgan to the house for a dinner party and watching him gawk shamelessly at Emma, following her around the house at a distance as if his heart would stop beating if he lost sight of her. Shaw took it as a compliment. That was, after all, the primary reason he had married Emma.

If only Jorgan knew the truth. If only he knew what Emma had tried to do to Shaw.

Pulling his eyes away from the picture, Jorgan said, "Project Biofire is not moving along as quickly as we'd hoped. We've made a lot of progress, but not enough to satisfy the...the, uh, client."

"You can speak freely in here, Alan. You know this office is safe."

Jorgan nodded and cleared his throat. "The Pentagon is getting impatient. The progress we've made is enough for us to know that the project is a viable one. The desired result is very likely, in fact. Everything is ready and waiting. Even the synthetic virus was completed over a month ago. But we need human subjects. At least one. There's no way around it." He looked down at his lap, as if he were ashamed. He was not. He was simply searching for the right words so none would be wasted. "The Pentagon is unwilling to arrange for...well, the necessary *accoutrements*," he said, giving a perfect French pronunciation of the last word. "They're feeling a little skittish these days, what with the recent change of hands in Washington and the opposing viewpoints of the new administration. They're not about to give us the same cooperation they gave us with the subway project. In spite of that, they want OdysseyCorp to produce." He took in a deep breath and his belly rose, then he let the air out slowly through pursed lips. "I'm afraid this project will die if we can't come up with at least one subject. On our own. Otherwise, they'll pull the money. They're giving us a week. I thought I should talk to you. How would you like me to proceed?"

Shaw nodded slowly. "Well, we can't let this one go. It's too big." He held the cigar between his teeth a moment, running his tongue around the tip, puffing gently. "Normally, I'd suggest we go to Terrance at the prison, use somebody on Death Row. But ever since he got sacked we haven't gotten too far with his successor. What about getting someone from down under?"

Many of the subjects used in projects at OdysseyCorp came from beneath the city, where homeless people huddled in the dark. Most were mentally ill, addicted to drugs, or near death from exposure, but they could be used in most projects. It originally had been Shaw's idea to get subjects from down there. He had gone down alone a few times, even when a subject was not needed. Just for sport.

Jorgan shook his head. "We need someone in good health. Good health is pretty scarce down there."

Carmen's voice came over the intercom. "The car is here to take you to your meeting with the vice president."

He hit the button and said, "I'll be right out."

Jorgan's eyes had returned to the picture of Emma.

"Tell you what, Alan. I'm going to think about this. I'll be in touch with you by this evening. Is that all right with you?"

"Fine. Just fine."

Shaw put his cigar out in the marble bowl of an ashtray on his desk, then stood. Jorgan stood with him. They shook hands over the desk.

"Try to come up with something yourself," Shaw said. "I have a lot of faith in you."

Jorgan nodded but did not smile. He never smiled. "Thank you," he said. Then he turned and left the office, pulling the door closed behind him.

Shaw turned and walked around the desk to get his coat and meet his car, when his eyes caught the portrait of his wife on the shelf. His eyes narrowed as thoughts began to churn in his head, to boil and stew. He ran the tip of his tongue slowly over his lower lip, back and forth, as he stared at the picture.

Then Shaw spun around and punched the intercom button.

"Carmen, get Dr. Jorgan back in here immediately."

"Yes, sir."

A moment later, the door opened again.

"Alan, don't worry. I have your subject."

"Really?"

"Yes, really. I'll call you tonight. Take care."

Jorgan nodded and backed out of the office, pulling the door closed slowly.

Shaw whistled a tune as he put on his overcoat.

"Carmen, empty the ashtray," he said as he left the office on his way to meet with the vice president of the United States.

7.

LIFE IN PRISON

Emma never realized before just how small a forty-three-room house could be, nor how fond she could become of a large lizard named Rupert.

"Bologna sandwiches, Rupert!" she called as she entered the greenhouse. "I made them myself."

She could hear his tail swishing through the bushes, his claws clicking on the floor as he hurried toward the sound of her voice.

Pulling up the white plastic chair she had brought into the greenhouse weeks ago, she sat down and placed the tray on her lap. On the tray were four bologna sandwiches with mayonnaise, mustard, and American cheese on white bread, a plate of raw vegetables and a large bowl of potato chips. The chips were the plain kind, very thin. She had found that Rupert preferred them over others she had given him.

The enormous iguana appeared from the small jungle of greenery and shuffled toward her, smiling the whole way. Emma leaned down and held out a sandwich. Rupert plucked it from her hand and ate happily.

"And chips," she said. "I've got your favorite kind." She took a handful of potato chips from the bowl, leaned down, and dropped them in a pile before the iguana.

As soon as he was done with the sandwich, Rupert cocked his head and locked an eye on the small mound of chips. He poked his head forward and closed his mouth on a few of them with a loud crunch, paused a moment, then began opening and closing his mouth as he drew the chips in with his pink tongue. As he chewed, Rupert tilted his head this way and that, sometimes looking up at Emma.

Popping a chip into her mouth, Emma chewed as she watched the lizard. "If you pretend they're Landon's bones, that crunch sounds pretty good, doesn't it, Rupert?"

He looked at her with his left eye as he crunched, smiling.

She used to hate the iguana. Not that she had anything against reptiles in general or lizards in particular. In fact, she had always admitted that Rupert was a beautifully colored animal and had a rather charming face that seemed to be forever smiling. She had hated it because it was part of Landon's collection of possessions, part of the display he put on for everyone around him. His obscenely large and odd-looking house, his collection of vintage cars, his green iguana, which, at six feet, two inches, was the largest in captivity, and, of course, Emma herself, among so many other things. With the exception of his cars, he really cared for nothing. His possessions were only for show, to impress people, to give him something to talk about between business deals. He cared deeply for his business, of course, but that was not a possession. Landon's business was his life.

Rupert was kept in a sprawling greenhouse attached to the rear of the house in which a small tropical forest had been created for his comfort. Someone on the groundskeeping staff took Rupert for a walk twice a day on a dog leash attached to a halter and fed him fruits, vegetables, and grub worms. The only time Landon saw the lizard was when he brought someone into the greenhouse to show him off.

That was why Emma had always hated Rupert. The iguana was a reflection of her, of what she was: a possession of Landon's.

But over the past few months, Emma's feelings toward the long, smiling, lazy-eyed, green and yellow reptile had changed. He had become a partner, a cell mate. Even a confidant. He had proven to her that she still had some feelings left, just when she had become convinced that they had been extinguished.

Emma's father and grandfather had smoked cigars, and she had grown up with their aroma, had even come to find it comforting. But she had never smelled cigar smoke with the pungent odor of burning flesh.

Landon had pressed the burning end of his cigar to the bottoms of her feet, in the gently curved arch where the skin was smoothest, softest. Emma had no idea how long he had pressed that red ember against her skin, but it was long enough for the burns to throb steadily for days after, long enough for her to be unable to walk properly for weeks. Her feet were still sore and she walked slowly and with care, mostly on the balls of her feet.

For all the pain that came afterward, the night he had burned her had been the worst. After he left, she had screamed in agony, writhed on the bed, calling for help, until her voice became a raspy croak and her throat was raw. Though she had lost consciousness from the pain early on, once she regained consciousness it was days before she got any real sleep. The fire still burned in the bottoms of her feet, driving its pain up into her legs like red-hot spikes.

The next morning, Landon had come to her room with a man from the lab, just as he had said he would: a thin, short, balding man in a white lab coat whose name she was never told. The man went about the business of examining her feet as Landon watched, each of them behaving as if she were not there at all.

For the first few days, she'd had to crawl on hands and knees to get to the bathroom. She did not bother trying the bedroom door, assuming it was locked, but Mrs. Babcock did not use a key to get in when she brought Emma her meals and a snack if she wanted.

Mrs. Babcock was sidling up to fifty, widowed and childless, and looked like a woman who was never meant to have children. Thin, stringy, and shapeless, she never smiled; her face did not seem built for it. She had gone to work for Landon years before Emma had met him, and her loyalty to her boss was quiet, unspoken, but utterly complete.

When she had brought Emma's breakfast in on a tray the morning after the burning and beating, she had said good morning, asked Emma if she needed anything else, then left. Each time she came in, she behaved as if nothing was wrong or out of the ordinary, as if the bandages on Emma's feet did not exist, as if Emma's face was not puffy from crying and lack of sleep. She was never in the room for more than a minute before going back to her work.

Emma had rejected the idea of pleading for help from Mrs. Babcock almost as soon as it had occurred to her. She knew Mrs. Babcock would do nothing to help her, she would only run to Landon and tell him that Emma had asked. That might result in more physical punishment.

She remained in her bedroom for a little over two weeks, watching TV, listening to the radio, and trying to ignore her pain. Her feet showed some quick improvement, though, more than she had expected. After a couple of weeks, she was able to stop crawling to the bathroom, as long as she walked only on her tiptoes. Even that was painful, but she was determined to get used to the pain because she wanted to be able to walk again as soon as possible.

The man from the lab came back every couple of days to change her bandages, examine the burns, and apply some kind of cream, always without Landon. He never spoke or made eye contact with her. His visits became less frequent as her burns improved, and then he stopped coming. It felt good for the first few days to be free of him. No lab guy. No Landon. Just Mrs. Babcock popping in and out now and then. But then it began to make Emma nervous.

What was Landon doing? Why had he not shown himself, come to gloat over her wounds? She remembered Landon making some threats of some kind the night he had taken The Towel to her, but she could not remember specifics; that night had become a blur of pain in her memory.

From that moment on—when she realized that, like a problem child in the next room, Landon was being *too* quiet—Emma was unable to feel comfortable, to relax, to lose herself in a movie on TV, or even in the pain in her feet, however diminished it might be. She knew he had something planned, or was in the process of planning it. Her discomfort became agitation, and then paranoia. Late in her third week of isolation in the bedroom, Emma realized she had to get out before her paranoia became abject fear and she was too afraid to leave the room.

That was when the lab guy returned and spoke to her for the first time.

"Let's get you on your feet and see if you can walk."

As her ability to walk improved, she found that she was free to leave the bedroom and roam the house. It was a big house, and once she was out of the bedroom, she began to relax again.

Then she met her guardian. He was tall, blond, in his thirties, with broad shoulders and muscles that pressed nicely against the yellow cotton shirt he wore. She first saw him in the kitchen when she made her slow way down there to fix herself a snack. He was mixing some beige-colored drink in the blender. Probably a protein shake, or something; he looked like the type. He smiled, nodded, but said nothing. When he did not speak, she knew he was there for her, one of the many thugs who worked for Landon whose job it was to make sure she did not try to hot-wire one of the cars or hike into the city to tell the editor of the *Tribune* all of Landon's deep, dark secrets. He probably had been there from the beginning, but having been cooped up in the bedroom for so long, this was the first time she had seen him.

Emma returned none of the man's smiles, and except for that first time, never made eye contact with him. She behaved as if he were not there. It was difficult at first, but what she faked early on became quite natural with time.

She wandered the house day and night over the following weeks, moving slowly, having to stop frequently to take the weight off her feet. Her blond shadow was never far behind. She explored parts of the house she had never seen before, reclined on the sofa in the library with a stack of books on the floor beside her, reading a few, skimming through others. She took time to appreciate Landon's spectacular art collection, knowing that the price of each painting was far more important to him than its beauty, which he hardly noticed, if at all. Emma wandered and explored, day and night. And that was how

Landon's audaciously unconventional and stunningly original forty-three-room, two-story, giant maxi-pad of a house came to seem so small to Emma. The housekeeping staff, the kitchen staff—they all seemed crowded into this mansion, bumping into her. Emma decided it was time to go outside.

On her first day out it was raining, as always. The sky over this part of the country never seemed to run dry, was forever drenching the city and its outlying areas, filled with dark, bloated clouds that only seemed to part long enough to give a teasing, taunting glimpse of the beautiful sunlight on the other side, only to close again and continue their onslaught. But Emma did not care. She bundled up and grabbed an umbrella on the way out, ignoring the man who followed.

Emma crossed the veranda, walked carefully and slowly through the flower garden, every move calculated to protect the painful burns on the soles of her feet, stopping now and then to lean against something and give them a rest.

Eventually, she made her way to the greenhouse. She had gone in there only once before, and that had been years ago. Emma had never been comfortable around Rupert and had always avoided him. But she was bored, lonely, and depressed. Sick to death of the inside of the house, she wanted to do something unusual, look at something she did not see every day.

She opened the greenhouse door, collapsed her umbrella and glanced surreptitiously at her guardian, who stood a few yards away, trying to look casual under his umbrella, like some B-movie private eye. She went inside and closed the door. It felt nice not being able to see him lurking nearby. The only other time she had that luxury was in the bedroom.

It was just Emma and Rupert.

She heard him before she saw him, moving toward the sound of movement, toward company in the greenhouse. His heed peered out between green stalks of something or other—plants were not an interest of Emma's. The lizard watched her as she made her slow, unsteady way through the lush greenery toward him.

The rain falling on the greenhouse roof filled it with a loud but not unpleasant roar that seemed appropriate amid all the jungle like green and colorful orchids and other large, exotic flowers.

She stood before the lizard and said, "Hiya, Rupert. How's life in the jungle?"

Rupert shuffled toward her, stopped at her feet, and cocked his head so that his right eye stared up at her. He wore a halter to which a leash was attached two times a day to take him outside for a walk, as per Landon's orders.

"Sorry, I didn't bring any treats. Is that what you're waiting for? I promise I won't make this mistake again."

Rupert followed her as she made her way through the greenhouse, ambling along at her heels or just beside her, tipping his head to look up at her expectantly with one upward-blinking eye. He accompanied her on her entire tour of the greenhouse.

She stood just inside the door wondering if food was all he wanted. Maybe he was waiting for her to hook a leash to his halter and take him outside. She understood the need to get out; Emma was just as much a prisoner as the huge, lonely lizard smiling up at her.

After that, she took a daily walk to the greenhouse for a visit with Rupert. She talked to him, fed him, ate some of her meals with him. Rather than hating Rupert for being another one of Landon's possessions, as she had before, Emma came to love him for that very reason. She did not belong in that rambling, maze-like house with Landon's employees and flunkies; she belonged with one of her own, like Rupert, even if he did live in a greenhouse. She came to feel such affection for the iguana that she regretted ever referring to her husband as "Mr. Lizard"; it was an insult to Rupert and reptiles everywhere. As her feet improved, she began taking Rupert for short walks over the grounds, walks that grew longer each week.

That was why, nearly six months after she had been beaten and burned, Emma sat in a folding chair in the greenhouse sharing her lunch with Rupert. And it was on that day that their quiet refuge was invaded for the first time by someone else.

"Hello, Emma."

Landon stood inside the door in his ash-gray cashmere overcoat, looking at Emma with something that resembled a smirk. Or perhaps it was the beginning of a sneer.

The man from the lab—the one who had cared for her feet—stepped through the open door behind Landon carrying his bag, and pulled it closed.

Taking a few steps toward her, Landon said, "I see you've made friends with Rupert. That's nice. I've always had the impression that you didn't approve of my lizard. I'm glad to see I was wrong." He walked slowly over to her chair and stood in front of her.

A blade of ice cut into Emma's chest, but she struggled to keep fear from her face as she looked up at her husband.

Behind Landon, the lab man leaned against the wall, waiting, pretending to see and hear nothing. Beneath his overcoat, he wore his usual white lab coat.

Landon frowned as he looked down at Rupert, who was chomping on part of a bologna sandwich.

"You really shouldn't feed him garbage like that," he said with annoyance. "It'll make him sick. I hope you don't do it every day." He looked at her, waiting for a response.

She gave none and silently stared up at him, waiting for whatever was coming.

"Oh, well," he said with a sigh, "I didn't come to discuss Rupert. Do you remember what I said, Emma? On that night? You know what night I'm talking about."

Although she could not prevent her eyes from widening slightly, she did not respond. But fear scooped out her insides and then took their place, snuggling into her gut.

"I told you I'd figure out a way to handle the problem you had become. I told you that things would change drastically for you. Soon. Do you remember that?"

Still, she only stared him silently. Fear seemed to have stiffened her neck, preventing her from nodding.

Landon's jaw flexed and his lips paled as they pressed together tightly. "Have you gone deaf and dumb?" he said through clenched teeth. "Answer me. You remember all that, don't you?"

Emma felt Rupert's nose nudging her leg, waiting for another bite to eat. She glanced down at the iguana, leaned forward with a bowl of potato chips in hand, and upended it in front of the lizard.

"For God's *sake*, Emma do you know how much that damned thing is *worth*? He has a very specific diet and you're gonna make him sick if you feed him that crap. He's the biggest goddamned iguana in captivity, and if you—" He stopped, took a breath.

Emma leaned back in her chair and looked up at him.

"Are you going to answer my questions?" he said, voice lower now, more controlled. "Or just sit there like a spoiled child."

Her natural response was to say yes, she remembered all the things he had said. That was what she normally did, and then she would apologize for everything. But she saw no point in apologizing when she had done nothing wrong, and when apologizing made no difference, anyway. She said nothing.

"All right, fine," he said. "I don't care. It doesn't matter."

Emma saw Landon's left arm jerk twice behind him, in the direction of the lab man. Over Landon's shoulder, she saw the lab man move away from the wall and toward her, slipping a hand inside his coat.

"I've been true to my word, Emma," Landon said. "Things change for you as of today. Drastically. You and I have filed for divorce. It's in all the papers. On the news. Even Liz Smith wrote about it. But within two days, you're going to be killed in a tragic auto accident. At least, as far as everyone else in the world is concerned, you'll be dead. But, of course, you'll really be working for me. And in a much more important capacity than you have in the past."

His smile was shockingly warm and genuine, broad and bright and full of satisfaction.

"Don't make this hard on yourself, Emma. Okay?"

Then Landon stepped aside as the lab man moved toward her with a hypodermic in his right hand.

8.

COMING BACK TO LIFE

The main entrance to the South Street Mission was located on the corner of South and Beacham. Two sets of large glass double doors, long ago blackened with paint, were built into the corner of the building.

Once, the doors had opened to a grand, two-story department store filled with clothes and toys, hardware and sporting goods, cosmetics and furniture. Back then, there had been three other entrances for customers, but two of those had been boarded up for years. Now, it was a man-made cavern, a cold and massive place that seemed too big to be filled with anything.

But Reverend Wilton Childs and a woman called Mama Charity had given the lie to that impression. Now, instead of dealing in appliances for the home, it dealt with homeless people; instead of selling clothes and toys, it gave them away. The same people who would have been kicked out of the department store that existed thirty-eight years ago were now welcomed into the mission with open arms and given as much help as possible. The walls of the old department store's cafeteria had been torn down to expand it into an enormous dining room where people who had not had a balanced meal in days or weeks or months could eat comfortably and sit afterward over a hot cup of coffee while they digested their food.

McNolte was not only impressed with the place, he was sorry he'd ever had doubts about it. But his feelings toward the South Street Mission had not been so enthusiastic or positive when he first arrived.

P.W. had driven him from the hospital in a hulking, rusted 1953 Chevy Bel Air that looked like it would collapse into a heap of parts if the doors were slammed too hard. He had led McNolte through the painted glass doors of the mission and into what looked like a small-town bus station. McNolte later learned it was called the "receiving room," where volunteers greeted the incoming needy and determined their needs.

Benches and folding chairs and stools were occupied by the tenants of the city's streets: shuddering alcoholics and corpse-thin junkies, as well as the perfectly clean and sober; homeless men, women, children, and families, some wearing rags, some dressed in clean and tidy clothes that would make them impossible to identify as needy among the other pedestrians on the street, while still others wore once-pristine business suits, now dulled and stained by life on the sidewalks and in the alleys, as if they had gone to work one day weeks or months ago to find that they had no job, and then had returned home to find that they had no home. They still looked stunned, as if they had not yet figured out what had happened.

Although most of them were seated, there were not enough chairs and benches for everyone. Their faces spoke louder than their clothes. While the attire differed, the chalky faces were all the same. From the youngest to the oldest, their eyes were alive with fear and confusion, surrounded by darkened, yellowish-gray flesh, some wrinkled, some puffy, but all shaded with despair.

Throughout the crowded room, there were a number of people who looked different from the others; McNolte assumed they worked at the mission, probably volunteers. They were handing out Styrofoam cups of coffee, bandaging wounds, feeding babies, leading people out of the room to other parts of the building.

As McNolte stood there looking around at all the faces, hollow-cheeked and stripped of their dignity, he began to feel short of breath, as if he had been running. Running, in fact, was precisely what he wanted to do. He wanted to turn and run back through those blackened glass doors, away from those faces, away from the feeling of claustrophobia that was beginning to embrace him. Mostly, he wanted to run away from the cold, slobbering, fanged reality that had just bitten a chunk of flesh out of the back of his neck.

I've hit bottom. Rock bottom. This is it. I'm one of them.

It cut through the layers of grogginess caused by his painkillers, shot a current of electricity into his numbed brain, reached between his healing ribs and clutched his heart in its vulture-like talon. His mouth opened slowly as his eyes passed over the faces, the desolate expressions and hopeless eyes.

Do I look like them yet? he wondered. *Will I? Soon? Is that expression frozen onto your face when you lose everything? Does it ever go away?*

McNolte was about to tell P.W. thanks, but no, thanks, and leave the building when he was jarred from his growing panic by the sight of a woman shouldering her way through the crowd in his direction, her eyes meeting his. He was startled, even vaguely frightened by the sight of her bearing down on him and he prepared to jump out of her way.

Her skin was dark. It was not mocha, it was not chocolaty, it was black. She could not have been more than an inch taller than five feet or an ounce under three hundred pounds. She wore a flowing black caftan with gold trim, and everything underneath it jumped with each quick step she took. Her hair was pulled back tightly and exploded in a full, frizzy mass behind her head. Moving with surprising speed, her legs pumped beneath the black material, thick arms slightly outstretched at her sides with small hands open, fingers splayed. Her smile grew wider the closer she got and when she was about ten feet away, she spoke.

"You must be the Mr. Magnolia Willy been tellin' me about!" she said. Standing before him, she clutched his hands between hers. The fragrance of orange and cinnamon hovered about her, like a cozy kitchen at Christmas time. "I am so glad you got here in time for lunch so you can sit down to a good meal before you get to know the place. I don't know what's on the menu, but I'm sure it's better than hospital food, huh?"

McNolte nodded uncertainly, opened his mouth to speak, but did not get a chance.

"I'm Mama Charity," she went on, squeezing his hands, "and I help run this joint, ain't that right, P.W.?"

Grinning, P.W. started to respond, but waited a fraction of a second too long.

Mama Charity quickly hooked her arm through McNolte's good one and began to lead him deeper into the room full of people as she continued: "Why don't you let me take you to Willy, introduce you, let him know you're here, 'cause he's gonna wanna welcome you, too. I know this must look like a strange place to you right now, Mr. Magnolia, but if you're willing to do your part, this can be almost like home, if you let it."

He pounced on that second-long pause as Mama Charity took a breath: "McNolte," he said.

She stopped walking and looked at him. "Whassat?"

"McNolte. It's McNolte, not Magnolia."

He heard P.W. chuckle on the other side of Mama Charity as her round, black face broke into a big grin. "Is that right? Well, I'm sorry about that. But you know what? If you don't mind, I kinda like Magnolia. You mind if Mama Charity calls you Magnolia? Don't think of it is as sissified, or nothin'. It's a real pretty flower, a magnolia, don't you think? And that's what we do here, we take care of flowers. The good Lord sends 'em to us, and we do the gardenin'. Would that be okay with you? Magnolia? 'Cause tell ya the truth, I'm prob'ly never gonna remember your name."

McNolte did not respond at first. He leaned forward and looked to P.W. as if for help, for confirmation that this mile-a-minute woman was not really one of the people who had come in off the street, that she was, indeed, one of the people in charge.

P.W. laughed and shrugged. "You could be called worse."

When McNolte looked at Mama Charity again, she was laughing. It was quite a sight. Every part of her beneath the caftan quaked with her laughter. It was contagious and he felt a smile begin to spread over his lips without any conscious help from him. Pretty soon, he was grinning; it still hurt his ribs too much to laugh.

"Okay," he said. "I guess if you don't mind being called Mama Charity, you can call me Magnolia."

The Reverend Wilton Childs was not nearly as colorful as Mama Charity. They found him in his office talking on the phone, securing a donation of potatoes for the kitchen. The office was a cluttered mess of books and papers, magazines, file folders, all in haphazard stacks that threatened to topple over under the force of a mere breath, and the desk was hardly better. There were no windows and the slightly yellowed walls were bare except for a framed painting of a black young man with a thick beard wearing a ragged cloak. It took McNolte a minute to realize it was a painting of Jesus—a realistic one, for a change. A light fixture holding three bare bulbs was in the center of the ceiling. The only other light came from a bright lamp on his desk. The sweet-smelling ghost of pipe tobacco lingered in the air.

Willy was a broad-shouldered black man, about six feet tall, with a band of black-and-silver hair growing around the back of his otherwise bald head from ear to ear. He was in his early sixties, and though there were bags beneath his eyes and the flesh of his face sagged as if it were simply too exhausted to be supple anymore, his large bright blue eyes glimmered with youth and vitality. His voice was deep; it seemed to erupt from some rumbling pocket of seismic activity deep in his big chest, and his movements were quick, agile, those of a much younger man.

Once off the phone, he stood, smiled, and introduced himself—as Willy, not Wilton or Reverend Childs—shook hands and offered McNolte a seat. P.W. excused himself and Mama Charity went to get them some coffee.

"Dr. Liu told me a lot about you," Willy said. "I'm glad he thought of us, because I think we can help you. If you'll let us. Of course, that's up to you."

"Well, um, everyone seems very nice. But to be honest, I don't like the idea of my personal problems being spread among strangers."

"Yes, my fault. Mama and P.W. were in here when I took Dr. Langley's call. They overheard, and I suppose I overspoke. But please understand, Mr. McNolte, that everyone here has personal problems. Humiliating, sometimes dehumanizing problems. The very act of coming here is seen by most as an admission of failure, defeat. Our job is to make sure everyone knows they're not alone, that they have value, and that we're all in this together. So we don't spend too much time trying to keep every little detail confidential. If that's a problem, then you might not be too comfortable here. But I hope you'll give it a try. Of course, we'll want you to pitch in. We'll give you all the help we can. Food, board, counseling, limited medical care. But this is a big operation, Mr. McNolte, and running it requires a great deal of work. Unfortunately, we're always short of volunteers. That's why, with the exception of those too ill or disabled, we ask everyone who comes here for help to pitch in. Anything you can do. Cleaning, cooking, helping out with new arrivals. Of course, you don't look to be in any kind of shape for that at the moment. But when you're able, we would appreciate any help you can give us. If you will. If not, we'll still help you, because we don't turn anyone away. But if you want to stay for an extended period of time, you'll have to do your part. So, tell me, Mr. McNolte. Are you willing to let us help you?"

McNolte gave it a few moments of thought. He could stay with Richard for a little while, maybe even borrow some money. Once he was in better shape, he might even be able to get a job. But how long would it be before he had enough to get a place of his own with the medical bills hanging over his head and the fine he would have to pay for driving under the influence? And what about that other thing...that shadowy, ominous, hunkering thing in the very back of his mind...that thing he had refused to think about while in the hospital: the money he owed Mr. Trafficante.

Willy was right; it was humiliating to come to a mission, an admission of failure. But if he could get used to the lack of privacy, it might be a good thing. It would mean he would have a place to stay and food to eat while he went about the arduous task of repairing the battered wreck of his life.

More importantly, the South Street Mission was a place Mr. Trafficante, or anyone in his employ, would be unlikely to look for him.

That had been months ago.

During that time, McNolte had burrowed his way deeply into life at South Street, both as a recipient of the help it had to offer and as a volunteer worker.

P.W. had become his best friend. The man was not the grinning simpleton McNolte had first thought him to be. He was bright and possessed a razor-sharp wit; he was well read and had an impressive collection of books that he kept in the trunk of his Bel Air, and he shared them with McNolte. They spent hours discussing everything from the classics to bestsellers, from nonfiction to pulp fiction.

One evening before dinner, McNolte said hesitantly, "P.W., you said you were in pretty bad shape by the time you got here."

"Oh, yeah," P.W. said, nodding. "I was the walkin' dead."

"Well, if you don't mind my asking, how did you get that way?"

"I don't mind at all." He took a few bites of food and chewed thoughtfully before answering. "Everybody figures I hit the bottle 'cause of some traumatic experience in 'Nam, but...hell, the whole thing was a traumatic experience. I know people who had a tougher time over there. In some ways, I think I came out of it a better person. I sure as hell came out of it *different*. Maybe stronger. And probably more sensitive to things. To other people. Maybe that was the problem. I started looking around me with different eyes, realized Vietnam wasn't the only place where the shit was hittin' the fan on an hourly basis. Wasn't until I got home and started looking around like that, with more open eyes, that I got messed up. People didn't care about the hell that was goin' on in their own front yard. Starvation right here in our own streets, politicians smilin' and lyin' like there were no consequences, and there never are—not for *them*. Meanwhile, everything around 'em just turned to shit. Most people, long as they had their TVs and their frozen dinners, a car that worked, and a nice coat of paint on their house—hell, they didn't care what was goin' on across the street, let alone across the globe. So it was sure as shit no surprise that they were watchin' what was goin' on in 'Nam on TV while they ate their frozen dinners.

Made me sick. Not like...well, it wasn't righteous indignation, nothin' like that. I didn't wanna grab a sign and start picketing, or anything. It just...*scared* me, that's what it did. Scared the hell outta me. 'Cause it made me realize what was coming."

"What was coming?" McNolte said after P.W. paused to take another bite of his dinner. "What do you mean?"

"Hey, babe, we're in it. Things just keep gettin' worse. As long as Joe Q. Public's got his cable and a VCR, maybe a computer, a six pack of cold beer in the fridge, he don't give a flying frijole *what's* goin' on outside his front door. *That's* what I saw coming. I just got a little carried away with that fear, is all, with bein' afraid of all that...*apathy*. So I tried to drown it in booze, which—for a while, anyway—made me no better than anybody else. Made me a hypocrite. But once I got that behind me, I decided the best I could do was...the best I could do. Which is why I stay here and do my best. That's also why I don't watch the news anymore, McNolte. A day, an hour...a *minute* doesn't go by that I don't crave another drink. That numbness. It was cozy while it lasted, I'll tell ya. But I can't go back to that, and I'm afraid the news might just push me over the edge."

McNolte was familiar with the cravings. Although his physical recovery was satisfactory, his craving for cocaine did not go away. Shortly after coming to South Street, the need for that precious white powder returned like an old lover who, after breaking his heart once, had come back to do it again. It was usually his first thought in the morning, and it stayed with him all day long. At night, as he slept, he often dreamed of it so vividly that he could still feel the sting of the cocaine in his nostrils as he woke up, could still taste it in his throat. He often craved a drink, any kind of booze at all, just something that would dull his thoughts and silence the whispering voice in his head that told him how much better things would be with a gram, just a gram, or a bottle of...anything.

"It gets better," P.W. assured him. "It never goes away, but it does get better with time."

A support group for recovering addicts met three times a day at South Street. The meetings helped somewhat, but McNolte found that the best therapy was to simply throw himself headlong into the work that needed to be done around the mission. In the process, he got to know all the regulars.

There was Irving, a stocky, fifty-nine-year-old homeless man with a gray crewcut who had come to the mission during its first year and had been there ever since. Willy and Mama Charity had helped him find several jobs in the past and Irving had done his level best to keep each one. But his efforts were always undone by his affliction: Tourette's syndrome, a neurological disorder that caused facial tics and body jerks, as well as a tendency to repeat words that others said to him and to blurt obscenities uncontrollably. Now, South Street was Irving's home and he was in charge of maintenance.

"Hey, how you doing?" Irving said to McNolte one day during his first week there. The man smiled and reached out to shake his hand. "Never seen you around here before. I'm Irving. I clean up the place."

McNolte shook Irving's hand, impressed by the strength in his calloused grip. "I'm Neil McNolte. Everybody calls me McNolte."

"Well, then I don't want to be any different, McNolte. Nice to meet you, you *shit-eating asshole!*"

Startled into speechlessness, McNolte hurried away from the man as soon as he could. Later, Willy explained Irving's condition and assured him that the man had meant none of the unpleasant things he had said. After that, McNolte and Irving became fast friends, and McNolte helped him around the mission whenever he could, joining Irving's ever-changing staff of maintenance workers.

The staff included a young man named Juarez. He was in his early twenties but had more years than that on his hard, cold face. He wore a black patch over his right eye, which was sinister enough, but not as sinister as the look that sometimes came from his exposed left eye, so dark it was almost black. As with Irving, though, McNolte found that his first impression of Juarez was wrong.

When he was fourteen, Juarez had run away from his cruelly abusive home in a small Texas town and come to the city, where he lived on the street, and lived *off* the street, as well, eating when he could, sleeping anyplace he could find. He joined a gang—one of the many that prowled the city's streets—and became addicted to drugs. Losing his eye saved his life. It had been in a gang fight. Juarez was stabbed in the eye and left behind for dead by the members of his own gang. He woke up in a hospital, ending up at South Street in much the same way McNolte had, later going on to get a job at a fish market on the wharf. But even after he could afford his own room at a boarding house, Juarez returned to South Street almost every day.

"Coming here keeps me off the streets," he told McNolte. "I'm used to the streets, I know 'em. Hell, I know every inch of this city by now. I even been in the sewers and down under the subways. Slept down under a few nights. See, I'm not used to sitting in a room watching TV and eating Cheese Nips. That's not me. Once you get the streets in your blood, night rolls around and you wanna feel 'em under your feet, be walkin' 'em. But comin' here reminds me what kinda shit happens out there. Yeah. Keeps me off the streets."

There were other regulars, and many more newcomers every day, each with a story to tell. In all his years of reporting, McNolte had never been to the city these people knew. He had lived there, walked there, driven the same streets, breathed the same damp, dirty air, but he came to realize that through their eyes, it was an entirely different city. Perhaps even a different culture, a different country. Maybe a different world altogether. They inhabited a parallel universe, an alternate dimension. While McNolte and everyone else like him had been going to work and living in their apartments and houses, buying groceries and filling their cars with gas, tipping cab drivers and waiters and waitresses, the people who came to South Street were living among them, invisible because they had been there so long, silent because no one listened anymore, with their own laws and traditions, their own ways of living and eating, surviving and dying. They were two worlds occupying the same space.

At night, lying in one of the many beds in the enormous second-floor section of the building that made up the men's quarters, McNolte propped a flashlight on his shoulder and wrote his impressions of these people in a spiral notebook. He wrote every night before going to sleep: character sketches, descriptions of the mission and the people who worked there. Before long, he needed a new notebook.

By that time, his arm, still achy but mobile, was much better, and his hair had grown back over the closed-up cut in his skull. He still went to the meetings and had to admit that, although a day did not go by when the whispering voice did not tell him that things always went better with coke, the urge gradually became weaker. And all the while, his writing was getting stronger.

Wily spotted him writing in the notebook at lunch one day and asked if he could read some of it. After reading a few pages, Wily asked McNolte to come to his office.

With Wily behind his cluttered desk, McNolte in a chair in front of it, and the spiral notebook open before him, Wily read some more. Then he focused his attention on McNolte.

"You know, you've been with us a year, McNolte. And I've been thinking, that's a long time. Especially for someone with your abilities and background. Now that I've seen what you can do first-hand, I'm even more puzzled."

He was quiet for several seconds, then nodded slowly and said, "Yeah, I know. I've been thinking about that, too. I guess I've been waiting for you to kick me out, or something."

"Scared, aren't you?"

"Scared? Oh, boy, am I scared. I owe a lot of money. To the hospital, to Dr. Langley, to that nice judge who hit me with a twenty-five hundred dollar fine and didn't put me in jail because it was my first offense and no one else was involved but the deer."

"Lucky for you. Lucky you didn't go to jail and he didn't charge you double what he did. After all, you were at the wheel while blasted out of your mind, right?" Wily leaned back in his chair. "Well, I'm not going to talk to you in bumper stickers and platitudes, McNolte. You're too smart for that. We're here to give you whatever help we can, and we *will* do that, but when it comes right down to it, you're in your own hands. Moving forward is up to you."

McNolte nodded with a dreary sigh.

"Okay, let's think about this, now," Willy said. "You've got your fine for driving under the influence, the hospital bill, and Dr. Langley's bill. For one thing, Dr. Langley treated you for months after your surgery, but you're only being billed for what he did in the hospital. The rest was here at the clinic, free of charge, so you've got that to be grateful for. Okay, you owe all this money that you can't pay. What are they going to do? I mean, think about it. Until you've got the money to pay them back, what are they going to do to you? Send some big thug out to beat you up for it?"

McNolte shrugged slightly, his blood chilling as his mind wandered elsewhere, to someone who would do that very thing.

"Now, you've written this," Willy said, tapping a finger on the open notebook. "And I think it's wonderful, McNolte. It's beautiful. Most of the stuff written about the homeless and about addiction—it usually misses the boat. All those chest-beating articles and books asking, 'What are we going to do about this problem?' Asking that question *for* the reader. That doesn't work. What the readers need is something that will make them ask that question for *themselves*. Something like this," he said with another tap of the finger on the notebook. "You paint a picture here, McNolte, a real and vivid picture. If you could sell this, you'd be doing two things. You'd be putting yourself back on your feet, and you'd be showing your readers what's going on around them, things they don't even see anymore. And you could do it without whining at them, without telling them about something you've learned second hand, through a filter. And if you could sell that one article, then you could sell another, and another. Pretty soon, you'd have enough for a book. And you'd have a place of your own. You'd be making payments on those debts."

"Those debts," McNolte muttered.

"Is there something wrong, McNolte? I get the feeling... you're not telling me everything. You got something else on your mind?"

"No, no, I'm fine. You're right. I'd like to whip this into an article. You wouldn't happen to have a spare computer I could use?"

Willy laughed. "A spare computer? We don't even have an electric mixer for the kitchen. Those mashed potatoes you eat are done by hand. I have an old Royal typewriter you can use if you'd like, but I bet you've got a friend or two in this city with computer."

"You're right. I do."

"Good. The Royal's available if you want it, though."

McNolte was on his way out the office door when he stopped and almost turned back, almost told Willy everything, about the money he owed Trafficante, about what Trafficante had promised to do if he did not pay it back, and that the only reason he had not done that already was that he probably could not find him. But he kept going. He knew there was nothing Willy could do for him except maybe pray, and once he stepped outside of the mission, McNolte strongly doubted that would be enough.

He worked on the article, using Willy's battered Royal to condense his work into a solid and potent piece. Nothing in it revealed the fact that he was living at South Street. When it was done, he called Richard, who agreed to let him come over and use his computer. Once the article was printed up, McNolte hand-delivered it to a friend of his at the *Tribune*, Diane Shackley. When he was at the *Tribune*, Diane worked in entertainment writing puff pieces about celebrities. Now she was editor of the Sunday magazine supplement, *Skyline*. She was not as friendly as she used to be, probably because she had heard about what had become of McNolte and decided he was a lost cause. She was a bit chilly, a little condescending, and not interested in a conversation that went beyond small talk.

But she shocked McNolte by buying the piece. He was almost as thrilled as he had been when he sold his first story. The elation soon passed, though, and was replaced by fear.

This is the first sale of the rest of your career, he thought.

And that meant that his days at South Street were winding down. After selling one article, he would have no excuse for not writing and selling another, and another, and pretty soon people would start asking if he was working on the inevitable book yet. He would have to go *out there* and live, work, produce, and wait to be found by someone sent by Mr. Trafficante. Someone who would start with McNolte's fingers.

But he did it, anyway. His article on the homeless was the talk of every radio talk show in town, and it even snagged him a couple of radio interviews by phone. It led, as Willy had predicted, to other articles, and even a few assignments.

Leaving South Street felt a little like leaving home to go to college. Exciting, but scary as hell. He was given a small party at lunch. Marcy, the chief cook, baked him a cake. Everyone shook his hand, gave him hugs. Mama Charity showered him with kisses. Willy gave him the old Royal typewriter as a going away present.

He had struck bottom and worked his way back up again, but he knew that, just like Irving, just like Juarez, just like P.W. and so many others, he would be back. He would return to South Street often to help in any way he could.

McNolte moved into a studio apartment furnished with a bed, a chair, and a rickety card table in a part of the city he would not choose under normal circumstances—but circumstances were hardly normal. It was the best he could afford at the moment, and he did not plan to be there long.

A block away from his apartment building, McNolte discovered Wee's Café and quickly became a regular. It was a tiny place owned by a loud Chinese fellow named Wee. The Chinese food was greasy enough to give a bear a stroke, but it was surprisingly cheap. McNolte stuck to the American menu, having salads, sandwiches, and breakfast food, and he ate only one meal a day aside from fruits and snack foods he kept in his apartment. He wanted to save a little money while making small payments toward his fine and medical bill.

But all the while, he was nagged by two things: the needling hunger for cocaine, and the gnawing fear that he was living on borrowed time. Every day, he fought hard to push both of them aside so he could work. If he had the money, he would have purchased a gun—providing the city's stiff-as-steel-pipe gun laws allowed it.

Through the fear and occasional paranoia, he worked. That was all he did; he sat at the card table clacking away at the Royal, proofreading his pages with a pencil.

Until one day when he was able to do something different: answer the door.

When he heard the three solid knocks, McNolte froze, fingers on the typewriter keys, and turned his head slowly to look at the door.

"Who is it?" he called.

"Messenger. A package from the *Tribune*."

He pulled away from the table, frowning. He was not expecting anything, but there was always the chance it could be another assignment from *Skyline*. He stood, walked to the door, still frowning, moving slowly, cautiously. He considered asking the messenger for the name of the person who had sent the package, but he knew if it was someone who worked for Mr. Trafficante, he probably would be ready with a real name. Even if McNolte did not open the door, the voice on the other side would get to him sooner or later if that was his job. As he stood there staring at the door, he decided to take the chance, because it was coming sooner or later. If this was it, so be it.

Everything inside McNolte's body tightened into cold, hard knots as he unlocked the door and pulled it open. He only got a glimpse of the man outside the apartment.

The door was shoved open and a hand clamped onto McNolte's throat and pushed him backward. The door was kicked shut as the hand pushed McNolte backward until he tripped over his own feet and fell to the floor, gagging because the man's hand was closing so tight, holding on all the way to the hardwood floor until McNolte's back hit with a hard thump and all the air exploded from his lungs.

The face that stared down at him was young and smooth and without character. Pale skin, blank, heavy-lidded, wide-set eyes, an expressionless mouth with thin lips, dark hair combed straight back and shiny with some kind of product. His lips occasionally pulled back far enough to give McNolte a look at his silver-capped incisor.

The man produced a gun, but McNolte only glimpsed it before the barrel was pressed to his lips.

"I want you to pretend this is a cock," the man said quietly, eyes looking sleepy, as if he were bored. "And I want you to suck on it."

McNolte's eyes crossed as he tried to look at the gun and his lips trembled and wiggled.

"Open up or I fire it," the man said.

McNolte parted his lips, felt the barrel bump his teeth before he opened them. The barrel clacked against his teeth as it entered his mouth, cold on his tongue, slick with the taste of gun oil. He could not keep his lips from pulling back over his teeth.

"Okay, now," the man said. "Suck on it. Remember, it's a cock. *Suck* on it."

McNolte gagged a little as he closed his lips around the barrel. It made a hollow, breathy sound as he sucked on the tube of gunmetal, so he pressed the tip of his tongue to the end to make the sound stop. He sucked as he pressed the back of his head against the floor, and his lips made quiet kissing sounds against the outside of the barrel.

"No, no, no," the man said, shaking his head slowly. "Man, haven't you ever had a blowjob? They don't call it giving head for nothing. Now, let's see some head action. Take that cock into your mouth, move your head, press the back of your throat to it like you mean it, man, suck on that thing, show it a good time."

McNolte did as he was told, clenching his eyes shut as he gagged again and again, belching, his teeth clattering against the metal, tongue pulling away from the end and sliding under it so he could take it deeper as he lifted his head slowly, lowered it slowly, lifted it, lowered it.

The man leaned close until his face was less than an inch from McNolte's, breath hot and moist. As he spoke, his silver tooth flashed again and again.

"Now, I got something to tell you. But I want you to keep giving head to this cock, here, you understand? Don't stop. Just keep taking it in. Attaboy. Mr. Trafficante has been considerate of your situation this past year," he said, voice flat, as if saying something nice to an ugly aunt at his parents' prompting. "He's still being nice, in fact, 'cause this is—hey, hey, keep moving that head, buddy. You don't want this cock to go limp, do you?

Okay, yeah, that's better. He's still being nice, 'cause this is only a warning. He's giving you a chance. The next time will hurt. It'll hurt bad. Mr. Trafficante wants his money."

McNolte's head stopped moving, his eyes widened, and his voice squeezed through his constricted throat. But it came out as nothing more than a muffled, rat-like squeak with the barrel of the gun pressing against the back of his throat. He gagged again, belched again, and his head dropped back to the floor.

"Mr. Trafficante wants his money," the man repeated. Then he pulled the gun from McNolte's mouth, stood, and quickly left the apartment, quietly closing the door.

"I can make payments," McNolte said in a tremulous rasp, still lying on the floor, sick with fear and ready to vomit from all the gagging. But the man was gone; McNolte was talking to himself.

He wondered how much longer he would have all ten fingers. Or his life.

9.

DAMSEL IN DISTRESS

Dr. Alan Jorgan knocked some books off the sofa in his office and flopped down, first sitting, then lying back with his head on the curved armrest. He stared at the speckled tiles on the ceiling through heavy-lidded eyes, unable to work another second without some rest.

Nearly two hours ago, he had completed the operation on Emma Shaw. It had never been done before, so it would take a little time to see if it was going to work. But Jorgan felt confident.

Minutes after the operation, he had passed Dr. Benjamin Mason in the corridor. He and the tall black man usually exchanged little more than guarded glances and spoke only when absolutely necessary. But Jorgan felt so confident and elated at the moment that he had given the doctor a smile, a friendly nod,

In the beginning, Mason had tried to make Project Biofire his own, insisting that the introduction of the synthetic virus was unnecessary and risky. When Mason approached Shaw about it, his argument had fallen on deaf ears, because Jorgan had already convinced him of his argument. Jorgan had no doubt that Mason was keeping track of the project as closely as possible, looking for a weakness, a reason to go to Shaw and say, "I told you so," but Jorgan had no intention of giving him that chance, that satisfaction. He hoped his confidence had been evident in his smile, and he hoped it was still eating at Mason.

For the last two hours, he had been sitting at his desk, trying to get some work done while his patient recovered. But he could not do it. He was too tired, and too soul-sick.

Jorgan had always known that Landon Shaw was an evil prick. He had known that even before he had begun to work with the man. After all, the only reason Jorgan was working at OdysseyCorp was because Shaw had blackmailed him into it, and was still blackmailing him. If he were to quit that very day, tell Shaw he would never do another minute of work for OdysseyCorp and walk out the door, the feds would be at his door the next day and his name would be all over the media because, by then, Shaw would have released all the information he had about Jorgan's illegal dealings in human organs. He would hand the authorities all the proof they needed: Jorgan's means of acquiring the organs, how he had sold them, and who had helped him.

Between his problems with the IRS and alimony from two failed marriages, Jorgan had needed the money desperately thirteen years ago. He had become involved with a group of doctors that harvested kidneys, eyes, skin, and sometimes lungs, hearts, and livers for the black market. Sales took place immediately upon a patient's death, and each one was risky, but an enormous amount of money changed hands. The way Jorgan saw it, he was hurting no one. The donors were dead, the recipients would die otherwise, and the buyers were filthy rich, otherwise they could not afford the prices. He was depriving no one of anything, he was helping to save lives—even if they were the lives of rich, arrogant people who, unlike the average patient in need of a transplant, could afford to get what they needed immediately. It was illegal, of course, but he did not think it was immoral. As far as he was concerned, the law had little to do with morality. The dead were dead, the living were saved.

But Landon Shaw knew the authorities would not have the same attitude, and that was how he convinced Jorgan to work at OdysseyCorp.

Jorgan knew Shaw had done the same with many other employees. The man employed an army of top-drawer private investigators and he used the information they gathered like a sword. Once he had gotten someone in his employ at

OdysseyCorp, that sword kept their mouths shut, and kept them dancing to Shaw's tune. He could not have his employees sharing the details of their work at OdysseyCorp with friends and relatives. Before being hired, everyone who worked at OdysseyCorp had to sign a non-disclosure agreement, vowing secrecy about everything they saw, heard, and did while there. But most had already been informed of what Shaw knew about them, and they were well aware of how drastically their lives would change if they did not sign the agreement. It was nothing more than a piece of paper, of course, a prop, for show. Shaw's knowledge was what *really* kept them in line, and everyone knew it, although it remained unspoken, a well-known secret among OdysseyCorp's employees. Even after he had convinced them to sign the agreement, Jorgan knew that Shaw kept a close eye on everyone and continued to gather information on them. That was why Jorgan had chosen to live in a small apartment connected to the OdysseyCorp building; it seemed pointless to find a place of his own and pay rent when he knew damned well Shaw would have everything bugged all the time, anyway—his phone, his furniture, his clothes, everything.

Although he knew Shaw was a monster, Jorgan had managed to keep his feelings toward the man to himself during his years at OdysseyCorp. As a result of his hard and productive work, he knew he had Shaw's respect. Sometimes it almost felt as if Shaw liked him, but Jorgan knew the man too well to believe that for a moment.

But months ago, Jorgan had begun to re-evaluate his dark opinion of Landon Shaw, making it even darker. He had thought he knew Shaw and could deal with him because he had him outlined clearly in his mind, had him pegged. But he had been wrong.

What kind of man used his own wife as a guinea pig for a risky scientific experiment, one that could possibly kill her or, if she lived, turn her into a freak for the rest of her life? And what kind of man faked her death, apparently with the intention of making her "body" show up much later so that no one would question her disappearance?

It was not the kind of man Jorgan had figured Shaw to be;

it was someone much worse, someone who had no soul. It was someone who was human in appearance only.

It made Jorgan's bones cold to think about it. Not just that Shaw would do such a thing to someone, but that he would do it to his wife, to Emma. To *her*, that particular woman. That wonderful woman.

Jorgan had seen only her picture at first, the portrait on the shelf in Shaw's office. Once he had seen her face, he could not get it out of his mind. Pale skin, thick, wavy auburn hair that tumbled past her shoulders and somehow seemed to glitter. Large brown eyes with dense, luxuriant lashes, and the most sensuous lips he had ever seen, full and plum-colored.

He had met her only once, at the only dinner party to which he had ever been invited at Shaw's enormous, weird house, and he had not been able to take his eyes off of her. They had shaken hands and spoken only briefly to exchange clumsy small talk, but his eyes had followed her everywhere. He had been unable to stop watching her, listening to her whenever she spoke at the exclusion of all other sound, following her around like a puppy, staying just close enough to always see and hear her. She had been so much more beautiful in person than in the photograph, almost a different woman, with a voice that sounded like velvet felt. Seeing her hair up close made him want to touch it, stroke it slowly, slide his fingers through, press it to his face, and deeply inhale its fragrance.

That hair was gone now. It had been shaved off, all of it. Her head was bare except for the ugly incision, which had been opened twice. Jorgan had not slept the night her head had been shaved. He had sat up in bed, holding a thick lock of her hair that he had snatched when Miranda was not looking. He had held it between his fingers and thumb, stroking it, occasionally smelling it, brushing it against his cheek, his lips, even his tongue, tasting it.

Lying on the sofa in his office, Jorgan lifted his right hand and looked at it. It was still trembling slightly. That was because he hated his hands now. They were dirty. He had never had a sip of alcohol or taken a drug stronger than aspirin in his entire life, but his hand trembled as if experiencing withdrawals because it was guilty of a crime. A horrible crime.

"Hey, Dr. Jorgan, are you all right?"

He dropped his hand and sat up on the sofa.

Miranda Otter was his assistant, a young woman in her late twenties, short and rather squat, with shiny black hair that was straight and flat and cut like a helmet around her face. Her green eyes looked intelligent above her pug nose. While her behavior often seemed immature, she was brilliant, and Jorgan put great value on her assistance, her judgment. The only problem was that she was quite obviously in love with him. And the thing he disliked most about it was that he had allowed it to happen and had even taken advantage of it.

"Yeah, Miranda, I'm fine, fine," he said, annoyed. "How is she?"

"She woke up just a few minutes ago. Said a few words. Didn't make any sense, but she spoke. She's back in her room now. She's fine."

As always when the subject was Emma, Miranda spoke flatly and with an expressionless face. It was her jealousy showing, Jorgan was certain. She had become terribly possessive of him lately, greedy for his time and attention. Her behavior annoyed Jorgan, even angered him at times. His relationship with Emma Shaw was really none of her damned business, and her behavior made him bristle, as if he had caught her going through his drawers, inspecting his private things.

Miranda sat close beside him on the sofa and ran four fingers through his unruly hair.

"You sure you're all right?" she said.

"I'm *positive*," he snapped. "You said she spoke, that it didn't make any sense. Did you understand anything she said?"

"I made out a little of it. Something about a guy named Rupert."

Jorgan's head turned sharply to face her. "Rupert? She said something about *Rupert*?"

"Uh-huh. 'Just you and me, Rupert,' she said. 'Prisoners, both of us. Just you and me.' Something like that. I was only there long enough to take blood, so she might have said more. I don't know."

Jorgan stared at his lap, smirking. He knew who Rupert was; anyone who had ever gone to Shaw's house knew who Rupert was. Shaw was so proud of that damned oversize lizard that he showed it to anyone and everyone who came through the door.

She had been talking to Rupert as if the two of them were equals, both held prisoner by Shaw.

"You know what you need?" Miranda said. "One of my massages."

"Not now, Miranda."

Jorgan regretted ever surrendering to Miranda's advances. He had not been attracted to her then and was not now. She was built like a fire hydrant. Undressed, that was what she looked like, a human, flesh-and-blood fire hydrant. But the sex had been good, he could not deny that, the best he'd had since he was a kid, as long as he kept his eyes closed. And God knew he had needed it. It had been a tremendous release at the time. That was why he had gone along with it in the first place, he supposed: the need for release and for human contact, hoping it would fill the empty crevasse his life had become.

But there was no place in his life now for sex, or for Miranda Otter. He still had the utmost respect for her. She was the best assistant he had ever had and he did not doubt that she would go far. She was a fast learner, a quick thinker; she was resourceful and imaginative in ways that most scientific minds were not.

She was allowing her emotions to get in the way of their work together, which was unacceptable. This crush of hers was becoming a problem. Sooner or later, he knew he would have to discuss it with her. He had come close to doing that three times already. Each time, he had rehearsed in front of his bathroom mirror what he would say to her. But he had not actually done it yet.

"Well, of course not *now*," she said, a bit of a purr in her voice, "because every time I give you a massage, we end up fucking." She smiled, leaned over and licked his earlobe. "Unless you'd like to do that here. In your office. It's been a long time."

"Goddammit, Miranda," he said, jerking away from her as he pushed her in the opposite direction with one hand on her shoulder, "I said not *now*." He stood and went to his desk, back to the work that he had been unable to concentrate on before. Dropping into his chair, he said, his voice more controlled now, "Look, why don't you go round up some lunch. We can eat together—" He tapped the open folder on his desk. "—and go over the details of these tests, make sure we're on top of things."

"Okay," she said, standing. Once again, her voice was flat, her face without expression. "Be back in a few."

When Miranda was gone, Jorgan got up, walked around his desk and stretched out on the sofa again. He stared up at the ceiling, thinking about Emma, about her husband and their marriage.

During his time with Emma, he had learned a lot. In spite of her circumstances, she had treated him with nothing but kindness, had always been cooperative. Jorgan liked to think the reason for that was the way he had treated her: like royalty. No matter what he might want Miranda to think, Emma Shaw was not just another subject. She was the face he had seen so many times in Shaw's office, the woman with the velvety voice. And although she had never told him directly, he knew how Emma felt about her husband. He could feel it, smell it on her. It was something he sensed in the air whenever Shaw's name came up, even if it was mentioned only in passing. Emma despised Landon Shaw, even more than Jorgan did. That made him feel good. Whenever he felt it—like a fetid breeze wafting out from a fly-buzzing garbage dump—his heart swelled. She hated her husband.

Jorgan knew what kind of man made his wife the subject of a dangerous experiment like Project Biofire. But what kind of man made his wife into the kind of creature that Project Biofire was meant to create?

Only an idiot. Evil, perhaps. But an idiot.

And it was in that knowledge that Jorgan found some consolation.

What Shaw had done to Emma was unthinkable. Although Jorgan had been through two nightmarish marriages himself and knew all too well the boiling hatred that could arise from them, no matter how blissful their beginnings, he never would have considered doing such a thing to either of his ex-wives, even in their worst moments.

But in doing this to Emma, Shaw had handed her over to Jorgan, put her in his care. Emma had resigned herself to her situation and had been almost zombie-like in her surrender at the beginning. But Jorgan had drawn her out of that, gotten to know her slowly. And she had not disappointed him; the woman inside was every bit as lovely as the face in the photograph.

Jorgan had to go through with the project, he had no choice. He knew that were he to follow his gut, take Emma, and run away from OdysseyCorp, Shaw would have found and killed them before they got far, and the vacancy he left would be filled quickly by someone else who would carry on the project with other subjects. If it was to be done, it was best that he do it; that way, Emma would be in the hands of someone who truly cared for her, someone who could make an unpleasant situation as tolerable as possible, maybe even comfortable.

Then, when it was finished, when Jorgan had the results he fully expected, he would act.

Then he would be able to help Emma, and she would be able to help them both. In the process, he would be able to hurt Landon Shaw. *Emma* would be able to hurt him. Even kill him— and probably quite willingly, he guessed. And only because Shaw, in his cruelty, had chosen her as the subject of his project.

Jorgan looked forward to that time, lived for it, and knew that when it finally happened, it would make him the happiest man in the world.

10.

FINGERS

McNolte walked through the front entrance of the South Street Mission just as Mama Charity was beginning to get tough with an unruly drunk.

The majority of the people who came to South Street were either drunk or on drugs, and they were never turned away—unless they persisted in causing trouble, in which case the police were called to haul away the troublemaker. When that happened, the police were always told to call the mission when the troublemaker was ready to leave so someone could drive to the station and pick up the man or woman once he or she dried out.

McNolte stood just inside the glass doors and watched the confrontation. He knew better than to step in when Mama Charity was on a roll.

"Now, if you can't tell me why you'd do that to somebody," Mama Charity said firmly, her voice growing louder as she stood close to the much taller drunk, head tilted back so she could look him in the bleary eyes, "then I think you're just too damned drunk to be walkin' around among good decent people. So why don't you just *git*." She stabbed a finger toward the doors.

The drunk was stoop-shouldered and wore a filthy raincoat. His red, matted hair grew wild and he wore a Brillo-like beard with bits of...something caught among its tiny curls. He swayed back and forth in a slow-motion way as he stood before Mama Charity.

The large, bus station-like room was much quieter than usual as the despairing faces watched to see how Mama Charity would handle herself. McNolte noticed that some of them were actually smiling wearily, so the old girl must have done fine so far.

"C'mon, hon," the drunk slurred, resting a hand on Mama Charity's shoulder. "I juss wanna hot cuppa coffee, mebbe sumpin t'eat, I'm not gonna—"

"There you go *touchin'* again," she said, slapping his arm down hard. "Don't worry, you'll get somethin' to eat when you come back *sober*, hear me? I take you in now and you're just gonna wander around gropin' people, so—"

The man put his hand back on her shoulder, but this time it slipped down onto her enormous breast and he made a comical face as he squeezed. "Whoops," he said, laughing and squeezing.

Mama Charity gripped the hand in hers and bent it backward hard at the wrist and continued to bend it back until he dropped to his knees with a gurgling wail.

"You won't *ever* be welcome here again, you keep that crap up, you understand me?"

The drunk was staring at his hand, pain beginning to register slowly on his dirty face, jaw slackening.

Smirking, McNolte went to her side and said, "You need any help here?"

"Oh, Magnolia!" She grinned up at him, never letting go of the drunk's hand as he continued to cry out in pain. "It's been a few days."

"I know. I've been busy working."

"On the new book?"

"Well, that, and looking for other work, too. Can I give you a hand?"

"No, honey, you know Mama Charity don't need no help with this fella. The police are on their way, should be here any second."

"Good."

"Oh, by the way, you've got a package in Willy's office. I think he's in there now talkin' on the phone. He's trying to round up some veggies for the kitchen 'cause the last batch we got was already spoiled."

"A package? From whom?"

"I don't know, Magnolia, I haven't seen the thing." She still held the man's bent hand in an iron grip as he groaned on his knees. "You go along and find out while Mr. Touchy-Feely and I wait here for his ride."

"Please...*stop* that, willya?" the drunk cried.

"I'll stop when the police get here and not until, you hear?"

McNolte gave her a peck on the cheek, then headed for Willy's office. But he was no longer smiling.

He was not expecting any package, and certainly not one to be delivered to South Street. The fact that one had arrived made his palms moist.

McNolte had continued to get work writing articles, and he was making much better money now. He had tried to get back into advertising, but no one would have him. The only agency he had worked for refused to take him back because of the trouble his cocaine problem had caused, and word of that had gotten around the business quickly, so nobody else in the city would take him, either.

Having put himself on a tight budget, he continued to write diligently, and every penny that he did not absolutely need went to Milo, the small, dark-haired young man who had throttled him to the floor in his apartment nine months ago. Milo always passed the money on to Mr. Trafficante, but not before doing something to McNolte that would stay with him for a while and remind him of the importance of his debt. Once, he had knocked McNolte unconscious with a frying pan and then left. Another time, he had stayed in the apartment for over an hour having a casual conversation with McNolte while pressing the barrel of his cocked and loaded gun against McNolte's right temple. And once, he had simply beaten McNolte nearly senseless with his small but capable fists.

McNolte had spent months turning his observations of South Street into a novel. Once he had nearly two hundred pages and an outline, he shopped for an agent. The only one to express interest was Warren Steinberg, who soon made a deal with LeGassi and Kriesh, a New York publisher with an office there in the city: eighty-five thousand dollars, half on signing, half on delivery of the completed manuscript.

That did not come close to what he owed Trafficante, but it was the biggest success he'd had in a long, long time. Nearly all of it would go toward his debt.

He had finished that novel almost two months ago, then begun another while waiting for the second half of the advance. He almost had another proposal on his hands—sample chapters, an outline—and he was looking forward to another advance, even though he had not yet received all of the first.

McNolte was surprised he still had all of his fingers. That had been Mr. Trafficante's promise, after all, and a lot of time had passed since then. But Mr. Trafficante had other things on his mind.

Some cocky young fed had teamed up with a vote-hungry congressman and had targeted Trafficante in an apparent bid for recognition. He was charged with racketeering, and the witnesses and evidence began coming out from under rocks all over the country. He was arrested, released on bail, and immediately went into hiding, surrounded by a battalion of high-priced and fiercely loyal attorneys.

McNolte knew his debt was a fly on the ass of Trafficante's business empire. The only reason he was still being harassed by Milo, he suspected, was that Milo enjoyed it. That was pretty obvious.

But a little over a week ago, Mr. Trafficante's highly publicized trail had ended and he had been found not guilty. He was free now, and somewhere in the city, some or all of the twelve former jurors were most likely driving around in much nicer cars than before and doing significantly more shopping than usual.

And now there was a package waiting for McNolte in Willy's office.

His palms were moist as he entered Willy's cluttered, badly lighted office, a headache beginning to throb in the center of his head.

Willy was still on the phone, speaking rapidly and with

great enthusiasm, seated behind the desk.

"No, please don't apologize," he said as he looked up and smiled at McNolte, beckoned him to sit down. "I understand your situation perfectly, and I'll take you up on that generous offer of two freezers, because we—" He stopped and listened a moment, then pressed a palm over the receiver's mouthpiece and whispered to McNolte, "Be with you in a second. Oh, and that's for you." He gestured toward the package, which was perched atop a tall stack of folders.

Willy went on with his conversation, but McNolte heard none of it.

The package was the size of a regular business envelope, but it was not an envelope. The contents were wrapped in brown paper and taped up carefully, even stapled at both ends. A rectangular, white, adhesive label was attached to the package. It read: NEIL McNOLTE.

Maybe it's a gift, he thought. *Maybe it's from somebody I helped here, somebody who moved on and was just nice enough to send me something. Or maybe it's from somebody who's here now, somebody who wanted me to receive it anonymously.*

His thoughts went on and on, running in circles as he stood just inside the door and stared at the package while Willy went on talking.

McNolte reached out and touched it lightly with his fingertips. Pressed just a bit. Whatever was inside was soft and pliable.

"Who delivered this, Willy?" he said.

Willy held up a palm, telling him to wait.

But the baby snakes writhing around in his intestines told McNolte that he could not wait, no matter how much the prospect of opening the package frightened him.

He picked it up to find it was light, then pried at the tape with one finger, then two. Then he pulled the wrapping apart and tore one stapled end open.

A small, white card, like a business card, fell out first and landed at McNolte's feet. He stared at it a moment, then leaned down, picked it up, and read the handwritten line: "You might be needing these."

Placing the card on the desk, he reached hesitantly into the brown wrapping, closed his fingers on soft, smooth material, and removed the contents.

He became light-headed as he looked at what he held in his hand, flopping backward into the folding chair in front of Willy's desk. His mouth hung open and his skin felt too tight over his body.

In his hand, McNolte held two black calfskin gloves with cashmere linings.

All five fingers had been cut off of each of them, and the holes had been sewn shut with thick, red thread.

11.

MIRANDA AND EMMA

Miranda Otter was doing her job, as always, but she did not have to like it. And she had liked nothing about it for a while.

She made her way through the maze-like corridors of OdysseyCorp, followed by two silent armed guards. They took one elevator, walked for a while, then took another. None of the elevators in the building went directly from the first floor to the third; she had to use her card-key as well as her palm print to get into them, and a guard was stationed outside each one. The building's security measures were just as stiff for employees—even those as high on the ladder as Dr. Jorgan—as they were for outsiders. Nothing was taken for granted and no one was trusted.

Miranda was on her way to Emma Shaw's room. She was to take Emma from there to a conference room on the first floor to meet Dr. Jorgan.

She would do it, but she would not like it. Because Miranda did not like Emma, not one bit. She had done something to Dr. Jorgan, this woman, she had...clogged the man up. He had not been the same since her arrival at OdysseyCorp. He had been preoccupied, morose, even volatile. For that reason, she hated Emma Shaw.

When Miranda had come to OdysseyCorp almost three years ago, she had been assigned to work as Dr. Alan Jorgan's assistant. He had seemed nothing special at first, just another doctor so obsessed with his work that it never occurred to him to get a haircut or buy new clothes. She had known nothing about him at first, but it did not take long for her to get a feel for the man as she watched him work. He said little to her, just assigned her work and expected her to finish it. She never knew very much about anything she worked on with Dr. Jorgan. OdysseyCorp was fiercely protective of the work done there. Only a select few knew the true nature of any given project, and the rest simply performed whatever job was assigned them, like cogs in a giant clockwork, never really knowing what they were doing, to what they were contributing, without even knowing exactly who *did* know those things. But that mattered little to Miranda, because her attention was soon captured by Dr. Jorgan, and there it stayed.

He was brilliant. She knew little of his background, his education, but it was quickly apparent that the man was brilliant. He said little as he worked, his movements were economical, and his work, no matter how intricate or complex, no matter how revolutionary, seemed as natural to him as breathing.

All the other women in the country could have their Tom Cruises and Leonardo DiCaprios. Miranda looked to the mind for her turn-on. And she had found arousal in Dr. Jorgan.

It had not been easy to get his attention. He lived in a small apartment in the back of the OdysseyCorp building, so he never really left his work, not physically; he certainly never left it mentally. He was his work. She had found that sex, like getting a haircut, simply never occurred to him. But Miranda had changed that.

She had waited for one of those late nights, when the work took them well past the witching hour, and when they were finished up and just about to part, when she knew they were alone, she had kissed him. It was a hard, passionate kiss, wet and open-mouthed as her hands moved searchingly over his body. Miranda did not have a great deal of carnal experience behind her, but she guessed she had a better handle on things than Dr. Jorgan, who failed to respond at first.

Realizing she would have to go even further, Miranda threw caution to the wind and placed a hand between his legs as she kissed him, massaging him through his pants, gently at first.

When there was no response beneath her palm, when she began to fear that he had no sex drive whatsoever—or, God forbid, that he was gay—she was not quite so gentle. Finally, he began to grow hard, and she suggested they go to his apartment. He said nothing, just nodded, and they left.

Dr. Jorgan said nothing until they'd had sex twice. And what sex it had been. Although he had not spoken to Miranda, his cries and wails as they writhed and rutted together on his bed had been communication enough. She wondered how long since he had been with a woman; he behaved as if he had been starving for affection, physical contact, loud and ungentle sex, which was what they had engaged in that night.

After that, things went back to normal. Almost. He looked at her differently as they worked. His eyes were softer, warmer, and they held hers for long moments at a time rather than simply glancing for an instant.

The experience had made her feel things she had not felt since high school. She wanted to stay with him, never leave his side, go straight from work to his apartment, his bed. But that did not happen.

Though he behaved differently toward her after their first time together, Dr. Jorgan never touched her, and he seemed uncomfortable whenever their arms brushed together or their hands touched. She knew then that her work was not over. The man was wrapped so tightly that one sexual encounter alone would not be enough.

She waited a few days before striking again. And then a few more days after that. He seemed to loosen up a bit then. He would only touch her during their lunch breaks—pat her shoulder, her hand—but only now and then. He never, ever instigated anything himself.

Efforts to discuss the situation with him were met with silence. When the subject of their relationship came up, his eyes grew dark and pensive and he avoided the topic, simply refusing to discuss it. Miranda came to the conclusion that he had been badly hurt before, and that had resulted his complete immersion in his work, casting all else aside.

Miranda adjusted herself to the situation. She knew she

could break him eventually, she simply would have to keep trying. And try she did, again and again. The sex was always great, but it did not happen unless she made it happen, and afterward it was as if it had never happened at all. Outside of the bedroom, he was a slave to his work. Except for the occasional touch of his hand or brief eye contact between them now and then, he had a one-track mind—and it was not on the same track as most other men's minds, that was obvious. It certainly was not on the same track as Miranda's.

But she was determined. More than that—she was in love. The only competition she had was his work, and she could deal with that. She was no fashion plate, no beauty queen, but she could handle going up against Dr. Jorgan's work.

Even in bed she called him Dr. Jorgan. She was not sure why. Just saying it made her tingle, but saying it while they lay naked in bed together made her wet. It was more than that, though. She not only loved him and delighted in feasting on his body in bed—however pale and flabby it might be—she respected him, as well. Calling him Dr. Jorgan, even after they had been so intimate, was her way of showing that respect.

The change she saw in him was slight, but unmistakable. The change she felt in herself, though, was quite astounding. She felt a sustained giddiness she had never experienced before—not for that long, anyway. She felt...solid.

Sometimes, Miranda felt as if she were as ethereal as a ghost, as if, should she try to pick something up—a pen, a cup of coffee, a book—her hand would pass through it without feeling anything. She felt as if she could pass through walls from one room to the next, as if she could walk right through an embankment of solid rock. She did neither of those things, but she felt as if she could. Sometimes, she felt no more real than the vaporous exhalation of her breath on a cold morning.

It came and went, this feeling of not being solid, of being a mere wisp of smoke. There were times when she felt perfectly normal. Quite happy, in fact. Able to work hard, accomplish so much, always eager to move on to the next task once she was finished. That was how she had felt when she applied to OdysseyCorp: normal and happy. Otherwise, she never would have considered it. And even if she had tried to get work there while in one of her vaporous periods, she would not have been considered for a moment, she knew that now. The screening process at OdysseyCorp was rigorous; every aspect of her life had been carefully explored, from her school records to her credit rating, from her medical history to her political affiliations. She was tested for everything from drugs to loyalty, from skill to psychological make-up. But she was fine then, feeling good about herself, and confident that she would be able to do some excellent work at OdysseyCorp. She was shameless in her self-confidence, unafraid to show them how eager she was to work at OdysseyCorp, where she could do the kind of work she had always wanted and planned to do. Had she been in one of her shadowy states, that never would have happened, even if she had somehow miraculously mustered the courage to apply while in such a condition. She was aware of it, knew when it was coming on, when it had her in its clutches, but she was helpless to combat it or even lessen its intensity. It was while her ghostly, vaporous state seemed far, far away that she had successfully approached OdysseyCorp for a job.

Since she had started working there, however, those feelings began to return. She could sense them, feel that state of mind coming, moving in like a fog rolling in over a dark, still sea, growing nearer, closing in on her steadily.

Then Dr. Jorgan had entered her life. He had changed everything. Upon meeting him, she could feel the fog receding until it was a safe distance away. And, once again, Miranda felt real. The shadows did not come. Miranda was safe and solid. Her relationship with Dr. Jorgan held all those murky, dream-like things at bay, kept the light bright in her life. She knew that if she tried to explain that to anyone—like a friend, if she had any, although aside from Dr. Jorgan, she did not—it probably would sound silly, crazy. But when that darkness overwhelmed her, life became something like a waking nightmare. It had happened before she had come to the city to attend the university. It had happened several times, the dimming of the light, the closing in of those shadows.

But not now, not for a long time. Not since she had fallen

in love with Dr. Jorgan. Not since she had shown him how much fun life and love could be. The shadows had not come into her life, and she thought they might never return again, if only she could continue her tutorial in carnal delights with Dr. Jorgan, softening him more and more until he told her what had happened in his past to make him so cold and afraid of warmth; until he finally realized—and *admitted*—how much she, Miranda, had done for him, how much she meant to him. How much he loved her.

That had been her fuel ever since their first time together. It had been her reason for waking up brightly in the morning and going to work and being productive. It had been the reason her hands had not passed through coffee cups and books, the reason her body had not walked through doors and walls.

But lately, things had been different. For the past year, Dr. Jorgan had changed. First he had become distant, even in bed. His wild behavior—the wailing and writhing, the crying out as he came—gave way to quiet grunting, and he was quick to leave the bed afterward, wanting her out so he could go to sleep.

All that had started with the arrival at OdysseyCorp of Emma Shaw. Beautiful, doe-eyed, auburn-haired Emma Shaw.

She was not beautiful anymore and hadn't been for some time. Her hair had been shaved off twice and was now growing back in a spiky mess, and those doe eyes were puffy and usually looked confused and frightened.

Miranda had no idea what Landon Shaw's wife was doing at OdysseyCorp as a subject in one of the lab's projects and she did not care. That was none of her business. After signing the stiff non-disclosure agreement when she started working at OdysseyCorp, Miranda knew that if she breathed a word of what went on there she would be fired and would never work in the field again, so she simply ignored a lot of things she saw and heard at work. For all she knew, this was just Mrs. Shaw's way of getting involved with her husband's work. It did not matter.

The only thing that really mattered to Miranda was what Emma's presence had done to Dr. Jorgan. Or, more importantly, what it had done to Dr. Jorgan's feelings for Miranda. *That* was all that mattered.

It was almost as if he had known Emma Shaw well before she had shown up at OdysseyCorp. Their relationship was friendly, sometimes even warm, and the warmer it got, the colder his relationship with Miranda became. Dr. Jorgan did not treat Emma with the cool, professional detachment he reserved for all lab subjects. He even allowed her more freedom than any of the others. He had given her a room and moved her back and forth from the lab rather than quarantining her in a single location in the building. And he treated Emma with far more gentility than he had ever treated Miranda, even after they had begun their affair.

Although she did not know what it was, there was something between Dr. Jorgan and Emma Shaw that Miranda seemed unable to touch, because nothing she had done over the past seven months or so succeeded in getting him into bed. And the last time it had happened, Dr. Jorgan had behaved in a surprisingly uncharacteristic and even frightening way. He had held Miranda's arms down on the mattress and pounded into her with a growling violence that had nothing to do with sexual passion. It had been angry, bitter sex, and afterward, Miranda had been sore and her inner thighs had been bruised; she had walked unsteadily for a whole day.

Since then, Dr. Jorgan had seldom heard anything Miranda said and she found herself repeating her words to him often. Too often. Sometimes he even became angry at her, usually for no discernible reason, like a cranky child in need of a nap. His moods had grown worse as time went on. Nothing she could do or say seemed to get through to him; she was either snapped at angrily or ignored altogether. It became apparent to Miranda that Dr. Jorgan had lost interest in her.

It was almost as if she were becoming a ghost again, fading to transparency.

But Miranda refused to believe that, or to let it happen. She might lose Dr. Jorgan's attention for a little while, but she was determined not to lose him. Certainly not to some spoiled rich bitch whose husband owned the lab. Not as long as she could still hold a pen or a coffee cup or knock on a wall with her knuckles and hear the sound. Not as long as she was solid.

Miranda stepped out of the elevator and started down the third floor corridor toward Emma Shaw's room, the silent guards at her heels.

The thing Emma missed the most since being brought to OdysseyCorp was a window. Her room was small, with bare walls papered a pale blue. Her bed was comfortable, she had a bathtub and shower, and she was provided with any reading material she requested. There was a TV set, but it showed only movies and TV shows that had been edited of all commercials and news broadcasts. She had no idea what had been happening in the world while she had been there in that small, windowless room. She craved a view of the outdoors to remind herself that the sky was still there and the sun still occasionally shone through the clouds.

Emma lay on her bed, eyes closed, but she was wide awake and alert. She knew that at any moment now, someone would come for her, either Dr. Jorgan or Miranda, and she would be pushed out of the room in a wheelchair and taken downstairs to continue working with Dr. Jorgan. She would kill more laboratory monkeys as he led her through further steps designed to help her tighten her control over her ability.

It would be different this time, though, if all went well. Emma's palms were slick with perspiration as she lay in bed waiting, wondering if she could go through with her plan.

On her first day there, she had awakened in that small blue room quite suddenly, sitting up with a harsh gasp of terror. Dr. Jorgan had been smiling down at her, pressing a cotton ball to the stinging flesh of her inner elbow as he put a hand on her shoulder and gently pushed her back down onto the bed with quiet reassurances. He had explained to her in soft tones that she was simply startled by the stimulant he had injected to revive her from the soporific she had been under while being brought to the facility. As she calmed down slowly and shakily, the way one does after experiencing a surge of adrenaline, Dr. Jorgan introduced himself in a soft voice and told her he was in charge of the project in which she had become involved. He seemed almost ashamed and apologetic as he informed her that, whether she could see them or not, there were armed security guards just steps away from her at all times. When she was not being watched directly, she was being observed on security monitors. If she made any attempt to escape or even resist, guards were under orders to shoot and kill her immediately, without hesitation, and she would be replaced. He assured her he did not want that to happen because he was her friend, and although she would be undergoing some uncomfortable and even unpleasant procedures while she was there, he promised to do his best to make the experience as tolerable and comfortable as possible for her—if only she would cooperate. For her own good.

Emma had felt confused as she listened to him, as if she had come in on the middle of a conversation and did not know the topic being discussed.

His name was vaguely familiar and, though it took a moment, she remembered Landon mentioning it, even remembered seeing him a time or two, somewhere, sometime. As her mind cleared, understanding came to her, unemotionally and without shock, as if she had known all along, even though she had not. Landon was using her, like some kind of lab rat, in one of his projects. That made sense, and everything Dr. Jorgan said made sense. But something was not right.

As Jorgan continued talking, telling her that she would begin a series of tests in about an hour, he looked every bit the wild-haired scientist in his thick glasses and white lab coat. He was restless, unable to hold still, shifting his weight from one foot to the other, jittery hands nervously fussing with each other, an uncertain smile coming and going on his face, eyes darting all around. She did not know what was disturbing her until his restless eyes settled on her and met with her own. Then she saw it.

His eyes softened, widened slightly, and the muscles of his face relaxed as his nervous movements fell still. He stopped talking for a moment, although his mouth opened and closed, as if struggling to speak. Then even that movement stopped and he simply stared at her for several long seconds. He finally pulled his eyes away from her, cleared his throat, and continued speaking, but now in a breathy, tremulous voice.

It scared her at first, his obvious attraction to her. But as he led her through the initial tests that day—blood, urine, X-rays, a brain scan—she realized he was not at all dangerous. Just the opposite, in fact. He made such a gallant effort to see that she was always comfortable that she was not afraid of anything being done to her. The attention he paid her, clumsy and halting as it was, held a certain charm, and in an odd way it eased Emma's mind, because, although she did not show it outwardly, she was terrified.

Jorgan's assistant Miranda was clearly unhappy that he was treating Emma. She maintained an icy demeanor throughout the battery of tests, and as time went on, she only became icier and her glances at Emma became deadly glares. While Emma became more comfortable with Jorgan in time, her discomfort with Miranda became fear.

Once finished with those first tests, Emma was allowed to "get a night of solid sleep," as Jorgan put it. That was the last time she remembered having any sense of day or night. After that, she soon lost track of time altogether.

When Emma awoke, Miranda silently shaved her head, then Jorgan took her to a room filled with surgical equipment and complex-looking machinery, seated her in a reclining dentist-like chair, gave her a mild sedative, then administered a number of stinging injections into her scalp. Then he opened her skull. She remained reasonably alert and hooked up to something like an ECG as Jorgan attached ultra-fine wires to various parts of her brain; then they left her alone while he and Miranda, in surgical greens, went into an adjoining room to watch her through a rectangular window with a thick, tinted pane, and speak to her through an intercom. Emma remained seated in the chair facing a large white rat in a small cage on a metal table a few feet in front of her.

After instructing Emma to tell him of anything she felt or smelled or heard, anything at all, Jorgan began to stimulate those tiny spots in her brain by sending a small electrical current through the wires. In a low, slightly slurred voice, Emma described every sensation she experienced. The electrical stimulation made her limbs jerk and her face twitch; it made her smell bacon frying and rubber burning, hear bells and squawks, and made her melt with an overwhelming, uncontrollable orgasm. But none of it seemed to satisfy Jorgan—although he apologized profusely for the orgasm when he came back into the room. He adjusted the wires several times before finally getting the result he seemed to want.

Emma was overcome by a draining sensation, as if something were sucking the very soul from deep inside her, and the pacing, nose-twitching rat in the cage before her suddenly reared up on its haunches and began to screech. After several seconds, blood spurted from the rat's eyes and ears. It fell on its side and convulsed violently. But it did not die. Not right away. That, it turned out, took time and practice.

The experience had exhausted Emma, but it excited Jorgan. He hurried back into the room, muttering to himself about locating the origin, tapping the source, and he asked Emma rapid-fire questions about how she had felt at the moment he had made the connection. Had her vision been affected? Had she felt the muscle? Emma had no idea what he was talking about and did not care. She felt anger growing within her, anger about the fact that she was reclining in a chair with the top of her skull opened up like a humidor and a dead rat in front of her while he asked about some *muscle*.

Later, Emma lay in her bed sedated while Jorgan explained, slowly and patiently, that he had found in her brain the source of an untapped ability, and he wanted her to get a hold of that ability and nurture it. Eventually, she would be able to do that without the aid of external stimulation.

"But first," he said, "I will have to perform an operation. It's a complex operation, somewhat risky, but I don't want you to worry. You'll be fine."

"Operation? Why?"

"I'm going to introduce a synthetic virus that will act as a catalyst. It will help to enable you to do on your own what you did in the lab today."

"With…the rat?"

"Yes."

Upon hearing the word "virus," something in the back of Emma's mind prickled, recoiled slightly. But she was in no condition to ask about it or discuss it. All she wanted to do was sleep. When she woke later, she had no memory of the "synthetic virus," and Jorgan did not mention it again.

Although Jorgan was pleased with her recovery after the operation, Emma felt she might never recover. She thought often of the white rat that had died in its cage before her, eyes and ears bloodied. There were so many after that—the early ones paralyzed, some bloodied, but not killed right away; Jorgan had to finish the job on some—but it was the first one that haunted her, perhaps for no other reason than that it was the first.

She had not known what she was doing the first time, had not even been aware of doing it because she had felt so bad, so depleted so suddenly that she teetered on the edge of unconsciousness. So little was explained to her—Emma simply did as she was told because she had no alternative—that it took a little while for her to understand what was going on. *She* had killed the rat without lifting a finger, and the endless replications of the test helped her to understand the process and learn how to manipulate it. Sometimes before a test, Dr. Jorgan would tell her, "Feel that muscle. *Feel* it."

Emma came to understand that she did, indeed, have a new muscle, and she was learning to flex it. The procedure she kept repeating was not a test. She was exercising that new muscle.

Her thoughts returned repeatedly to that first white rat. She felt a great deal of sympathy for that rat—caged, toyed with, and finally killed to further a project in a lab—because she knew she had *become* that rat, and it probably was only a matter of time before she fell, twitching and bleeding, to the floor of her cage.

That became her life—eating, sleeping, and being escorted to the lab, usually by Miranda, occasionally by Jorgan, and always followed closely by two armed guards, to that reclining chair where she felt for that muscle and taught herself to use it. Each time she was taken from her room to the lab, Jorgan gave her an injection that made her suddenly alert and able to concentrate, but it always wore off by the time she went back to her room, where, once again, she was sluggish and somewhat disoriented, unable to concentrate on one thing for very long.

That bothered her, at first in a vague way in the back of her muddled mind. But before long, it bothered her enough to *force* herself to think about it, try to work it out in her head. The only injections she ever received came before each trip to the lab. She assumed the purpose of that injection was to bring her out of her stupor and allow her to think clearly enough to focus on what she was doing. But what was causing the stupor? What was draining her of energy, of her will, making her unable to think clearly enough to read a trashy paperback or watch a mindless sitcom on TV? What was doing it, and how were they administering it?

Jorgan was such a gentleman that it became embarrassing at times. When he touched her—not often, but occasionally he would pat her on the hand or gently touch her shoulder—his voice became breathy, almost reverent. Sometimes she caught him staring at her, either through the rectangular window that separated them during her exercises, or while standing right next to her. He always looked away quickly with a stung expression. But before long, his gaze always returned to her.

His feelings for her were painfully obvious, but they both pretended otherwise. He was happy with Emma's progress, and on especially good days, he seemed giddy with excitement.

For a while, Emma had a small, pillbox-like device attached to the top of her head where a hair-like wire remained in her brain. The pillbox protected the wire and her brain from harm. She felt like one of the capuchin monkeys she had seen once in a National Geographic special on laboratory animals; they'd had similar devices attached to their poor tampered-with little skulls.

The "muscle" in her brain came to life with the help of external stimulation. After a while, with practice, she was able to kill the rat before her almost instantly. Still later, the rat was caught so off-guard that it did not have time to make a final sound, or even react to what was happening to it. It simply died.

"Tell me how it feels," Jorgan asked her one day. "What sensations do you experience when it happens?" His intense eyes remained fixed to hers as he waited for a response.

"Well, at first," she said, "something inside my skull seems to grow warm and…swell. It's just a sensation, I know, because that would be…well, impossible. But it *feels* real. The swelling continues until it becomes uncomfortable. Almost painful. Not quite, but almost. And then there's this abrupt release. A gushing release. Kind of like reaching the crest of an orgasm—" Jorgan's head turned sharply as he averted his gaze, pale cheeks growing pink. "—but without any pleasure. That's when it happens. With that rushing release. The rat dies. And then I feel…so tired. Diminished. Like I've shrunk."

Jorgan began to pace in front of her. "That feeling. You need to get a hook into that feeling. Study that feeling. Make it your goal. Your purpose."

It was not long before she did exactly that. The feeling became part of her. Even when she was not experiencing it, she thought about it, remembered it, until she could conjure it in her mind in a heartbeat. Soon, the pillbox was removed, the small piece of skull that had been cut out was replaced, and her scalp was sewn over it. At first, she was able to "flame," as Jordan called it, only for short periods of time before she was overcome with exhaustion and her head began to ache. Then she would take a break and rest a bit until the ache was gone and she could try again.

They worked on her control. That was the worst part, the part she hated most. She learned how to withhold that final release, then allow it to come slowly, in stages. She learned to make the rats suffer. It made her sick at first, watching them writhe, hearing them squeal, and finally seeing them die. She learned to hold back just enough so the rat would not hemorrhage, and there would be no external sign of injury. Sometimes she heard those squeals in her sleep.

With each attempt, she was able to flame a little longer before the aching began and she had to stop. It was a deep ache in the center of her brain, slow in coming in the beginning, expanding and growing steadily worse; once it gained momentum, it was blinding and made her eyes tear up. As her ability improved, she could flame for longer periods of time without pain, but when it arrived, it came instantly, detonating inside her skull, pushing at the backs of her eyes, digging down into the roof of her mouth, making her ears ring. Jorgan assured her he would find a way to stop the headaches, but until then, he was always considerate, allowing her to rest as long as she needed.

Emma progressed from rats to guinea pigs, then to rabbits, later graduating to monkeys. By then, she had grown so accustomed to killing animals that it was almost easy to ignore their curious, darting eyes, their childlike facial expressions. Almost.

Jorgan began to get under her skin. Just a little. He was the only other person with whom she had contact besides Miranda, who spoke to her only when necessary, and then in cold, steely tones. Jorgan's eyes were cloying as they stared, sometimes making her want to scream at him to stop. He eased up a bit with time. His manner became less formal. But she still caught him staring hungrily at her now and then, and it made her feel claustrophobic.

Only one thing made her stay there tolerable. The food. It was like eating out three times a day, only at the best restaurants. Delicious breakfasts of eggs benedict, or sumptuous crepes stuffed with lobster or crab, mouth-watering fruit and pastries as light and fluffy as clouds; lunches of salads made with produce that seemed only minutes from the garden, sandwiches so delectable that it seemed criminal to call them mere sandwiches; and the dinners—the tenderest veal, perfectly seasoned pasta dishes, calamari that melted on her tongue.

At first, she worried about her weight. She knew that if she ate that extravagantly three times a day while being so sedentary, she would be as big as a house by the time she left. Then it occurred to her—she would not be leaving. Landon had already told her that, as far as the world was concerned, she was dead. Corpses did not worry about their waistlines. Corpses also had nowhere to go but into the ground.

One evening during a dinner of filet mignon with tender new potatoes bathed in seasoned butter, juicy asparagus drizzled with cheese sauce, a flaky dinner roll and crisp green salad on the side, topped with a slice of cheesecake covered in cherries, it occurred to her that she was eating her medication three times a day—and enjoying it so much that she had to resist the urge to lick the plates. That was how it was being administered, keeping her in a twilight state.

The deviousness of it made her cringe, but not for long. She had figured it out, even in her weak and foggy state.

All she had to do was stop eating.

Emma picked at her filet mignon as she fought for clarity, fought to think her newfound problem through to a solution.

She went into the lab each morning, broke for lunch, then returned in the afternoon for what seemed an eternity before stopping in time for dinner. With each meal, clarity faded and the brain fog rolled in.

Landon had told her that security guards were watching her on monitors, which meant that cameras were trained on her at all times. When she looked around her small room, she saw none, but she knew they were there. That meant she could not openly dispose of her food. They were watching, and they expected her to clean her plate, as always. It took a few meals, some practice, and a tremendous effort to remain focused on her task before she finally worked out a system.

Emma always ate while sitting up in the adjustable bed with the rectangular table wheeled to her bedside and stretching across her lap. She went to the bathroom before each meal and sat on the toilet. When she reached between her legs with toilet paper as if to wipe herself, she carefully tucked rolled-up pieces of tissue between her buttocks. It remained there as she got into bed and was served her meal. She removed the pieces of toilet paper as she situated herself on the bed and placed them in her lap beneath the table.

She had been terribly clumsy at first. She coughed into her hand; another time, she picked her teeth; still later, she wiped her mouth, then sneezed. Each time, she placed a mouthful of food in her lap as surreptitiously as possible, then wrapped it in the toilet paper. She could not get all the food, of course; she ended up eating some of it. Emma had to eat. But considering how thorough she had been in finishing her meals up to that point, it was a vast improvement. She knew she would not be getting nearly as much of whatever drug was in the food as she had been ingesting, and she hoped to see an improvement in her state of mind.

The first time she tried it, she had succeeded without incident. In the bathroom, she had sat on the toilet and allowed the concealed food to drop into the bowl. It worked beautifully the next time, too, and the next. Each time, she got a little better at it. Then, on her way to the bathroom after dinner one evening, two of the moist, tissue-wrapped lumps dropped to the tile floor between her feet with ugly plopping sounds.

Emma froze. Stood there. Forever. Resisting the temptation to look around the room, as if the cameras might suddenly be visible now, glaring at her with condemnation.

Leaning down carefully, she picked up the globs of tissue and food, carried them into the bathroom, dropped them into the toilet, and flushed. She expected the door to burst open and guards to rush into the room at any moment, demanding to know what she had flushed down the toilet. But no one came. Nothing happened. She wondered if perhaps she was not being watched quite as closely as she had been led to believe.

The grogginess began to recede, but she could not let that show, so she continued to shuffle around slowly and maintained an expressionless face, heavy-lidded eyes. As clarity returned, Emma became more adept at disposing of the food with each meal, but it became harder to do because she was so hungry. Starving. Her stomach growled first, then roared so loudly that she feared it would give her away. She nibbled just a bit from each plate to give the illusion that she was actually eating, and to appease the grinding hunger in her gut, if only a little. But not enough to return her to the hazy state she had been in since arriving.

With clarity came anger. She was able to think lucidly about what Landon had done and continued to do to her. And with her anger came a hatred that eclipsed anything she had felt for Landon in the past, anger that bubbled inside her like lava over what he was doing—using her like a lab rat to develop something that would no doubt be used as a weapon, something that would fatten Landon's already bulging bank accounts and, as a result, give him even more power than he already possessed.

She kept her anger and hatred inside—she had no other choice for the time being—but there, it swelled and festered.

Landon was so arrogant and smug that it probably never occurred to him that, once he had given her this power, she might use it to save herself. Landon did not think that way. He always assumed success in everything he did, never for a moment considering the possibility of failure or catastrophe. Besides, he owned her, and he no doubt assumed that he had so cowed her by now, she would never consider retaliating. In business, Landon trusted no one, but when it came to his possessions, he was supremely confident; they were his subjects and he their king, and like any king, he never entertained doubts about his dominance. Landon knew that Emma would be locked away and under constant surveillance, never far from an armed guard who would follow his orders to the letter.

But with Emma's newfound clarity, the rules changed. And no one knew but Emma. She planned to use that advantage as best she could. She looked forward to surprising Landon.

In the lab, her control improved. She was able to manipulate the flaming well, but so far with only one animal at a time. Jorgan began to bring in more than one monkey. Just two at first. She killed them both at once. He brought in two more and told her to kill them one at a time as they sat side by side. She tried, but failed. She could control the flaming but was unable to aim it at one monkey without affecting others as well.

Jorgan said they would work on that later, but for the time being, he wanted to concentrate on her strength, on the force of her flaming. He brought in three monkeys at once. Then four. Until finally she found herself facing a wall of cages stacked to the ceiling, a chattering monkey in each cage. Twenty in all. He talked her through it, telling her to hold back, let it build but keep holding back until she could hold it no longer, until she felt she were about to explode, then let it go in a great, fanning wave. She did. All of the monkeys fell silent at once and died without a struggle.

An instant later, the headache rushed in, making Emma slump in the chair, exhausted, emptied, crying silently because it hurt too much to make sounds. Jorgan was elated and congratulated her as if she had just won the lottery. Then he gave her the rest of the day off and let her sleep.

Although her stomach never stopped burning with hunger, Emma regained much of her strength and awareness. As a result, the stimulant she was given each time she was taken to the lab became harder and harder to endure. She had to conceal the fact that with each injection her heart rate increased, she felt hot and her skin seemed to shrink like melting cellophane over her muscles and bones, all the while burning as if on fire. Jorgan was no longer monitoring her vitals every time she entered the lab, otherwise she would not have been able to hide it. And if the explosive reaction had not been reasonably brief each time, it would have been impossible to keep from screaming. Somehow, she managed.

Another problem was weight loss. When she arrived at OdysseyCorp, eating such rich foods three times a day had caused her to gain weight. Once she started to dispose of her food, though, the weight began to come off quickly. She was not weighed regularly, but one day Jorgan mentioned it, said she looked thinner, frowned and had her get on a scale, checked her chart, scribbled a note on it as he muttered to himself about the possibility of flaming affecting her metabolism. He said he wanted to start monitoring her weight each day, but said nothing more about it.

Emma knew if she continued to lose weight, Jorgan would know that something was up and, before long, she would be found out. She had no choice—she would have to put her concealed clear-headedness to use sooner than she had hoped, before she was completely ready. And she knew she would not have much time in which to do it.

Miranda would be arriving soon to take her down to the lab. Emma waited on her bed, eyes closed as if napping, chest rising and falling rhythmically, but wide awake, thinking, planning, and worrying. She still had a long way to go before she could control the flaming the way she would like, but she had no time.

Emma already regretted what she would have to do to Jorgan. He was as pathetic as a teenager with a crush on a movie star, but under the circumstances, he *had* been terribly kind to her and always seemed to have her best interests in mind.

Don't kid yourself, she thought. She knew if Jorgan were forced to choose between saving her from her inevitable fate and remaining loyal to Landon, she would not stand a chance.

She would try not to kill him, but she was still a novice, and a desperate one, as well. If getting out meant killing Jorgan, that would be one person fewer to blindly follow Landon's every order. As sweet as he had been to her, Emma figured that would be a kind of public service.

Waiting for Miranda to arrive, her thoughts were dominated by one question: Would it work? It worked on the monkeys, of course, but they were chirpy little capuchin monkeys and he was a grown man. She had never tried it on a human before, of course, although she was certain that would be the next step in the project. And she knew the person she would be made to kill would be innocent, a victim. Her way—even if she failed—at least provided a modicum of justice.

Emma heard the door of her room open, heard Miranda's hushed footsteps on the tile floor. Without opening her eyes, she knew Miranda was wearing her white lab coat with her ID badge pinned to the lapel, her face as unsmiling in the small photo on the badge as it no doubt was at that moment in Emma's room.

"Okay, time to go," Miranda said in her usual flat, emotionless voice. "We're going down to one of the conference rooms today, not the lab. Dr. Jorgan wants to see you there. So get up."

Emma made a show of slowly getting off the bed, with effort, eyes half-closed.

"All right," Emma said quietly. She had found that she never quite sounded like herself when she spoke to Miranda; the squat young woman put her on edge and made her stiffen, inside and out. "Just let me put on my robe and slippers."

"Hurry. I don't think Dr. Jorgan's in a very good mood this morning."

She donned her heavy forest-green terrycloth robe and moccasin slippers, both given to her by Dr. Jorgan. He had thought the robe and slippers issued by the lab too uncomfortable for the amount of time she would be there.

As she walked with Miranda, two guards followed them, as usual, down the sterile white corridor with its shining tiles and blinding white walls, bare except for an occasional bulletin board or red, glass-covered fire alarm or extinguisher.

The guard posted outside the elevator nodded at Miranda from his chair, where he sat reading an issue of *Sports Illustrated*. Miranda slipped her card into the slot in the wall beside the elevator, then pressed her palm flat against the black rectangle above it. There was a sharp beep, the card was ejected, Miranda returned it to the pocket of her lab coat, and they waited for the elevator doors to slide open heavily. The guards followed them in, then stepped to the rear of the car, backs against the wall. They gave Emma the creeps.

Once inside, Miranda hit the appropriate button with a stubby forefinger, then joined her hands behind her back.

Although she stood still and calm beside Miranda, Emma's thoughts raced chaotically through her mind.

She could wait until she was alone with Dr. Jorgan, but even then, Miranda and would not be far away, and the guards would be even closer, waiting just outside the door for any sign of trouble. Once she started, she would have to follow through, providing it worked at all, which meant she would have to go through a lot of other people, not just Jorgan and Miranda and the guards—other doctors, lab techs, assistants. Once the commotion started, they would be pouring into the corridors to see what was going on. Guards would be called and would respond from every corner of the complex, and they probably would keep coming. Emma balked at the thought of having so many people to deal with when she was so unsure of her strength and ability, but she had no choice if she hoped to get out.

And the sooner she started, the better.

Emma knew they would be in the elevator for only a couple of minutes at most, then another corridor, another elevator, then the conference room, none of which would take long. But if she could at least disable them, they would not pose much of a problem once things started to move quickly. And if it worked, things would move extremely quickly.

Emma leaned her right shoulder against the wall of the elevator car, slumped a bit, let her head droop, eyes close, as if she were barely able to stay awake. And then she began.

12.

TOUGH TALK

"Why didn't you tell me sooner?" Willy said. His voice was ominously quiet and his usually bright, open face was tense and unsmiling.

"I figured there was no point in telling you," McNolte said. He held the fingerless gloves in one fist. "I figured there was nothing you could do, anyway, and maybe...you'd even kick me out."

As he spoke, Willy became increasingly upset, his voice steadily louder. "Well, I wouldn't have kicked you out. But there was something I *could* have done, and I *would* have if I'd known. I would've made damned sure word didn't get out that you were here. When necessary, we can be just as secretive as we are open here. And if you'd told me about this, I would've seen to it that we *were*." He barked the last word, slamming his palm down on the desk as he stood so suddenly that his chair rolled backward.

McNolte leaned forward and dropped the gloves on the desk—he did not want to touch them anymore—as Willy rounded the desk, frowning and tugging thoughtfully on his lower lip with thumb and forefinger. He perched on the corner of the desk and scowled down at McNolte.

"First of all," he said, "you were an idiot to go to somebody like Trafficante for money. An *idiot*. But I understand. At the time, you were a complete mess, I'm sure, probably walking around with only half your pistons firing. I just wish you'd been as honest with us about your money problem as you were about your drug problem. Because now, Mr. Trafficante and his friends have connected you to South Street. Otherwise, this package wouldn't have come here. And I have a great deal of responsibility to the people here, McNolte, you know that. I don't need thugs showing up who don't value the lives of others, not to mention the lives of drunks, drug addicts, and street people."

Willy fell silent and stared down at his lap for a moment. His face slowly relaxed, then he looked down at McNolte with a gentle smile.

"I'm telling you this, McNolte, only because...I want you to take responsibility for the things you do from now on. Drug addicts don't do that. They have no sense of responsibility, do whatever they want, hurt whomever they please, then smile and shrug and tell charming lies as they walk away from the wreckage. Well, you're not on drugs anymore, McNolte. You have responsibilities. Don't ever do anything like this again."

McNolte stood and paced, ran a hand through his hair. "Look, I didn't realize...I mean, I really don't think anybody here is in danger, Willy. Except me. If you want me to stay away from the mission I will. But I had no intention of putting the mission at risk."

"We have to worry about you right now. Do you have any plans?"

McNolte shrugged. "I'm just gonna keep making payments. That's all I *can* do."

"From the looks of those—" Willy jerked his head toward the gloves on the desk. "—payments aren't exactly what Trafficante has in mind."

McNolte stopped pacing and sighed. "He's closing in. I don't have the rest of the money in one lump sum. And with the interest Trafficante charges—well, I guess I'll be paying it off for the rest of my life. Which may not be long."

"There are people here who can help you, McNolte."

"What do you mean? Do you have some generous rich people tucked away here at the mission, Willy?"

He chuckled. "I'm not talking about money. I'm talking about protection."

McNolte cocked his head slightly as he frowned. "Protection?

You've got bodyguards here, thugs, something like that?"

"I'm talking about preventive measures that may protect you. Juarez, for one thing. He knows this city intimately, every corner of it, it's in his blood. If you don't mind moving around so you can keep a step or two ahead of Trafficante's people, Juarez would help you out."

"Oh, jeez, Willy," McNolte leaned wearily back against the wall and rubbed his eyes with his knuckles. "I'm working again. I have an apartment. I just got back into real life. I admit, it feels like I stepped into a party where I don't know anybody, but at least I'm back. I don't know if I can start living like some kind of nomad again. I mean, I know what's at stake, here, I know what I'm up against, but—" He looked at Willy and everything in his gut was visible in his eyes, raw and unhidden. "—I'm exhausted, Willy. I don't know if I can start doing it again."

"All right, then," Willy said without a moment's pause, nodding slowly, "I have another idea. P.W."

When Willy did not continue, McNolte said, "What?"

"P.W. I think he should stay close to you. From now on."

"P.W. Why? I mean, I love P.W. to death, I think the world of him, but...why?"

"You don't *know* P.W. He's tight-lipped about his past. Mostly because he's tried so hard to put it behind him. P.W. is one of the most cheerful men I know, probably as likable a fellow as you'll find in this city. But he spent some time in Vietnam, stayed in the military and did some work for the government. Covert stuff. Some pretty scary stuff, from what little he's told me."

"During the war?"

"Yes. He fought for his country, but not as a simple soldier. He wasn't your average G.I. Joe. He rarely talks about it, but every once in a while the mood will strike him, and he'll tell a story. He's got stories that make Stephen King look like Dr. Seuss. He's only told me a few, in confidence. And never without breaking down in sobs. It haunts him, his past. There's more to P.W. than meets the eye. He's content to be seen as a kind of smiling simpleton who likes a good joke and is willing to help out when he can. I think he'd help you. I don't know if he's told you this, but he's terribly proud of the work you've done since you came here, the articles, the book. He has a lot of admiration for your talent. And for you."

"Well, I like him, too, he's become my best friend. But I don't know...."

"You see P.W. as a big, jolly fellow with a white beard and a ready laugh, but he could have you dead on the floor before you knew his mood had changed."

McNolte took a moment to digest that. When he thought of P.W., he certainly did not think of...someone like that.

He said, "You want me to use P.W. was a kind of bodyguard? Is that it?"

"You're in danger, McNolte. You realize that, don't you?"

"Realize it? It's all I think about."

"I can have someone else take over P.W.'s responsibilities for a few days. I think you should take him home with you."

"But all I have is a studio apartment with a sofa that opens into a bed and—"

"He would happily sleep on the floor. He'd sleep in the sink if he had to, and he wouldn't let you out of his sight. If that young man you told me about were to show up again, he'd have to deal with P.W."

"Yeah, but Willy, that guy always has a gun."

Willy smiled. "P.W. can take care of himself *and* you, take my word for it."

"Look, Willy, not to diminish anything P.W. has done in the past, but...he's older now. And fatter."

It was Willy's turn to pace. "You know how we sometimes get troublesome people coming in here, right? A drunk, a drug addict, somebody who's maybe not quite himself when he gets to the mission? One day, a man came in—a *big* man, tall and muscular—out of his mind on something, I don't know what. Mama Charity approached him and with one swipe of his hand, he knocked her to the floor like a beanbag. So you *know* what kind of problem he was, to do that to Mama Charity. Well, P.W. was there. He stepped forward without a word, smiling as always. I was watching the entire time, and to this day, I'm not sure what he did. I mean, this guy was much younger than P.W., in much better shape, and even *bigger*, if you can believe that. He was so wild, on some kind of drug that had turned him into a machine, you know the type? P.W. walked up to this man, made one small movement with his arm, and that drug-crazed gorilla hit the floor like a side of beef. He was still unconscious when the police arrived, but he was completely unharmed, didn't have a mark on his body. All P.W. would tell me was, 'I just calmed him down for a while, that's all.' So don't tell me about P.W. being too old and fat. He might look fat, but he's *not*. The man's like granite, no matter how he looks. And I have a feeling that if he wanted to, he could make a tuna sandwich out of your sadistic friend before the guy knew he was invited to lunch."

McNolte laughed in spite of his dark mood.

"Besides," Willy said, "you don't have a car. P.W.'s big jalopy could save you on cab fare."

McNolte decided he would not mind having a roommate.

13.

BACKFIRE

Dr. Jorgan waited in the conference room, seated at one end of the eight-foot-long table, studying his notes and looking grim, forehead creased, the corners of his mouth pulled downward.

Something was wrong. He was trying not to panic, trying to keep his composure, but something was definitely wrong. He had before him computer printouts, test results, and his own notes. His eyes shot back and forth over them as the creases in his forehead deepened, looking for something to prove his suspicions wrong, to ease the tension he was feeling. He had been looking over them again and again for more than two hours, searching for a mistake, something he had misread, anything that might make everything all right. But there was nothing there. Nothing at all.

For the first time he could remember, the first time in his life, including his entire childhood, Dr. Alan Jorgan was deeply, coldly afraid. But he held the fear back, refused to acknowledge it fully just yet.

He had a list of questions to ask Emma Shaw, because if what he suspected were true, then there was a good chance she would be showing symptoms that might tell him how far along the problem might be.

Jorgan had been just short of frantic all day, ever since discovering the possible problem during the sleepless early morning hours as he pored over the material at his desk. Miranda had reacted to his distracted irritability, as usual, with her flat voice and expressionless face, no doubt attributing his mood to Emma in that particular schoolgirl-crush way of hers. But she could not be further from the truth. This problem made his feelings for Emma irrelevant, vaporized them for the time being. This problem went far beyond him, and even OdysseyCorp.

Jorgan looked up as Miranda and Emma entered the room. He smiled at Emma, but her lips merely squirmed beneath blank eyes. Her face was slack and there was a glimmer of perspiration above her upper lip. He did not even glance at Miranda; he was staring too intently at Emma's face, fearing that she might already be experiencing the symptoms that would prove his horrible suspicions to be correct.

They came toward him and Emma seated herself—rather clumsily, he noticed—in the chair directly to his right.

"I...I've gotta go," Miranda said quietly, her voice thick.

Jorgan glanced in Miranda's direction without seeing her. "Okay, fine," he said, turning back to Emma.

"I don't...feel well," Miranda said. "I might be getting the flu, or something."

"Fine, fine, then go," he said, his voice firm now, eyes never leaving Emma's face. A moment later, he heard the door close.

When Miranda left the conference room, she noticed vaguely, peripherally, that the two guards were nowhere in sight. Normally, they would be posted just outside or just inside the door. She would have looked for them, or at least told Dr. Jorgan they were gone, if she did not feel so ill. It was getting worse by the minute, weakening her knees and slightly blurring her vision as the nausea escalated. She had to get to a restroom. Quickly.

On her way there, Miranda hurried past the men's room, hardly noticing at all the muffled retching sounds coming from inside.

"You don't look well, Emma," Jorgan said after a long silence between them. She looked directly into his eyes, her own eyes blank, empty. "Are you feeling all right?"

She did not respond for a long time. Then: "Okay...I guess." Her lips, slightly parted, did not move at all.

Jorgan's frown grew even deeper as he began to find her gaze unsettling. He looked down at the papers before him for a moment to collect his thoughts, decide what to say next, how much to tell her, how to explain the questions he was about to ask.

The room grew warm rather abruptly. Or was it just him? The collar of his shirt felt tight and he curled two fingers beneath it to scratch an itch on his throat, just above the collarbone.

"You guess," he said without looking up. Finally, he raised his head and allowed his eyes to meet hers, which were trained on his face. "You, um...seem to be perspiring a bit. Do you feel hot? Or do you feel as if you might have a fever?"

The tip of her tongue ran slowly back and forth over her lower lip. She inclined her head slightly toward him, holding her unblinking stare.

"A little warm...I guess," she said.

He nodded, relieved that it was not just him. "Again, you say you guess. Um, Emma, I have some questions I need to ask you. About how you've been feeling. They're important. I'm going to need you to do a little more than guess at the answers. I need you to...uh, I need to know..."

Removing his glasses, he turned from her and wiped his moist forehead with his sleeve, then rubbed his eyes with the thumb and forefinger of his right hand. They burned, and his vision was somewhat blurred.

Not enough sleep, he thought.

Slipping his glasses back on, he looked down at the handwritten questions again, then at Emma.

"I need you to answer these questions honestly and concisely, Emma. The first one: Have you been experiencing headaches that feel as if—"

It struck him hard, all at once. An overwhelming weakness, a sudden hammering of his heart in his chest, and a cloying sweat that broke out all over his body.

Emma's eyes did not move from his. She stared at him with a sort of blank-faced determination.

Jorgan slumped back in his chair with a quick exhalation of breath, slid down into a slouch as his left hand clutched his chest, heart going off like a machine gun behind his ribs.

"Oh, my God," he croaked, head falling forward slightly. His wide eyes stared at Emma with understanding now. "Don't do this." His voice was little more than a coarse breath. "You don't...know what...you're doing."

Her head remained perfectly still and when she spoke, her lips, once again, did not move. "Yes. I do."

"No, Emma, really...I want...to help you. That's all I've... ever wanted to do." Jorgan's knuckles went white as his hands gripped the ends of the armrests on his chair. He pulled himself forward with great effort, flopped both arms onto the table, and reached for her hand, clutched it weakly as pain exploded like a bomb in his chest and stabbed its way down his left arm. "I swear to God," he said, barely whispering now, "I'll get you... away from him. But not...now. Not...yet."

Emma slid her hand out from beneath his

"Emma, I-I...I love you...I *do*...I love you and want...to save you...from him."

She pushed her chair back from the table slightly, away from him.

Jorgan felt something delicate break deep in his face, and warm blood rolled from his nostrils, over his upper lip, and into his mouth.

"Something's wrong, Emma, you...you can't...do this...not now. Something has gone wrong...with the synthetic virus... that we injected...into you."

Emma rose slowly to her feet.

Overcome by a nauseating dizziness, Jorgan's head lolled. His blood was warm and coppery in his mouth, slick against his teeth.

"Please...listen to me...Emma...you can't...leave now."

She took one step backward, away from him, then another, and another. Small steps toward the door.

"You're...in danger...the virus...it could hurt you...hurt others."

When she bumped into the door, Emma reached behind

her clumsily for the knob. Her head was still tipped slightly forward, eyes holding his, unblinking.

"Emma...don't..."

He leaned forward, pressed his hands to the tabletop and tried to push himself to his feet. But the room tilted sharply like a jarring carnival ride. His vision blurred further, swirled sickeningly, then began to darken until he lurched forward.

Jorgan was unconscious before his head *thunked* onto the table.

14.

GETAWAY

The OdysseyCorp complex was a massive five-story L-shaped building. During the day, there were five hundred and thirty people employed there, two hundred and ten after business hours. It was surrounded by a massive paved parking lot and landscaping that made sections of the grounds look like a park, all of which was surrounded by a cyclone fence with strips of barbed wire at the top which slanted both inward and out. Security cameras were mounted all around the exterior of the building, as well as on the lamp posts of the parking lot.

It was from this imposing complex that Emma Shaw needed to escape now that she had dispatched Dr. Alan Jorgan, who was slumped, unconscious and bleeding from his nose, over the table.

Emma pulled the door of the conference room open cautiously and leaned her head out of the room to peer up and down the corridor. She was afraid the two guards might be waiting just outside. They were not. Apparently, she had, at the very least, made them sick enough to abandon their post.

There was no one in sight at the moment, but across the corridor and to her right, a door was open wide and voices came from inside the room. Emma's abdomen tightened at the thought of having to pass that open door as she headed for the front of the building.

Glancing over her shoulder at Jorgan one more time—he had not moved—she stepped into the corridor and pulled the door closed silently behind her.

A faint, not unpleasant tingling sensation began inside her head accompanied by a low hum that she felt rather than heard. Dr. Jorgan had referred to those symptoms as "your brain's way of telling you that the pilot light is still lit."

She feared that if she lost the ability, if it simply stopped, she would not be able to get it back when she needed it. And Emma was sure she would need it. Making Miranda sick enough to get her out of the way and flaming Dr. Jorgan at the same time was much easier, she was certain, than it would be to hold off security guards and whoever else might come after her once she was discovered, because she knew they would not come one at a time, and the security guards would have guns drawn and ready.

Standing straight, Emma turned right and headed down the corridor, walking with the kind of self-assuredness that would make her look like she belonged there even though she was wearing a robe and slippers.

The closer she got to the open door on her left, the clearer the voices inside became, until she recognized one of them.

"—any better now?" a man asked.

"A little," Miranda said, sounding wary. "Maybe it's a touch of the flu, I don't know. It hit me all of a sudden."

"Can I get you something? I've got Alka Seltzer cold medicine in my locker."

"No, I think I'll be okay."

Emma passed the door and, with a flick of her eyes, glanced into the room. From what she could see, it was a small lounge with a round table, some chairs, a small refrigerator; the rich aroma of brewing coffee wafted through the open door. Miranda was seated at the table. Michael Finch, one of the lab techs, stood beside her with a can of soda in hand. Miranda began to raise her head, turning toward the open door.

And then she was out of sight and Emma was past the door, quickening her pace as she walked on.

"Hey," Miranda said, quietly at first.

Emma heard a chair scrape over the tile floor in the lounge.

"*Hey!*" Miranda called sharply. "What are you doing?" Her voice was much clearer and louder now and Emma knew that if she turned, she would see Miranda in the corridor, hurrying toward her.

Emma did not look back or hesitate; she kept walking fast.

Miranda ran past her and spun around as she stepped in front of her, pressing a hand to Emma's shoulder to make her stop walking.

"You can't just walk around here like this," Miranda said, glaring at Emma. "Where's Dr. Jorgan?"

Emma said nothing. She clenched her teeth and continued the process. The tingling increased. The hum seemed to vibrate just behind her eyes. Dr. Jorgan had said it was entirely psychological, that there was no hum, not really. But it felt real to Emma.

Miranda's frown dissolved, returning her face to its normal expressionless state. She looked past Emma at someone behind her and said, "Michael, get Dr. Jorgan. He's in conference B." Miranda lifted a hand and wiped the back of it across her forehead, which glistened with perspiration. Looking at Emma again, she tried to sound angry, but her voice was weak and growing hoarse. "I don't know what you think you're doing, but you're gonna get yourself...in trouble if...if you think—"

"Get security!" Michael shouted behind Emma.

She assumed he had found Dr. Jorgan.

Miranda's already pale face became the color of milk and beads of perspiration trickled down her forehead and cheeks as she swayed on her feet. Her eyes and mouth all opened wide at the same time. Then her eyelids began to flutter.

Emma did not move, did not even blink as she aimed a narrow beam of intense concentration directly at Miranda. Her body was relaxed, only now beginning to perspire under her arms and down the center of her back. Breathing steady, heartbeat regular. She was not panicking. It was going well so far.

"Think of your brain as a computer," Dr. Jorgan had told her. "I have upgraded your computer and added, say, a modem. Now you just have to *adapt* to the advancements, adjust to the faster speed. We'll take it a step at a time, but before you know it, it'll be second nature to you."

She was still learning, but now she was not in a lab. This was not a test.

Blood dribbled from Miranda's left nostril as she collapsed to the floor, unconscious.

"Goddammit, somebody get security!" Michael shouted behind her, still in the conference room.

Emma moved forward as she heard a group of rapid footsteps behind her, far back at the other end of the corridor.

She turned right as she picked up her pace.

Voices chattered behind her and the footsteps grew louder, closer.

Emma took another corridor, this one to the left.

A door opened inward on her right and an Asian man stepped into the corridor wearing a lab coat as white as his hair. He looked like a doctor. Emma kept her eyes front as she hurried past him, but he reached out and grabbed her elbow, jerking her to a stop.

"Excuse me, Miss," he said, "but...where are you supposed to be?"

She said nothing, only clenched her teeth and closed her eyes for a moment.

The man said, "I don't think you're supposed to be—"

His hand dropped her arm and slapped to his chest as his voice caught in his throat with a croak. He took one step back, then fell backward through the door.

Emma hurried on, ignoring the woman's voice behind her.

"Dr. Im? Oh, my God, Dr. *Im*! Help! Somebody help!"

The tingling sensation in Emma's head was becoming more intense and would soon edge into a headache. During the tests, Dr. Jorgan had always told her it was important that she speak up when that happened; it meant she was overdoing it and it was time to take a break. But she did not have time for a break now.

What if I can't pull it back? she thought. *What if I can't make it stop when I want it to?*

Emma tried to ignore the growing pain as she walked faster. The footsteps were catching up with her and had been joined by urgent voices. As she turned down another corridor, she broke into a light jog. Not too fast—she was still weak from inactivity and did not want to tire herself. She wanted nothing to interfere with her ability to concentrate.

Jogging did not help. They were gaining on her fast. Faster.

Then, behind her, "*Stop!*"

More footsteps, grouping together, then closing in behind her.

She did not stop, did not even slow down, just kept jogging.

"I said *stop*! I'll shoot!"

Emma stopped. She turned around slowly.

A sweeping gesture, she remembered.

That was what Dr. Jorgan had told her the first time he had left her in that room with the wall of cages, a monkey in each cage, twelve monkeys in all.

"Now, I want you to think in terms of a sweeping gesture, does that make sense?" His voice had come through an intercom as he stood in the next room, watching her through the thick, tinted glass. "Like I told you before, Emma, you have a brand new muscle now, and I want you to use it, exercise it. But I want you to use it in a much broader way than you have before. *Sweeping.* Think *sweeping.* Okay, now. All the monkeys at once. Take your time."

Only three monkeys had been mildly affected the first time. The next time, seven monkeys died. The third time, all twelve within two and a half minutes. That time had shortened with each exercise, until it happened in less than a minute. Then less than thirty seconds.

But now, there were no monkeys. Instead, she faced four men wearing the black and gray uniforms of OdysseyCorp security. Two of them had guns drawn, and all four rushed toward her.

Sweeping...

One stopped. Two stumbled to a clumsy halt. The fourth fell sideways against the wall, dropping his gun as he slid to the floor.

By the time Emma turned her back to them, they were all on the floor, one of them making a low, sickened groaning sound, the other three still and silent.

She continued walking, worked her way back up to the light

jog, and rounded another corner to the right.

Dr. Jorgan had been right. It really *was* like having a new muscle, like learning to use a third arm, or to see out of a new eye in the back of her head.

Another corner, another corridor.

"Hold it right there, lady, or I *will* shoot, I *mean* it!"

Two more guards were about five yards ahead of her and closing the gap fast. One held his gun between both hands, elbows locked, aiming at her. The other held a small walkie-talkie in his right hand as he moved toward her, grabbed her arm, spun her and pressed her against the wall with his hand between her shoulder blades. Emma's breath burst from her lungs when her chest hit the wall.

The radio released a staticky blurt, then the guard holding her to the wall said, "This is 22. We found her heading for the front exit."

Emma recognized Michael's voice over the radio: "I'll be right there. But for God's sake, be *very careful*! She'll be dangerous until she's sedated."

The guards had distracted Emma and her concentration had faltered. The headache was worse now, becoming harder to ignore, making her eyes hurt. It was unlike any headache she had ever experienced before the second operation: millions of tiny pinprick aches grouped together behind her forehead, each one throbbing to its own individual rhythm, the pain filling her head.

She fought to peel her attention off of it so she could concentrate, otherwise the headache would be her undoing. It would keep her from flaming again.

Her face was wet with perspiration, mouth so dry that she could not swallow, and her lips felt burnt and swollen. Her entire head felt swollen and heavy, as if it might flop to the side, useless under its own weight.

Emma clenched her fists, her teeth, her eyes, pressed her forehead harder against the wall.

The guards, the two guards—both stood close behind her now. The one who had pushed her against the wall still had his hand in the center of her back, pushing.

She had never tried to direct a flame at a target that was behind her before—Dr. Jorgan had not taken her that far in the tests yet, although he had said they would. Now the pain was singing like the fat lady in an opera and Emma found it difficult to focus.

The other guard said, "Where the hell did you think you were going, anyway?"

She ignored him, made his voice grow distant, as if it were coming from another room.

Then, in the distance, she heard more voices, growing louder, coming from the direction in which she had been hurrying when the guards stopped her. One voice was louder than the others, and angry. That voice broke her concentration like a dry twig. Her eyes snapped open and she pulled her head up straight, looked to her right, toward the approaching voices.

"—you imagine if I *hadn't* come here today?" the angry voice was saying.

Another voice replied, muffled.

Closer.

"Jesus H. *Christ*! What do I pay you bastards for, anyway?"

Another garbled reply.

Closer...closer.

"I don't give a damn if she only got three *feet* from where she was supposed to be! You guys aren't worth the price of your fucking *uniforms*!"

It was Landon. And he knew. She had not even gotten out, and already he knew she was trying. As always. He knew everything. Everything she did, every move she made...for all she knew, he had a record of her every thought in some encrypted computer file, ready to use against her.

Emma watched the corner twenty yards down the corridor as the footsteps and voices grew louder and closer.

Landon rounded the corner with two more guards. He wore his overcoat, umbrella in his left hand, car keys dangling from his right. He had just arrived.

Even at that distance, his eyes bored into Emma's as he hurried toward her taking long strides, back stiff, arms swinging at his sides. His face darkened as he neared her, became a sinister mask, jaw set.

Emma shriveled inside. She could feel the tingling dissipating as the headache grew worse. As he came closer, tucking the umbrella beneath his right arm, she began to lose control of her breathing. Landon gestured commandingly to the guard holding her against the wall. Her knees felt weak with fear and she could feel the muscles in her back involuntarily tensing in anticipation of a blow.

The guard stepped away from Emma and Landon did not stop until his body was pressed against hers and his breath was hot on her cheek. He grabbed her arm with his free hand and dug his thumb deep and hard into her soft inner elbow.

"God damn you," he whispered into her ear. There was a slight growl to his voice, but it was so low that no one heard it besides her. It was the voice he had always used as he wrapped the oranges in The Towel. "What the fuck do you think you're trying to do? Just walk out of here? You forget. I own you. You can't *function* without me, bitch."

Her fear stopped suddenly, as if it had been cut off at the source. It simply turned off, like the lights in a power outage. A bilious, burning hatred rose in her gut, rushed up into her chest and threatened to spew from her throat in one great, gushing, burst. The tingling filled her head almost instantly, stronger than before. Then it happened, before she even thought about it, before she had a chance to *make* it happen. It just happened.

Emma felt something...*release* in her head. No, it was not in her head, it was not a physical feeling. Something released in her *mind*.

At that moment, Landon stopped, his mouth dropped open and his eyes bulged, as if someone had stabbed him in the back. The keys and umbrella dropped to the floor as his knees buckled and he dropped to a kneeling position before her.

The guards did the same, collapsing one after another.

Emma's eyes were tearing up as she turned around to survey the damage. Landon and all four guards were down. She spotted a gun on the floor and quickly swept it up, clutching it tightly in her hand.

The headache had become an exquisite, shrieking pain that threatened to crush her beneath its weight.

Fighting to get her breath back under control, struggling to focus once again, she went to Landon's side. He lay face-down, head turned to the side, a puddle of blood growing beneath his bleeding nose. She leaned down and snatched up his car keys. She recognized the key chain; he was driving the Bugatti today.

As she started down the corridor again, she broke into a run; she did not have time to jog.

Emma passed others in the corridor, employees in their white coats, visitors in street clothes, all of whom quickly moved out of her way when they saw the gun. They spoke to one another breathlessly, some calling out for security. Some of them dropped to the floor as she passed.

I'm still flaming, she thought. *Not trying to...but still flaming.*

A female voice spoke calmly over the P.A. system: "Security to all exits. Security to all exits immediately. Security to all exits."

Emma's vision became fuzzy as she ran, and she feared the pain in her head would worsen until she fainted, and then they would find her and she would wake up in her room and never have this chance again.

She started trying doors as she passed them with no idea where they led, only that they might lead her out of the corridor and away from them. One led to a utility closet, another to a stairwell that went down to the basement, and a third opened on what appeared to be a storeroom.

Corner after corner, all the corridors looked the same. She had no idea where she was in that meandering, maze-like complex.

Then she saw it: an exit. It was a metal door at the end of the corridor—far away at the end, a hundred and fifty yards away, maybe more—with a green EXIT sign on the wall above it.

And three guards standing in front of it.

"Stop right there or I'll take you out, lady!" one of the guards bellowed as all three of them raised their guns.

Instead of slowing down or stopping, Emma raised her own gun and began to fire.

With the first shot, all three guards dropped flat onto their bellies. One of them managed to get off a single shot, but that was all. They were too busy staying as flat against the floor as possible while Emma continued to fire at them as she approached.

The metal door grew larger in Emma's tear-blurred eyes as she continued to flame. She could feel it draining her, making the pain in her head worse, pressing on the backs of her eyes, spreading into her teeth and jaws.

The guards did not move on the floor. One of them whimpered quietly as Emma hurried past them and pushed on the metal bar that stretched across the door. She did not know if she had shot one of them or if the noisy one was simply miserable from being flamed, and she did not care.

Outside the door, she was bathed in cold, damp air. She kept running into the rain, into the gloomy, ash-colored light of day.

She slowed only briefly to look around, get her bearings.

Cars. Everywhere. The parking lot.

To her right stood the front gate, where a guard stood in his kiosk, another stood outside, and a black-and-white–striped security arm blocked the entrance. A tall cyclone fence with barbed wire strung along the top went all the way around the lot and the building.

Before one of the guards at the gate spotted her, Emma hunkered down and hurried along the side of the building, her moccasin slippers slapping on the wet pavement.

Landon would not park among the other cars in the lot, especially in the Bugatti. He had to have a private space separate from the others.

The wall went on forever.

The pain in her head seemed to have reached a plateau, but it was not receding. Her chest burned, her legs ached, and her hand had gone numb from gripping the gun.

She had almost reached the corner of the building when she heard a door open far behind her.

Voices, footsteps. Shouting.

A gunshot.

She rounded the corner and there it was, the shiny black

Bugatti EB 110, parked all by itself near the door. As she stumbled toward it, her left hand fumbled with the keys, hit the button in the middle of the fob, and heard the short blip that meant the car alarm was off.

Emma had the car door open and was getting inside when she heard the nearby door of the building open. Two more guards came out, guns drawn. She fell into the driver's seat of the Bugatti and leaned out just enough to point the gun in the general direction of the guards and fire.

The gun gave a solid click, but nothing more. It was empty.

"Drop the gun, lady, right now."

She did. Emma did not realize she had fired the gun that many times, but it was okay. Her head, though pounding with pain, was still tingling and humming. She was still flaming.

The guards were on the ground in seconds.

She slammed the door and started the car, put it in gear and shot away from the building, driving away from the guards on her tail, who would no doubt round the corner behind her at any moment. She drove away from the U-shaped building and down the center lane of the parking lot between columns of cars, heading straight for the gate.

The guards were ready for her. One stood on each side of the gate, guns drawn. They began to fire.

Emma hunched down behind the wheel and the tires squealed as she swerved to the left, then the right, then left again. The passenger-side window shattered and she heard bullets hitting the car. Emma tensed, waiting for one to hit her.

The Bugatti slammed through the security arm with a horrible crunch. The arm broke away, leaving the left front corner of the car mangled. She did not ease the pressure of her foot on the accelerator and put OdysseyCorp behind her fast.

It occurred to Emma that, providing she had not killed Landon back there, then seeing his precious Bugatti drive through that security arm under a hail of bullets probably would be enough to make him drop dead.

That made her smile as she sped on.

The headache receded quickly. By the time she reached the freeway and had dropped the Bugatti's speed to the legal limit, the tingling and humming had stopped. The headache had left her weak, and her hands were trembling fearfully, but she felt fine. Better, in fact, than she had felt in a long time. Because she was free. She had done something Landon had not expected, something he would have laughed at had she told him in advance that she was going to try. His overabundance of self-confidence was Landon's biggest weakness, and perhaps one of his worst enemies.

The needle on the gas gauge indicated that the tank was full and the Bugatti ran purringly; Landon never let the needle drop below three-quarters full in any of his cars. Emma could not help wondering how Landon was—not that she cared, but because she knew that if he regained consciousness and found that she had taken his Bugatti, that might require hospitalization and medical attention more urgently than anything she had done to him. He would no doubt have a hard time deciding what to be more furious about: that Emma had escaped, or that she had stolen his precious car. The windshield wipers were on high-speed to keep up with the downpour of rain and Emma was careful to drive a little slower than the speed limit. She could not afford to have an accident now, she was still too close to OdysseyCorp.

An army of Landon's people would be after her in no time, if they weren't already, and Landon, if he were healthy enough, would call the police and sheriff's department to pull every string within his reach.

Emma's plan had been flawed. It had only gone as far as her escape from OdysseyCorp. Now that she was out, she had no idea what to do, where to go.

But she had to lose the Bugatti, and soon. They were not exactly a dime a dozen on the roads, and if she did not get it off the freeway soon and abandon it someplace, she would have police cars with lights flashing and sirens wailing hot on her tail in no time. But where could she go in her thin hospital gown, terrycloth robe, and moccasin slippers?

Although it was not quite noon, the day was almost as dark

as dusk. Emma felt disoriented, not even sure which freeway she was on or in what direction she was headed.

There had been two eighteen-wheelers ahead of her ever since she had pulled onto the freeway, but when they finally moved, she could see the hulking specter of the city ahead in the distance; that gave her a reference point.

Now she needed a destination.

On each side of the freeway were empty fields, real estate developments, clusters of gas stations convenience stores, and fast food restaurants. Then she saw the enormous, brightly lit sign. She had seen it a million times before, but never once had she thought to read it. She did now:

K & L TRUCK STOP
FUEL – FOOD – SUPPLIES
FAMILY RESTAURANT
FULL SALAD BAR
FRESH BAKED PIES
* NEXT EXIT *

Before she reached the exit, she could see the truck stop off the freeway to her right. It had two massive parking lots: one for trucks, one far cars and pickups. Both were full.

Emma took the exit and pulled into the crowded parking lot, avoiding the deep potholes and sections of pavement that had broken away to be replaced by large patches of mud. She parked the Bugatti between a white Chevrolet pickup truck with a camper shell on the back and an ancient Mustang of indeterminate color. The black beauty she was in would shine like a neon light in the truck stop parking lot.

Once she killed the engine and headlights, she sat back in the seat, the key chain still dangling from the ignition, and closed her eyes. Emma had no doubt that walking around in a robe and slippers in the pouring rain at a truck stop would get her plenty of help, from truckers if no one else. But would it be the kind of help she needed? She did not even know what she was looking for, or what kind of story she would tell to anyone who offered assistance.

"First things first," she muttered with a sigh. She looked around in both directions. There was no one nearby, so she opened the door and got out of the car. She left the door open. She wanted to make sure that any passersby could see the keys in the ignition. Then Emma got away from the Bugatti as quickly as she could.

She was soaked through long before she reached the glass doors of the truck stop. She stopped in the foyer and leaned against the wall, wiping a hand over her face, then back over her hair.

A new kind of headache began to bother Emma. Although not nearly as bad as the last, this one was nevertheless agitating. It was a...*crackling*...headache. Something inside her head actually seemed to *crackle*, like a blinking electronic sign with a short in it, blinking and crackling. It affected her eyes as well as her head, made them ache, as if she had been staring into a bright light. She rubbed them slowly, her eyes, trying to push the crackling headache away, out of her head.

Emma did not see the two police officers until she had pushed halfway through the door and into the restaurant and gift shop. She froze in the doorway.

They were standing with their backs to her at the counter, talking to the blonde girl behind the cash register. One was leaning forward over the counter, the other stood straight.

They're not here because of me, Emma thought. *They can't be. They just came here for coffee and now they're flirting with that cashier. But...I can't go in. Not like this. They'll notice me, maybe stop me. Ask questions. What if they've already heard? What if a call's already been put out?*

She turned away from them, then went back outside before they turned around and saw her. She turned to her left and hurried along the front of the building, staying on the covered sidewalk. She passed window after window, and on the other side, people sat in booths in the restaurant, looking away from their food to watch the drenched woman in her robe and slippers hurry by.

The sidewalk came to an end. So did the cover.

Ahead, she saw the fuel island where two trucks were parked beneath the brightly lighted shelter to be refueled. Other trucks were lined up behind them. She looked around the corner of the building and saw the other parking lot in the back. It was much bigger than the one in front and filled with scores of eighteen-wheelers.

She ran across the pavement, looking for a truck with someone in it or around it. They all seemed dead, like giant metal coffins lined up neatly, ready to be buried.

Emma rushed between two of the trucks, then stopped to rest, leaning on one of the trailers. She was about to push away and go deeper into the truck lot when she heard a voice.

"You okay?"

Emma spun around to face a man standing beside the cab of the trailer she had been leaning on, gripping the handle of the door, his head turned to face her. He wore a puffy down jacket and a cap with a long bill that stuck out over his face.

"Hello?" he said. "You okay?"

His face was in the shadow of the camp's bill, but he sounded like an older man, voice thickened by a heavy Texas accent.

"No," she said reluctantly. "No, I'm not. I was just...trying to get out of the rain."

"Well, now, what're you doin' out here dressed like that?" he said.

"Um, well..." She thought hard and fast, searching for something sympathetic and believable. "Somebody's after me. I need help."

"Hellfire, why didn't you say so? Come on into the cab and get outta these elements." He opened the door and helped her up, climbing in after her.

Inside, the air was made of body odor, cigarette smoke, and the smell of strong coffee.

Emma stood hunched over between the seats as he slid behind the wheel, reached up, and flicked on the small light in the middle of the ceiling.

"You're soaked to the bone, honey," he said, looking at her with concern. "You want some dry clothes?"

"Oh, yes, please, anything you have, even if it doesn't fit, I can—"

"Hey, hey, wait just a second, now. You said somebody's after you. Who might that be?"

She did not hesitate. "My husband."

He nodded slowly. She could see his face now. It was ruggedly pleasant with silvery stubble on his chin. He smiled.

"Climb on up into the sleeper, there," he said. "Light's above your head. Switch's on the right. Turn it on."

She did as he said.

"Now, just to your left, there's a bundle of clothes. Grab yourself a shirt. One of them quilted flannels. But first, you get ridda that wet stuff. Throw it out here and I'll dump it. Sure ain't no good to you."

Once again, she did as he said, tossed the soaked robe and gown into the cab, never giving modesty a thought, and put on one of the quilted flannel shirts, blue plaid with lots of red and yellow stripes. It felt wonderful, glorious, so soft and dry against her flesh.

"Do you have something I can wear, um...from the waist down?" she said. "Some pants, maybe? Anything?"

His head rose from the opening that separated the cab from the sleeper.

"Well, now, honey," he said, grinning as he pulled himself up into the sleeper with her. "You don't need them just yet, do ya?"

Emma crawled backward, away from him. She felt a tingling in her head, and a faint humming.

15.

AFTERMATH

Jorgan was in the same chair in which he had collapsed almost two hours ago. His legs were stretched out and spread, and his head was hanging back limply, a cold, white cloth over his eyes and forehead. The cloth was darkened with blood.

Miranda stood beside him. She did not look too healthy herself, but she had held up better than Jorgan.

"Feeling better?" she said.

Jorgan slurred, "The explosions have stopped going off in my head."

"Shaw's down the hall. I heard him yelling earlier. He sounds pissed off."

"Oh, I'm sure he is." Jorgan touched his mustache with his fingertips. Blood from the nosebleed was beginning to dry among the scraggly hairs. He took the cloth and scrubbed around his mouth. "Are they absolutely sure she got away?"

"Gone with the wind. She took Shaw's Bugatti. From the way he sounded earlier, he may be having a stroke soon."

"Damn," he muttered, shaking his head. "This was the wrong time for her to pull something like this." He glanced up at Miranda. "Did she flame anyone else?"

"Everybody who got in her way. Even Shaw. He was out as long as you were. Two of the guards went into cardiac arrest, and she shot another one. In the hip. He'll live, but one of the other two is dead, and the third is pretty iffy, from what I hear."

He pulled his legs in and leaned forward in his chair, elbows on the table, palms pressing to the sides of his aching head.

"How did she *do* it?" he said. "I mean, she was doing well in all the tests, quite well, better than I'd expected. But...*this*. She always became symptomatic after three or four mild tests, sometimes even fewer. She wasn't *ready* for this much activity yet."

Miranda pulled out the chair to Jorgan's left and seated herself heavily. She was pale and looked weary.

"Well, you could've fooled the security staff," she said. "*They* seem pretty convinced she was ready."

Jorgan shook his head, confused.

"Maybe it was just beginner's luck," Miranda said quietly, reaching over to stroke his hand.

"This has nothing to do with luck, dammit." He dropped his hands to the table, pulling them out of her reach. "The only time she could've exercised was with me, during the tests. If she'd tried anything with anyone, we would've found out, it would've gotten back to us. How...in the hell...did she *do* it?"

When she spoke again, Miranda's voice was level and a bit cool. "She should've been isolated. That's what you were *supposed* to do. And you know as well as I do that Shaw's gonna throw all of this into your lap because you *didn't* isolate her properly. All because of whatever little...*crush* you have on her."

"Oh, thank you. I'm being accused of having a crush by the *queen* of the crush? Queen Miranda?"

She flinched slightly at his words, then seemed to shrink.

Jorgan leaned back in the chair again and his voice contained an element of fear along with exhaustion when he said, "My God, what have I done?"

"You made a mistake, that's all," she said. But there was very little comfort in her flat, cold voice.

"No, no, no, that's not what I mean," he said, waving vaguely toward his open briefcase.

She frowned then and for a moment looked as if she were going to pursue that. But she seemed to think better of it.

"By the way," she said, "looks like you've got a burst blood vessel in your left eye. You look like Christopher Lee, or something. Does it hurt?"

Before he could reply, Landon Shaw's voice began shouting obscenities in the hall outside. The door of the conference room was open and they heard his footsteps stalking over the tile floor as his voice grew louder.

Jorgan sat up straight in the chair and handed the washcloth to Miranda. He stared at the door, bracing himself.

Shaw's fists were clenched at his sides as he stormed into the room. Apparently, he'd had a bloody nose recently because there were streaks of blood above his upper lip. He took long, angry steps to the table and stopped beside Jorgan, glaring down at him. He pressed his fingertips to the tabletop, fingers stiff, palms tented.

"I'm only going to ask this question once," Shaw said, his voice a low grumble. He sounded more threatening than if he had been roaring. "I don't want any stuttering or stammering, just a straight answer. If I don't get that, and if I don't get it immediately, I may very well kill you with my bare hands. Right here and now. Do you understand?"

Jorgan nodded.

"All right, then." Shaw took in a deep breath and screamed, *"What the fuck happened here?"*

Jorgan did not even blink. Watching Miranda hurry out of the room, he envied her. He leaned his head back and looked Shaw in the eye.

"She flamed me, just like she flamed you. And the guards. And God knows who else."

His voice was low again, but it gradually grew louder: "And exactly how the hell did she do that? I mean, I thought you were just testing her. I didn't think you were giving her fucking *lessons* so you could turn her loose on the fucking *world*."

"We don't know how she—"

"What is this *we* shit? *You* are in charge of this project, nobody else."

Jorgan closed his eyes a moment and nodded. "I don't know how she learned to use the ability so well so quickly. In fact, as far as I can tell from all the tests, she *can't*. But...she did. I guess she just...took a chance. And it worked for her."

"Son of a *bitch*!" Shaw shouted, pounding a fist on the table.

He turned away and began to pace. "You were the one who insisted she was under control. *You* were the one who said she didn't have to be confined. I mean, we've got the fucking facilities, she could've been in one room the whole time, never completely exposed to you or anyone else. But *no*! No, you wanted her to be comfortable, like she was Liza Minelli at some fucking rehab clinic. *You* didn't *want* her locked up in confinement, which is where she should have been, and—" He spun around and stabbed the air with a stiff forefinger aimed directly at Jorgan's face. "—*you* are the fucking reason this happened!" He stood frozen in that position for several long seconds, like an evangelist waiting for his point to sink in, then dropped his arm and began pacing again. "You think I haven't noticed? You think I'm blind? Or stupid? Back when she used to come here every Thursday to have lunch with me...Jesus, you were like some fucking dog waiting for its master to come home. Wandering around in the corridor, *knowing* she'd arrive at the same time on the same day ever week. Staring at her like she was a movie star, or something, a fucking *goddess*. I mean, my God, I kept expecting you to drop your pants and start beating *off* for Christ's sake! *Oh!*" He stopped and turned again, glaring at Jorgan. "That time in the parking lot! I was on my way out, I happened to run into you on your way in, remember? *Jesus!* Soon as you saw her, you said you had to go back into town. You followed us all the way into the *city*! You kept passing us on the right, gawking at her like an ass. Passing us, then slowing down, then passing us *again*." He shook his head slowly, narrowing his eyes, his face a mask of angry disgust. "She didn't notice. I mean, why *should* she? But I did." He turned away, started pacing again, ran a hand through his hair again "My God. You get a hard-on for my wife and I have to pay the fucking bill!"

Jorgan said nothing. He just watched as Shaw continued to pace manically, following with his eyes, back and forth, without moving his head.

"We'll find her," Shaw said, sounding determined. "She can't get far in that Bugatti. It's not like everybody's got one." In a whisper, he added, "That miserable cunt. Taking my Bugatti."

Jorgan had been dreading giving Shaw the latest piece of bad news. He knew it would infuriate the man, making him helpless with rage. For one thing, he would be unable to understand it. Shaw was a barracuda in the business world but when it came to science he was dead from the neck up. When something was explained to him that he did not understand, Shaw angrily blamed everyone around him for making the information too complicated. But Jorgan did not think he would mind taking the heat again. Not this time. It was going to be fun watching the bastard lose control.

"There may be another problem now that she's out," Jorgan said.

"Yeah, you're damned right. The problem is that she's *out*."

"No, that's not what I mean. This would be a problem under any circumstances. But her escape...complicates things."

Shaw turned and faced Jorgan, waiting for him to continue.

"The problem involves the synthetic virus that was used as a catalyst in the infusion. "When she, erm, *left* this morning, I was about to question her regarding possible symptoms that might confirm the suspicions raised by the latest tests."

"Suspicions? About what?"

"Well, all test results indicate...that the virus has mutated."

"Virus? Mutated?" His roaring voice filled the room: *"Why wasn't I told that a fucking virus was involved in this project?"*

Jorgan did not take his eyes from Shaw's and did not raise his voice. "You were told. Long ago. At the very beginning. A synthetic virus was used as a—"

"I thought all you had to do was connect two parts of her fucking *brain,* or something! Nobody said anything about a goddamned *virus!"*

Jorgan continued to speak quietly in spite of the overwhelming urge to scream at his idiot boss. "Oh, I'm afraid I did, Mr. Shaw. I explained to you that the fusion on its own would not be enough. I explained to you that the synthetic virus—which, by the way, was designed specifically for this purpose and with your authorization, however perfunctory that might have been, it's all a matter of record—was needed to generate the desired result from the two surgically fused portions of the brain. It was created to do its job, nothing more. Now, if you'd like, I can go into great detail and describe to you the make-up of the virus and its intended interaction with chemicals in the brain. An interaction that *did*, by the way, occur, and which was responsible for the success of the project up to this point. But I know how much you hate that sort of thing. Details, I mean. I know how, uh, difficult it is for you to understand that sort of thing."

Jorgan waited and watched as Shaw's face darkened, as his eyes became silently murderous. But Shaw said nothing. So Jorgan continued.

"As far as we can—er, as far as *I* can tell at this point, judging by the results of the tests we've been conducting ever since this stage of the project began...the virus is mutating."

Shaw stared silently at Jorgan for a long time. When he finally spoke, his voice was barely a whisper. "Mutating. What... does *that* mean?" He began pacing again.

Jorgan thought before he spoke, turning possible responses over in his mind, trying to find the one least likely to get a violent reaction from his boss. Finally, he decided to simply say what he had to say, straight out. "That means there's a chance that the virus might become contagious."

Shaw stopped at Jorgan's side and looked down at him. "Contagious? *How?* In what way *might* it become contagious?"

Jorgan leaned back in the chair with a long sigh, then said, "I don't know."

"Oh, for...Jesus *Christ!* Give me an educated *guess*, goddammit! If someone were to catch this virus, what would happen to that person?"

"There is a chance that the abilities given to Em—er, to the subject may be passed on to those exposed to the virus. Most likely, those abilities would be weaker in them, perhaps not even noticeable. After all, even after I'd tapped the source, it took rigorous training before she was even able to—"

"Holy shit," Shaw interrupted. He lost some of the color in his face. "Holy *shit*. You're telling me...that she might be able to make others like her just by...*coughing* on them?"

"I'm *telling* you nothing. I'm saying that *might* be the case, and even if it is, I'm not sure how the virus might be transmitted. I really don't know *anything* yet. I was in the process of trying to answer all these questions when she decided to take her little trip. Now that she's gone, I can't be sure how much of a threat the virus poses to others. If any. I don't know how it might be transmitted, if at all, or how strong it might be if it is transmitted."

"What do you mean?" Shaw said.

"I mean, it could be passed in saliva, or maybe through an exchange of bodily fluids, like AIDS. Sexual contact or blood transfusions, that sort of thing. Or, God forbid, it could be airborne."

Shaw lifted his hand and stared at it as if it were an unfamiliar object. "I touched her," he whispered shakily, staring at the hand with a fearful expression. "Out there in the corridor, I...I *touched* her."

"The chances of her passing the virus to you that way," Jorgan said haltingly as Shaw continued staring at his hand, "are...well, minimal. At the *worst*. Not impossible, but... extremely unlikely. However, if you want me to speak with certainty about this...well, the only thing I can tell you with any certainty is...I can't be certain."

Shaw slowly lowered his arm at his side and turned to Jorgan, serious now, his fear suddenly gone as if it had never been on his face, hidden away now like a family secret. "What about Emma? How strong is she?"

Jorgan shrugged. "She's never experienced this much activity in one sitting. For all I know, she could be a gibbering mess by now. She might have fried her own brain just getting out of the complex. On the other hand, maybe *she* doesn't even know her own strength and she could kill everyone within a city block of her with a sneeze. If she'd done this later, after I'd had a little more time to work with her, I could give you some idea of how powerful she is. But now...it's just too soon to tell. Like I said, she might have already wiped herself out. Or she might just be getting started."

Shaw licked his lips and asked, "What can you do?" There

was something new in his quiet voice, something Jorgan had never heard coming from Landon Shaw before: desperation.

"All I can do is extrapolate from the data I have and see what might hap—"

"Never *mind*, goddammit. I don't want to hear all the technical shit. You do whatever you have to do, and do it *now*. I don't even want you taking time out to take a *piss*, do you understand me? Wear a diaper, catheterize yourself, just stay focused on *this*. In the meantime, I'm going to make sure she's found if I have go out and find her *myself*." He turned and went to the door, stopped and turned to Jorgan again. "I'm not jerking around here, Jorgan, this is all your fault. All because you've got the quivering hots for my fucking wife. You've gotta make good on this. I'll figure out how to deal with you later. After you've cleaned up your fucking mess. You've already been sitting in that chair *way* too long. Get the fuck to work. *Now*." Then he stalked out of the room.

But Jorgan sat in the chair for a while longer. He stared at the open doorway, despising Landon Shaw and wondering what had become of Emma.

16.

WEE'S CAF□

McNolte sat in his usual booth by the front window, but on this Tuesday night, he was not alone. Across from him sat P.W. and Irving, each with a cup of coffee.

It was 7:43 according to the Coca Cola clock on the wall behind the coffee counter. Outside, gusts of wind blew the pouring rain against the windowpane in sheets; the water crawled slowly and sadly down the glass, making the lights outside bleed together into a dirty, melting neon rainbow.

The sounds of traffic whooshing back and forth outside came into the café whenever someone opened the door, like the throaty hisses of a great reptilian beast angered by the rain.

McNolte had just eaten a bowl of clam chowder and P.W. was finishing a chicken salad sandwich, while Irving had decided on coffee only. The three of them had split up Wee's copy of the *Tribune* and were still browsing through it, switching sections now and then.

"Hey, Irving," McNolte said, "the clam chowder sure is good. You sure you don't want some? You should have something to eat."

"Eat *me* you cocksucker!" Irving snapped through clamped teeth, jerking his head. "I don't think so, McNolte. I've only got a little change on me. Hell, I've only got a little change p-p-puh-puh-*period blood!*" he added with a smile, convulsing once and then flapping his section of the paper uncontrollably.

McNolte knew that if he paid for the bowl of soup, it would make Irving feel bad. Early on in his stay at South Street, he had learned that, contrary to the opinions of so many angry, ranting radio talk show hosts, most underprivileged people did not enjoy taking handouts; they did out of necessity, but it only reminded them of how low they had sunk. As low as they were, they still had some pride. P.W. occasionally did odd jobs outside of the mission and gladly took his pay for them, because it was in exchange for work. But the only pay Irving received for his maintenance work at South Street was room and board. He was quite happy with that, but it prevented going out with friends for an occasional bite to eat, even at Wee's bargain basement prices.

P.W.'s primary job lately had been sticking close to McNolte and keeping an eye out for trouble.

He had taken a few changes of clothes over to McNolte's apartment and had moved in temporarily. McNolte had been reluctant, but on Willy's urging had agreed to do it because he knew what he was up against.

His reluctance was unnecessary. P.W. turned out to be the perfect roommate. Nothing bothered him. He brought a cot from the mission, along with his own pillow and a couple of blankets, and slept soundly through McNolte's late-night typing, the sound of the TV or radio playing, and even McNolte's habit of talking to himself as he wrote. P.W. left only to go to the mission when he was needed briefly, then came straight back. He read voraciously and shared McNolte's love for jazz. He did not talk much unless McNolte wanted to, and McNolte *did* want to—he was sure P.W. had some fascinating stories to tell about his time in Vietnam—but he had been so busy that he had decided to wait until he was done with the book before asking. P.W. also turned out to be helpful with McNolte's work, as well; he did not have much formal education behind him, but he was a great editor and McNolte was surprised by his insight and helpful suggestions.

"I'll be damned," P.W. said from behind his section of the paper.

"What?" McNolte said.

"They found that missing rich woman."

"Which one?"

P.W. laughed. "How many's missin'?"

McNolte chuckled, shrugged. "I haven't been paying much attention to the news, I guess."

"Well, 'bout a year ago, maybe more, this woman got into a fight with her husband and left. Just took off. She never came back. Nobody ever saw her again. Her husband's some fat cat, runs a big company outside of the city, some kinda research lab, somethin' like that. Anyway, says here in the paper there was some geologists divin' in the Thunderhead River a few days ago doin' some kinda research. They found her. Still strapped into her Mercedes. Identified her with her dental records just today. Shaw's her name. Emma Shaw." P.W. shook his head and whistled softly. "She musta been one hell of a smelly mess."

"After that long?" McNolte said. "I can imagine."

"No, I don't think you can. I seen a few waterlogged corpses, and they hadn't been in the drink *that* long. She was feedin' some fishies for a while, is what she was doin'."

"Mm. That's a pleasant thought after a meal."

P.W. said, "Oh, it's all part of the great food chain of life, McNolte. Nothing to squirm over."

Wee's Café was filled with noise, even though there were only two other customers there besides McNolte, P.W., and Irving. Kitchen noises clattered and sizzled from the rectangular stainless-steel-framed pass-through behind the coffee counter as an order was cooked and dishes and pots and pans were washed. From somewhere in the kitchen, a radio was playing a loud, tinny-sounding Chinese station on which voices yammered between twanging, dissonant songs.

Now and then, Wee's shrill voice could be heard shouting at one of his employees. He was a short, wiry Chinese man who moved quickly and appeared to be in a permanent bad mood. But anyone who knew him knew better. His English was broken and muddled, and newcomers often thought he was speaking in his native tongue. But the regulars, including McNolte, understood him perfectly.

On this particular night, Wee was annoyed at his waitress, Pam. She was a plump, round-faced blonde, twenty-one years old, sweet to all of her customers, even those who did not tip well. Tonight, she was experiencing an especially difficult period and had to retire to the restroom more often than usual. This annoyed Wee, and he was more than happy to let Pam know it, along with everyone else in the diner.

The air was thick with dark, greasy smells and haunted by spectral clouds of cigarette smoke. At the far end of the coffee counter, in the back of the café, sat a balding, middle-aged man in a brown suit that looked slept in. His overcoat was folded over the back of the counter seat and his umbrella was beside him, leaning against the front of the counter. He read a magazine as he waited for his order.

At the other end of the counter, the end by the cash register and closest to McNolte and friends, a scrawny old man sat hunched forward with both dirty, arthritic hands curved around a steaming cup of coffee into which he stared as if it held the secrets of the future. He had gotten his now-ragged clothes at South Street, where he was a frequent visitor. In fact, McNolte had found the clothes for him, although they had been in better shape then. The man was known only as Pooky—no one knew why—and he was a regular at Wee's because Wee often fed him leftovers. Wee did that for a lot of the street people in the neighborhood.

Wee's shrill voice began to rave in the kitchen. The swinging door that separated the back of the counter from the kitchen was suddenly kicked open loudly and Wee came out with a pot and ladle, shaking his head and complaining to no one in particular, " "*Period!*" He pronounced it "peeyud." Every fucking *month!* Period, period. I so sicka period I *vomit!*" He walked over to the booth and looked down at McNolte's empty bowl. "You want more chowder?"

"No, thanks, Wee," McNolte said. "It was delicious, but I'm full. However, my friend might want to take my refill." He looked at Irving and raised his eyebrows questioningly. "What do you say, Irving?"

"Oh, thank you, McNolte," Irving said, his eyes blinking rapidly. He glanced at Wee, nodded and smiled, then looked at McNolte again. "Fucking slant-eyed *shiteater!*" he said with a grunt, still smiling. "I should get to bed, though. It's late."

Wee shook his head with mock disapproval as he turned to McNolte. " Crazy people. Why you bring crazy people here? I got crazy waitress to deal with as it is. Crazy waitress on *period!*"

"Aw, c'mon, Wee," P.W. said. "Give her a break. Pam's a good waitress." He grinned as he spoke because he knew the tirade that was coming.

" Break? Give her *break*? What the fuck you talk about? She should bleed on her *own* time! Good waitress with period is same as *no* waitress!" He turned around and stomped back into the kitchen, still talking.

P.W. slid out of the booth and slipped his down jacket on as he said, "I'm gonna take Irving back to South Street, McNolte. See you at the apartment in, what—'bout half an hour?"

"Yep, I'll be there, P.W."

"Remember, go straight to the apartment and take the back way to stay outta sight."

"I'll remember. But thanks, P.W."

McNolte said so long to Irving, who left change on the table for his coffee and spontaneously and quite loudly impugned the marital status of McNolte's parents while twitching violently as he left.

McNolte had made a copy of his apartment key for P.W. He had tried to pay P.W. for the protection he provided, but the only compensation he would take was an occasional meal at Wee's and a movie now and then at the Liberty, an art house that showed everything from obscure foreign films to old Hollywood classics.

After gathering up the sections of the newspaper and setting them aside, McNolte put his spiral notebook on the table and opened it, removing a pen from his shirt pocket. He went back to work on the chapter that was currently in the typewriter back at the apartment, scribbling a few lines, stopping for a while, chewing on the pen, looking around absently, then chewing the pen more until he bent forward and wrote a few more lines.

"You want pie, Pooky?" Wee asked.

McNolte looked up to see Wee showing Pooky a thick wedge of pie.

"I got apple pie left over. You want?"

Pooky shrugged his bony shoulders, "Sure, fine with me."

"You want pie hot or cold?"

"Heat it up, please," Pooky mumbled.

As Wee put the pie in the microwave, McNolte pulled a pack of cigarettes from his shirt pocket, shook one out, and lit up.

Pam came to the booth with a pot of coffee and, in spite of her condition, a bright smile.

"More coffee, McNolte?"

"Sure, Pam, thanks."

For a couple of months now, Pam had been living with the café's dishwasher on her shift, Manuel, who was not exactly a catch to write home about. McNolte knew that Manuel was a heavy drinker, and he could not help noticing the bruises that showed up on Pam's arms and neck now and then, not to mention the swollen, purple eye she had been sporting last week. And yet, her pleasant mood never changed. McNolte pitied her, was angry for her—and a little angry at her for sticking around for such treatment—but he found her rather inspiring. She endured.

"You're not letting Wee get you down, are you?" he said.

"Oh, no," she said as she refilled his cup. "I know he doesn't mean it. Wee's a pussycat. He's just a really loud, yowling, cranky pussycat."

She went away, leaving McNolte with his thoughts and his notebook.

The microwave hummed as it heated Pooky's pie.

Voices chattered from the radio in the kitchen.

The door of Wee's Café opened and a figure stepped inside wearing a heavy, olive-green rubber poncho with a hood pulled up over the head, the kind of poncho that used to be issued by the military. The figure glanced to the right, turning its black sunglasses toward McNolte, and he saw a woman's face buried in the cave of the hood. It seemed to be a rather delicate face, although it was difficult to tell because it was darkened by the hood's shadow.

McNolte's journalistic instincts kicked in and he took a mental photograph.

She was about five seven and the poncho fell just above

her ankles, where too-large jeans bunched up over a pair of once-white Converse High Tops, which were not only filthy and soaking wet but about two sizes too big for her. The laces had been tied tightly, with plenty of string left over. Her arms, sticking out between the snaps that went up each side of the poncho, were enclosed in the baggy sleeves of a blue plaid, quilted shirt, the cuffs of which fell to her knuckles, leaving only her pale fingers visible.

She stepped forward and ducked into the first booth, the one closest to the entrance, so that she was facing the door. She made no attempt to remove the poncho or the hood, even though all that rubber made sliding into the booth difficult. She locked her hands together on the table, fingers and thumbs waggling nervously.

Her head leaned forward sharply, she raised a hand to her forehead, massaged one temple, then looked around quickly. Her face was tense, as if with pain, as she looked around the café, as if searching for something. Then she stopped looking and fixed her eyes on something.

McNolte followed her gaze until his eyes fell on the microwave oven heating Pooky's pie. He sipped his coffee as he watched her slide out of the booth, stand, and look around uncertainly. Finally, she walked all the way to the back of the diner, toward the single restroom just to the right of the door that read EMPLOYEES ONLY, past Pooky, past the man in the brown suit who was still reading his magazine, to the very last booth. She scooted into the seat facing the entrance. Her shoulders rose as she took in a deep breath, then fell slowly as she reached her hands into the hood and massaged her temples with her fingertips.

First, she fidgeted in the booth, head swallowed up by the rubber hood. She changed her position again and again, folded her hands, then placed them flat, then folded them again.

After sitting in the booth a couple of minutes, she pulled the hood back until it was bunched together behind her neck, and removed the sunglasses.

The sunglasses intrigued him most of all. Why was she wearing sunglasses on a stormy night?

She shook her head slightly and ran both hands roughly through her hair. It was short and damp, dark and spiky. She rolled her head in slow circles, as if trying to loosen up a stiff neck. Her large eyes, above high cheekbones, wore no makeup and looked puffy and stressed. Her face looked out of place in Wee's Café. In fact, it looked out of place in that neighborhood. She was dressed like a homeless person, and she had the jittery movements and trembling hands of someone struggling with a chemical addiction, but hers was the pristine, milky-skinned face of someone who took good care of herself and normally wore better clothes. McNolte had a feeling she was not homeless, and he even doubted that she was from that part of town.

Her hair looked expensive, probably done in a plush salon, and she looked like a woman accustomed to expensive things. These were gut feelings, of course, nothing more. But McNolte trusted his gut, even when he sometimes did not understand it.

Something about her was…odd. There had been something unusual about the way she walked when she came into the diner. Not too fast, and she had moved with purpose, back straight, chin up. Confidence, that was it. She moved with confidence, something rarely seen among the people who occupied this part of town.

From his experience at South Street, McNolte had learned that there was a certain similarity among the homeless. They usually kept their heads bowed, their shoulders were stooped, their back sometimes hunched, beaten down, defeated. Their movements were slow from constant fatigue brought on by spending every hour of every day and night in the act of surviving. They looked that way from the day-to-day humiliations of their lives, from the wear and tear on their souls. It was the mark of every person who lived in the dark corridors that separated wanting from desperately needing, success from failure, and civilization from savagery.

The woman wearing the rubber poncho did not bear that mark. If anything, she seemed its antithesis. There was pride in the way she held her head. Even the way she held herself as she sat there in the booth clashed violently with her appearance, in spite of her restless fidgeting, in spite of the costume she wore.

Her jitteriness suggested some kind of chemical withdrawals. Drug addiction was common among the homeless, but McNolte still doubted she was one of them. In spite of the clothes she wore—clearly a costume, as far as McNolte was concerned—there was a smugness about the way she held her head, the expression on her face as she searched for a waitress; it was the expression of someone not accustomed to waiting. She was troubled, maybe even afraid, there was no doubt about that, but she did not belong there.

The microwave oven beeped several times. The woman looked at it again, but now her face showed tremendous relief. McNolte noticed that her relief seemed to be triggered by the beeping of the microwave.

Wee appeared from the kitchen, opened the oven, and removed the plate.

"Here your pie," he said, slapping the plate onto the counter in front of Pooky. "You enjoy, cause it *free* okay? Okay." He glanced at the woman in the rear booth, then went back to the kitchen. "We got new customer! You stop bleeding and go wait on new customer! You do that now or you *fired*!"

A moment later, Pam hurried through the swinging door, order pad in one hand while she patted her hair with the other. Her uniform consisted of a white blouse, a black skirt that fell a few inches above her knees, and black sneakers. She swiped a menu from the rack at the end of the coffee counter as she passed.

McNolte watched carefully as Pam went to the woman's booth. He did not even try to hide his interest.

Pam spoke briefly with her usual smile, and the woman shook her head as she responded. Pam turned away just seconds later, still holding the menu. She replaced it in the rack, retrieved the coffee pot and an empty mug, and took them to the woman's table. Pam said something and the woman shook her head in quick, spastic jerks without looking up, and Pam turned and headed toward McNolte.

"Can I get you any dessert, McNolte?" she said.

"No, I'm fine, thanks. But, uh...what's her story?" he said, nodding toward the woman seated in the back booth.

Pam shrugged. "Doesn't even want to look at a menu. Says she just wants coffee. From the looks of her, I don't know if she can pay for that. But knowing Wee, he'll probably let her have the coffee, and I won't get a tip. Oh, well," she said with a shrug and a smile, "things could always be worse."

"Speaking of things being worse, how's Manuel?"

She averted her eyes and her smile faltered a bit. "He's, you know…still Manuel."

Pam walked away and replaced the coffee pot, then disappeared into the kitchen once again.

A moment later, Wee's voice wailed from the kitchen.

"Wah you do back hee? We got cussomuhs out deh! Dat man wah his oduh! Dey wah coffee! Dey wah dee-zut! No wunnuh we ahways hah so much pie leff ovuh! You no *sell* it! You go back out deh now!"

Pam came back through the swinging door carrying a plate of food. Got the coffee pot, put the order in front of the man in the brown suit, warmed up his coffee, warmed up Pooky's coffee, then grabbed a rag and started wiping tables, doing her best to look busy.

McNolte watched the woman in the rear booth as she sipped her coffee. It spilled now and then in her unsteady hand, and she glanced repeatedly out the window to her right, eyebrows gathered in a tight frown. They were not the absent glances a lone diner might toss out a window over coffee. They were nervous, expectant looks. Worried, frightened looks. She was waiting for something she did not want to happen, something she dreaded.

The poncho was so big that it completely concealed her body. But from the look on her face and the position of her feet beneath the table—they looked ready to push her out of the booth at any second—McNolte decided she was ready to bolt, ready to shoot out of that booth, perhaps even out of the diner.

This was not a homeless woman off the street who was happy to have a place to sit and a cup of something hot. This was a woman afraid of something, awaiting trouble.

She drummed the fingers of both hands on the tabletop, scratched the side of her nose or an eyebrow, ran her fingers through her hair again and again, tugged at her chin, at her ear. And she kept looking out that window, into the night and the small parking lot on that side of the diner.

McNolte tried again to take his attention away from her and put it back on his work, but failed. His gaze was always drawn back to that rear booth and the strangely attractive, frightened woman who could not seem to hold still.

McNolte was startled when their eyes met. He almost looked away, embarrassed for staring at her, but instead he smiled and nodded once.

She jerked her head to the right and looked out the window again.

McNolte sighed and looked over his shoulder at the clock on the wall above the pass-through. It was already quarter after eight, and he wanted to be home when P.W. arrived so the man would not worry about him.

Glancing at the bill, he pulled out his wallet and began thumbing through the singles. He heard the door of the café open, but was too preoccupied to pay any attention at first. He pulled out the appropriate number of bills, looked up, glanced at the man who had just walked in, then did a double-take.

He was tall and wore a black leather overcoat beaded with rain, and his shiny black hair was pulled back in a ponytail that fell halfway down his back. The lower half of his face was covered by a white surgical mask, and he wore latex surgical gloves on his hands.

The man began to walk toward the back of the diner with long, purposeful strides before McNolte had time to ponder the mask. Turning to the woman in the rear booth, McNolte saw her eyes become enormous with terror.

She knocked her cup over as she tried clumsily to slide from the booth, spilling coffee over the table. The man blocked her path before she could get out of her seat. He put a hand on her shoulder and pushed her back down. Hard.

The woman pulled away from him, slid backward over the seat, and pressed herself against the windowsill, but did not escape his hold. She said something and the man responded, leaning forward now, still clutching her shoulder, his fingers digging deep into the rubber poncho as he pulled her toward him.

"I will *not!*" she shouted, her hoarse voice rising above the Chinese radio station and the sounds of rain and traffic from outside. "Leave me alone! You know what will happen, you *know* what I'll do." She began to fight him, pounding him with her fists again and again.

The man let her go and stepped back, stiff now and fidgeting nervously in place. A long moment of silence stretched out between them as they stared fiercely at each other, still and deadlocked, the woman's wide eyes filled with naked fear and hatred.

"Calm down, now, just calm down," the man said, barely loud enough for McNolte to hear. He took a step forward and clutched her elbow, pulling her toward him again.

McNolte got out of his booth, stuffed his wallet into the back pocket of his jeans, and rounded the corner of the coffee counter in a hurry. "Hey," he said as he approached the woman's booth, "hey, come on, buddy, knock it off, okay?"

The man glanced at him for an instant, then continued to pull the woman from the booth. She was losing the struggle.

"Hey, *hey!*" McNolte shouted. "Come on, let her alone!" He stopped when he was standing two feet away from the man, whose jaw worked slowly and angrily as he glared at McNolte.

The man's face was narrow, with slightly sunken cheeks, which made the rounded surgical mask even more out of place than it already was, clinging to his nose and mouth with the aid of a rubber band. His close-set eyes were small, glimmering bullet holes in his face. "Back off," he said in a near-whisper. "This is none of your business. I'll only warn you once."

Behind him, McNolte heard the swinging door being kicked open in Wee's inimitable way, but ignored it.

"If you're going to rough this woman up," McNolte said, "once won't be enough. This is *anybody's* business, okay? That's the way things work. You can't go around—"

Still holding the woman's elbow with his left hand, the man reached inside his overcoat with his right and pulled out a gun, just far enough for McNolte to see it, just enough for McNolte to know he was armed and not in the mood for any differing opinions.

"Do you see this?" he asked, his voice a low rasp.

McNolte froze and stared at the gun.

"Well," the man growled, "do you see this or not?"

"Yeah," McNolte said, stiffening. "I see it."

"Then I suggest you back the hell off, okay, my friend? This is none of your business. You just back off now and I won't—"

He swallowed his words when the thick, threatening sound of a pump action shotgun being cocked went through the diner with an ugly crack.

With a flick of his eyes, McNolte saw Wee standing a few feet behind the man, aiming a sawed-off shotgun at his back.

"You no fuck with my customers!" Wee shouted. "You wanna show guns, do it in the street. You understand?"

McNolte watched the man's eyes roll to the left, watched his jaw slacken ever so slightly.

The man spoke cautiously: "Uh...I'm not sure I, uh... understood you."

"You get the fuck outta here!" Wee squealed. "You understand *that*?"

"All right," the man said slowly, putting the gun away. "I'll do that, I'll leave. I'd like to take this woman with me, though. She's sick and she needs help right away."

McNolte looked at the woman.

Her eyes teared up, jaws flexed as she clenched her teeth repeatedly. Her back was stiff and her wide eyes stared blankly at the cup of coffee on the table; they were blank in the way eyes got in moments of sheer terror and panic.

"She wanna go, that fine with me," Wee said. "She don't wanna go, then you get the fuck outta here."

No one moved or spoke for a moment.

Standing with the barrel of his shotgun in the man's back, Wee leaned toward the booth and asked, "You wanna go with him?"

The woman did not respond, only continued to stare blankly at her coffee cup.

"*Hey!*" Wee shouted. "You wanna go with him? Or you wanna stay here?"

Still, she did not respond. Her lips began to tremble and her eyelids fluttered, then lowered to half-mast.

"I don't think she wants to go, Wee," McNolte said. "But she's too terrified to say so. She's afraid of this man."

" What you want with her?" Wee barked at the man. To someone unfamiliar with his accent, it was garbled gibberish.

Standing stiff, the man stammered. "I-I-I'm sorry, but I...I don't understand—"

"He said, 'What do you want with her?'" McNolte repeated.

"I told you. She's sick. She needs help. I've been looking for her for days." He turned his head slightly toward Wee and raised his voice in the way some people do when speaking to a foreigner who has not yet mastered English. "Y-you can put your gun down. I'm going to leave, okay? And I'm going to take her with me."

Wee stomped a foot and stabbed the sawed-off barrel of the shotgun into the man's back. "I say you no fuck with my customers!"

McNolte turned to the woman, who continued to stare at the coffee cup. Trying to sound calm, he said, "Miss? Do you want to leave with this man? You don't have to."

Her eyes looked up at him, screaming silently. She moved her head minutely from left to right, then looked down at the coffee cup again.

McNolte looked at the man and smiled.

"You son of a bitch," the man said, "I *told* you this was none of your—"

" That's *it!*" Wee shouted, stabbing the man harder in the back with the gun. "You no use that kinda language with my fuckin' customers, asshole! Out! You get *outta* here now!"

The man reluctantly released the woman's elbow and took a sideways step away from the booth, never taking his eyes from McNolte's.

Wee poked him in the back again and again. "*Hey!* My place need paint job! You guts look pretty good on my walls You want me to do that? *Huh?*"

"I'm going, I'm going." He glared at McNolte a moment longer, eyes silently declaring McNolte's death, then stepped around him and headed for the door with Wee on his heels.

"You no come in here *no more!*" Wee yammered on at the top of his lungs. "I no feed you, I no pour you coffee. Know what I do? I blow you in *half,* that's what I do!"

The man pulled the door closed hard behind him. Wee turned and went back to the counter, replacing the shotgun beneath it.

McNolte noticed the man in the brown suit at the end of the counter for the first time since the stranger had tried to pull the woman from the booth. The entire incident had taken place just a few feet from the man who, a little more than a minute earlier, had been calmly reading a magazine while eating his meal. Now the magazine was crumpled in his lap between both hands and his seat was turned nearly all the way around. He looked pale.

"Holy shit," he muttered, voice trembling as he looked in McNolte's general direction. "What...the hell...was *that?*"

"No problem," Wee said, hurrying down the counter to stand in front of the man. He smiled, showing his crooked, yellow teeth. "You no worry about that. I give you discount onna chicken fry steak."

The man looked at Wee for several seconds. "What?" he finally said, turning to McNolte. "What did he just say?"

"He says not to worry," McNolte said, smiling. "He's giving you a discount on the chicken fried steak."

"Are you *kidding* me?" the man asked, doughy face slack. "He just pulled a sawed-off shotgun and—"

"It was nothing, really," McNolte said, waving a hand dismissively. His heart was still pounding from the whole thing, but he was not showing it. "Are you new to the city?"

"I'm a salesman. I'm just passing through. I didn't expect—"

"Well, there you go," McNolte said. "This sort of thing happens all the time here in the big city." He smiled. "But it's all over now. Everything's fine. And, hey, you got a discount for your trouble. Enjoy your chicken fried steak."

The man did not return McNolte's smile. He simply sat there

looking as if he had just been struck hard in the back of the head with a heavy, blunt object.

McNolte looked down at the woman.

She leaned both elbows on the coffee-puddled table, pressing her face into the palms of her hands. Her shoulders moved up and down rapidly with silent sobs.

He slid into the booth facing her. "Are you all right?"

She pulled her hands away and her teary eyes darted all around, but never met his.

"Don't worry, he's gone," McNolte said.

Her mouth worked as if trying to speak, but nothing came out for a moment. Then: "I'm fine. Thank you. For helping me, I mean." Her voice was cold, sterile, with no sign that she had been crying.

Pam appeared with a towel and quickly wiped the spilled coffee from the tabletop with one hand while filling the woman's empty cup with the other.

"Can I get you anything else?" she said.

McNolte said, "Would you mind bringing my coffee over here?"

She patted his shoulder. "Do you one better. I'll get you a fresh cup. Be right back."

The woman stared at the cup until Pam was gone, then picked it up between both hands and sipped.

With quiet caution, McNolte said, "Um, I'm Neil McNolte. Everybody around here just calls me McNolte. Look, uh…if you don't mind my asking, who was that guy?"

She still did not look at him and seemed not to have heard at first. Then she pressed herself hard to the back of the seat and muttered, "I should go."

"Wait a second," he said, "you don't have to tell me anything if you don't want to. But I really don't think it's such a good idea for you to leave here just yet. Whoever that guy was, he had a gun, and he seemed serious enough to maybe wait for you outside. So if I were you—"

"You don't understand," she whispered, bowing her head. "I have to leave. That's all. I just need to go."

She still twitched and fidgeted, and when she lifted her head again, her eyes shot here and there and back again, as if they were following a pinball bouncing around in a machine. Her eyes kept returning to the window to her right and the rainy parking lot outside.

McNolte looked through the glass to see if he could find whatever was catching her attention.

The single light in the lot had not worked since McNolte had been coming to Wee's, and with the intense rain, there was little to see. Some cars hunched in the darkness and a few lights beyond the parking lot glowed blurrily through the watery glass; other than that, he could not make out anything in detail beyond the cracked sidewalk that ran beside the diner.

"I might understand your situation better than you think," he said, smiling at the woman, although she did not seem to notice. When he continued, he was careful not to sound condescending or judgmental. "Look, I know of a place where you can get help."

Her eyes snapped open wide and locked onto his. She stared at him for a while, then said, "What...what do you mean, help?"

"It's a mission. It won't cost you a thing. I work there. They'll put you up and feed you. And there are people there who will help you with your addiction. If you let them. I had to. See, when I first got there, I was—"

"*Addiction?*" she spat bitterly. On the table, her hands curled into fists. "I'm not *addicted* to anything. You think I'm—oh, never mind. I've got to get out of here." From beneath the rubber poncho, she produced a worn black leather wallet, opened it, pulled out a dollar bill and dropped it onto the table. Then the wallet disappeared into her poncho again.

"At least let me walk with you," McNolte said. "I don't mind admitting that your friend nearly made me crap my pants a few minutes ago, but I don't feel right letting you leave alone."

"He's not my friend," she mumbled as she counted out some change.

"Where will you go?"

She sighed. "I have no idea. I've just got to get out of here. Now that they know I'm here, I have to leave the city. Tonight. Right away." She seemed to be talking to herself rather than

McNolte. "I need some sleep. That's why I couldn't flame him, dammit. Just too tired, that's all. Too fuzzy. I need some sleep."

"Leave the city?" he said. "I thought you meant leave *here*. This diner. Why do you have to leave the city? Now that *who* knows you're here? Who are *they*? And...did you say *flame*? That's why you couldn't *flame* him?" Noticing that questions were pouring out of him in a stream, he told himself to calm down.

She ignored him and started to scoot out of the booth.

Pam appeared then and placed a clean cup in front of McNolte and tipped the coffee pot over it until it was full.

"Anything else?" Pam said.

"I'll buy you a meal," McNolte said, speaking rapidly. "You can have anything on the menu."

The woman stopped and looked at him suspiciously.

"No strings," he said. "Just a meal. You look like you could use one. After that, you can do whatever you want. I just think you should wait in here for a while before going out."

He wanted to keep her there, talk to her some more, try to get her talking, find out as much as he could about her situation, about the man wearing surgical gloves and mask. McNolte hoped to keep her there long enough to convince her to let him help her.

She relaxed a little, put her hands back on the table. "All right," she said. "I'm...pretty hungry, so I'll take you up on it."

"Can we have a menu, Pam?"

After delivering the menu, Pam disappeared again. McNolte said, "If you're in some kind of trouble, I'd like to help. In any way I can. I don't know what that would be, though. You'd have to tell me."

She shook her head as she looked over the menu. "Thank you, but there's nothing you can do for me. Aside from the meal, I mean. I appreciate that."

"Well, maybe you should talk to the police."

Her head snapped around and she glared at him with heat in her eyes. "Listen to me. No police. If there are no strings attached to this meal, fine, but if you want to help me, then after I leave here, do *not* call the police. Don't tell them about me.

Please. I'm *begging* you." Her voice softened as she spoke until she was whispering.

Pam returned to the booth, her order pad ready. "Do you need another minute?"

"Yeah, stay right there," the woman said.

As she looked over the menu again, McNolte turned his head toward the window when he saw movement in his peripheral vision, then did a double-take when he saw the tall, slender man who had been in the diner only minutes earlier, still wearing his surgical mask and gloves. He stepped in front of the window and faced them, pulling a gun from beneath his leather coat. But it was not the same gun he'd had earlier. This one was much bigger.

McNolte glimpsed the retracted stock of the automatic weapon, and that was all he needed to see.

He reached across the table, grabbed a fold of the woman's rubber poncho, and pulled so hard that he grunted with exertion as they both headed for the floor, with Pam caught between them.

A heartbeat after that, the gunfire started and the sound of shattered glass cut through the night.

17.

RACING WITH BULLETS

The first scream came from the man in the brown suit at the coffee counter as shards of glass rained through the diner in a furious storm. Short bursts of rapid, thick popping sounds came from outside the shattered window.

McNolte was on the floor, his fist still clutching the woman's rubber poncho. Between them, beneath his arm, Pam lay on her side making small sounds of panic in her throat, struggling to turn over onto her hands and knees. A moment later, all three of them scrambled clumsily over the grimy floor, staying low, bellies scraping the dirty Formica. McNolte and Pam made their way toward the nearby restroom in an unspoken agreement, as if they were following some kind of instinct.

Pam worked her way ahead of them, with McNolte and the woman right behind her, his hand still clutching the rubber poncho. Somewhere in his confused and terrified mind, McNolte realized that the woman was simply wriggling over the floor in a wild panic with no destination in mind and was simply going wherever he pulled her.

The restroom was small and cramped, but McNolte knew there was a window in there that opened on the opposite side of the diner from the gunfire. He hoped it was big enough for each of them to get through.

Pam screamed as the automatic gunfire continued, but groped desperately for the restroom door.

More windows shattered.

McNolte heard Pooky release a long, garbled cry that sounded like his last.

Wee began to jabber in his native tongue, outraged at the attack on his establishment, and he fired his sawed-off shotgun once. His voice was silenced after an abrupt, gurgling cough.

More glass shattered and rained down on them, and pots and pans clanged in the kitchen as they scattered over the floor.

Pam reached the door of the restroom first and reached up for the knob, her hand slapping over the door's surface of paint that was peeling like old skin. She gripped the doorknob, turned it and pushed the door open.

McNolte followed her in, pulling the woman inside behind him, dragging her like a sack of potatoes as he stumbled to his feet, but remained hunched over. As soon as her feet were clear, he reached out and slammed the door shut, staying low.

It was a tiny cubicle of a room with a toilet on one side and a sink on the other; no mirror, just an old dented aluminum paper towel dispenser. A window on the far wall was set about eight inches below the ceiling. McNolte did not know how to open it, or if it opened at all—judging from the way the restroom always smelled, he guessed it was not designed to be opened—but he planned to get through it.

Pam stood, hands trembling as they raised to her mouth, her pudgy fingers curling over her lips. Her eyes widened slowly, as if something horrible were occurring to her.

"Manuel," she hissed. Then she screamed, "My God, *Manuel!*"

McNolte remained hunched over, ignoring Pam for the moment as every inch of his body tensed, waiting for the first bullet to hit him.

"Come on," he said, breathless from the adrenaline rush brought on by the gunfire, which went on and on outside the restroom door. "We've got to get out that wind—"

Several bullets punched through the bathroom door and McNolte flattened himself on the floor, pulling the woman down with him and crossing his arms protectively over her head.

Pam made a curt yelping sound as she fell back against the wall beneath the window.

McNolte craned his head around to look behind him. Pam had collapsed to the floor with her head and shoulders leaning against the wall, neck bent sharply, a stunned expression on her face. A dark red smear marred her white blouse just below the crest of her right shoulder, and blood ran from a small hole in her upper arm about two inches below her short sleeve. She started to get up even though she had been shot twice.

"Stay *down*, Pam!" he shouted.

The bullets kept coming in bursts, splintering the old door, sending bits of wood and old, peeling paint through the air like little missiles. McNolte heard the window shatter behind him.

After several seconds of bullets punching through the door and wall, McNolte realized that, while the gunfire continued outside the closed door, no more bullets were coming into the bathroom. McNolte got to his knees and pulled the woman up with him.

Pam was already on her feet and staggering toward the door, left arm outstretched in desperation, fingers splayed, while her right arm flopped limply at her side. She did not seem to notice.

"Manuel!" she cried.

"Pam, don't go out there," McNolte said. "Get away from that door, dammit. We're going out the window."

But Pam stumbled onward, apparently unaware of her wounds. She clasped the doorknob between both hands and struggled with it, muttering, "Manuel, oh, God, Manuel, my God, please, Manuel..." Her hands slid over the aluminum knob at first, then caught and turned it. She pulled the door open so hard, it slammed against the wall with what almost sounded like another gunshot.

"Pam, don't go out there," McNolte shouted.

She simply did not hear him as she lumbered out of the bathroom shouting, "Manuel? *Manuel!* Are you all right? Manuel?"

The gunfire continued.

"Son of a bitch," McNolte muttered as he hurried over to the toilet and stepped up onto the edge of the bowl. As he stood there precariously, left arm leaning against the wall above the toilet, he lifted his right leg high. Muscles that were no longer as limber as they used to be protested with pain, and he groaned quietly as he kicked the jagged edges of broken glass from the edges of the window.

It was while he stood there, a couple of feet above the floor, that he noticed he was sweating. At first, he thought it was natural under the circumstances. But it was not natural at all. Large sections of his shirt were soaked with sweat and clinging to his body. His palm, pressed against the wall as he kicked the glass spikes from the window, began to slip over the tile because it was so sweaty. And his head...the inside of his head...began to tilt ever so slightly. Or was it the room that was tilting?

Time passed sluggishly. Concentrating hard on the task at hand, he finished kicking out the glass as dizziness overwhelmed him. One moment, he was leaning his hand against the wall, and the next his left cheek was flat against the cold, moist floor of the bathroom, and the breath had been kicked out of his lungs.

Bones aching from the fall, McNolte got up on his hands and knees and saw drops of sweat fall from his face and neck to the floor. One drop of blood joined them from a small cut in his lower lip.

He looked over his shoulder and saw the woman crouching in front of the sink. She stared at him with gaping eyes wild with fear.

Waving toward the window, McNolte said, "Go! Go! I'll be right behind you."

She got up on the toilet quickly, leaned over the edge of the window with arms hanging out, then dropped her feet from the toilet. The toes of her sneakers kicked the wall as she pulled herself through the window clumsily, feet rising higher and higher, kicking and kicking, until they slipped out the window.

There followed the muffled sound of her body falling onto something wet and pliable.

McNolte got to his feet and tried to keep steady as he stepped over to the window, pulled himself up with his hands, got his arms out, then used his elbows to drag himself through.

He landed beside her in a garbage bin filled with old food and trash from Wee's kitchen. The stench made his stomach turn over.

Rain pelted his sweaty face. Ice-cold rain. It seemed to cut through his skin like the bullets from which they had been running.

The woman was already clambering out of the bin.

"You have a car?" she said, shouting to be heard above the relentless rainfall.

McNolte forced himself up and out of the bin even though he felt weak and shaky all over. Even so, he felt marginally better than he had inside. Standing beside the woman, he looked around them. They were in the alley that ran beside Wee's Café, and directly across from them was a dirty, graffiti-marred brick wall.

McNolte was winded and tried to catch his breath as he spoke. "A car? You kidding? If I could...afford a car...I'd drive the hell outta this city...and never come back."

It was not until that moment that McNolte realized the shooting had stopped. Cries and screams came from inside, voices that cut through the sound of pouring rain like knives.

McNolte was soaked. He had left his coat behind in the booth inside and his clothes were drenched, clinging to his body uncomfortably.

"Are you all right?" the woman said.

"I...think so. I was feeling pretty bad for a while, there, but now I'm—"

"I'm sorry!" she shouted, pressing clenched fists to her temples. "I'm so sorry, really. That was my fault. I didn't mean to, but I got so scared that I couldn't control it, and it just came out." She dropped her fists and turned to him with a look of anguish. "I'm so sorry, I really am. I'm just...glad it wasn't worse."

He cocked his head and frowned at her. "Worse? You couldn't control what? What the hell are you talking about?"

"I'm just sorry, that's all," she said, turning away from him, then gasping as she stared at the window through which they had just escaped.

Black smoke was beginning to ooze out of the small, rectangular opening.

"Oh, shit," McNolte said. He said it with sadness, but not without surprise. In a greasy spoon like Wee's Café, it was not surprising that the kind of pandemonium that had just broken out in there would end with a fire, most likely in the kitchen. Probably a grease fire, which could not always be readily extinguished. Especially by people who had been shot. He feared anyone who had not been killed by the bullets would be trapped by the fire, and he felt an instant urge to help them, to help get any survivors out before the fire got too big.

But he thought of that man in the white surgical mask with the machine gun. He was still around, not far away, and his target was pretty obvious: he was after the woman.

"Come on," he said, grabbing her hand. He led her in a hurry along the alley toward the front of the diner, toward 12th Street. "I live a block from here."

They hurried along 12th, hands clasped, and rushed up the steps of McNolte's building and through the entrance, up the stairs to his floor. He did not let go of her hand as he struggled in his soaked pocket for the keys, pulled them out, fumbled for the right one, then opened the door. He released her hand then and pushed her into the apartment, his hand flat against the back of her wet rubber poncho. He followed her in, slammed the door behind him, and flipped the light switch.

"Hello, McNolte," a voice said.

He looked past the woman at the smiling man sitting in his old, worn recliner.

It was Milo. He held a gun in his right hand, and in his left, the apartment's light reflected dully on the surface of the short, thick blades of the pruning shears he held.

18.

TAKING CARE OF BUSINESS

"Hello, Milo," McNolte said. "You look like a duffle bag."

The skinny young man was dressed in a baggy black suit with a black shirt and a narrow tie the color of dried blood. The baggy coat and pants were covered with little zippered and snapped pockets. He sat in the recliner, feet up. His overcoat was draped over the back of the chair. The zippers dangled and glinted as he sat up in the recliner, then stood, letting the gun hang at his side in his right hand. He made sure McNolte saw the pruning shears in his left hand. With thumb and fingers hooked through the handles, Milo chittered the blades open and closed rapidly several times, making sharp, metallic biting sounds.

"Yeah, well," Milo drawled, smirking, "you look like your evening's ruined."

"You're too late for that, Milo, believe me," McNolte said with a humorless chuckle. He turned to the woman and saw that the nervous fear had returned to her face, tightening her features.

"I figure I don't have to tell you why I'm here," Milo said, pacing slowly in front of the recliner, a few steps in each direction.

McNolte took the woman's elbow and led her toward the kitchen, whispering to her, "I'm sorry. Just bear with me, here." He took her around the short, stubby bar that was the only thing dividing the kitchen and living room in the small apartment. He led her to the small stove, put both hands on her shoulders, and said in a soft breath, "Stay right here." Then he turned and faced Milo, who was already sitting at the bar in one of the tall aluminum chairs, his left elbow propped on the edge, pruning shears clearly visible. He smiled, flashing his silver tooth.

"Maybe you weren't listening," Milo said. "You know why I'm here, right?"

McNolte went to the bar. "You want money."

"Very good. Tell him what he's won, Johnny!" He laughed at his little joke.

"I have money."

"Oh, really? You have all the money?"

Fear pierced McNolte's gut. "Not...*all* of the money. But you know every time you come I have money for you, right?"

"Look, McNolte, I'm just takin' care of business, right? You know my boss. His patience lasts only so long. So don't jerk me around, okay? I mean, I got better things to do with my time, too."

"Milo, what more can I do?" McNolte asked quietly, spreading his arms as if in surrender. "You know I don't have the balance, I can't get that kind of money together. The payments are the best I can do."

"Well, my boss thinks you can do a lot more. That's why I'm here." He raised the shears, aimed them at McNolte, and clapped them open and closed a few times.

The high, sharp, metallic sound made McNolte's scrotum shrivel as he imagined one of his fingers between the thick, powerful blades. He shuddered uncontrollably.

"I've got money in my closet. I'll get it for you, right now." McNolte's own words frightened him; he did not have very much money in the closet, just cash he had been setting aside for himself from every story payment, every advance, just a little from each so he would always have something for groceries when he needed it, and when Milo saw exactly how little there was, McNolte was afraid he would start using those shears.

Milo stood slowly, his heavy-lidded eyes giving away nothing. He shrugged with one shoulder. "Fine with me. Money's money, right?"

With a sigh of relief, McNolte hurried over to the closet,

opened the door, reached in and pulled the chain that turned on the light. A footstool stood in the middle of the closet so he could get to the top shelf, and he stepped up.

"Course, I'm not gonna make any promises," Milo sneered, snapping the shears a few times. "I mean, the boss wants it all. Everything you owe. Otherwise, he wouldn't have sent me over here with these." A single clack of the blades emphasized his words.

McNolte nearly fell off the stool when he heard that last sound. He knew the amount of money he had would not even come close to satisfying Milo if Mr. Trafficante had decided he wanted the rest of the money owed.

"It'll just take a second," he said, his voice hollow and rough, hoarse. "I've got it in a box up here. You can take all of it, Milo, all of it."

"Yeah, sure," Milo said. And his chuckle made McNolte's blood curdle.

Emma moved slowly away from the stove and made her way silently to the side of the young man in the black suit with all the zippers and snaps. As she stood beside him, she turned her head only slightly and looked at him from the corner of her eye.

The heavy, half-closed lids of his eyes reminded her, somehow, in an upside-down way, of Rupert, Landon's big iguana, right after he'd had a couple of sandwiches and some potato chips. But unlike Rupert, Milo gave her the creeps. He radiated smirking menace the way a space heater radiated warmth.

She looked down at his hands, at the gun and the shears. The gun she understood, but the shears...they were simply frightening.

Emma knew what she had to do, but she could not do it in such close proximity to McNolte. She had to get this Milo creature away from McNolte so she could deal with him herself.

"You're a little behind the times, aren't you, McNolte?" Milo said. "Keeping your money in a closet, I mean? You know, they got these places for that now. Whole buildings." He laughed again, amused at himself.

Sounding distracted, Milo said, "Well, I figure there's no sense in opening an account if I can't—"

Emma moved quickly, while McNolte was talking and Milo was listening to him. She threw herself on the closet door and slammed it shut before McNolte finished his sentence. Then she spun around to face Milo, her back pressed against the door.

His eyes were still half-closed as he looked at her with only the vaguest hint of surprise.

"That chair!" she blurted, pointing at the chair he had been sitting in at the bar. "Give it to me!"

"Hey, what the hell're you doing?" McNolte asked from inside the closet.

"Hurry!" she hissed at Milo. "Give it to me!"

He stared at her as if she had spoken in a foreign tongue.

"Damn!" she barked, running to the chair herself as sounds of movement came from behind the closet door. She grabbed it, took it back to the closet, and wedged the back of it hard beneath the doorknob. Then she turned to Milo again.

"The hell're you doing?" he said. He no longer sounded relaxed; now he sounded suspicious.

"You want your money?" she said. "I mean, all of it? He's just jerking you around, you know. I know where he *really* keeps the money. I mean, the big money. The money he doesn't want you to know about. All of it."

"Who the hell're you?" he said, eyebrows rising high above his sleepy eyes.

She rushed him, stopped an inch from his face, and he did not even flinch. They were eye to eye. She clenched her teeth and said, "I'm his ex-girlfriend. And the money's in the recliner. You were sitting on it, asshole."

He pondered that as he stared at her for a while, then: "What do you mean, it's in the recliner?"

"What did I just say? Did I stutter? I mean, yes, it's *inside* the recliner, you moron. Now, do you want it? Or do you want me to let him out so you can listen to his crap and be jerked around for a while longer?"

He turned and looked at the recliner, then at her, then at the recliner again.

"Okay," he said, nodding slowly. "I'll take a look."

Milo walked crab-like to the recliner, glancing repeatedly at Emma with suspicion. He tossed the pruning shears onto the sofa, then pushed the recliner onto its side with his foot. It fell with a thump, and somewhere inside, a weary spring twanged.

Emma walked toward him until only the recliner separated them. She hoped she was a safe distance from McNolte, who was pounding on the closet door from inside, cursing angrily.

"So where is it?" Milo asked. "In a box? A bag? What?"

Emma did not respond. She simply stared at him, focusing. Flaming.

"Hey, you deaf, or something?" he said. Perspiration was beginning to shine on his forehead. He swayed slightly, reached up and ran a hand down his face. He began to look pale, and a little worried.

Emma did not want to kill the guy, but he had to be taken out of the way fast. If he died as a result...well, she would feel bad. But not for long. Recently, Emma had passed a point of no return. She was far more concerned with survival than with morality.

"Hey..." His voice grew thick and ill-sounding. He frowned at her, eyes widening slightly beneath his furrowed brow. "What...what're you...doing to me?" he whispered.

She did not respond right away because she was too busy concentrating hard on what she was doing. Then, as he began to sway like a drunk, she said, "Just takin' care of business, Mr. Lizard."

About ten seconds later, Milo fell forward onto the overturned recliner with an ugly exhalation. His gun slipped from his hand and thumped to the carpet.

"Let me *out* of here, dammit!" McNolte shouted.

And she did.

McNolte rushed out of the closet as soon as the door opened, breathless and sticky with sweat. He had begun to feel claustrophobic and a little panicky; he was glad to see his living room again.

"What the hell was that all about?" he said. He looked at the woman, then turned around, looking for Milo.

He found him.

"My God," McNolte muttered, staring at Milo, walking around him with caution. "What...what did you do to him?"

"Do you really want to help me?" she said, approaching him. She stopped directly in front of him. They were no more than two inches apart. "*Do* you?"

McNolte took a moment to gather his thoughts. He had been locked in the closet, then had come out to find Milo lying unconscious on his overturned recliner. He shook his head in a jerky motion, like a cartoon character after being clobbered with a giant mallet.

The woman stood before him, darting eyes burning with fear, hands clutched together over her abdomen as her weight shifted back and forth from one foot to the other.

Her desperation was palpable, her fear a hot, foul breath in his face.

He looked at Milo, limp on the recliner, then turned again to the woman's face, raw with pleading.

"Is he dead?" McNolte said.

"No, just unconscious."

"What did you do to him?"

"Never mind. Do you want to help me or not?"

"Yes, I want to help you. But I don't understand what—"

"Then we have to leave. Right now. We have to get out of the city."

"What? You want to leave the city?"

"You have people after you, I have people after me. Isn't that right?"

"Where would we go?" He was not sure why he asked the question because leaving the city was absurd. He was still in the process of putting his life back together, and that life was right there, in the city. He did not know why he bothered to ask, but he was so caught up in her fear and desperation that it had come naturally.

"Who cares?" she said. "What difference does it make? Someplace far away enough so they can't find us. Anyplace. Someplace they wouldn't think to look. Right? Doesn't that sound good? I mean, I can't...do this...alone. I don't want to. I'm afraid. I'm going whether you come with me or not, but...I'm afraid."

McNolte placed his hands on her shoulders. "Who's after you?"

"That doesn't matter right now. We don't have time for talk. I can tell you later, I'll tell you *everything*. But not until we're on our way to someplace *else*. If they could find me in that diner, they can find me here."

McNolte squeezed her shoulders gently. They were warm beneath his hands. "Look, maybe that's not necessary. Leaving the city, I mean. I can't just pick up and...*go*. See, I know who's after me, I know what they want and what to expect from them. I've been dealing with it for a long time. But you...maybe we don't have to leave the city."

Her mouth opened to respond when a key rattled in the lock of the door.

McNolte was shocked when she released a sharp gasp, fell on him, and wrapped her arms around him, clinging tightly.

He turned to see P.W. enter the apartment with a smile, turn, and close the door.

P.W. said, "Sorry I took so long, but I was—" He froze when he saw Milo draped over the recliner. "Well, shit on a stick. Did I miss somethin'?"

McNolte welcomed the distraction. He turned to P.W. and said, "Look, we're gonna need a ride right away. To South Street."

"Okay, fine." He looked at Emma. "Who's this?"

McNolte turned to her and said, "Um...I don't know. Who are you?"

"My name is Emma," she said, sounding weak, deflated.

"And who the hell is *that*?" P.W. said, pointing at Milo.

"That's the guy I told you about. Milo."

"What'd you do to him?"

"It wasn't—" McNolte glanced at Emma and the look in her eyes, at once pleading and threatening, made him snap his mouth shut. Then he said, "Well, it wasn't easy, P.W."

P.W. looked at Emma with vague suspicion.

"We've got to get out of here, P.W.," McNolte said. "Emma's got somebody after her and I've got, well, an unconscious Milo on my hands."

P.W. said, "Okay, you wanna go? Fine. But let's take care of some bidness first."

He walked around them to get to Milo, leaned down and picked up Milo's gun from the floor, examining it carefully. ".45 automatic," he muttered. "Colt Commander. Well, this pup's gotta have some extra clips on him if he's any good at what he does." He leaned over Milo's still form and reached beneath his jacket, feeling around his waist. "Ah-hah," he said, standing. He held up two clips for McNolte and Emma to see. "Toldja." He slipped them into the pocket of his down jacket, then slid the gun beneath the waist of his jeans in the small of his back beneath his jacket. "Okay, then, grab whatever you need and let's hit the road. We'll talk in the car."

P.W. was no longer smiling. With more authority than McNolte had ever seen the man exhibit, he led them out of the apartment.

19.

AN ORAL REPORT

"I'm telling you, nobody got out of that place alive," Dunne said, his voice metallic and pinched over the speaker phone. In the background, sirens wailed and distant voices shouted. "There were only three other customers, plus people working in the back. Anybody I didn't hit died in that fire, Mr. Shaw, I swear. The place went up like a dead tree struck by lightning, and it's still blazing."

"But did you hit *her*?" Landon Shaw said as he pressed his fingertips hard into his temples and rubbed them in small circles. He sat in the back seat of a moving limousine with a pounding headache, mouth chalky from the four aspirin tablets he had just chewed up, which would play hell with his stomach if he did not get some food down soon.

Normally, he would rather die than have someone else drive him around; Shaw felt more comfortable behind the wheel of one of his cars than he did anywhere else in the world. But he had not felt like driving since his encounter with Emma. He had been unable to sleep knowing things were slipping between his fingers, just easing out of his control with each hour. He had just left a meeting after getting the call that she had been found in the city, so he had called for his Mercedes limo and one of his assistants, Edgar. It was not so bad—after all, the limo was his, and so was Edgar—but it wasn't the same as having his own hands on the wheel, his foot on the accelerator, comfortably in control.

Through the tinted window on his left, Shaw could see the

blood-red glow of the fire in the distance, oozing into the black sky.

"I don't give a damn about anyone else in there," he shouted at the speaker phone. "Only *her.*"

"I was right outside the window from her and that guy she was with," Dunne replied.

"Yes. That guy. I hope you got him, too, Dunne, whoever the hell he was, I hope you got him, too."

"Like I said, Mr. Shaw, she's gone. He's gone. The two guys sitting at the counter are gone. Everybody in that place is gone. They all had their last meal, whether they were eating it or cooking it."

"You're sure you didn't attract attention? With the gunfire, I mean?"

"I used the silencer, like you said. Nobody noticed. The traffic was loud."

"All right, Dunne, all right. Good job. Now go home and make yourself scarce. I'll call you when I need you."

"Sure, Mr. Shaw."

There was a click, followed by the hollow burr of the dial tone.

Shaw leaned forward and punched a button hard with a knuckle, cutting the connection. Picking up the remote, he turned on the small TV set before him and changed to a local channel.

"...burning steadily in spite of the pouring rain," a female voice said as the picture materialized rapidly on the screen. "Firefighters continue to battle the flames in an effort to keep the entire block from being consumed by the blaze."

The voice spoke over live footage of the fire. Shaw watched as great arcs of water were sprayed over the raging flames consuming what had once been a small greasy spoon diner.

Shaw looked out the window again, searching for the fire's glow, but he could not see it from inside the limousine anymore.

That was okay. He knew it was there.

He felt much better than he had felt in days. The thunderous ache in his head began to back off; he could feel it receding as he relaxed, relief flowing through his body like a soothing balm. Hunger struck him abruptly. He was ravenous. He hit the intercom button.

"Head for the wharf, Edgar," he said. "I want to go to Caldoni's for dinner."

"Yes, sir," Edgar said.

Shaw leaned back with the beginnings of a smile on his face. Although the wharf was, at all hours of the day and night, teeming with tourists and made up mostly of shops and attractions designed to drain their pocketbooks, there was, nestled in its tacky environs, the best seafood restaurant in the city, which served the best lobster dishes Shaw had ever eaten anywhere. His mouth watered as he thought of the lobster at Caldoni's, not to mention the delectable fresh-made bread and the sumptuous shrimp cocktails.

The problem was taken care of, and Shaw found himself feeling uncharacteristically calm. He looked forward to savoring that feeling over a delicious meal.

20.

ANOTHER ORAL REPORT

Milo sat in a chair in front of Mr. Trafficante's desk, waiting, trying to pull himself back from whatever pit he had been thrown into earlier.

He still felt queasy. His head did not seem to be attached to his neck correctly and everything still had a vague slant to it. There was still a fluttering feeling in his chest, as if his heart had been removed and replaced with a hummingbird whose wings fluttered at a blur against his rib cage; his heart was not beating fast, but that feeling remained unshakable, as if he had not yet recovered from a tremendous shock.

But there had been no shock. It had been something else far more disturbing than a simple shock.

Mr. Trafficante's office was huge and everything about it exuded power. Milo had been there only three times before, and it always made him nervous. He was especially anxious now because he was supposed to report his meeting with McNolte to one of Mr. Trafficante's assistants by phone, not by making a personal appearance in his office, and during a party yet.

Sitting in his boss's office, Milo could hear the thumping bass of a live band in another part of the house. And if he listened closely enough, he could hear the murmur of voices out there, talking, laughing, occasionally shrieking with delight.

All that noise outside the office made Milo even more nervous than he felt already.

He was not looking forward to telling Mr. Trafficante what he had come to tell him. But the experience had been so bizarre that he felt it was worth showing up and telling him in person.

Mr. Trafficante's enormous desk hunkered before Milo and appeared to stare at him. It was mahogany with intricate faces and figures carved into the side panels—faces both mournful and laughing, naked bodies that stretched their arms upward and reclined lasciviously—and they all seemed to stare at him with silent accusations.

Milo did not need any wooden faces giving him grief. He was certain he would get plenty of that from Mr. Trafficante for not coming back with a big chunk of McNolte's money.

The office door opened and the party sounds became much louder for a brief moment, only to be muffled again with the sound of the heavy wooden door closing.

"I hope you realize, Milo, that I'm having a party," Mr. Trafficante said as he went behind his desk and lowered himself into his chair. He leaned forward and put his elbows on the desktop, the white cuffs of his shirt standing out against the dark sleeves of his suit coat. He folded his hands on the desk and said, "What the hell's going on, Milo, that you had to see me tonight? You have any problems with McNolte?"

"Oh, God, Mr. Trafficante," Milo said, his words slurring. He reached up and rubbed his eyes with his left hand while massaging his temple with the fingertips of his right. "I'm not sure what happened, sir, but...I know there's a problem."

"He give you any money?"

"Well, he was...going to."

"Milo, what the hell's wrong with you. You look like shit. Have you been drinking?"

"No, sir. I've been...sick."

"Look, I'm throwing a party. You know who I've got out there right now? I've got movie stars and politicians out there, right now, waiting for me. Because I'm their host. But I'm in here. With you. Which means I'm not being a very good host, and that means you're skating on thin ice. You wanna tell me what the hell's going on, or not?"

"He's got a woman with him," Milo said, letting his hands drop heavily from his face and looking Mr. Trafficante, finally, in the eyes. "She says she's his ex-girlfriend, but if that's true, then

I don't know what she was doing with him tonight. Anyway, this woman...she did something. To me."

Trafficante pulled his head back sharply and frowned. "What do you mean, she *did* something to you? What'd she do, kick you in the nuts?"

Milo shook his head slowly and weakly. "No, sir, Mr. Trafficante, she didn't even touch me. I mean...she didn't...*touch* me. But still, she...*did* something to me. To my head. She made me sick. Made my nose bleed. Made me pass out."

"What are you talking about? You're saying she...what? Put a curse on you, or something?"

"No, no, she...I don't know, Mr. Trafficante. She told me the money was inside the recliner, and the last thing I remember, I was about to look for it when I got really sick really fast, and she's standing there staring at me like some kinda freak in a horror movie. I asked her, I says, what're you doing to me, and she says, 'Just taking care of business, Mr. Lizard.' And the next thing I know, I'm waking up on top of that recliner, and everybody's gone. They're just...*gone*. I looked at a clock and saw I was out for nearly an hour. An *hour*! I-I...I really don't know what she did, Mr. Trafficante, and I know it sounds crazy, but...she *did* something to me."

Behind the desk, Mr. Trafficante seemed to relax. His large shoulders slouched a bit and he leaned back in his leather-upholstered chair, folded his arms over his big chest as he muttered under his breath, "Mr. Lizard...Mr. Lizard..." He tilted his head to one side, eyes never leaving Milo, and became much more interested. "Tell you what, Milo. I want you to tell me everything that happened to you tonight. I want you to start at the beginning and go through every detail, until you got here."

Trafficante's request made Milo even more nervous. He was certain there was some sinister purpose behind Mr. Trafficante's sudden interest, and he was certain it had something to do with his, Milo's, failure to come back with a handful of money.

"Look, Mr. Trafficante, I know what I was supposed to do, but this woman, she really—"

"Milo, I'm not interested right now in what you were *supposed* to do. I'm interested in what you *did*. I'm interested in what happened, and especially in this woman. This ex-girlfriend."

Milo's mouth worked uselessly for a moment as he stared across the massive desk at his boss. Finally, he blurted, "Buh-but Mr. Trafficante, you've got movie stars and politicians waiting—"

"For the time being, I'm more interested in you and what you have to say. And to show you just how interested I am, I'm going to have some of the fantastic shrimp out there brought in here, and over that shrimp and a couple of drinks, you're going to tell me everything. Leave out nothing."

Mr. Trafficante leaned forward, hit a button on his speaker phone and asked that some shrimp be brought into his office.

They had drinks as well, as promised—expensive single malt scotch.

And Milo told him everything.

21.

LATE BREAKING NEWS

Landon Shaw knew that, because of his indulgence at Caldoni's, his insides would be screaming later that night, but he did not care. The extravagant meal he had just eaten had been worth whatever gastrointestinal grief he would have to endure later.

He ducked out of the pouring rain and slid into the backseat of his limousine, leaning back with a contented sigh as Edgar closed the door. Quickly rounding the rear of the car, Edgar collapsed the umbrella he had held over Shaw's head on the way from the restaurant to the limo, and got behind the wheel.

"Take me home, Edgar," Shaw said into the intercom.

"Yes, sir, Mr. Shaw."

Shaw settled himself comfortably into the seat with a gentle sigh as the engine started and the Mercedes pulled away from the curb. The rain made a quiet roar on the roof of the car. It was a soothing sound and Shaw leaned his head back, closed his eyes, and enjoyed it. Even with the windows rolled up, even in the pouring rain, he could smell the aromas of the wharf and hear its sounds; the salty scent of the sidewalk seafood stands, the smell of barbecue from the rib joint across the street from Caldoni's, the exhaust from the cars and buses that clogged the street, the muffled calliope music from the carousel on Pier 19, and the incessant barking of the sea lions that gathered around the pier, waiting to be fed by gawking tourists.

Shaw decided he would sleep in tomorrow, take the whole day off. After all he had been through, he deserved that. The last few days had been horrendously stressful and he was exhausted, completely drained. A day lounging around the house would do him good.

Slumped in the seat, he reached up and loosened his tie, unbuttoned his collar and pulled it away from his throat with two fingers. He opened his eyes and stared at the dead television screen before him, wondering what was going on with the fire in town. He lifted his foot and carefully tapped the button with the toe of his shoe.

"—fire that destroyed a small diner and the abandoned warehouse directly behind it," the male reporter was saying. At the bottom of the screen, white block letters identified the reporter as CHUCK DEKKER, who was reporting LIVE for ACTION 2 NEWS. Holding an umbrella over his head, he shouted into the microphone he held to his mouth, trying to be heard over the downpour as well as the commotion behind him, where flames still roared in spite of the rain and the firefighters still battling to extinguish them. "We want to ask our viewers once again, please, do not come near this part of the city. Although the fire in the restaurant has been extinguished, the warehouse is still ablaze. We've had a problem with sightseers, but they've all been sent away. Not only do we still have a fire burning here, but the police have cordoned off the scene of the shooting. The entire area has been blocked off, so it's impossible to get within two blocks of the scene of the crime."

Shaw felt his body grow slowly and steadily rigid. He felt his insides shift around, the first signs that his ill-tempered stomach was waking up from its slumber.

The scene of the shooting? he asked himself silently. *The scene of the crime?*

"What crime?" he muttered. "What fucking crime?"

The camera cut to a shot of the anchor desk, where a Latino man and Asian woman sat watching Chuck Dekker on a monitor set in the wall behind them.

"Chuck?" the male anchor said solemnly. "Can you tell us if the police have gathered any further details about the shooting?"

"No, Rico," Chuck replied, pressing four fingers over the small receiver in his ear, "the police really know little more than they've already told us. To recap, there was a shooting at Wee's Café, but we don't know yet if it was a robbery, or perhaps gang related—we just don't know. Some people who were nearby, right here on this very block, came forward to say that they heard what sounded like machine gun fire, and it appears that at least four victims suffered gunshot wounds, including the only survivor of the fire."

"Survivor?" Shaw croaked as he ran a hand nervously through his hair, licking his suddenly dry lips.

"As you might expect," Chuck continued, "there's been a great deal of confusion around here, but I actually had the opportunity to speak with that survivor briefly a few minutes ago, just before she was put into an ambulance and taken to the hospital. Her name is Pamela Connor, a waitress at Wee's Café. Uh, I think that tape is—" He looked at someone off camera for a moment, then nodded. "—yes, that tape is ready, so why don't we have a look at it now."

"Son of a *bitch*," Shaw growled as he leaned forward even further, the burning ache in his gut growing steadily worse.

The anchor desk was replaced by a full-screen shot of Chuck Dekker hurrying toward a transport gurney at the back of an open ambulance. An EMT was leaning into the ambulance, his back to the woman stretched out with a white sheet over her. The camera jittered as the operator jogged behind Chuck Dekker, finally stopping to look down over the reporter's shoulder at the woman on the gurney.

Her face was blackened around her mouth and nose and her eyes were swollen. There was blood on the gurney around her right shoulder

"Miss, can you tell us what happened?" Chuck Dekker said, holding the microphone close to her face.

Her head rolled back and forth slowly and her red, moist eyes blinked.

"Somebody...shot at us," she said, her voice weak. "And then...the fire started."

"Why was someone shooting at the diner?"

She shook her head and made an inarticulate "I don't know" sound.

"Did anyone get out of the building? Are there any survivors besides yourself?"

Shaw's hands curled into fists as he leaned even closer to the television, waiting for her answer.

She tried to speak, stopped to lick her lips, then said, "One of...the regulars. McNolte. And some...woman."

"Can you tell us why the—"

"Hey!" the EMT barked at the reporter. "What the hell you think you're doing? This is an injured woman, here. Get the hell outta here, now." He was joined by another EMT, and they quickly hefted the gurney into the ambulance and slammed the doors.

"Oh, my God," Shaw said, his voice a low, dry rumble as he fell backward into the seat. He ran his right hand through his hair and grabbed a clump of it, holding tightly as he hissed, "Oh, my *God*."

The news broadcast had cut back to the anchor desk, but Shaw was paying no attention now. He sat clutching his hair with one hand while the other moved to his stomach, which was beginning to bubble and roll with molten lava.

Suddenly, he let go of his hair, jerked forward, hit the button on the speaker phone and punched in seven numbers.

"Yeah," Dunne said after three rings.

"Are you watching the news?" Shaw said hoarsely, his breath short.

"No. Should I?"

"You're goddamned *right* you should."

Dunne's casual tone became tense. "Hey, Mr. Shaw, what is it? What's the matter?"

"You fucked up, *that's* what's the matter. At least three people got out of that diner."

Dunne gasped and sputtered. "B-but...huh-how can that be? How do you know?"

"Because unlike you, *I* watch the fucking news. I found this out from the waitress who survived. Along with her were a man and woman. My God, I thought this was over and done with, taken care of, I've actually been *relaxing*, for Christ's sake, while she's out there somewhere, getting father away every minute."

A tense silence stretched out over the speaker phone. When Dunne spoke, it was with a formal stiffness.

"What would you like me to do, Mr. Shaw?"

Shaw's hand clenched and unclenched again and again as he thought. Finally, he snapped. "She's in one of the hospitals. Find out which one. Then get the doc. Tell him the situation and he'll know what to do. I'm going home. If anything goes wrong, call me, understand?"

"I understand, Mr. Shaw."

"Hell, call me no matter what. I won't sleep until I hear from you. Call me the second it's done, all right? *Understand*?"

"Sure thing, Mr. Shaw. I'll call you."

Shaw hit the button on the speaker phone with the side of his fist, then pressed the intercom button.

"Edgar, I want security doubled on the house immediately until further notice. Call ahead. I want that place air-tight by the time I get there."

"Yes, Mr. Shaw."

Shaw threw himself back into the seat hard, folding his arms tightly over his chest as he turned his attention back to the television."

"—can only hope that Pamela Connor, the only survivor to whom police have access," the male anchor was saying, "will be able to shed some light on this tragedy, and perhaps even identify the shooter for—"

Shaw lifted his foot unsteadily and poked at the button to turn off the television, but he missed. Once, twice, a third time, his foot trembling. Finally, he released an angry growl through clenched teeth and stabbed his heel through the small picture tube with a thick *whump* sound. Shaw sat stiffly in the seat, staring as thin tendrils of smoke curled slowly from the jagged opening.

After a full minute had passed, Shaw hit the intercom and said, "Edgar?"

"Yes, Mr. Shaw?"

"As soon as you drop me off...get a new TV for the car."

22.

QUESTIONS

Willy leaned back in his chair at his desk and folded his arms across his big chest, looking somber.

"What do we do, P.W.?" he said quietly, almost as if McNolte and Emma were not in the room with them.

Emma was seated in one of the folding chairs while McNolte stood beside her leaning against the wall.

P.W. stood casually in front of Willy's desk. He took his time lighting a cigarette, then took a couple of puffs before responding, wearing his happy smile the whole time.

"Well, I'll tell ya, Willy," P.W. said, "I wasn't there and I still don't know what they did to that little guy. They took care of him really good, but..." He turned his head to look at McNolte and Emma. "...they won't tell me how they did it. Will ya?"

McNolte looked down at Emma. He could tell she knew he was looking at her because her shoulders stiffened slightly. She did not make eye contact.

"You saw him, P.W.," McNolte said. "He had a bloody nose. He was out like a light. It wasn't easy, like I said, because...well, I'm just not much of a fighter, but, uh..." McNolte left his words dangling in mid-air, unfinished, because of the way P.W. was looking at him.

P.W. kept smiling, but it changed just a bit, became a *secret* smile, one that told McNolte that P.W. knew he was not telling the truth, and McNolte *knew* that P.W. knew it. He turned to Willy again.

"Whatever they did to that little fella," he said, "I can tell you this. He'll be back. And there'll probably be more with him. The guy—what was his name?"

"Milo," McNolte said.

"—he had a pair of prunin' shears. For McNolte's fingers."

"So if we keep them here, there might be trouble, right?" Willy said.

P.W. shrugged. "Oh, there's gonna be trouble, yeah. These guys've already connected McNolte to this place. They might already be here, for all we know. As many people move in and out those doors here day and night, we'd never know. Somebody could be here now, waiting for the right moment. But that don't mean we can't hide 'em here. For a while, anyway." He turned to Emma. "Now...our new friend Emma, here...I'm not sure about her, 'cause I don't know what the hell she's runnin' from."

Willy leaned forward, put his elbows on the edge of his cluttered desktop and turned to McNolte. "Well?"

McNolte shrugged. "I don't know what to tell you, Willy. I don't know any more about her than you do."

It was true, he did not. Emma had not spoken a word in P.W.'s car all the way to South Street. He had asked her question after question—"Who was the guy with the gun? Why was he trying to kill you? What does he want? What have you done?"— but she had sat slumped in the back seat, staring out the window blankly, silently, as if she were in some kind of trance. At one point, he reached out to touch her shoulder to get her attention, but then remembered how much she disliked being touched and snapped his hand back and put it in his lap. Once he had decided he was going to get no information from her, he wondered what the hell he was going to tell Willy once they got to South Street.

McNolte was wondering that now as he stared at the large minister behind his messy desk.

"She won't tell me anything," McNolte said, glancing at Emma. "We nearly died in Wee's tonight and it was because somebody was trying to kill her, but she won't tell me who or why or...anything." He said the last word with a sigh in his voice. "I just met her. I don't know anything about her. I don't even know—"

"Okay, okay, McNolte," Willy said, "this isn't the McCarthy hearing, so let's go easy on our friend, here." His eyes moved to Emma, who looked at no one and nothing in particular. She seemed to have shriveled up in her poncho, as if hoping everyone simply would forget she was there. He stood, walked around the desk and crossed the small office, stopping before her. "Emma?" he said, his deep, resonant voice now soft and gentle as he smiled tentatively. "I hope you don't mind if I call you Emma, but I don't know what else to call you. Unless you'll tell me."

She did not look at him, did not move.

He spoke slowly as he continued: "You know, we can help you. We want to do our best to protect you. But Emma, you need to understand...first we have to know what we're protecting you *from* before we can do it effectively."

She turned her head slowly to the left, then slowly to the right. But she did not look at him or speak.

"Please understand, Emma, I'm your friend," Willy said. "I want very much to help you. That's all we do here. It's our job. It's what I've devoted my life to, and I really—"

"You can't help me, nobody can help me." She ran her words together into one long word as she shot to her feet and rushed toward the door of the office.

McNolte stepped in front of the door and put his hands on Emma's shoulders, bringing her to a clumsy stop directly in front of him.

"Wait, Emma, please," he said, but she fell away from him, slamming her back into the wall as she said in a high, quiet voice, "Don't touch me, please, don't touch me! I-I'm scared and I'm up-upset, so pluh-please don't tuh-touch me!"

McNolte looked first at Willy, then at P.W., both of whom were staring at Emma with deep frowns; even P.W.'s seemingly relentless smile had disappeared.

Willy stood slowly, stepped around the desk, and approached Emma cautiously, arms spread, palms open upward in a gesture of surrender.

"Look, dear," he said, "I don't know exactly what your problem is, but I've seen enough of them to have an idea, and

I want to tell you something. We've helped a lot of battered women here. We've given them shelter until they could get their lives together. We've protected them from their husbands and even helped put some of those husbands away. So, Emma, you're really in the best possible place you could—"

"You don't understand, it's not that kind of problem," she said, pressing herself even harder against the wall, as if she were hoping to disappear into it.

"The details don't matter," Willy said, stopping a couple of feet from her. He smiled gently and his voice was low and warm. "I *want* you to stay here so we can take care of you. But it would be a big help if you told us—"

"You wouldn't *believe* me!" she shouted.

All three men flinched at the sharp sound of her voice in the small office, but none of them spoke.

"Look," P.W. said quietly, "if we're gonna tuck you two away, we're gonna have to do it fast. Like I said, they might already be here in the building. Now, my idea is, we hide you both down in the basement until we can find someplace to take you, and in the meantime, we watch everybody who comes in the door closely. Look for somebody who seems to be looking for something or someone. But if we wait around much longer, we might as well not even try." He turned to Emma. "So, listen, young lady, you're gonna have to *talk* to us, do you understand."

Emma's eyes, wide and terrified, moved over their faces. "I'm getting upset," she whispered. "You're upsetting me. Please let me go, please, before I...hurt you. Please. I can't get upset. I don't want to hurt you."

Willy took a step toward her, but McNolte said, "Wait. Just a second, Willy." He turned to Emma and said, "Something happened when we were getting out of Wee's. I got sick for a few minutes in the restroom. I was dripping sweat and felt weak and shaky. You asked me about it once we were outside, and...you apologized for it. You said you didn't mean to, or you couldn't help yourself, something like that. Isn't that right?"

She nodded.

"I couldn't figure it out," McNolte went on. "Why you were apologetic, I mean. You couldn't have known I was sick...but you *did*. And you apologized as if it were your fault. As if you'd somehow done it to me."

She nodded again, once, slowly, then said, "You wouldn't believe me. I could tell you, but you'd think I was crazy. You'd... you'd probably call somebody, a doctor, or something...have me put in a hospital." Her eyes narrowed as she glared at McNolte. "I didn't want to come here in the first place. I wanted to get out of the city, but you dragged me *here*. Now, why don't you just let me out? Let me *go!*"

"Hey, whatever it is," McNolte said, "I'll believe you. I can't speak for them—" He gestured to P.W. and Willy. "—but *I* will listen and I'll believe you. Really, however weird your story is, it couldn't be any weirder than what we've been through tonight."

Willy said, "Really, dear, we've dealt with this kind of thing so many times before. If you'll just—"

"Hold it, Willy," McNolte said, raising a hand. "I have a feeling this isn't exactly the kind of thing you're used to dealing with here. Let me talk to her." He turned to Emma. "That's right, isn't it? This is something...unusual."

She did not take her eyes from him, but she said nothing. When he spoke again, he lowered his voice to little more than a whisper.

"Emma, you don't have anybody else. Like Willy says, you'd be surprised how safe this place is. That's why *I'm* here. Please, tell us. Who are you running from? What is it that you think we'll find so hard to believe?"

She licked her lips once, twice, chewed lightly on her lower lip for a moment. "That I can hurt you. If you upset me, I might... lose control, and you might get sick or...drop dead where you stand. You won't believe me until it happens, though. And I don't want that. Really, I don't want to hurt any of you."

"Is that what you did to Milo?" McNolte said.

She nodded cautiously. "I knew he was trouble. For you, I mean. And as long as we were together, that meant he was trouble for me, too, and I just couldn't take any more." She seemed to sag against the wall, as if her knees were giving out. "Not after...everything. I just couldn't take any more. But I didn't kill him. Because I tried not to. If I get angry, though...or scared...I don't know what I'll do. I'll lose control and...I could hurt all of you. Maybe even kill you."

"How?" McNolte said. "How would you do that?"

She lowered her eyes then, and McNolte was afraid she had decided not to answer, to say no more than she had said already.

"Please, Emma," he said, "tell us. We want to help you, and I know we can. But you've got to tell us."

Finally, she did. She told them everything.

Well...almost everything.

23.

THERAPY

Pamela Connor swam back and forth between sleep and consciousness, never knowing when she was peering into the murky dream world of her sleep or rising blearily into wakefulness. It was only after long minutes of trying to force her eyes to stay open, blinking rapidly, and licking her parched lips repeatedly, that she realized she was in no dream, no matter how much she wished she were.

She was in pain, and she was in a hospital. That was obvious from the long, rectangular lights overhead and the sheets on her bed, which were so crisp they nearly crunched beneath her when she moved. Another giveaway was the slender IV tube in her left arm. And the smell: the stinging odor of medicine and rubbing alcohol. It was a familiar smell. She had been in hospitals before, and like motel rooms and pizza parlors, they all smelled the same.

There was activity all around her, but she did not have the strength to lift her head to see what it was. She did not care, anyway. All that mattered was the incredible pain in her upper chest and left shoulder.

Once she was fully awake, though still groggy from anesthesia, she closed her eyes tightly and tried to remember what had happened that brought her to the crisp, clean bed and the bright room with the stinging odors.

But she could not. She kept dozing and waking, dozing and waking.

After a while, she realized her arms hurt. They did not just hurt, they burned. They felt twice their normal size, as if the skin were about to split open like that of an overboiled frankfurter. But even with the burning pain, Pamela dozed some more.

"Pamela," a soft, female voice said. When Pamela opened her eyes, a pleasant face appeared over her, hovering like dream image. "How do you feel?"

"I...hurt," Pamela said, her voice raspy, throat soar and dry.

"I'm not surprised. You've just had surgery."

"For...what?"

"The bullet that passed through you chipped your collarbone. A couple of bone fragments had to be removed."

Bullet? Pamela thought, confused. *I've been shot? Why? Who shot me? Where? When?*

A male voice began to groan from another part of the room.

"You're going to be fine, Pamela." The nurse continued to smile as the groaning male voice grew uglier. She glanced over her shoulder. "You just rest, and we'll take you to your room in just a little—"

The male voice vomited. The sound was unmistakable and was immediately followed by a wet splashing sound on the floor.

The nurse's smile disappeared and she said, "S'cuse me," then hurried away from Pamela's bed.

After that, Pamela fought to keep her eyes open as she struggled to remember what had happened. For just a fleeting instant, she thought she smelled something besides the chemicals in the air, something familiar, dark, and threatening. Smoke? Had she caught a whiff of smoke? The thought made her shudder, gave her goosebumps—but why?

It came to her as a hot knife of memory stabbing downward into the top of her skull, through the bone and into the soft tissue of her brain. Everything returned to her so quickly and vividly that, for a moment, she thought it was all happening again. Her heart pounded rapidly and her breath became short for a moment, then she slowly calmed.

Manuel! she thought, then said it out loud, struggling to lift her head off the pillow. "Man...uel? Manuel?"

A man leaned over her bed and smiled down at her. He had

curly gray hair, ruddy cheeks, and wore a white lab coat with a stethoscope dangling from around his neck.

"Miss Connor?"

Her voice was a croak. "Yes?"

"I'm Dexter, your respiratory therapist."

"Hi, Dex...ter."

"I know you don't feel like talking, but I want to examine you, make sure your lungs are still functioning properly, and ask you a few questions." He kept smiling as he fitted the stethoscope over his ears and pressed it to the top of her left breast. It was cold and made her body stiffen.

"Mm-hm," he muttered, moving it around on her chest, listening. "Mm-hm. Deep breath, please." She took a deep breath. He asked her to do it again, and she did. He lifted it from her chest and looked into her eyes, but left the stethoscope on her chest. "You were shot and burned in a fire, eh?"

"Yes. I need to...find out about Manuel. How is Manuel?"

"Who's Manuel?"

"My boyfriend. He w-worked in...the kitchen. At Wee's."

"I wouldn't know, Miss Connor. All I know is, you're an extremely lucky woman. Not many people survive a fire and a gunshot wound in one night, you know."

"But how is Manuel? Did he get out?" She tried to sit up as she began to cry. "Was he hurt bad? D-did he—"

"Sh-sh-sshh, you just calm down, now," he said, placing a hand gently on her right arm.

Pamela tried to relax and pull herself together, took a deep breath and stopped crying.

"Maybe I can ask around about Manuel," Dexter said. "Would that make you feel better?"

"Oh, yes, would you? Please?"

"I'm just the respiratory therapist, remember, but I'll see what I can do. First, I've got to finish with you."

He slipped the stethoscope underneath her, pressed it to her back, and asked for a couple more deep breaths. When the examination was finished, he said, "What about the others in the diner?"

"Others?"

"Well, yes, there were others, weren't there? What about the man in the back booth with the woman? Was he a regular?"

She frowned as she turned his questions over in her mind. Then: "Oh, you mean McNolte? Yeah, he was a regular."

"McNolte? What's his first name?"

"I don't know. Just...McNolte. I'm pretty sure he and that woman got out."

"Really? How?"

"Well, I was standing at their table when the shooting started and...they tried to drag me into the bathroom because there's a window in there, yeah, we wanted to get to the window. It opens on the alley. But I left them to...to find Manuel. And then...I don't remember anything else."

"You're sure they got out?"

"Pretty sure. That's why they went into the bathroom. To get out the window."

"Where do you suppose they went? You know, it's possible that they saw something they could tell the police. Something helpful."

"Oh. I don't know. McNolte...if he was hurt...well, I know he probably can't afford a hospital bill. I doubt he went there. Maybe the mission."

"Mission? What mission would that be?"

"Well, he works at this mission, see, it's...well, I can't remember the name."

"A homeless mission?"

"Something like that, yeah. The big one. It's on that street, um..." Her eyes closed for a moment and her thoughts drifted dreamily.

"What street is that?" Dexter said after several seconds.

She opened her eyes again. "Um...South Street, yeah, that's the one. The South Street Mission. He works there, see. Volunteer work, that sorta thing."

Her eyes started to close again. All the talking she had been doing had drained her of energy.

"McNolte, huh?" Dexter muttered, sounding preoccupied as he looked over her chart. Finally, he turned to her and smiled as he removed something from the pocket of his white coat.

A syringe. Its plunger was already pulled out. He popped the small, narrow cap off the needle, then took her IV tube in his left hand and stuck the needle into the small, rubber-ended port with his right. Pressing the plunger, he injected the syringe's clear fluid into her IV tube as he continued to smile. The second it was empty, he pulled the needle from the port, replaced the cap, and slipped the syringe back into his pocket.

"Thank you so much, Miss Connor," he said with a nod. Then he disappeared.

She closed her eyes and dozed...until she felt the sudden fluttering in her chest, which quickly became a sledgehammer-like pain.

That was the last thing she ever felt.

24.

DIAGNOSIS

Dunne waited in a parking lot across from the main entrance of the massive hospital, hoping all was going well inside. The rain pounded deafeningly on the roof of the car and poured over the windshield, distorting the world, making everything look blurry and nightmarish.

Dunne could not afford another mistake, not even an unavoidable one. Mr. Shaw would not be so forgiving the second time, especially in the same night. In fact, he was not sure Mr. Shaw *was* being forgiving. Dunne was well aware of Mr. Shaw's reputation for reacting violently when things did not go his way. He had only spoken to the man on the phone, and if Emma Shaw really *had* escaped the mayhem at Wee's Café, there was no telling how Mr. Shaw might choose to handle Dunne's mistake once they met in person.

Dr. Dexter was his only hope.

Now in his sixties, Dexter had lost his license to practice years ago for his liberal distribution of prescription drugs. He had been an excellent doctor then, and he still was; he simply could not practice legally. Ever since losing his license, he had been a doctor for hire, available to anyone who needed medical help off the record, or in this case, someone who could insinuate himself into a hospital without attracting attention, someone who could get information from, or even eliminate, a patient. Or both.

Dunne spotted Dr. Dexter as he came out of the hospital and hurried across the street holding his umbrella over his head.

Once he was in the parking lot, Dunne realized the man was smiling, for God's sake. He kept smiling as he approached the car, collapsing his umbrella, and even as he got into the car and pulled the door closed.

"I require a libation, my friend," the doctor said with a breathy sigh.

Dunne reached behind his seat for a brown paper bag and handed it over to Dr. Dexter. It contained the quart of whiskey that was always required when working with Dexter.

The doctor unscrewed the cap rapidly, leaving the bottle in the bag, then tipped it up to his mouth for a moment. He lowered it with a satisfied smile, a delighted exhalation of breath, and wiped his lips with the sleeve of his lab coat. Then he offered the bottle to Dunne and said, "Have a dose. Doctor's orders."

"No, thanks. I'm driving. So, how'd it go."

"Thanks to a large dose of Digoxin, your witness is no longer a witness. To anything." He took another healthy swig from the bottle, then rested it between his thighs.

"Okay, great. But were you able to talk to her?"

"Oh, yes, we spoke. Had a pleasant little exchange. Seemed like a nice girl."

"And? What did you learn, dammit?"

Dr. Dexter smiled at him. It was a cruel smile. "Well, considering what you've already told me, my diagnosis would be that you are up to your patellas in gastrointestinal byproduct."

Dunne pounded his fist on the steering wheel hard as he shouted, "Don't fuck with me, Doc, I'm not in the mood for it."

Dr. Dexter paused to take a few more swallows of his medication, then said, quietly, seriously, "You're in deep shit, my friend. Up to your knees at best. It seems this woman you're looking for got out of the diner, accompanied by one of the regulars. Some fellow named McNolte."

Dunne leaned back his head and groaned. "Son of a bitch."

"But if they stayed together, I know where you might find them. Or at least where you might find someone who knows where they are. I suggest you convey this information to your employer before any more time passes. You wouldn't want this woman to get any further out of reach, now, would you?" He kept smiling, enjoying Dunne's discomfort.

Dunne picked up his cell phone and punched in Mr. Shaw's number, waiting with dread for the man to answer.

25.

ANSWERS

Willy's office was as silent as a tomb. The smell of coffee from the pot Mama Charity had brought them mixed with the sweet aroma of Willy's pipe and the harsher smell of the cigarettes McNolte and P.W. had been smoking to form a bitter, caramel-like swirl in the air.

Emma had taken her time, talking in long rapid spurts, pausing now and then, as if to gather scattered thoughts into a coherent whole. She had told them everything that had been done to her in her husband's lab, everything she knew about the project, although she admitted that her knowledge was sketchy, made up largely of things she had overheard, and that her conclusions were mostly speculation. But she was done now, and she sat slumped in a folding chair, still buried in the rubber poncho, which she had refused to take off. She had lifted the hood again in a gesture of withdrawal, as if she might be safer completely engulfed in the enormous garment; her face was a mournful, ghostly apparition in the hood's cavernous darkness.

No one spoke. Willy's pipe had gone out again as he clenched it between his teeth and stared at Emma from behind his desk, but strands of smoke still rose from McNolte's cigarette, which had a long, drooping, neglected tube of ash clinging tenuously to the filter. P.W. sat on the very edge of his chair, forearms resting on his thighs, hands dangling between his knees, head hanging low. He had been in that position for a long time, and when McNolte looked at him now, he wondered if P.W. had fallen asleep.

But he wondered that only distractedly as his mind returned again and again to the tale Emma had just told them. That was exactly what it sounded like: a tale. It smacked of campfires and S'mores on a crisp autumn night. It was a modern version of one of those urban legends kids were always telling each other, stories that began with, "I had a neighbor whose friend's aunt was..."

But McNolte believed it. He had no choice.

For one thing, he strongly suspected that the usual obsessive, abusive husband stalking his wife would not have access to automatic weapons. And he vividly remembered the feeling that had come over him so suddenly in the restroom of Wee's Café, a feeling that he was experiencing some life-threatening illness, or perhaps a stroke.

Emma's story could have come from a comic book or a science fiction movie, but McNolte did not doubt it. In fact, it was his gut-level acceptance of it as truth that made him inclined to consider his own protection and survival first and foremost, especially after what had happened back at Wee's.

But as he looked at her soft eyes, nearly invisible in the hood as she cowered in that rubber poncho like a terrified child, he knew it would not be possible for him to send her away to face them on her own. McNolte would understand if Willy did not want them hanging around South Street. He would go with her.

Still, no one spoke. Emma remained motionless, waiting patiently for some kind of reaction.

"You're dead," P.W. said. Then he lifted his head, sat up straight, and leaned back in his chair, looking blankly at Emma.

After a long moment, she nodded somewhere inside that bag-like rubber hood. "I know," she whispered. "I know I'm probably going to end up dead, which is why I don't want to endanger anyone else by—"

"No, no," P.W. said gently, smiling, "that's not what I mean. I mean, you're *supposed* to be dead. I read about it in the paper. Just tonight, in fact. They found your remains buckled up in a Mercedes at the bottom of the Thunderhead River."

Emma's hand rose slowly and peeled back the rubber hood. Her face was a mixture of shock and fear and deep pain as she leaned toward P.W. slightly.

"Are you sure it was…supposed to be me?" she said.

"Your name was in the article. Emma Shaw." P.W. stood and turned to Willy. "You got today's paper?"

Willy spun around in his chair to the credenza behind him, gathered the scattered sections of the paper together and handed it to P.W., who turned to the article and handed it over to Emma. They gathered around behind her, McNolte, P.W., and Willy peering over her shoulder at the paper.

Her eyes darted back and forth as she read the article quickly. Accompanying it was a wedding picture of Emma and her husband, a tall, handsome man who looked crisply businesslike in spite of his smile and the occasion.

"Sounds like your husband meant it when he said you were dead," P.W. said. "He just took his time proving it to everybody. Looks better that way, too, letting some time pass before your corpse is pulled outta the river, all bloated and fish-eaten. Harder to identify by sight. He probably arranged for the identification. Money exchanged hands, you can bet your butt. I'd say he did a pretty damned good job."

The ash fell from McNolte's cigarette and he dropped the dead filter into the ashtray on Willy's desk.

"You think she's telling the truth, P.W.?" Willy said.

"She's shook up, not crazy," he said. "I don't have any problem with her story."

"Neither do I," McNolte said. "I believe her."

Willy frowned. "I…I don't know. People have come through here with all kinds of stories, people who seemed perfectly sane, but whose stories were…not so much, if you know what I mean." He looked at Emma, who was reading over the article again, eyes glistening with tears.

Emma crumpled the paper in her lap and looked at Willy. "I'm not lying. And I'm not crazy. Landon did this. I don't know who they found, but it wasn't me. It was somebody he had killed, that son of a bitch. Somebody he had put in that Mercedes and dumped into the river in the middle of the night. The dental records…that had to be faked. He managed that somehow. He has so many connections and so much money, that wouldn't be hard for him to pull off."

"And this project he used you for," P.W. said, "you say it might have been commissioned by the Pentagon?"

"Yes. I've overheard him talking about Project Biofire several times before he took me. A couple of times while I know he was talking to the Pentagon, and then with others, when he *mentioned* the Pentagon. And I know how important this project was to him. The ones that he really values, the ones he tries the hardest to protect and keep secret, they're almost always for the Pentagon. I just never knew what Project Biofire was. At least, not until they locked me up in that building and started doing things. It didn't take long for me to start putting it all together in my head. Things I'd heard, documents I'd seen, and what he was doing to me. Or having done."

P.W. scrubbed a hand up and down over his face as he exhaled explosively.

"What?" Willy said to him, standing behind the desk. "What are you thinking, P.W.?"

He sighed. "As a Vietnam vet, I can say from experience...I wouldn't put a thing past the goddamned Pentagon." He began to pace the cramped office. His usual happy smile was nowhere in sight. Instead, the corners of his mouth seemed to be turned downward behind the wiry hair of his mustache and beard, which he tugged at nervously as he walked back and forth. Finally, he turned to Emma and said, "We can hide you, but I gotta ask—if they come for ya, and they got you cornered, can you take care of 'em?"

"Well...yes. That's how I got out of the lab. The only thing is...I can't contain it very well. I can flame them, but I'll flame anybody else in range, too, and I'm not even sure what that range is. I don't want to do that. That's why I shouldn't be here. I should—"

"Let us worry about that," P.W. turned to Willy. "Let's put 'em in the basement. Keep 'em there for a while, isolated and put away from the others, at least long enough for Shaw and his people to decide she's gotten out of the city."

"Why both of them?" Willy asked.

"Well, McNolte's situation might not be as dramatic, but if he'd been alone tonight, he might be missin' some digits. I think his creditors have run out of patience and are getting serious. It'd be a real bad idea for him to go back home. But if we're gonna do this, we gotta do it *now*. We've wasted enough time, 'cause they're gonna show up here, I got no doubt about that. I'm just wondering, like I said before, if maybe they already have."

McNolte watched P.W. with amazement. He was no longer the grinning, carefree fellow with whom McNolte had been rooming, no longer the quiet smiler who had an occasional joke to add to the conversation, or who sometimes laughed at a joke that he kept to himself. Now, he was deadly serious. His large body had a tautness to it that had never been evident before, his eyes a thoughtful determination that McNolte had not seen until now. His voice was solid with confidence, and he was speaking and moving with the fluidity and assurance of a man in his element.

"P.W., I'm not really sure about this," Willy said, his voice uncharacteristically quiet. "This will endanger all of us, everyone here. If I thought we could actually *do* something about Emma's predicament, I might feel differently, but as it is—"

"Maybe we can," P.W. interrupted. "I know some people. I have some connections, too, you know. Just like Mr. Shaw. Maybe we *can* do something. For now, we get 'em in the basement and keep 'em there. Nobody, and I mean *nobody* can know they're here. Tell everybody they've left, I mean, really get the word out right away that they took off forty-five minutes, an hour ago." He turned to McNolte and Emma and added, "And once you're down there, you *stay* there until further notice." To Willy: "Is the basement fit for company, Willy?"

"Certainly. We always keep it clean and ready for guests if we get overrun. There are bathrooms and beds, even a television set and ping pong table."

"And we'll see that you two are fed well," P.W. said to McNolte.

"Jesus, P.W., you sound like you're shipping us off to some gulag, or something," McNolte said. He was uncomfortable with the way P.W. had quickly taken over and begun making decisions for McNolte and Emma, as if they were not even in the room.

"Don't worry, it ain't a gulag," P.W. said, smiling again, more like his old self, "but you're gonna feel like prisoners. I just want to prepare you for that. We put you down there, you don't exist no more far as anybody's concerned. Least, not until we can think of something else. And we will, don't worry. You're gonna be invisible for a while, one way or another. Then, pretty soon, your friends," he said, nodding at Emma, "are gonna give up on the city and take their search someplace else."

"You don't know what you're doing," Emma said, voice hollow and breathy as she shook her head slowly back and forth. "You don't know who you're dealing with, here." Her weary eyes moved slowly from P.W. to McNolte to Willy and back to P.W. again. "You're very nice to want to help me, I really appreciate it. But these people...my husband and the men who work for him...they will hurt you. Kill you. Without a thought. What I really need to do is get out of the city, that's all. If you could get me on a train, or on a plane out of the country, Mexico, maybe—"

P.W. said firmly, "If your husband and his people are so determined to find you, how long do you think you'd last in a train station or airport. He's probably got people there looking for you right now. Look, Mrs. Shaw, I know you're real scared, and rightfully so from the looks of things. But can you think if any reason why your husband would look for you here at South Street? Huh?"

Her face tensed as she considered the question. "No. But still...I know what he can do."

"Your problem is, you don't know what *I* can do," P.W. said, giving her a good-natured wink. He turned to McNolte. "Any reason you can think of that these fine folks looking for Emma might connect her to you? To South Street?"

McNolte looked at Emma, who was staring with a frown at nothing in particular.

"I've never even seen her before tonight," McNolte said. "I didn't even know her name until we got to my apartment. No, there's no way anybody could possibly connect the two of us."

"Then all we gotta worry about for right now, McNolte, are your friends," P.W. said. He turned to Willy and asked, "Can we get them settled down there right away?"

"Yes, of course," Willy said, still sounding hesitant. "If you think this is the right thing to do."

"If we don't want Emma, here, shot full of holes, or McNolte walking around with a stump on the end of each arm, then I think this is definitely the thing to do. The *only* thing to do. And the sooner, the better." Not only was there no smile on P.W.'s face as he said it, but there was none in his voice, either. He was serious, firm, and did not sound like he was in the mood to hear any argument from anyone, not even Willy.

McNolte watched Emma. She looked wilted, withered, and lost in the tent-like poncho. In spite of her aversion to being touched, he reached over and put his hand on her shoulder and squeezed warmly.

She looked at him for a moment and almost smiled.

26.

SAFE HAVEN

The basement of the South Street Mission was vast, divided up into five large rooms.

In one room were piles of folding chairs along one wall, and along another were stacks of folding tables of all sizes, with ping-pong table in the middle. Cupboards were filled with supplies like paper plates, plastic silverware, Styrofoam cups, packages of coffee filters, containers of sugar and artificial sweetener, boxes of napkins, paper towels, tablecloths, and cases of cleaning fluids and dish soaps, sponges, and scouring pads, all of which had been donated by church groups or local merchants.

Boxes of holiday decorations were stacked against the wall of another room. Most of it was Christmas stuff, but there were also flags and banners for Independence Day, Veterans Day, and Memorial Day, because such a high percentage of the people who came to the mission were veterans. Mama Charity handled all the holiday chores and had already had a couple of the boxes taken upstairs, leaving behind dusty, empty spots among all the others; those boxes contained the fall decorations—plastic pumpkins, stuffed scarecrows, artificial autumn leaves, plastic cornucopias, and orange crepe paper—which she would put up within the next few days.

Across the room from the boxes was an old, tired-looking delivery elevator that rose up through big metal doors to the sidewalk outside for large deliveries.

Still another room, dark and musty and humid, contained

the building's only furnace. It made a rackety humming sound as it sent warmth up through the ducts and out of the vents all through the mission.

The other two rooms contained beds with bare mattresses ready and waiting to be made for an overflow from upstairs, along with a few chairs, a couple of card tables, and cupboards of blankets and towels. Each of the two rooms had a bathroom and single shower. The floors were cold, uncarpeted concrete, but mismatched throw rugs had been spread around to cover most of it.

"I've been meaning to get some carpeting down here," Willy said as he flipped a bank of light switches, turning on the long fluorescent lights suspended from the ceiling. "But it seems there's always something more important to do with money."

Mama Charity stood behind Willy, and behind her was P.W.; McNolte and Emma stood facing the three of them at the foot of the sturdy wooden stairs that led down from the laundry room.

"You have plenty of beds to choose from," Willy continued. "There are a couple dozen in each of these two rooms. That room is for the men, the other is for women. I suppose since it's just the two of you...well, I'll just leave the sleeping arrangements up to you."

Mama Charity slapped Willy's shoulder as she pushed by him, saying, "Oh, just *stop* that silliness, now, they's *adults*, for pitysake." She continued as she waddled hurriedly to a cupboard. "I think they got other things on they mind than playin' Post Office in the basement." She pulled two cupboard doors open and turned to McNolte and Emma. "Towels and wash cloths are on this side, and blankets, sheets, and pillowcases are all over here. I'd make up a couple of beds for you, but it's startin' to get pretty busy upstairs. Now, you just go ahead and pick a couple beds in one of these rooms. No sense in sleepin' on opposite sides of this big, creepy dungeon." She started for the stairs again. "I'll bring down some nightclothes for you later. Robes, slippers, pajamas. I'll bring a few, you can take your picks. I'll see y'all later." She moved up the stairs rapidly in spite of her girth and was gone in seconds.

Willy pointed to some cupboards. "There's a television and

a combination radio-tape-deck in the cupboard right there, and an old Mr. Coffee in the cupboard next to it. I think it still works. I'll bring some coffee and tea and all the fixings down a little later. And I'll make sure you get your meals, one of us will bring them down to you. Um...are you hungry right now? Either of you?"

McNolte looked at Emma. She either ignored the question or had not heard it; she was turning her head this way and that, looking all around her. But McNolte knew she had not eaten, so he answered Willy for her. "I think some hot food might be a good idea."

"No problem. I'll go up to the kitchen right now and see what I can find."

"Thanks, Willy," McNolte said.

As Willy went back upstairs, P.W. approached McNolte, smiling. "Feel like we're lockin' you up and throwin' away the key?"

"Yeah, a little."

"Don't worry, McNolte. It won't be for long. And it's a good way to avoid trouble for a while. Can I get you anything from your apartment?"

"My typewriter. I'd appreciate that."

"Anything else? Paper? Notebooks?"

"Just bring everything that's on my work table. All of it. Oh, and in the bathroom, get my toothbrush. It's just over the sink. While you're at it, bring the unopened one from the medicine cabinet, too, for Emma."

"Toothpaste?"

"Yes, please. Maybe some floss, too. And the mouthwash."

"I'll just pack a bunch of toiletries for you."

"Thanks, that'd be great."

P.W. turned to Emma and his smile grew a bit, eyes softened and became warmer than usual. "Listen, Mrs. Shaw, uh...would it be all right if I called you Emma?"

She nodded. The rubber hood was still crumpled behind her shoulders.

"Okay. Can I ask you some questions, Emma?"

"If you want."

"Good. Tell you what." P.W. stepped over to a stack of folding chairs against the wall and brought back three of them, opening them one at a time. "C'mon, let's all get comfortable."

Emma lowered herself wearily into the chair, then McNolte and P.W. seated themselves.

"Do you know the names of any of the people your husband works with?" P.W. said. "Can you identify any of those...what did you call those clients of his?"

"Shadow clients."

"Yeah, shadow clients. Can you identify any of them?"

She spoke slowly and lazily. Her eyelids looked heavy and her mouth sounded dry. "Some. Not all. And I can only identify most of them by their faces, not their names. He invites some of them to the house now and then. A few of them don't even speak English."

"Do they have interpreters?" P.W. asked.

She nodded. "And bodyguards and limos. Sometimes whole entourages. They're important people." After a pause, she said, "Well, they're powerful, at least. I guess their importance depends on your point of view." She took a deep breath, sighed, and met P.W.'s gaze. "Like I said, my knowledge is limited. Landon rarely discussed his work with me, and he got angry when I asked questions. I tried not to make him angry. It never ended well for me."

"I'm not surprised. Tell me, do you happen to know who his contact at the Pentagon is? Who he deals with there when he's working on a project for them?"

McNolte watched her bow her head for a moment, then finally shake it negatively.

"Do you know the names of the particular office or division that he deals with?"

Another silent shake of the head.

P.W. leaned back in his chair and joined his hands behind his head, wearing a strained look of frustration.

"What is it, P.W.?" McNolte said.

"I don't have a whole lot to go on," he muttered, sounding as if he might be talking to himself.

"What do you mean?"

P.W. ignored him and leaned forward again, looking at Emma. "Listen, Emma, I know you're tired. You take yourself a long hot shower, eat some food, and get a good night's sleep. But try your best to think about this, okay? I want to help you, and I think I can, but I need more information about your husband's work and associates. If you come up with any names you might have overheard, anything at all, even if you don't know who they are, I want you to write them down. I'm gonna run over to McNolte's apartment and I'll come back with lots of pads and pens, okay? You just see if you can come up with some names, anything at all for me. Will you do that, Emma?"

After a moment, she pushed the words out with effort: "I can try."

"Good, that's good." P.W. stood and McNolte followed him to the foot of the stairs.

"What do you have in mind?" McNolte said.

"Don't know yet until I can get some more information. Like I said upstairs, I've got some connections, too. You want me to grab some reading material while I'm at your place?"

"Good idea. Oh, and cigarettes. There's a carton in the freezer."

"Freezer?"

"Keeps them fresh."

As P.W. went up the stairs, McNolte turned and went back to his chair rather cautiously. Her head was still bowed, and he wondered if she had fallen asleep. As he seated himself, the folding chair made an abrupt creaking sound, and Emma's entire body jerked with surprise. She lifted her head and turned to him, eyes wide, dry lips parted slightly, and she stared at him for some time, as if for a few seconds, she did not know who he was or what he was doing there so close, staring at her. Fear and confusion welled up in her eyes for just a moment, then melted away. Her eyelids lowered and her momentarily rigid back slumped a bit.

"I'm sorry," McNolte said. "I didn't mean to startle you."

"That's okay. I dozed off, that's all."

"Willy'll probably be back with food after a while. Would you like to take a shower?"

Emma cocked her head toward him and her right eyebrow lifted elegantly in a high arch.

"Oh, no, *no*, I don't mean with *me*. Jeez, look." He stood, walked around his chair and leaned both hands on the back. "I don't know you, you don't know me, but...we're kind of in a mess together. Like you said before, we're both running from somebody. I guess we got off to a bad start. I mean, it's a little hard to exchange pleasantries and get to know one another while running from a guy with a machine gun, right?"

Emma did not move; she continued to look up at him with her head cocked and one eyebrow raised. McNolte waited for a response—a word, a nod, anything—but she gave him nothing. He shifted his weight from one foot to the other and back again, unnerved by her stare.

"Okay," he said, standing straight and taking a step back from her chair, and from her, "do whatever you what to do. Take a shower, go to bed, wait for food. I don't care. All I'm saying is...we're probably going to be here for a while, so we could at least try to get along."

She closed her eyes and sighed, then stood. "I'm sorry," she said, peeling the rubber poncho over her head clumsily, noisily. Once it was off, she let it drop to the floor in a weighty heap. "God, it feels good to get that thing off." Her baggy plaid shirt and jeans clung to her perspiring skin. She loosened the top button on her shirt and plucked at the flannel here and there. Approaching McNolte cautiously, she offered her hand and he shook it a few times, then let go. "Thank you. For bringing me here, I mean. I know I gave you a hard time about it, but that was only because I was scared and wanted to get out of the city. When you said you wanted to go to a mission...well, I just thought it was a stupid idea. And I guess I was, um...I was wrong. I haven't been able to stand still for days, and this is—" She shrugged as she looked around again. "—perfect. A perfect hiding place."

"I'm glad you think so."

She went to the cupboard Mama Charity had pointed out, opened it, and removed a towel and a wash cloth. "I think I will take a shower." On her way to the bathroom, she said, "Keep that food warm for me when it comes," her voice fading as she disappeared around the corner.

McNolte walked over to the closest bed and sat on the edge. His right shin was aching, had been for a long time now, and he pulled up his pant leg and pushed down his sock to reveal a swollen bruise that had spread over his skin in a mottled purple oval. In the middle of the bruise, blood oozed slowly from a cut about half an inch long. He touched it gingerly and winced with the pain, assuming it had happened while going out the window in Wee's bathroom and into the dumpster outside. He decided he would ask Mama Charity or Willy for some alcohol and Band-Aids as he fell back on the bare mattress and closed his eyes, telling himself he would rest only for a minute or so, just long enough to ease the tension in his aching back and neck.

The bottom fell out of the blackness of his mind and the plunge was a sudden one, swift and inexorable, and on the way down, he heard Wee shouting something unintelligible from the noisy kitchen, saw Pam filling his coffee cup with a smile even though she looked dead on her feet, and as he tumbled downward into sleep, he felt a deep longing inside him, a pain, because he missed them, they were gone and although he was not sure why, or where they had gone, he knew he missed them. And just before the blackness swallowed him, there was another face, one that was not as familiar, but somehow connected to the others. The face rose up before him in the darkness wearing an enormous hood, eyes frightened as the sound of an automatic weapon shattering glass came from somewhere in the distance. A final thought occurred to him, floating by, directionless and brief, but quite vivid as he saw that face staring at him from out of the oval of darkness, clean now, pale, smooth-skinned and lovely:

She's beautiful.

27.

IN MCNOLTE'S APARTMENT

As McNolte was falling asleep, P.W. was entering his apartment.

At the card table where McNolte worked, P.W. stacked all the scattered papers together and slipped them into a manila envelope from a stack beneath the table. He put the typewriter's case onto the table, lifted the typewriter into it, then closed it up and flipped the latch. In the closet, he found McNolte's box of money, took three tens, and stuffed them into his pocket. After giving it a second thought, he decided to bring the whole box, just in case McNolte ended up in a position where he needed some fast cash in the near future. In the bathroom, he stuffed toiletries into McNolte's black vinyl shaving kit, then switched the light off on his way out and went to McNolte's single bookcase. On top of it was a stack of dog-eared paperbacks McNolte had brought home the last time he and P.W. had visited the Paperback Trader, and P.W. knew McNolte had not read them yet. He picked out a few and put them on the table beside the typewriter case.

He took a suitcase of his own, large and heavy, from beneath his cot and set it beside the card table. It looked like nothing more than a battered old Samsonite, but P.W. thought of it as his armory. He had not used it in a long time—there had been no need—but he wanted to take it with him now, just in case.

He retrieved a small telephone and address book from a box of books beneath his cot. Paging through it, he went to the recliner, still lying on its side, and turned it upright so he could sit in it.

His bushy silver eyebrows huddled together above the bridge of his nose and curled down over the wire frames of his glasses as he looked over the names.

They were the names of people he had neither seen nor talked to in so long. Buddies he had gone through hell with in jungles that rendered the enemy invisible. There weren't many, just a small group of guys he had stayed in close touch with for years...until he fell into that bottle of booze and disappeared from the world for a while. He had not been in contact with them since then.

P.W. knew that if he had called them during that time, when he was so troubled, they would have done anything for him, given him money, put him up for as long as he needed, put him in rehab, anything at all. But he had not wanted them to see what he had become. Instead, he had gone deeper into that bottle until he had been dragged in off the street and brought back to life by Willy and Mama Charity and the others at South Street.

Of course, P.W. would have done the same for his friends, anything at all, anytime, except they'd had no way of contacting him or even knowing if he were dead or alive for...how long now? Four years? Five? Maybe closer to six, he decided, counting back those blurry years in his head.

P.W. picked out three names, the three he used to get together with a couple of times a week to play cards or watch a ball game, the three he had been thinking about most lately. He spent some time there in the recliner staring at those names, wondering how they were doing, if they still lived in and around the city, if one of them was still married and if the other two were still single, if any of them had died. And he wondered if he had let too much time pass to ask them for a favor.

He picked up the phone reluctantly, punched in a number, his eyes moving back and forth between the buttons and the number written in his book.

The phone ran three times, then a deep, stony voice at the other end said, "Yeah?"

A TV was playing loudly in the background; P.W. could hear a studio audience laughing about something.

"Hey, Ty. It's P.W."

"P....W.?" The TV noise stopped abruptly. "*Pee-Dubbuyah?*"

He chuckled. "Yeah, that's right. How's things?"

"How's things? How's *things*, he's asking me!" Ty roared with laughter. "I'll be damned, you moth-eaten son of a bitch, where the hell you *been*? I was starting to think you were—hell, we *all* figured you were dead, or something."

"You wanna know the truth, I was kinda dead for a while."

"Yeah, well...we were pretty worried about you, P.W. You seemed to be keeping to yourself for a while, there, after Dolores left you. Hitting the bottle pretty hard. Then all of a sudden you were gone. Just disappeared, you miserable bastard, you. We looked for you, too, but no luck. What the hell *happened* to you?" Although his words were harsh, there was laughter in Ty's voice.

"I would've said something to you guys, but...well, I wasn't talking so well back then. I made noises like a duck and puked a lot, but that's about it. Tell you the truth, I was too busy pissing my pants to make any phone calls."

"Aw, jeez, P.W., I wish I'd known. I coulda done something, I coulda—"

"Hey, nobody could've done anything but me. And I finally did."

"Well, how are things now?"

"They're a lot better than they were, that's for damned sure."

"You still in the city?"

"Yeah."

"Where you living."

He did not reply for a moment, just togged on his beard a couple of times. "Oh...I'm around. Look, Ty, I was thinking maybe, uh...maybe the four of us could get together soon. Catch up."

"That'd be great, P.W. Did you know Jess moved upstate? He's got a little place in Burkett. He's a suburbanite now."

"Does that mean he's unavailable?"

"Shit, no. He gets a haircut twice a week just to get away from his wife."

"He's still married, huh?"

"If you can call it that. She's turned into one of those crazy cat ladies. She's got about twenty of 'em. And that's just *inside* the house. Plus, she's ballooned up to about the size of a Baltic state. When do you wanna get together, P.W.? This weekend? Next weekend?"

"I was thinking more along the lines of right away. As soon as possible. Would that be okay?"

"Sounds like something's up. You in trouble, P.W.?"

"Not me, no. But I've, uh…stumbled into a situation, here. I'm gonna need some help."

"I'll call Jess right away, you want me to."

"Call Buddy, too. I'd like to get together tomorrow night, if it's okay with everybody."

"Okay with everybody?" You disappear for years, now I get a call from you out of the blue and you wanna know if it's okay? It's fan-fucking-*tastic!*"

P.W. laughed, but this time it sounded different than his usual chortles. It came from deep inside him and had a joyous life to it.

"Hey, one more thing," P.W. said. "You heard anything about Travis?"

"Travis? Not since you told me you'd talked to him. You said he was still at the Pentagon. That was about, oh, seven years ago, maybe more."

"That long?" P.W. muttered, frowning.

"Yeah, that long."

"You don't know if he's still there?"

"Nope. Why do you ask?"

"Just curious. I may look him up."

"Jeez, P.W. what's going on that you need to look up somebody at the Pentagon?"

"It's a long story, and I'll tell you the whole thing tomorrow night. I'll give you a call in the morning, okay, Ty?"

"It's sure great to hear from you, P.W., really great. Just… don't go disappearing again, okay?"

"You got a deal."

After hanging up, P.W. leaned back in the recliner again and paged through the book for another name, but he was distracted by the blinking red light on the answering machine beside the telephone. Thinking there might be a message on the machine that McNolte needed to hear, P.W. reached over and hit the play button.

The first message was from McNolte's agent, and it went on and on. P.W. hit the FWD/SKIP button. There was a sharp beep, then the second message began. It was a man's voice, unfamiliar to P.W., low, even, and ominous. P.W. frowned as he listened, but at one point, his eyebrows popped up high on his forehead.

The message ended. It was the last one on the machine. P.W. rewound the tape and listened to it again, more carefully this time.

When it finished, he leaned back in the recliner, tugging on his beard thoughtfully. After a moment, he returned his attention to the book, thumbing through it until he found the name he was looking for.

Leland Travis. He had been a warrant officer when P.W. had met him, but he was a full colonel now. P.W. was uncertain what he did at the Pentagon, but if he was still there, he might be able to help. After all, he had owed P.W. a favor since 1972.

P.W. was a staff sergeant in the army back then, doing his time in Vietnam. He was heading up a Long Range Reconnaissance Patrol team—known as LRRPs or "lurps"—with Ty and a guy named Wilby. They had been behind enemy lines for days, quietly observing, gathering intelligence on an enemy troop build-up. When the time came, they were picked up by a Huey "slick" on a designated hilltop.

As the Huey lifted off from the pick-up point, a barrage of heavy machine gun fire came from the ridgeline opposite them. Inside the chopper, ballet-like bursts of blood and bone accompanied the barely audible gunfire from the ridge. P.W.'s forehead was badly cut and a grazing bullet cut a trench across his thigh, another passed through the beefy flesh of Wilby's upper right arm, and Ty came through it untouched, but the pilot and door gunner were killed instantly. The co-pilot was badly injured and bleeding, but not dead.

The chopper nose-dived toward the ground as the co-pilot cried out in pain and horror, vomiting on himself and his controls. But he maintained enough presence of mind to pull the nose up enough so the chopper belly-flopped onto the ground.

The lurps were shaken, but P.W. knew they did not have time to pull themselves together; they had to move immediately, because the gunfire continued, and it would only get closer. He snapped his teammates into action and they carried the bloodied, groaning co-pilot from the chopper and across the deadly clearing in which they were so vulnerable toward a thicket of small trees and underbrush. They were a few yards from cover when the chopper, which stood between them and the machine gun fire, exploded with an ear-popping *whump*, and the impact slammed all of them to the ground. They scrambled the rest of the way clumsily, pulling the co-pilot with them.

When the enemy soldiers got too close, Wilby moved on with the co-pilot while P.W. and Ty stayed back and set up an ambush. They killed three NVA troops silently, quickly, and efficiently, leaving their bodies behind in the kind of shape that would make the rest of the troops continue their pursuit with great caution and fear. P.W. and Ty caught up with the others and together, they moved on.

P.W. and Wilby began popping their Benzedrine tabs like jelly beans, and they stopped long enough to give the co-pilot a shot of morphine to keep him from crying out in pain.

"Goddammit, leave me," the co-pilot rasped after getting the injection. "I'll lay low, you can go ahead and get help. I'm just slowing you down."

"No offense, babe," P.W. whispered, "but shut the fuck up. You're comin' with us."

Several times, P.W. and Wilby held back to delay pursuing NVA troops, but finally caught up with Ty and the co-pilot.

The three moved as fast as they could to reach the next landing zone far enough ahead of the enemy troops so they could be picked up safely by another chopper. The next one lifted off with machine gun fire right behind it, but the second time, they escaped without a hitch.

The co-pilot was Leland Travis, and that was the last action he ever saw. But he stayed in the military, working his way up through the ranks. He had told P.W. and Ty back then—and had repeated it several times since—that he owed them big-time and would be happy to oblige anytime they needed a favor, as long as it was within his ability.

P.W. finally was going to call in that favor all these years later. Travis was not going to like it, but it certainly was within his ability, and although it was against P.W.'s nature to insist, in a situation like this he would if he had to.

P.W. punched the number into the phone and waited through two rings.

"Travis."

"Hello, Colonel. P.W. Meredith calling."

"P.W.?" His voice boomed pleasantly over the line. "God*damn*, it's been a long time!"

"I know, and I'm sorry for losin' touch."

P.W. learned that Travis was, indeed, still at the Pentagon, where he had worked his way up even further since they had last spoken; he walked with a cane now instead of a crutch and a brace, but his leg gave him hell in the cold winter months. When Travis asked about P.W.'s life, P.W. gave amiable but evasive answers. The only thing that connected the two of them was that one experience in 1972 when their lives had crossed paths; beyond that, they were little more than strangers. There was not even enough small talk to last long.

"Hey, Colonel," P.W. said, "you know, I'm not one for callin' in favors, especially when it's for something anybody in my shoes woulda done, but I—"

"Bullshit, P.W. I owed you then, and I owe you now. I haven't forgotten. By the way, it's General Travis now. What can I do for you?"

P.W. paused to choose his words, deciding how best to approach the favor.

"I need someone to tell me about OdysseyCorp Labs and a man named Landon Shaw."

The ensuing silence from Virginia was long, so long that for a moment P.W. thought the connection had been severed.

"You still there?" P.W. said.

"Yes, still here. Uh…I'm not sure I understand."

"Look, we don't need to dance around this. I already know a lot more about this than your average civilian, and I know I'm

puttin' my ass in the crosshairs by talkin' to you about it, but…
you said you owed me, and you said you'd do anything within
your ability, so I—"

"What do you know, P.W.?"

"I know that OdysseyCorp does weapons research and
development for the Pentagon."

"That's not exactly top secret information."

"Oh, I know that any reporter worth his salt could dig up
that much. But I also know that the work OdysseyCorp's doing
for the government is being sold under the table to outside
interests. The highest bidder. One of the projects underway there
has gotten some friends of mine into trouble. And it's gotten a
lot of people killed. Just tonight. And the night is young. Now,
I don't give a bug's behind what new toys the government's
cooking up, I really don't. Hell, even if I did, what difference
would it make? I haven't thought of it as *my* government since
my junior high civics class, know what I'm sayin'? It's just that
my friends are in some pretty hot water and they didn't do a
damned thing to get themselves there. I just wanna help them
out, okay?"

Another long silence, then: "Why don't you tell me what
you know."

"I don't know everything, keep that in mind. I sorta came in
on the middle of this movie."

"Let's hear it."

He began telling General Leland Travis what sounded to
P.W. like a tall and preposterous tale.

28.

JORGAN AND MIRANDA

As P.W. talked with his old friend on the phone in McNolte's apartment, Dr. Jorgan, too, was talking on the phone in his office, but not with a friend.

"Are you sure?" Landon Shaw said. "Are you absolutely *positive*?"

Jorgan rolled his eyes, wanting to slam the receiver against the desktop until it shattered, as if it were Shaw's skull. It was not the first time during the conversation that he had felt such an urge.

"I *said* that I am *not* positive," Jorgan said, speaking slowly, as if to a child. "I am as sure as I can be given the time constraints."

"Time constraints? What the fuck are you talking about, *time* constraints? Is that some kind of excuse, or something, Jorgan?"

"Four days. That's all I've had, Mr. Shaw." *You miserable fucking demon*, Jorgan added silently. "In four days, I've done more than most could in four *weeks*. I cannot guarantee you that it will work flawlessly, but it's all we've got right now, until I come up with something more solid. But that will take time and this is ready now. I can say with some degree of certainty that it will—"

"All right, all right." Shaw sounded winded and his voice was ragged, as if he had been shouting a lot lately. "You've come up with something that will stop that-that-that...*thing* she does, yes?"

Jorgan rolled his eyes. Truly, the man was a moron. It was

frightening to think that Shaw was overseeing an operation as awesome as OdysseyCorp but understood so little of what was going on within its walls. Worse, the man had pathetic listening skills.

"As I said a moment ago, Mr. Shaw, it will not *stop* her abilities, but it will likely curtail them."

"Curtail? What the hell does that mean."

"It will severely reduce the impact of her abilities. Do you understand?"

"With a single injection?"

"Yes. You can use it in a dart gun. One shot *should* do the trick."

"Well, it's the best we've got right now, I guess. But you'll keep working." It was a firm order, not a question.

"Of course I will. But before this can work, you have to find her."

Shaw sighed. When he spoke again, all the angry, bitter energy that made his voice the harsh, ugly sound that it was seemed to disappear. He sounded exhausted. "Yes, I know. And I think we've found her."

"Oh? That's remarkable. So soon, I mean. Where is she?"

"Some big mission in the city."

"A mission?"

"Yes. With a man who—" Shaw made a primitive grunting sound into the phone, then his voice returned in all its ugliness: "Goddammit, what business is it of yours? You handle the mad scientist shit and leave the rest to me, Jorgan, you got that?"

Jorgan did not reply immediately. He did not want Shaw to hear his smile in his voice.

"Yes, Mr. Shaw. I've already put vials in the drop box in my lab. You can send someone to pick them up."

"I will. And you'd better hope it works." His last sentence was spoken with little conviction, as if only out of duty. He hung up.

Jorgan stood behind his desk and started to make his way around it to leave the office when Miranda appeared in the open doorway.

"What are you doing?" she said, her voice heavy and

completely without inflection. It was a dead voice, as flat and cold as a slab of concrete.

Jorgan stopped and blinked several times as he looked at her. She was almost unrecognizable.

Face red and puffy, the flesh around her eyes appeared swollen. Several strands of her black hair, which was so thick and straight that it was hard to muss, were tossed and tangled, in disarray, as if she had been scrubbing both hands through it viciously before stepping into the doorway. Her round shoulders sagged more than usual as she leaned heavily against the doorjamb, staring at him.

"What are you talking about?" he said. "And what are you doing here at this hour? Shouldn't you be home in bed? We've got a lot to do tomorrow."

She neither moved nor spoke, and her eyes continued to stare at him, looking as dead and cold as her voice sounded.

"I was in your apartment a little while ago." Her lips hardly moved at all. "You've packed two suitcases. And I was standing out here. Just now. I heard what you said to Mr. Shaw. I know it's a lie. The whole thing. You haven't been working on anything. You've been brooding, that's all. Like a lovesick teenager. Silent all the time. Sad eyes. Shuffling around. Not eating. Not talking. To me. Not spending time. With me." Her tongue moved slowly over her lips and she gulped thickly. "Ignoring me. Like I'm not here. Even when I get in your face and talk to you, yuh-you're like…like a zombie. So, Dr. Jorgan. What are you doing?"

His mind raced, too unnerved by her to lock onto a satisfactory reply.

"What are you giving them?" she said, pushing herself with some effort from the doorjamb and moving toward him slowly. "What are you leaving in the drop box? Saline, maybe? Just some kind of saline solution? You know Shaw wouldn't know an effective serum from Gatorade, right? So maybe it's nothing more than plain old tap water. They'll shoot her with it. It won't work. Won't do a thing. And then she can flame them. Kill them. Is that what you have in mind, Dr. Jorgan?"

"That is ridiculous," he said, surprised by how calm he sounded. Beneath the weight of Miranda's dead stare, it was a calm he did not feel inside. "I won't dignify it with a response." He turned to his desk and swept up a couple of file folders. He was not even sure what was in them, but he wanted to look as if he had purpose when he left the office. Facing her again, he started forward and stepped around her.

She grabbed his arm, clutched his elbow with surprising strength, her short, round-nailed fingers digging into his flesh hard, hurting him. When he tried to wrench his arm from her grasp, he was startled—and a little frightened, he admitted to himself—to find that he could not. He looked down at her hand, about to shout at her, but when he looked into her eyes, much closer now than a moment ago, he thought better of it and simply remained silent, lips pulled back over his clenched teeth.

In spite of the strength with which she held him, her face had not changed. Her eyes were two dead orbs, glistening only with the moisture that clung around their lower edges. Her bloated face remained expressionless as she stared at him from beneath the hood of her brow.

Jorgan had seen eyes like Miranda's before. They had belonged to patients he had seen in psych wards, people so deeply immersed in depression, despair, and delusion that they were no longer seeing the world around them as it really existed, but only as a world of dense, cloying darkness in which every detail was part of an endless conspiracy against them, the victims of uncontrollable dark forces, unholy powers, angry Fates.

Miranda's eyes were washed out, the deep brown now looking diluted, as if half the color had been sucked from the irises and replaced with murky water, giving them a paleness that looked cold and empty. Like all the others Jorgan had seen, these particular eyes, Miranda's eyes, did not even blink as they stared unwaveringly at him. Not once.

"Where are you going, Dr. Jorgan? Why did you pack your bags?"

"I do not have to report my every move to you, Miranda," he said, teeth still clenched to make his unsettled voice sound more confident.

"Of course you don't."

Neither of them moved for a while. They stared at one another as Miranda's fingers dug deeper into Jorgan's elbow. Then, quite suddenly and without any gradual lessening of pressure, she dropped her hand so heavily that it slapped against her thigh. But her gaze held firm.

Jorgan debated with himself: simply walk away without looking back, or say a few words to remind her who was in charge and to let her know she was walking on very thin ice. The words won out.

"I can't say much for *your* behavior, either, Miranda," he said, his teeth apart now, but with a definite edge to his voice. "You're a bright girl with quite a future ahead of you, but not if you make a habit of this kind of insubordination and...well, frankly, erratic behavior."

Finally, he pulled his eyes from hers—but not without difficulty—and went to the doorway, where he stopped and turned around slowly. Her back was to him, head bowed low now. "Why don't you go home to bed, Miranda. That's where you belong. You look as if you could use some sleep."

Her head was sagging so low now that, from behind, it looked as if she had been decapitated, leaving only her round, dropping shoulders and no neck. Her head hung so low that Jorgan half-expected to hear the wet sound of it peeling off her neck, the crack of it hitting the floor, and the muted, lumpy, shuddering sound it would make as it rolled under his desk.

"And why aren't you in bed, Dr. Jorgan?" she said, her body remaining so still that her voice seemed to come from another part of the room.

"That's none of your damned business," he said, genuinely angry now. "Now go home. I'll see you in the morning."

"Will you?" She still did not move.

Jorgan's lips parted to speak, but he paused a moment as he stared at the back of her headless body—to steady his voice, to make the lie work.

"Well, of *course* I will. Where the hell else would I be?" He started to leave, but stopped long enough to say, "And stay out of my damned apartment unless you're *invited*."

Then he left quickly, slapping the light switch hard with his palm, turning off the office lights, as if to emphasize his words by leaving her in darkness.

Jorgan was anxious to put as much distance between himself and Miranda as possible. He had long known that his involvement with her was a mistake, but he had never been as certain of that fact as he was at that moment. Something was not right about that girl. That familiar and disturbing look in her eyes was a sign of real trouble, evidence of a flaw in her wiring. Under different circumstances, he would have fired her on the spot. Under *these* circumstances, there was no point. As of that night, he was no longer an employee of OdysseyCorp Labs, so whether or not she remained was no concern of his.

As anxious as he was to get away from Miranda, Jorgan was even more anxious to get back to his apartment, get his bags, get into his car, and go find Emma.

A mission in the city. He knew of four, although he was sure there probably were more in a city of such size, and with so many homeless winos and druggies staggering through the streets and alleys. But there was one mission in particular that came to his mind. A big one. Huge.

The South Street Mission. That was where he would begin his search.

Miranda stood in Dr. Jorgan's office and listened to his footsteps fade down the corridor, just as she had stood outside his office earlier, listening to him talk to Mr. Shaw on the phone. She stood there for a long time, just listening, until his footsteps became ghostly taps in the distance, and then faded away.

When there was only silence, she raised her head a bit and walked slowly to the window. She looked through the pouring rain to the parking lot, where rows of bleary pools of light were cast by the tall lamps. A few small clusters of cars, hers among them, were parked around the lights. But she did not remember driving back to OdysseyCorp. She knew she had done so, but could not remember doing it because everything was simply too dark inside her head.

The rain, of course, only made her feel worse. But the rain was the least of it now. If it were only raining—if that were all, and nothing else—Miranda knew she would not be nearly this bad, because it rained most of the time in this city. But there were so many things, so many other factors piled one atop the other, so many bad, dark things that were making everything around her dim, as if God himself had turned down the lights on the world, casting those long, engulfing shadows everywhere, shadows that went from a pale gray to a deep purple to the deepest, blackest black imaginable. Cold shadows that made her bones hollow and her chest thick with so many things: bitter anger, strangling sadness, overwhelming self-loathing, utter helplessness…and a rolling desire in her gut to banish that helplessness, to exorcise it like a possessing demon by taking things into her own hands and *doing* something, *anything*, whatever it might take to make things better, to make the shadows go away and bring back the light that was now missing from her life only, no one else's, no one else in the world.

That one feeling, of needing to take control and do something about the problem, was very strong now, perhaps stronger than it ever had been. It was drawing her mind out of its darkness, forcing it to think in that direction, to consider ways of brightening the darkness by her own hand rather than waiting for it to happen on its own.

She had awakened that morning with a horrible feeling she had not experienced in a long time. She had opened her eyes and stared up at the ceiling of her bedroom with the absolute certainty that she was not lying *on* her bed but was actually a *part* of it. *In* it. She had awakened with the feeling that she was no longer solid—a bad sign. The fact that it had been a long time since she had experienced it was no comfort, because the longer it was gone, the longer it stayed when it returned. She had been unable to shake the feeling before going to work.

She had gone through the day quietly, hoping no one would notice how terribly thin her existence was, hoping no one would catch a glimpse of something *through* her, and hoping things would not get worse. Because what typically followed the realization of her vaporousness was much worse. Much darker. It was followed by the shadows. They came next.

But in spite of her efforts early in the day to fight off what she knew was coming, they had come after all, those shadows, in spite of her Herculean efforts to maintain a pleasant disposition and go about her business. They had come when she returned to the building that night and had gone into Dr. Jorgan's apartment, expecting to find him, planning to throw herself at him, to have rabid, noisy, unashamed sex with him in order to repair her ghostly state of being. Instead, she had found his packed suitcases waiting by the door while he was away doing something else. No doubt preparing to go away. To leave her.

And she had little doubt that he was preparing to go away with that bitch, that rich, spoiled cunt who probably had been solid every second of her life. Emma Shaw.

Miranda had gone to Dr. Jorgan's bed, which was the biggest piece of furniture in the small, cramped apartment, and planted her behind onto the edge of it, fighting to retain her posture as she stared at the suitcases. She cried silently at first, then sobbed, and felt her body curl up on the bed like a singed string. She felt her muscles melting and her bones becoming soft, pliable shafts of warm clay, felt herself dissolving into Dr. Jorgan's mattress, becoming part of it. Disappearing.

So Miranda had stood to prevent herself from disappearing, and brought her violent crying jag to an abrupt halt. She had gone to Dr. Jorgan's office and stood outside his door, listening to him talk. Miranda had heard everything he told Mr. Shaw, and she had known it was a lie.

But she knew what he was up to. She had known that as soon as she heard the lie, and Dr. Jorgan had confirmed it when he had asked Mr. Shaw where Emma was.

That was what she thought about as she stared out the window at the wet and glimmering parking lot with its tall, glowing, bone-thin sentries—what Dr. Jorgan was up to.

He was trying to find that whore so he could save her, that bitch, that cunt who was so rich and so spoiled and so solid.

Not like Miranda, who was little more than a cloud of smoke. She knew it was true now, because she had seen the utter shock in Dr. Jorgan's eyes when she had tried to touch his arm and her hand had simply oozed into his elbow with hardly any impact at all. Soon, it would pass right through. He had looked at her with absolute horror. Miranda knew now that it was true. She was a ghost. Nothing more.

She knew, also, that Dr. Jorgan was leaving. Running away from his job and from Mr. Shaw to look for that woman.

And she knew where that woman was. In a mission. Somewhere in the city, there was a mission in which that woman was being cared for, as if she were not rich enough to buy the place, tear it down, and put up a luxury high-rise condo. As if she were not solid enough to take care of herself. Someone was taking care of her as if she needed it. As if she deserved it. And she probably thought she was hidden from everyone.

Well, if that was what she was thinking, then she was wrong. Because Dr. Jorgan knew. And Miranda knew.

She was certain she could find that rich, whining twat with no trouble at all and take care of her before Dr. Jorgan found her. He would know then—she would *make* him know—that Emma Shaw was not what he needed. He would learn that Miranda was the only one who really mattered, who really cared for him, loved him, who could give his life meaning.

Although she was sure there were plenty of others, Miranda knew of only one mission in the city. The big one. In that huge, ominous old building. She thought it was South Street, but she was not certain. It hardly mattered. She knew where it was, and she would find it. She would start there, and if she could not find Emma Shaw there, Miranda would work her way through the phone book if necessary.

Miranda knew she could find Emma Shaw before Dr. Jorgan because she was almost completely invisible. And she could pass through walls.

29.

DINNER CONVERSATION

When he opened his eyes and saw all the pipes and wiring running along the ceiling above him, McNolte bolted upright on the bed and wondered how long he had been asleep.

"I was about to wake you."

Emma stood at the foot of the bed, facing him. Behind her, a card table was set up with two trays of food on it. He caught a whiff of something that smelled delicious and his stomach rumbled.

"Are you hungry?" she said.

He rubbed his bleary eyes and yawned, his hands feeling heavy, as if he had been drugged. "Doesn't seem like that long ago that I was eating," he said, standing and stretching his arms above his head, "but I'm starving."

"Well, soup's on."

"How long was I out?"

"Oh, about an hour, a little less, maybe."

McNolte's pant leg was still rolled up, so he leaned down and tugged it back into place.

"I couldn't help noticing you'd hurt yourself," Emma said, nodding toward his leg, "so I had Mama Charity bring down some bandages. I've got some bumps that could use a little attention myself. I'll wrap that ugly lump on your leg, if you'd like. But if you don't mind, I need to eat first because I'm starving."

Seating herself at the table, she began scooping food onto her plate.

There was something different about her. He watched her closely as he took his seat, trying not to be too obvious about it but wanting to identify the subtle change in her.

Emma seemed much more relaxed, for one thing. Perhaps the shower had helped. Even her voice sounded more natural. She still looked exhausted, but there was something else, too.

The plaid shirt and jeans were gone. Now she wore a pair of baggy men's pajamas, dark blue with large gray buttons down the front. And the auburn hair that looked so spiky and jagged and greasy before was now smooth and shiny and had a slight bounce to it when she moved her head. It was growing wild, with no order to it, no direction, which somehow served to give it a more intriguing look. Her face was clean and her skin was pale and smooth, without a blemish. Her hands were clean, too, and he watched them a moment as she put food on her plate, marveling at the length of her lovely fingers, which somehow had appeared short and stubby earlier, when they had worn a thin layer of mottled grime. She did not look at all like the woman he had met, the bundle of nerves and fear in the rubber poncho.

"Do you know that you're staring?" she said softly as she set her plate before her with one hand, picked up her fork with the other, and began to eat without hesitation or shame, unlike any woman McNolte had ever eaten with before. She shoveled the food from her plate into her mouth, and her face took a sublime look of almost sexual pleasure.

"I'm sorry," McNolte said. He lifted his plate and dished up some food: a couple of slices of pressed turkey breast meat, mashed potatoes and gravy, jellied cranberry sauce, mixed vegetables and a hot roll. There were two cans of generic cola in the middle of the table. Emma had not touched hers, but McNolte grabbed his and snapped it open.

Emma chewed for a long time, her eyes closed beneath raised brows. She swallowed, then dabbed a napkin over her lips.

"If it's my hair," she said, "I don't blame you. It looks terrible. I used to have long hair. Really full, too." She picked up her knife, pinned down a slice of turkey meat with her fork, as if it might get away, and sliced with rapid, emphatic strokes of the blade. "But they shaved it all off for the two operations. Now it's growing back like wild shrubbery, or something. I despise it. But I suppose it's better than being bald." She speared a couple of chunks of the meat, slid them into her mouth, and chewed with great relish, eyes closed again, jaw working slowly behind lips that only barely remained together.

"No," McNolte said. "It wasn't your hair. It's just that you seem so...different now. Than before, I mean."

"Amazing what a shower will do, huh?" she said with half a smile, mouth still full.

"And I think you're being a little hard on your hair. I'm sure it looked fine before, but it looks good now. Very, um...hip, I think."

"Hip. I've never been hip in my life. Whether I try or not, I'm never hip."

He spent a few seconds staring at her again and muttered, "Timeless."

"I'm sorry?"

His neck burned with embarrassment. He was not sure why he had said the word. He had thought it, but had not meant to speak it aloud. Apparently, he was still groggy from his hour-long nap. He avoided her eyes as he took another bite of the food.

"What did you say?" she asked.

He swallowed, cleared his throat, and said, "Timeless. You strike me as a woman who doesn't take to passing fads. You know, timeless. The kind of, um, beauty that's always in style. That sort of thing. That's what I meant."

She laughed as she put a forkful of mashed potatoes into her mouth and chewed, making the tendons in her long, slender neck stand out against her pale skin, then swallowed. "That's very nice of you to say. But I'm afraid my hair is still atrocious."

"You seem much more relaxed."

"I think that's because we're down here."

"Oh? Why is that?"

"I've got a slight buzz in my head right now. It's very quiet, probably just from the fluorescent lights. They do that, you know, especially when there are a lot of them, like the long tube lights in here. But other than that, I'm fine. We're pretty isolated down here. There's not a lot of interference. I can think clearly. Have a conversation."

"That kind of thing really bothers you, huh?" McNolte said. "Like the microwave back at Wee's?"

She dabbed her lips with the napkin again, then reached for the cola and opened it with a hissing pop.

"You know how an AM radio station sounds when it's just in range enough to hear the voices, but just enough out of range for the voices to be garbled by static?"

He nodded.

"That's what it's like inside my head when I'm around a lot of electrical appliances. When I was on the street in the city, I really thought it was going to go insane, because I had nothing but garbly static in my head all the time. It varied in intensity, but it was always there. I could barely hear over it. And it got worse if I was around something like, um, say, a radio or TV station, something like that. Nothing but constant hissing static, everything so garbled. My head felt...swollen. Like it was inflated with static and might just split open at any second. Like a melon. And all this wiry electrical stuff would just tumble out of my broken skull." She chuckled shaking her head, as if embarrassed by her own words. "That probably sounds crazy, but that's how it felt. And because of that, my nerves were raw all the time. Like every single nerve in my body was exposed and had cold air blowing over it. The biggest toothache in the world inside my head. At the lab, it was much different. Quiet and calm, no interference. It's not as quiet here, but at least I can think."

Emma sliced into the turkey meat again. "To tell you the truth, I don't care if I ever leave this basement. Really, I don't. At least, that's how I feel right now. It's quiet, and I feel safe." She lifted the fork and plucked the meat from it with her teeth.

McNolte smiled as he watched her enjoy that single bite of food more than he had ever seen anyone enjoy anything. Her face seemed to glow as she chewed with her head tilted back slightly, muscles in her neck working slowly, luxuriously beneath her pale skin.

"You know," she said, "not long ago, I probably would have been horribly offended by this food. I mean, compared to what I'm used to, I probably wouldn't even have touched it. But right now...well, this is maybe the most delicious meal I've ever had in my entire life. I was living on candy bars and the occasional bag of chips or teriyaki beef stick. My God, it's amazing the things people put into their bodies as snacks, isn't it? *This*, however... is *delicious*."

"I'm glad," McNolte said with a chuckle.

She put her fork and knife down and sighed. "I just hope all these nice people don't get killed because of me."

His smile dropped off his face as he put his knife and fork down. "You sure know how to spoil a mood."

"Why do you think I didn't want to come here in the first place? I mean, now I know it's a great place to hide for a while, but that's only because it's so comfortable for *me*. That's my selfish streak showing. I know my husband too well, McNolte. I know what he can do. Apparently, your friend P.W. doesn't believe me. He seems to think he can do something to keep me safe. Your friend is a nice man and I know he means well, but he has no idea what we're dealing with, here. And after all, he's just a homeless guy, right?"

McNolte felt a tentacle of anger and another of loyalty make vicious swipes inside him, but he buried them. "No, he's not just a homeless guy. I'm not sure exactly *what* he is, but there seems to be a lot more to P.W. than meets the eye."

"That's the problem with my husband. There's more to him than meets the eye, too. What meets the eye is charming and sophisticated and engaging. But beneath that..." She took another drink rather than finishing the sentence. "He's going to find me. Eventually. I...I guess I've resigned myself to it. That way, it won't be such a shock when it happens. But I know it'll happen. Sooner or later."

"Why do you say that. How is he going to find you in the basement of a mission, for God's sake? There's no reason for him to look here, or even consider this a possibility. Unless you're the charitable type and you spend a lot of time in missions."

A cold laugh bubbled out of her. "Hardly. I mentioned my

selfish streak earlier. Normally, I'd never step foot in a mission."

"Then why would he look for you in one?"

"I know Landon. I've known him a long time, and I know that if he wants to find someone, he will. Especially if it's his wife who's supposed to be dead...and who's carrying around one of his precious projects in her head. He's big on ownership, my husband, and the way he sees us, he owns both of us. His project and me. And he wants us back. He found me in that little greasy spoon, didn't he? That man with the gun?"

"Why was he wearing a surgical mask, by the way," McNolte said.

"I have no idea. Maybe as some kind of disguise, something to confuse witnesses. I don't know."

"Did you recognize him? Have you seen him before?"

"Oh, yes, I've seen him before. I don't know his name, but I recognized him right away. He works for Landon, of course." She scooped up a second helping of mashed potatoes, speared a second slice of turkey with her fork and put it on her plate. Her mouth was soon full of turkey and mashed potatoes again.

"What if your husband *doesn't* find you?"

Her chewing slowed as she narrowed her eyes at his question, frowned. She stopped chewing altogether for a moment, thinking about the question.

"You're dead, right?" McNolte said. "Let's say he turns the city upside down, doesn't find you, looks everywhere else, then finally gives up, figures you're *really* dead, or something. Just think, you could do whatever you want then. You could start your life over. Right?"

Emma looked him in the eye and laughed, covering her mouth with a hand because she had not swallowed her food yet.

"I'm sorry," she said, after gulping the food down. "I just found that funny because...well, see, Landon never gives up. Never. He just *doesn't*. Especially if he's hunting for something that belongs to him that he's lost, or that's been taken away from him. You don't know him, McNolte." She put her knife and fork down and leaned back in her chair. "He collects collections. He has a car collection, an art collection, a rare books collection. He drives the car, but he doesn't read and he hates art, doesn't see any point to it. Because he's an empty human being. Empty of everything but greed for more. He has a thimble collection. Sounds stupid, doesn't it? But it's a thimble collection worth millions. He lost one of those thimbles once. We looked and looked, but couldn't find it. He moved us into another house and then tore that one apart looking for his thimble. *Literally* tore it apart. He found the thimble, but the house was destroyed. He had it demolished and sold the land. He never gives up. That's the kind of man he is, and that's the way he does things."

McNolte frowned as he leaned back in his chair and folded his arms over his chest. "You say that as if you admire him for it."

Emma flinched and her pleasant smile was swallowed up by a look of fiery anger. "I don't admire that son of a bitch for *anything*. I'm simply telling you how things are, trying to make you understand what he's like, what you and your friends are up against with me around. I would've gotten out of that marriage a long time ago if I weren't so damned afraid of him. And as you've seen, there's plenty to be afraid of. The man is evil." She shook her head. "No, that's probably the wrong word. It suggests something supernatural. He's just empty, like I said. Empty. And evil is what results from that emptiness."

"Um, I'm sorry," McNolte said, squirming in his seat. "I didn't mean...I just misinterpreted you, I guess. I apologize. Please, eat your food. You were enjoying it so much."

After about thirty seconds, she leaned forward and began to eat again. In a moment, she seemed to be unaware of anything being wrong in her life, even unaware of what she had just said a moment ago. The food made her happy. Soon, she was smiling again, and she shared that smile with McNolte, locking her eyes with his as she chewed.

"You see?" he said. "Things aren't so bad after all, are they? You should stop assuming that everything is hopeless. You'll end up fulfilling your own prophecies."

She shook her head as she swallowed her food. "Good Lord, I've gotten myself hooked up with an optimist. What do you do for a living, anyway? Clean chimneys in a Disney movie, or something?"

"No, I'm a writer."

"A writer? An *optimistic* writer? Isn't that like military intelligence? Judging by the writers I've known, that's quite an oxymoron you've got there. Shouldn't you be inebriated and brooding about the meaningless of existence? Something like that?"

"I'm not that kind of writer. Besides, that's a stereotype. The only writers I've known who were drunk all the time were that way because they were always broke. I'm optimistic only because...well, I've had to be. I guess if you find yourself in a hole, you either have to look up and start climbing or, sooner or later, it'll fall in on you. I have a pessimistic streak, believe me. I've just found out that I don't have much use for it, so I keep it in a closet, you might say."

She rested her hands on the table, one holding the fork and the other the knife, and looked at him curiously. "Bad things have happened to you, haven't they, McNolte?"

"Hey, I crawled through a bathroom window with you while being shot at, didn't I?"

She laughed. "I mean before that. Tell me your story, Mr. McNolte."

"It's more a case of me being my own worst enemy."

"Let's hear it. We've got time."

"Oh, take my word for it, you don't want to hear the story. It's very boring. Full of clichés. Sort of like a network TV movie of the week, but without the pretty stars and dramatic music. You've heard it all before, I'm sure. Usually with several commercial breaks."

"No, really, tell me. After all, I had to bare all to you and your friends upstairs. Not necessarily of my own free will, either. You practically had me imprisoned in that office. So...I showed you mine, now you show me yours."

Reluctantly, McNolte told Emma his story, keeping it short. She listened with interest, interrupting at times to ask questions or make comments. When she finished her meal, she removed her tray from the table and put it on the floor so she could prop her elbows on the tabletop and rest her chin on her joined hands, eyes looking sleepy but attentive, her unfinished soda on the table before her.

When McNolte was done, she said nothing, but continued to look at him. Her eyes were heavy-lidded but alert as she searched his face, as if trying to decide what to make of his story, his misfortune.

Finally, she said, "It's amazing. It's like I've been living with blinders on my whole life."

"What do you mean?"

"I always thought my life was so different from everyone else's. Not *everyone's*, exactly, but different from the lives of people who weren't...like me."

"You mean poor people."

She sighed. "I was born into a wealthy family. Ridiculously wealthy. Then I married a wealthy man. I've been wealthy my whole life. And I've always assumed that people who *aren't* wealthy have very different lives, worlds apart."

"We do. Trust me."

"The only real difference is the tax bracket. The problems pretty much stay the same. Wealthy people just have more options open to them when they deal with those problems, that's all. Well, better drugs, too. That's usually different."

"I always thought rich people snort coke, too, right? From what I've heard, that's how a lot of them get poor."

"Some, I suppose. But not in the circles I've moved in all my life. Illegal drugs can be messy. We prefer the prescription variety, and we can afford doctors who'll be generous with their prescription pads. For a while, I had a rather serious relationship with Xanax. I had to go into rehab in Colorado for that. Which wasn't so bad, because it got me away from Landon. But it was a problem nonetheless and it messed up my life for a while. After that, I had a fling with OxyContin and went back to see my friends at the Colorado rehab facility. Some of the same ones were there, too. I had a friend, a rich woman, even richer than us, and she had a drug problem, too. She was involved with a variety of prescription pills. One night a few years ago, she took too many Halcions with her Remy Martin. She was on life support for about six months until her family decided to pull the plug. She died the same day. And there've been others, too. Some close friends, some who were just acquaintances. I guess pain is pain and drugs is drugs, huh? And the results are usually the same, no matter how rich you are. I guess I'm just a little surprised to come to that realization."

McNolte saw the conversation taking a serious, even dark, tone and he was not in the mood to follow it in that direction, so he smiled and said, "But how many people do you know who have been stupid enough to burn up a suitcase full of cocaine about forty-five minutes after buying it with money borrowed from a vicious loan shark?"

She laughed. "You really think this guy will have you killed?"

"Eventually. He's told me he'll start with my fingers."

"Your fingers?"

"Yes, he'll break them."

"If I had my checkbook with me, McNolte, I would happily solve your problem with a few scribbles."

"Dead women don't write checks."

She chuckled.

"What about you, Emma? Why do you suppose your husband wants you dead? Seems to me he's got a lot invested in you. Why doesn't he just round you up and take you back to his lab instead of blowing a whole diner away to kill you?"

"Obviously, I'm very important to him, but I'm a danger to him. What I've overheard alone is probably enough to ruin him, if I could get the right people to believe me. But that's not the only reason. I've also defied him one time too many. I'm afraid this is the last straw. He's probably already got my replacement picked out. Somebody who will be afraid of him and acquiesce to all those disgusting procedures. That's how I used to be. Until recently. He'll find someone who doesn't know him as well as I do. Or hate him as much." She sipped her cola. "And this time, thanks to what they learned from working on me, his drones at OdysseyCorp will probably be much more efficient. Only one operation instead of two. Twice the results in half the time. In the end, Landon will get exactly what he wants. And so will the Pentagon." Her voice lowered to a near-whisper. "And so will his miserable goddamned shadow clients."

"Shadow clients?" McNolte said. "You mentioned those

upstairs. What kind of people does he sell OdysseyCorp's work to under the table? Are we talking about foreign governments, or enemies of the country, or organized crime? That sort of thing?"

"All of the above," she said. "Whoever can put up the most money. That's all the morality Landon has ever known. The morality of the highest bidder. Of course, these days, that's just about all the morality we've got left in this country."

"I don't understand why you don't pull the rug out from under him," McNolte said. "You just said you know enough to ruin him. Why don't you?"

"*If* I could get the right people to believe me. I don't have any proof I can hand them. Besides, I never know who might be in Landon's pocket. The police department in the little town next to the lab? He owns them. If I went to them, they'd just take me right back to him."

"I think you've got plenty of proof. What you can *do* is proof. You've done it to me twice and even though it still sounds like science fiction to me, I—hey, wait a second. Why haven't you done it to *him*? Why is he even a problem? Why haven't you—"

"Yes, I know. It's the logical question. I've considered it. I even came close to trying it once. Nothing I can say, though, will make you understand my reasoning. I can't even call it that, it's unreasonable. It's irrational. But it's natural given my experience with Landon."

"I don't understand, what do you mean?"

"I was afraid."

"But what's he going to do? This isn't like a gun he can grab out of your hand. This is right inside your own—"

"I know, I know. But it's not that simple."

Emma told him about The Towel.

"Oh, God, I'm sorry," he said, wincing.

"That's just one example of my life with Landon. And I never knew when he was going to surprise me with a new one. When he wasn't actually physically abusing me, he was threatening physical abuse. And he was good at that. He could make my knees shake with his cruel threats because I knew he might actually carry out those threats. I was terrified of him,

McNolte. I still am. All I have to do is *think* about him and my skin tightens. Do you know how powerful that kind of fear is? I was in training to fear Landon the whole time we were married. That's what our marriage was. Fear training. And it worked. Now, I've got this bizarre ability inside my head that I could use on him in a second, but just being in the room with him freezes me up. Does that make any sense at all?"

"It does, yes. I'm sorry for making you go to such great lengths to explain it. You're the victim here, you shouldn't have to explain anything."

"But even though I couldn't use it on him, I still used it," she said. "That's how I got out of OdysseyCorp. I don't know how badly those people were hurt, or if I killed any of them." She massaged the back of her neck with her left hand for a moment. "To be honest, I don't care. They're all nothing but sycophants."

With a heavy sigh, she began eating again, but after a couple of bites, she put down her fork and pushed the plate away. "I think I've eaten too much."

"You had quite an appetite."

"Normally, I wouldn't be caught dead eating that much in front of someone. But, yes, I was very hungry." She folded her arms on the table and leaned forward. "So, McNolte, tell me, who should I go to with my story? The Pentagon? They're the ones who commissioned the project. If I went to them and showed them what I can do, it would be like Santa Claus dropping in a couple of months early. They would be *thrilled*. And I would never be seen again. Who else? The FBI? The president, maybe?"

"I see you've given this a lot of thought."

"I have. I've had plenty of time to think locked up in my house for so long, then at OdysseyCorp. And the one conclusion I come to again and again is this: get the hell out of the city, out of Landon's reach, before he even knows I'm gone. Go somewhere far away. Start over."

"What about your family?"

"They're all dead. And Landon and I have no children. Thank God."

"Friends?"

"All of my friends were Landon's friends first. And they

remain Landon's friends first, trust me. Going to them would be like going straight to Landon."

It would be easy to believe that she *wanted* her situation to be hopeless, so determined was she to shoot down his every suggestion. But he knew she was telling the truth, that she had thought it all through, considered every possible option, and found them all to be dead ends.

Frustrated, Landon said, "Please don't think I'm trying to blame you for your situation. I'm not. I'm just curious. Why didn't you leave him years ago? When you found out what a nightmare he is?"

"Oh, I tried. I tried to leave him once. I was going to fly to Florida to be with my sister. She was still alive then. But he had a couple of goons catch me at the airport and drag me back to him. I have no idea how he knew that's what I was going to do, but he did. I even tried to have him killed once, but that didn't work, either."

McNolte's surprise registered on his face. "You tried to have him killed?"

Without a word, she said yes—with a twitch of the brow, a smile that played about her eyes, a tilt of her head to one side and back a bit. It was a mild look of defiance, as if she were daring him to make a castigating remark, to pass judgment on her.

"You hired somebody?" he said.

"Not exactly. There was this man, a very powerful man, a lot more powerful than Landon but with too much class and self-confidence to go around shoving it down people's throats." She finished off her cola, then leaned forward and rested her chin on her arms. "He was one of Landon's shadow clients. Had been for a long time, for years. An older man. Older than me, I mean. I had an affair with him. I was the instigator. That was hard. I did *not* feel attractive. Landon had worn me down into such a state of self-loathing I could hardly look in the mirror. But I forced myself. It had been so long since I had pursued a man that I wasn't sure I could do it without making a fool of myself. I thought of myself as an aging, faded movie star trying to make a comeback. That's how I did it, joking myself through it like that. I was Norma Desmond trying to get her Salome movie made. But what I was *really* doing was trying to train myself to be sexy again. I wasn't sure it would work. But I thought this shadow client would get a thrill out of nailing Landon's wife. I figured he *had* to know what a prick Landon was.

"I was right," she said with a slight smile. "He took the bait. I was afraid it would end up being a one-night stand, but he came back for more. I was surprised, but relieved. I wanted to work on him, soften him up, and somehow push him into the idea of having Landon killed, but in a way that would make it look like his idea. The amazing thing...the really *stunning* thing...was that it worked *too* well."

McNolte smiled. "You mean, he fell in love with you?"

Pressing her lips together so her cheeks dimpled a bit at each end of her mouth, she shrugged and said, "He *said* he was in love with me. And he acted like it, too. So when he found out that Landon beats me, that I was afraid to leave him because he would find me and kill me...when I told him about The Towel... he offered to have him killed for me." She laughed. "Can you believe it? It worked."

"Did you, um..." McNolte cleared his throat. "Did you fall in love with him?"

"Oh, God, *no.* Like I said, he's a lot older, and big fat guy. I mean, *big.* He's sweet, a real gentleman, interesting company. But even if there was a chance in the world that I might have fallen for him, I wouldn't have had time. I was too busy trying not to think about who and what he was. The shadow client. We're talking about a very powerful man who has killed people, had people killed. He calls himself a businessman, and technically that's true, but all of his business dealings are as crooked as can be, and some of the people involved in them die simply from being involved in them. Being in the wrong place at the wrong time. On the surface, he's different from Landon, but when it comes right down to it, they're exactly alike. Both of them... scum."

"Why isn't Landon dead?"

"Because he had something the shadow client wanted more

than me. Project Biofire. It's something he would be extremely interested in. A way to kill people with natural causes? Are you kidding? A guy like him would have to have something like that. I've given it a lot of thought and gone over the timeline. I'm not *positive*, but I'd bet serious money that my knight in shining armor dropped me and his plans for Landon because it got in the way of his chances of obtaining the results of Project Biofire."

"You're kidding me."

"Of course not. He always said he was married to his work, that it came first. That's what he said in his so-long note to me. Business first, before everything else, including me. So he didn't kill Landon because he was more useful to him alive."

"But…I thought this guy was in *love* with you."

"He probably was. For a little while. But it was eclipsed by his need to stay on top, to murder the competition without getting caught."

"Does he know Landon used you in his experiment?"

Emma shrugged again. "I suppose so. Like Landon, all that matters to him is the result, not the way it's achieved."

She stared at her hand for a while as she made invisible doodles on the table with a fingernail.

"That must have been upsetting."

"Oh, I've been through worse." She stopped doodling and looked at him. "Like what Landon did to me when he found out."

McNolte watched her, waiting for her to continue.

Instead, she stood and stretched her arms out straight at each side, saying, "I don't know about you, but I'm going to whip out some of those sheets and blankets, make my bed, and then get into it. I'm exhausted. I'm sure you feel the same. Is someone going to come down and clean up the food?"

He smiled. He doubted she was accustomed to clearing her own table or doing her own dishes. "Don't worry, I'll take care of that before I go to bed. Right now, I think I'm going to take a shower."

Her face brightened. "Yes, do that. It's wonderful. After tonight? Best shower I ever had."

"Like the food."

"Yes, exactly. I'm going to remember every detail of this night for the rest of my life." Another sigh. "However long that might be."

McNolte headed for the bathroom, but Emma stepped directly in front of him, forcing him to stop abruptly with maybe four inches between their faces. She smiled, but when she spoke, her breathy voice quavered and her lips trembled slightly.

"Thank you, McNolte," she whispered. "Thank you for everything you've done." She put first one hand on his left shoulder, then, after a moment's hesitation, the other hand on his right shoulder. "I can't stay here forever, you know that as well as I do, but thank you for bringing me here. It was just what I needed, even if it's only for a little while." Emma leaned forward and gave him a brief but warm kiss on the corner of his mouth and squeezed his shoulders once. "Thanks. Now, go take your shower."

She stepped around him and shuffled wearily to the cupboard that held the sheets and blankets.

McNolte wanted to turn around and stop her, tell her that she did not have to stay there forever, just long enough for her husband to lose interest. But after their conversation about Landon Shaw, that would be a stupid thing to say. The man was not going to lose interest.

Still, he worried she would try to wander off on her own in the middle of the night. Not tonight, certainly, because she was probably going to sleep like a corpse after her days and nights on the street. But maybe tomorrow night, or the night after that. He wanted to tell her what a mistake that would be, a bigger mistake than staying at South Street for a while, because then she would be alone, on her own again, with no help at all.

He said none of that, though, and he did not move. The spot at the corner of his mouth to which she had touched her lips was warm and tingly, and he could still smell her soapy scent, the shampoo she had used, could still feel her hands on his shoulders. Those sensations held him in place for a while.

This is a mistake, he thought, after a quick inventory of his feelings at the moment. *You're still too messed up yourself to be attracted to a woman as messed up as she is.*

McNolte decided he needed a shower more than ever.

30.

HEAD GAMES ⬜ PART 1

Landon Shaw chewed up his sixth Gaviscon tablet after hanging up the phone. He lay back in a plush recliner in his living room while some soothing Haydn played softly from speakers hidden in the walls all around him. He closed his eyes, chewing the tablet slowly, letting it foam up in his mouth a little and ooze down his throat.

But even after six Gaviscon tablets, the volcanic activity in his gut did not subside, and he knew it would not.

Dunne had told him everything Doc Dexter had learned from the waitress in the hospital, and Shaw had told him to go home for the night. Then he had put a couple of men on it. He was confident everything would be cleaned up within the next hour or two.

But now...all he could do was wait. Shaw had never been very good at waiting for things—waiting, by definition, was the absence of control—and in this case, it was going to be harder than usual. He had no control over this, not even a modicum of it. The whole thing was out of his hands and he was helpless. He had done everything he possibly could, which was less than usual. Under normal circumstances, he would call in a favor from the police department, have them keep an eye out for Emma in the city. But her corpse had just been pulled out of the Thunderhead, and the police were not involved in that particular sleight-of-hand trick, so they would look askance at such a request, to say the least.

His hands were bound and he was gagged. That was exactly

how he felt, bound tightly and gagged with some foul, balled-up rag and left in the dark, helpless to manipulate the events going on around him, unable even to monitor them. It was an unusual position for Landon Shaw to be in, and it made his whole body feel clogged up, dysfunctional.

"You don't look well, Mr. Shaw."

He opened his eyes to see Mrs. Babcock standing beside the chair, hands joined behind her.

"I don't feel well at all, Mrs. Babcock."

"Your stomach again?"

"That, and a very...*very* bad evening."

"I'm sorry. Can I get you anything?"

"No, I don't think so."

"Maybe you should go to bed, Mr. Shaw."

"I don't think I would be able to sleep, Mrs. Babcock. Besides, I'm expecting a phone call. Sooner or later."

"Why don't you take a couple of your sleeping pills, soak in a hot tub for a bit, then go to bed, anyway. I'll wake you if anyone calls."

He closed his eyes again, finding the idea of a bath and a good night's sleep appealing. He felt like he had not slept in weeks. He would have to sleep partially sitting up on pillows, though, otherwise the sizzling acid inside him would creep up slowly until it was in his throat, then his mouth, where it probably would dissolve his tongue if it he let it.

"You know, Mrs. Babcock," he said, sitting up slowly, then rising to his feet, "that may be just the thing I need to do right now. Try to get some sleep."

"Would you like me to run the bath for you?"

"No, you don't have to do that," he said, leaning back, stretching his aching muscles. A few muted pops went off in his back. "But bring me some chamomile tea. Put it on my nightstand. And remember, Mrs. Babcock, it's terribly important that you wake me when—"

"I'll be waiting for it to ring, Mr. Shaw, and I'll wake you immediately, don't worry."

He muttered his thanks, then dragged his feet upstairs to his bedroom. After undressing, he hung his clothes meticulously in his closet, with half an inch of space between the items of clothing. He removed his pajamas from a drawer and put them on, slid his feet into his slippers, took his robe from the closet and shrugged into it, tying the belt, then went into the bathroom and flipped on the light.

The spacious bathroom was tiled in cream and sky blue. To his right upon entering, along the bedroom wall of the bathroom, there was a long tile counter with two sinks to his right, with a three-sectioned mirror stretching above it. Each of the end sections opened on a deep medicine cabinet. Above the mirror was a panel of seven globe lights. The toilet was at the far end of the counter, against the wall. Across from the counter, a wall of glass bricks opened in an arch. Shaw passed through the arch and up the three tiled steps to the luxurious oval-shaped bathtub. There was a shower of chrome and frosted glass in one corner. Instead of windows, there were strips of glass bricks in the tiled walls that let in light during the day.

Shaw turned to his right and slid a rectangular panel of the wall upward. Beneath it was a control panel. He punched a button and, instantly, the music he had been listening to downstairs began to play from speakers concealed in the bathroom walls. He closed the panel, turned, stepped along the tub, hunkered down and turned the ceramic handles on each side of the chrome faucet. Testing the water with his fingers, he adjusted the handles, tested it again, then stood as steam began to billow up from the tub.

He untied the belt of his robe, smacking his lips a few times. His mouth had the familiar, vaguely foul taste that was caused by the acids roiling inside him. As the bathtub filled, Shaw went back down the steps, through the arch, and to one of the sinks to brush his teeth, quietly humming along with the music. He gently punched the bottom edge of the mirror with his thumb and the section swung open as he reached up to take his toothpaste from one of the glass shelves.

Something fell out of the cabinet, something oval-shaped and heavy and green. It landed in the sink with a loud, sickening *crack*. Blood splattered over the tiles.

A soft, abrupt sound of surprise came from Shaw's throat,

but he did not move for a moment. His hand remained frozen in the air, halfway to the medicine cabinet. Staring into the sink. Eyes getting gradually wider. Mouth opening until it could open no further. Lips twitching as they pulled back over teeth. Bath water running. Haydn playing softly.

"*Jesus!*" He stumbled backward suddenly, slamming into the wall of glass bricks. He slid down until he was sitting on the floor, knees jutting upward, legs spread. Then he released a long, loud cry of anger and disgust, clenching his eyes shut, trying, but failing, to block out the image that remained before him as clearly as if he were still looking at it.

The image of Rupert's severed head staring up out of the sink with dead, open eyes that had retreated deeply into their sockets, a cigar clamped tightly in the lizard's mouth.

31.

CONNECTIONS

When McNolte came out of the bathroom after a long, soothing shower, he was surprised, and a little alarmed, to hear voices. But when he heard P.W.'s laughter, he knew nothing was wrong. He wore a pair of baggy pajama bottoms and a white terrycloth robe, and his wet hair sprang from his head in thin, worm-like tangles. He roughed it up with one hand to flatten it a bit, surprised to find himself feeling self-conscious about his appearance in Emma's presence.

She and P.W. were facing one another, each of them seated on the edge of a bed, knees nearly meeting in the middle. Emma was seated on the same bed on which McNolte had napped. P.W. was surprised to see that both beds had been made up with sheets, blankets, and pillowcases. He had not expected Emma to be comfortable sleeping right next to him, even if in a different bed.

Beside P.W. on the bed was a cardboard box, and next to that, a bulging grocery bag.

P.W. looked over his shoulder as McNolte approached and stood, stuffing his hands into the back pockets of his jeans. "Hey, babe, feel better after your shower?"

"Much. What'd you bring, P.W.? It looks like you emptied the apartment."

"Only by half. I also took some money and went to a stop-and-rob, got you a carton of cigarettes, a paper, a few magazines, and some snack foods and drinks. Oh, and a *TV Guide*, just in case you wanna know what's on the idiot box while you're holed up down here."

"Thank you, P.W., that's great," McNolte said as he went to the bed and peered into the bag. "I appreciate this."

"Hey, no problem."

When he looked in the cardboard box, McNolte was puzzled to see his answering machine on top of his typewriter case. He lifted the machine, frowning, and said, "What's this for? I don't think I'll be getting any calls down here."

"I thought you'd want to hear the messages on there, so I brought it with me."

"Anything important?"

"A couple of calls. One from your agent, and, uh...one from your favorite creditor."

McNolte felt his shoulders fall. "Oh, great. Wonderful. What did *he* have to say?" He was in no mood to hear Trafficante's voice at the moment.

"Oh, some pretty interesting things." P.W.'s smile grew and he released a quiet chuckle. "*Real* interesting. Just think of it as a surprise, 'cause I'm not gonna tell you."

"What, he's gonna forget all about the money I owe him?"

"Sort of."

McNolte's eyes widened. "You're joking."

P.W. shook his head. "Listen to it. There's a plug in the wall over there." He nodded toward a socket on the other side of Emma's bed. "I think both of you should listen to it."

McNolte found that last remark disturbing, and when he looked at Emma, he saw that she felt the same way. She wore a worried, questioning look as she stared up at P.W.

After plugging the machine in, McNolte sat on the bed and hit the ON button. Emma stretched out behind him on the mattress, propped her elbow on the pillow, and watched the machine on McNolte's lap.

"Hello, McNolte. It's me. I'm calling for two reasons."

McNolte was not surprised to hear Trafficante's voice because P.W. had warned him. But he nearly fell off the bed when he heard Emma's sudden jagged gasp as she sat up and pressed her back to the wall and hugged her knees to her chest. Her eyes became so wide, they nearly swallowed her face, and they sparkled with sudden tears, mouth hanging open like that of a marionette with a broken string. He saw all that in a fraction of a second and felt a bubble of unidentifiable dread rise up in his throat. Before he could react to her behavior, Trafficante continued.

"First of all, I want to remind you that you still owe me a great deal of money. Secondly...you have something I want. Something I want very, very much. I think, McNolte, that we might be able to work out a deal, here." There was a smile in his voice when he said, "I understand you've been keeping company with a certain woman."

McNolte's head snapped around and he turned his eyes to Emma, who looked numb with terror.

"I'd like to propose a trade. You hand over the woman and I forget about the loan. Simple as that. The only reason I ask is that I'd like to speed things up, save some time. I'll find her with or without your help. The only difference is, if you don't hand her over, I'll stick to my schedule and collect on your debt. And you know what that means. It means you've given your last piano recital. You decide, McNolte. Let's see, it's twenty minutes to eleven now. I'll give you until midnight."

A soft click was followed by the machine's piercing beep. Then silence.

P.W. checked his watch and muttered, "Ten to twelve."

"Leo," Emma said, forcing her voice out in a dry croak.

"Yes," McNolte said, mouth dry as sandpaper. "Leo Trafficante. How do you know him? How does he know you?"

Her lips moved but nothing came out. She put both hands over her mouth, fingers interlocked, and closed her eyes as tears spilled down her cheeks.

McNolte was stunned by the change in Emma. Before his eyes, she had become a third person—not the jittering nervous wreck he had met in Wee's, and not the defiant and pleasantly manipulative woman with whom he had shared dinner. Now she was a vulnerable innocent, a woman cornered. She spoke haltingly, pushing the words out a few at a time.

"Leo was the man...I had the affair with. The shadow client...who was going to have...Landon killed."

Individual pieces fell together in McNolte's mind, forming

a larger whole. Everything changed in an instant, as if he had been walking around with a blindfold that was ripped from his face without warning.

"And somehow," McNolte said slowly, "he knows we're together. He probably knows I came here. And he works with your husband."

Emma rolled off the bed and began pacing the concrete floor. "My clothes, where did I put my clothes," she muttered, voice quivering as her eyes searched the room frantically, darting in every direction. "I have to get out of here. Where did I put my damned *clothes*?" Then she cried out and bent forward as if she had been struck by terrible abdominal cramps. She tried to say something else, but her voice collapsed in a fit of sobs as she fell back on her behind, hitting the hard floor with a pained grunt and falling on her side. She curled up like a crying baby, body convulsing with her sobs.

McNolte was startled to see P.W. step forward. He had forgotten that he and Emma were no longer alone.

P.W. knelt beside her and McNolte joined him.

P.W. closed his large hand on her upper arm, still smiling, but gently now, calmingly. "Hey, look, sweetie, you gotta calm down or you're gonna make yourself sick."

"Let me go," she said, jerking away from P.W.

"Careful, P.W.," McNolte said, standing. "She's already upset. You don't want to get her too worked up."

"You two have gotta get outta here right away. I don't know where yet, but I'm thinkin'. I got some friends comin' to help us tomorrow, but that'll be too late. Let me see if I can get 'em here right away. Be back in a minute." P.W. stood and went upstairs.

McNolte cautiously placed a hand on Emma's arm. "It's all right, don't worry," he said, "we're gonna be okay, don't worry."

He wished he could believe his own words.

32.

HEAD GAMES – PART 2

Landon Shaw, standing once again, shoulders rising and falling with angry, trembling breaths, stared into the sink at the cigar that was stuck in Rupert's smiling mouth. It was still wrapped in cellophane, with the familiar black-and-silver foil band wrapped around it sporting two ornate silver letters: LT.

Mrs. Babcock hurried into the bathroom, her usually stern face now tense, its color a bit mottled. She rushed to Shaw's side and started to speak, but before she got the words out, she saw the lizard's head and made a gulping sound as her back stiffened, and she stared at the head, open-mouthed and stunned into silence.

Beyond the glass brick wall, bath water was still running. Shaw did not take his eyes from Rupert's cigar-chomping smile as he reached out and closed his left hand on Mrs. Babcock's shoulder and spoke in a wet, guttural voice.

"How...did this...happen...Mrs. Babcock?"

"I-I-I...I swear, Mr. Shaw, I don't have a *clue*! No one has been here, not even at the door, and I haven't—"

Two of Shaw's security men rushed into the room with guns drawn, wearing immaculate dark suits, and Shaw was on them in a heartbeat, pushing his face into the face of one while clutching the front of the other's shirt in a fist. He screamed at them before they could ask what was wrong, and they took it with the stony faces of employees riding out a professional storm, while Mrs. Babcock hurried through the glass arch to turn off the bath.

"How did this happen?" Shaw bellowed, furious. "*Huh?* How in the *fuck* did this happen here in my *house*? How did somebody cut the fucking head off my lizard, come into this fucking house, and put that thing in my fucking medicine cabinet without being *noticed*? *How?*"

He stopped only for a breath, not long enough for either of the security men to respond.

"How did this sick fuck even get on the *property*? I want to know how in the hell somebody got into that green house and chopped the head off my—do you know what that *was*?" he shouted, pointing into the sink at the green head that ended in an abrupt, bloody stump. "That wasn't just any fucking lizard, you know, that was the biggest fucking iguana in *captivity*. You know how much that thing was *worth*?"

Cautiously, the two security men followed the direction of Shaw's finger with their eyes until they saw the severed lizard head.

The first security man, the tall one in whose face Shaw had been shouting, removed a small walkie-talkie from beneath his suit coat, held it to his mouth, and pressed a button, speaking firmly.

"This is Number Two. Red alert. All units on the perimeter *immediately*. Repeat, all units on the perimeter immediately, this is a red alert. There has been a breach. Intruders have been on the property and have broken into the main house," he said, reaching into the sink to touch the bloody stump. He rubbed his thumb and first two fingers together to see how congealed the blood was. "And the breach was recent. Number of intruders unknown, no descriptions. Armed and dangerous. Over."

Number two waited as the three security units spread over the property acknowledged his transmission, then he said, "Number Two, out," and replaced the walkie-talkie beneath his suit coat.

Mrs. Babcock returned and stood just inside the arch.

"Mr. Shaw," Number Two said, "I assure you that if whoever did this is anywhere in the vicinity, we will—"

Shaw spun away from him and paced frantically, shouting,

"What do you mean, whoever did this? I know damned *well* who did this because he *wants* me to know!" He went to the sink and plucked the cellophane-wrapped cigar from Rupert's mouth. The sudden jerk made the lizard's head roll onto its side with a thin, wet sound as the drying blood peeled away from the curved bottom of the bowl. Shaw went to Number Two and shoved the cigar in his face. "You see that? You know what that is?"

"It's...a cigar, sir."

"No, goddammit, it's a fucking *calling card*. You see those two letters right there, that L and that T on the band? Those letters stand for Leo Trafficante—" He threw the cigar to the floor so hard that it bounced over the tiles, then he stomped on it with his right foot, grinding it into the floor. "—and *he's* the fucking son of a bitch who did this." He paced again, breath coming in heaves as his hands closed into fists, opened, closed again, over and over. "That miserable fucking...why would he...who does he think he *is*?"

"Uh, Mr. Shaw," Number Two said, "we're going to take care of this, I assure you."

Shaw rushed Number Two and got in his face again. "How the fuck're you gonna do that from my *bathroom*, you bonehead?"

Number Two nodded once stiffly and said, "Thank you, sir." Then he and his partner hurried out.

Mrs. Babcock turned to Shaw then, joining her hands behind her, and watched as he paced. "Why don't you let me clean up in here, Mr. Shaw."

"Yes, please do, I'd appreciate that, Mrs. Babcock." He stopped and pointed to Rupert's head. "Keep that. I want it stuffed."

She nodded once, then said, "You can sleep in one of your guest rooms, if you prefer, Mr. Shaw. You have your health to consider. You'll be no good for anything if you don't get some sleep and if you allow the stress of this situation to exacerbate your stomach condition. You took a sleeping pill?"

"No, not yet." He stopped pacing and scowled down at the sink, disgusted. "Look at all that *blood*," he hissed.

"Don't worry, it'll all be gone in no time. Why don't you take that bath in one of the other rooms."

"Yes." His eyes fell on the crushed cigar on the floor. "What the fuck am I saying? I can't take a bath. I can't do *anything*. Because I've gotta call this son of a bitch and find out what the hell is going through his fucking dago head."

Shaw tied the belt of his robe and hurried out of the bathroom.

In his office, he dropped into the chair behind his desk, picked up the cordless receiver from its base, and hit the appropriate speed dial button.

The phone at the other end rang once. Twice. Shaw was standing impatiently by the third ring, ready to shout out at the fourth.

"Hello, Landon," Leo said.

Shaw flinched at the greeting.

There was a smile in Leo's voice.

Shaw could not find his own voice for a moment. He began to stalk around the office, clutching the receiver so hard that the plastic case creaked in his grip. "You bastard," he said. "You miserable fucking—"

"Please don't waste my time with one of your adolescent, foul-mouthed temper tantrums, Landon. It would be pointless given the fact that I have the upper hand here, and *you* are the miserable fucking bastard in this particular situation."

Shaw's teeth ground together, making thunder rumble in his head. "You killed...*my*...iguana. The largest fucking iguana in captivity."

"Not anymore. And what did *you* do, Landon? Tell me. Tell me what you did, Landon. Tell me now."

"I don't know what the fuck you're talking about."

"Then maybe you're not as bright as I thought. What I did, Landon, I did to let you know that *I* know what you've done."

Shaw knew exactly what Leo was talking about. So did his churning, burning stomach, and it said so. But he was determined not to back down, to let Leo know that it wasn't important and that he really had nothing on Shaw.

"That sounds like an Abbott and Costello routine, Leo," he said. "What are you drinking? Or are you getting senile already?"

"No, Landon, no. What this is, it's me reading you the

fucking riot act. I know what you did to Emma. I know you faked her death so you could use her as a guinea pig for your fucking project. After you'd sucked me into it, knowing how I felt about her. And the moral of this little story is that I think *you*, Landon, are one sick fucker."

"Now, wait just a second, here, Leo," Shaw said with a smirk, realizing he had that fat gangster over a barrel all of a sudden. "You can't go throwing morals around like that. You gave me a wink and a nod when you found out Emma was missing. Like you knew I'd handled it. So now that you know she's still alive, that those weren't *her* remains pulled out of the Thunderhead, *now* you're calling me a sick fucker?"

Leo sharply drew in a deep breath and let it out in a big sigh, then said, "Business is business, Landon. You know that and I know that. I thought maybe you *had* to get rid of her after what happened between her and me, after the trouble it caused. I told you how I felt about Emma. That I loved her. That I let her go for the business, which has been my life for longer than you've been alive, you cocky little shit. I figured you'd done the same. In whatever way you had to do it. But I was wrong. I was *really* wrong.

"Your own wife, Landon...using your own wife in an experiment like that. And *that* is why you're a sick fucker. And that's why I did what I did to your lizard. I did it to let you know that I *could*, in spite of all your security cameras and laser beam trip alarms, and all your fucking fine-suited goons. I did it to remind you that, in spite of whatever you might think, Landon, you are not in charge. And to let you know that all bets are off. All deals are canceled. All transactions are null and voice. I'm not interested in your fucking project anymore. I'm only interested in Emma's safety. She's out there somewhere. And I know where. I'm going to find her. And I'm going to keep her from you, just like I took your lizard away from you. Your precious, biggest-in-captivity fucking lizard."

"*You're* going to find her?" Shaw shouted. "Look, I've got my best people on this, Leo, and we know exactly where to find her now. If you think you're going to save her from her plight like some kind of knight in shining armor, you're crazy. All you're going to do is endanger yourself and everyone with you. You know why, Leo? I'll tell you. Because the experiment didn't work. Something went wrong. Emma's condition is contagious. You hear me, Leo? *Contagious!* There was some kind of virus used in the operation, a synthetic virus. Hell, I don't know the details, I hire people to keep up with that shit. But they tell me the virus has mutated. You hear that, Leo? It's mutated, and it's contagious."

Leo laughed a quiet laugh filled with a blend of mockery, genuine amusement, and threat.

Shaw could hear the grin in Leo's voice and, in his mind, he saw both rows of Leo's small teeth.

"I told you that I was in love with Emma," Leo said, still quiet, as if he were building up to something, "and I still am. I thought you got rid of her for your own legitimate reasons. But all you did was use her like some kind of animal." His voice grew louder, harder, angrier. "And now you try to tell me that *she's* a danger? That wonderful woman? *She's* a danger to me and the people around me?" He laughed again, but it was a dry, bitter sound. "You are some piece of work, Landon. Let me tell you what's gonna happen."

Shaw stopped pacing and seated himself at the desk again because his legs felt week.

"I'm gonna find your lovely wife. I'm gonna take her in and try to repair the sick, perverted damage you've done to her. And I'm gonna give her the kinda life she deserves. The kinda life you would've given her if you were half a man. Or if you were a *normal* man. But you're not, Landon. You're a sick fucker. I'm gonna take care of your wife. And then…I'm gonna take care of you."

The brief silence that followed made Shaw's head hurt and stirred up his burning stomach.

"You know, Landon, I'm really kinda sorry that I had to do that to poor old Rupert. I mean, you think about it and you gotta ask yourself, what did that poor, sad-eyed fuckin' lizard ever do to anybody? But you, on the other hand, Landon… you're different. What I did to Rupert should've been done to you a long, long time ago. And now I'm gonna make sure that it happens. Finally."

Leo hung up with a soft click.

Shaw lowered the receiver from his ear slowly, leaned forward and replaced it on its base, then leaned back in his chair and cover his face with his hands.

His stomach raged and the headache in the middle of his forehead increased its intensity. He knew it would spread quickly until it encompassed his entire skull, like an invisible vise. He rested his feet on the lump beneath his desk and massaged his temples, pressing hard with his fingertips, trying to calm himself and forget what he had just heard, even if only for a few moments, just long enough to let himself calm down to a level where he could sleep.

But then, something occurred to him, something disturbing. It had to do with his feet and the lump upon which they were resting.

There was no lump beneath his desk.

Shaw wheeled the chair back and bent forward to look under the desk.

Through the murky shadows under there, he could see that the thing he had been resting his feet on was long and bright green, and to the left, it ended in an abrupt, flat stub.

He scrambled to his feet and made a move to get around the desk and rush to the bathroom, but he was too late.

Shaw vomited his dinner, along with a lot of hot, burning stomach acids, all over his desk. He vomited with a loud, wet, warbling sound.

Mrs. Babcock was at his side in a moment and she put her hand on his shoulder.

"Mr. Shaw, what can I do?" she said.

"You can…clean up this…fucking mess."

33.

IN THE DARK HOURS

The city thrived beneath the stormy cover of night. Many slept in their suburban homes and urban apartments and slums, recharging for the day to come. Others worked behind cash registers in fluorescent-lit convenience stores, guarded darkened buildings, poured drinks in bars, drove the streets in taxi cabs and patrol cars, cleaned darkened, empty offices, nursed the sick, and made record of the dead. But many others haunted the streets like ghosts, souls trapped between life and death in a world in which rest was rarely found and the only job was to stay alive. They sought shelter from the rain beneath cardboard and newspapers, and occasionally dined on scrapings from the plates of others, and many of them retreated to the South Street Mission.

No city remains utterly sleepless twenty-four hours a day; there are dark hours in which its pulse slows, its functions relax, and it dreams for a brief time.

But South Street Mission could not rest. It was the city's true heart, and it beat round the clock in its endless attempt to pump healthy blood into the city's decay and sickness.

It was no busier than any other night at the mission, but it was no less so, either. Every night, like every day, was busy. The usual shortage of volunteers worked long shifts to keep up with the influx of homeless and needy people.

Mama Charity had no shift. She slept, but never for more than four or five hours at a time, because that was all she needed. From the moment her alarm clock went off, she was alert and

full of energy, always anxious to start her long and full day.
Whenever anyone commented on her initiative and stamina,
Mama Charity told them God had made her that way because
he had so much work for her to do.

Her birth certificate read Evangeline Maybelle Carter, but
she had not answered to that name, or even heard it, in years; she
had put it behind her just as she had put behind her the pain of
losing her husband, Amelio, then, a little over two months later,
her teenage son Russell. She had not lost them without a long
hard fight against the ugly powers that pulled them away from
her—drugs, the street, the darkness that seemed to be the city's
lifeblood—slowly at first, then with a frightening swiftness,
until they were both gone. But although they had left her, the
fight in her remained. The way Mama looked at it, she lost the
battle and not the war. She continued to fight and South Street
was her battlefield. As far as Mama Charity was concerned, she
had always been at South Street and she had always been Mama
Charity. She had nothing else, and needed nothing else.

Tonight, she was working the receiving room again, but
she would have to take some time off soon; she had been at it
for nearly fourteen hours with only a couple of short breaks.
She needed to get something to eat and then lie down because
her arthritis was starting to chew on her ankles and knees.
Dagmar and her son Boy were in the clinic; Boy had fallen
down the subway steps and had a gash on his forehead that
needed stitches, and he was near tears with fright at the idea
of someone working on him with a needle and thread. Mama
Charity wanted to check on him, maybe take him a Tootsie Roll
from the candy box.

Dagmar and Boy were regulars at South Street. They lived
down under in the filthy black belly of the city, with the rats and
the roar of the subway trains. Mama did not know exactly how
old Dagmar was, but she was no more than a girl, she knew that
much. And with a son. Dagmar did not talk about herself much,
about her past or how she fell on such hard times. But that really
did not matter. All Mama knew was that she needed help.

The problem was, Dagmar would not let anyone help them.
Mama had tried to convince her to move into the mission for

a while until she got back on her feet and could make a life for herself and Boy. But she always shook her head, silently refusing to stay. She never took any more than she needed, and always more for Boy than for herself. She accepted medical treatment only when it was necessary, and again, for Boy, never for herself. She protected that child like a lioness protecting a litter of cubs, but Mama wished she would take better care of herself as well, or one day Boy might end up on his own in the mean and heartless down under, the only home he had ever known.

Mama knew it was most likely pride that kept Dagmar from accepting charity, even if it was the kind South Street provided. Mama knew, because she had been through it herself. After her husband Amelio was fired as a truck driver for a furniture company because of his love for the needle, Mama took on two jobs. But after he was stabbed to death in a drug deal gone awry, she lost her night job cleaning a soft-drink bottling factory because the distractions of her life had made her sloppy. Then, after Russell, her sixteen-year-old son died of a drug overdose, she came to pieces, unraveled like a ball of string. She lost her second job, eventually lost her apartment, and found herself with nothing and nowhere to go. Except for South Street.

Mama could still remember the gnawing ache in her stomach when she had to admit defeat and move to the mission where she had been working as a volunteer. And she was sure that Dagmar felt the same ache whenever she was asked to stay at South Street. So many people, even at the end of their rope, wanted to hang on with their own two hands, their own strength, with no help.

But Dagmar and Boy came to the mission every two or three weeks for food or to see a doctor when they had infected rat bites or got too sick from eating garbage, and Mama helped them as much as she could, even though that was not as much as she would like.

She especially enjoyed spending time with Boy. It was an odd name, of course, but he did not seem to mind. Why should he? He had never been called anything else. Boy, as well was the other children who came to the mission, always reminded

Mama of her own son, and she always hoped she would be able to help them in some special way, do something, say something that would make their lives better. She wanted desperately to be able to touch those children in a way she had never seemed able to touch Russell, no matter how hard she had tried.

Hunger pangs rumbled in her stomach, and Mama Charity decided to grab herself a candy bar to hold her over when she got Boy's Tootsie Roll. That and a diet cola would keep her on her feet a while longer. Besides, she still had to check on those poor kids in the basement one last time for the night. What a mess *that* was. She knew it was worrying Willy into fits, which meant he would probably get even less sleep than usual, and with that temperamental heart of his, he needed a lot more of it than Mama Charity.

As Mama Charity headed for the clinic to coax a smile out of a scared, hurt little boy, P.W. climbed the stairs in the basement. His 9mm was tucked beneath his belt in the small of his back. He had given McNolte the .45 automatic Colt Commander, along with several clips and careful instructions in its use. He had considered arming Emma, but decided she was dangerous enough.

P.W. was especially concerned about Emma. The voice on the answering machine had spooked her, sent her into a panic. He was tempted to have Willy get one of the volunteer doctors to prescribe a sedative for her, but if the people on her tail were as serious as they seemed to be, P.W. wanted to make sure that thing in her head was loaded and ready to fire if they should storm the place.

He was going to tell Willy to call Juarez and get him down to the mission right away, maybe even suggest that he bring a few friends. Juarez still had the sharp, suspicious eye of the street kid he used to be, and P.W. wanted him on the door watching for anyone who looked the least bit shifty, somebody who looked like he did not belong there.

When he reached the top of the stairs, he pulled the door open, stepped out into the loud racket of the laundry room, and was jolted out of his thoughts, nearly reaching around to draw his gun.

Two men stood outside the basement door. One was tall and thin, with long, stringy dark hair that fell limply down his back; he wore a bulky, mud-colored sweater, a pea-green jacket, jeans, and a pair of old cowboy boots. The other was about the same height but heavier and unshaven, with short, curly, red hair and a long coat that looked like it was made of burlap, and his right eye socket was empty, covered by sunken, puckered flesh. They both looked to be somewhere in their thirties. Their clothes were filthy and barely held together.

"You gotta bathroom?" the heavier man asked

"Yeah," P.W. replied, nodding. His eyes raced over them warily. They looked pretty thrashed, and they smelled of rum. "You guys, uh..." He nodded toward the row of mismatched, battered washing machines against the wall he quickly hid his suspicion behind a pleasant, lazy smile. "...you washin' some clothes, or something?"

"No," the one-eyed man said, returning the smile. "Just lookin' for a bathroom, is all. Can we use it? Your bathroom?"

The man's teeth were uncommonly clean; it did not necessary mean anything, but P.W. noticed. "Sure, sure you can. You fellas been checked in yet?"

"No," the long-haired one said. "Just got here. Big place."

"Yeah, a real monster to heat, too, I can tell ya." P.W. stopped between the two men, turned, and placed a hand against each man's back gently. "Let's get you fellas checked in, okay?"

"Can we use the bathroom first? We just came in to use the bathroom, is all."

"It'll just take a minute. We like to know you're here before you go wanderin' around the place. It's an old building, so it's for your own safety, y'know." P.W. was not sure what the hell that meant, but it sounded good, and the one-eyed man nodded.

"Okay, sure."

"My name's P.W. How 'bout you two?"

"I'm Dennis," the long-haired man said. "This is Charlie. He don't talk much. But he's company, you know?"

"Sure, sure. Lotta people in the world could take a lesson from Charlie."

P.W. led them down the corridor and into the receiving

room, where he spotted Mama Charity heading into the clinic.

"Hey, Mama," he shouted, startling Dennis and Charlie.

She jerked to a stop, not certain she had heard her name called, and looked around. When P.W. shouted to her again, she hurried toward him, grinning.

"What do you need, P.W.?" she said.

"Dennis and Charlie, here, need to be checked in, if you've got a second."

"Hello, boys," she said, sharing her grin with the two newcomers. "Why don't you just come with me, okay?"

"Thanks, Mama," P.W. said as she led the men away. He moved as if to turn away, but stopped and glanced at them.

Dennis and Charlie had their backs to him as he watched them. Just to make sure. He heard Dennis laugh, saw Charlie nod his head a few times.

They had caught him off-guard in the laundry room and that made him angry at himself. He had gotten rusty. It had been a while since he had found himself in a situation like this and he had become easily distracted over the years. That would have to stop.

They did not look back at him; they seemed to have forgotten about him already. P.W. decided they were okay. But they might not have been, and he could be dead, or at least out like a light with a nasty headache in his immediate future. He reached up and tugged on his beard firmly, thinking, *Gonna have to pull the old head out of the old ass and get with the program.* Then he went off to find Willy, tossing one more look over his shoulder.

"I am Mama Charity, and I want you to tell me a little about yourselves," she said. "You boys feelin' okay? You wanna visit the clinic?"

"No," Dennis said. "We just came to use the bathroom. I gotta use it pretty bad, the bathroom. Do we gotta sign something first, or something?"

"Oh, no, no, not that kind of checkin' in. We just wanna find out if you need medical treatment, or food, or a bed, that sorta thing. C'mon I'll take you to the restrooms."

They followed her back the way they had come, down the

corridor and around a corner to the two labeled doors. An old porcelain drinking fountain grew from the wall between them.

"Here you go," she said. "When you get done, you come find me or talk to one of the volunteers if you need anything."

Dennis returned her smile as he and Charlie pushed through the door into the men's room.

Ignoring the deep ache in her knees and ankles, Mama Charity leaned over the drinking fountain for a few swallows of cold water before heading back to the clinic.

In the men's room, Dunne checked the stalls—they had no doors—to make sure they were alone, then said, "We hit the jackpot, Morrie. Did you see the way that guy looked at us when he came through the door?"

The black and white tiles were old and cracked and the glass mirror had been replaced by a rectangle of shiny, reflective chrome.

"For just a split-second, there, with that look in his eye, I thought he was gonna kill us both. Like Santa Claus on angel dust, or something."

"I say we go back and see what's behind that door he came out of."

"Looked like a stairway to me. The basement, maybe, couldn't tell for sure. But I bet our lady's down there. You think?"

"Yeah," Morrie said with a nod. "Looked like he was hiding something."

Dunne smiled and gestured at Morrie's face. "Hey, that's a nice touch, taking the eye out and not wearing your patch. I like it."

Dunne had known Morrie for ten years, but Morrie's prosthetic eye and the empty socket that held it remained a source of endless amusement and fascination. So did the story behind it. When he was twelve, as Morrie told it, he had run out of a classroom at school after being held for thirty minutes after the bell as punishment for disrupting class, with a pencil in his hand. In a moment of schoolboy clumsiness, he had validated the age-old warning given by every mother to every child about running with sharp objects: he had fallen and poked out his eye.

"Yeah, that's the great thing about disfigurements," Morrie said. "People either feel sorry for you, or it scares the shit out of them, which is good for a laugh."

"You think Mama Chubbycheeks is gone?"

"Should be by now, I'd think."

Each man removed a surgical mask from a pocket and slid the band over his head, fitting it over his nose and mouth.

The instant they stepped out of the restroom, Mama Charity rounded a corner, touching a knuckle to her lips as she belched after gulping water. She decided that while she was at that end of the building, she would duck into the basement to see how Magnolia and his friend were and if they needed anything.

As she stepped into the laundry room, she gave a bright hello to Margaret, a tough old volunteer who was unloading sheets into a basket from a dryer, and fished her keys from the enormous pocket on her thin, billowy, floor-length jacket. She slipped the key into the lock, pushed the door open, stepped down and swung it closed behind her, but stopped on the third step down because the door did not close, and when she turned, she got only a glimpse of Dennis's eyes above his mask before he punched her in the face.

Mama Charity slammed against the wooden rail and hooked an arm under it tightly when she felt her feet leave the step. She could already feel blood dribbling from her nose, but she fought the flashbulbs in her head and the slippery feeling of nearly losing consciousness before she bellowed, "Margaret, get help!" as she swung her left arm up between Dennis's legs and clasped a fist onto his crotch, squeezing hard.

Without making a sound, he raised his hand, which now held a gun, and brought the black butt down on Mama Charity's forehead, setting off more flashbulbs inside her skull. The pain finally arrived, lagging behind the actual assaults, and it exploded behind her face, pressing outward over her cheekbones and filling her sinuses with fire. She felt herself black out once, for just an instant, then again, but she bit her lip and desperately held onto consciousness, and the one-eyed man's genitals. And she pulled.

Morrie let out a small grunting sound as Dunne, who had come through the door behind Morrie, grabbed the door before it could swing closed and stepped out to the laundry room as the beefy old woman who had been pulling sheets from the dryer ran toward the corridor. Dunne swung out a foot and caught her shin with the toe of his boot. She slammed to the floor face-down and he kicked her in the side of the head hard before she could make a sound. When she did not move, he went back to the basement door, stepped through and closed it as Mama Charity's right arm slipped from the rail and she fell backward down the stairs, pulling Morrie with her.

"Shit," Dunne muttered, starting down the steps after them. When they slammed against one of the rail's supports with Mama Charity on top of Morrie, Dunne planted his foot on the fat woman's side and heaved, rolling her off of his partner. She tumbled the rest of the way down the stairs and sprawled onto the concrete floor below. "You all right, man?"

Morrie cupped both hands over his crotch as he took deep breaths and blew them out hard. His eyes bulged and his face had turned the color of boiled beets. He tried to speak to Dunne, to say, *No, I'm not, you fucking idiot*, but rusted blades of pain cut upward from his testicles, ripping through his guts. He rolled his head to the side and dry-heaved over the edge of the stairs.

Dunne hurried down the stairs toward Mama Charity, who was struggling to get to her knees. He hoped no one had heard them as he prepared to kick her in the face.

Mama Charity rose up on her knees, saw him coming, and threw herself forward, swinging her pendulous arms around Dunne's legs.

His back struck the stairs and he yelped with pain, but snapped his mouth shut instantly. He could not afford another fuck-up, not now, so soon after missing the woman in the café, and his mind clung to that, to the need to get the job done this time so he did not *really* piss off Mr. Shaw.

Mama Charity got to her feet, her face shiny with blood. Her teeth were bared, arms out at her sides like a Sumo wrestler's as she bore down on him, swallowing his field of vision, and he swung a leg up to kick her in the stomach. Instead, she grabbed his leg and dragged him off the stairs, the back of his head cracking against the edge of each step until it smacked flatly against the concrete.

Dunn rolled to his left, got on all fours and was about to get to his feet when she kicked him in the ass, flattening him to the floor again. When Dunne felt Mama Charity's hand close on a clump of his hair, he grunted, "Morrie!" as she pulled his head back and slammed his face to the concrete. Everything blurred inside and outside his head, and a sound like a tuning fork filled his ears.

Morrie staggered down the stairs clutching the rail and aimed his gun at her.

"Magnolia!" Mama Charity cried. "Magnolia, get in here!"

When the scuffle began, McNolte and Emma were sitting on the edges of their beds facing one another and talking softly, and it sounded to them like nothing more than someone clamoring back down the stairs, P.W. or Mama Charity. But when they heard a garbled sound followed by a loud crash, Emma said, "I think somebody fell," and they stood. By the time the gunshot cracked through the basement, they were jogging out of the room.

After the gunshot, there was a long moment of stunned waiting between Mama Charity, standing on the basement floor, and Dunne, who stood two steps up from the floor, gun still pointed at her, waiting for her to drop dead or start bleeding, but nothing happened and Mama Charity took advantage of that instant, not thinking about what had just *almost* happened, and launched herself forward, slamming into him. His gun clattered on the steps and they both fell on top of Morrie, who immediately groaned and began to drag himself out from under them. Mama Charity began pounding Dunne's face with her fist, growling, "You shot at me and missed, you must be blind as a *bat*, you damned son of a—"

McNolte shouted, "No!" as he and Emma rushed in from the other room just in time to see Dunne's switchblade knife click open and cut through the air, sinking to the hilt in Mama Charity's back.

McNolte immediately recognized the man with the knife as the same man who had shot up Wee's Café, but the thought barely registered in his mind as he was struck with paralysis and gawked helplessly, his voice lodged in his throat. He vaguely heard Emma release a childlike sound of horror as the second man, the one lying bloody on the stairs, rolled over and crawled up a few steps to snatch the gun.

Morrie sat up on the stairs and his empty eye socket, darkened by blood, looked like a gaping wound as he aimed his gun at McNolte and held it steady, calling, "Dunne! *Dunne!*"

The long-haired man left the knife in Mama Charity's back as she fell away from him, still bent over, landing on her side with a harsh coughing sound.

As Dunne pivoted, he reached beneath his jacket and removed the dart gun, then stopped once the gun was aiming straight at Emma. He fired.

Emma heard the soft *pphhutt*, glimpsed the projectile in a blur as it closed the distance between them, and her mind prepared itself for the bullet, anticipated it tearing through skin and muscle and bone and organs and arteries, and McNolte took a breath to shout again, only to flinch a heartbeat later when he realized there had been no gunshot.

Emma felt a child's fist punch her in the chest and she staggered back a couple of steps, looked down at what appeared to be a cross between a dart and a syringe jutting out of her chest just below her right collarbone, bobbing slightly from the impact. She looked up and saw the long-haired man still aiming his gun at her, saw the other man aiming his at McNolte, and something opened up deep inside her head.

McNolte saw the dart as he lunged toward Emma and began pushing her backward out of the room, until a blackness wrapped around his head like a soaked towel and he collapsed to the floor.

Dunne fell over backward and Morrie went limp as he slammed against the wall, as if a powerful wind had caught them off-balance and blown them over. On the floor, Mama Charity rolled to one side slowly, half on her back, the knife's handle scraping dryly against the concrete. Dunne's nose was bleeding before he hit the floor and Morrie went into convulsions on the stairs, his heels rattling against a wooden step.

Emma looked at the four still bodies and wondered remotely if she had killed them. Then she drew in a breath and screamed as P.W. clattered down the stairs, having dropped the telephone he had been carrying from Willy's office and drawn his gun the instant he saw Margaret bleeding on the laundry room floor.

P.W. bent down and picked up Dunne's gun on the stairs as he stepped around the man's now-motionless form and stuffed the gun under his belt, glancing at each body as he moved. When he saw Emma backing out of the room slowly, fists clenched and arms stiff at her sides, her whole body trembling as if she were being electrocuted, the dart sticking out of her chest, he hurried toward her, pausing to kick Charlie's gun across the room, well out of the unconscious man's reach. He turned Emma around, wrapped a big arm around her shoulders, and let her lean on him as he directed her back to her bed.

"C'mon, now, sweetheart," he said as gently as if she had just awakened from a nightmare and needed a little comforting, maybe a glass of milk. "C'mon, now, you just lie down here on the bed, okay?"

She started to cry then and tears rolled down her cheeks as she pushed him away, her eyes wide and panicky.

"No, no, don't do that, now, just calm down, lie back on the bed and don't move around, just stay right there for a minute, okay, just a minute, and I'll get help."

P.W. did not want to remove that dart too hastily; it might be safer to leave it where it was rather than simply pull it out. When her face relaxed and she met his eyes solidly and nodded, P.W. left her and crossed the hall, quickly surveying the damage.

The one-eyed man lay on the stairs, the other on the concrete floor near Mama Charity, each wearing a surgical mask slightly askew on his face. McNolte was beginning to stir, and P.W. wondered if the others would, too, or if they were dead. He rushed toward Mama Charity, gasping at the sight of her bloodied face, groaning as he knelt beside her and found the knife sticking out of her back.

"Oh, God, Mama. Mama? *Mama?*" He pressed three

fingertips to the side of her throat and felt for a pulse. He grabbed her thick wrist and tried there. "Oh, Jesus, her heart's not beating. *McNolte!*"

McNolte's mind grabbed onto the sound of P.W.'s voice and pulled itself out of its murkiness. He got on hands and knees and tasted blood dribbling over his upper lip from his nose. "P.W.?" he said weakly.

"Snap out of it, fella. Now." P.W. had put his gun on the floor, cleared the breathing passage, and held Mama Charity's mouth open as he leaned forward to blow into it. "Go to the clinic and get somebody." Another breath.

"What?" McNolte fought the lead weight of gravity to get clumsily to his feet.

"Get somebody from the clinic! Mama Charity is dying."

McNolte winced and blinked his eyes rapidly, swaying as he looked around the room. "Emma..."

"Emma's *fine*. Go get somebody."

McNolte's mind groped through its confusion, searching for a hold on what had happened. Mama Charity was dying and he had to get someone because she had been stabbed and he had to get someone, she was dying and he had to—

"*Get someone!*" P.W. shouted.

The pieces snapped together one after another as he made his way to the stairs and up toward the door, over the one-eyed man.

A hand clutched his ankle and pulled his foot out from under him. He fell hard to the steps, kicking as he cried out.

P.W. kept pumping Mama Charity's chest with both hands as he glanced at McNolte. He saw Dunne clutching McNolte's ankle, holding him back. P.W. pulled away from Mama Charity for a moment to grab his gun, lifted it, aimed, and fired.

Dunne's head jerked when a small hole appeared in the right side of his forehead, and his entire body became limp, hand dropping away from McNolte's ankle.

"Now, *go*, dammit," P.W. shouted as he went back to the business of keeping Mama Charity alive.

Outside the South Street Mission, Miranda Otter walked slowly around the building again and again as raindrops passed through her intangible, barely visible body. Her hands were buried in her coat pockets, the right fingering a hard, cold, blackjack, the left fondling the handle of a long, heavy knife. She walked around and around the building, thinking about Emma Shaw, who she was certain was inside. Miranda could feel Emma's presence in her chest, taste it like bile in her throat.

She remained outside the building only because she had not yet decided what she would do once inside. But she would soon. And once she was inside, Miranda would not come out until Emma Shaw was dead.

34.

SHELTER FROM THE STORM

McNolte had lost whatever sense of safety he had found in the old department store basement. He and Emma might as well be sitting in the middle of a busy freeway naked, for all the safety they had found down there. They were going to have to get out, and they both knew it. But they did not know where to go.

P.W. was working on it. After the ambulance had taken Mama Charity away, he returned to the basement and told them that, in addition to being kicked, beaten, and stabbed in the back, she was having a coronary when the ambulance took her away.

"Took all that to slow the old girl down, but she was still kicking when they left," he said, an emotional crack in his voice. "My money's on her to pull through. I'm not so sure about you two, though. One of the other volunteers went with Mama. I've gotta get you two out of here."

Emma was sitting on the bed with a couple of pillows between her back and the wall. A volunteer from the clinic had come down and removed the dart, then cleaned and dressed the wound. The dart itself was a mystery. It had not rendered Emma unconscious, which made them wonder what, if anything, it *had* done.

"The guy on the stairs," Emma said. "Is he, uh…dead?"

"Yep," P.W. said, balling up his right fist and massaging it with his left hand as if it hurt. He turned to McNolte. "The one you said shot up Wee's is tied up like a pretzel in one of the store rooms. When he feels a little more conversational, I might get something helpful out of him, but not for the next half hour or so. You really socked him in the brain hard, Emma. And I'm glad. Now, what am I gonna do with you two?"

"I still think we should get out of the city," Emma said, her voice little more than a shaky breath. "We should've done it before this."

"Let me ruminate on this a while," P.W. said. "I'm gonna go have a talk with Willy, maybe call a friend or two, see what they have to say about all this. In the meanwhile, you two stay here. I closed up the laundry room. Nobody gets near this basement. Don't you guys worry. I'm on top of this. McNolte, I want you to lock that door when I leave and don't open it for anyone but me. No exceptions. If you two wanna catch a little sleep, go ahead, but not both at once. Somebody needs to stay alert. Turn on the TV, or something. I'll call the hospital, let you know how Mama's doing. Okay, you two gonna be all right?"

McNolte, who had been sitting on the edge of his bed, stood and faced his friend. "P.W., I can't tell you how sorry I am for getting you into this. Maybe it *would* be best if we just left the city."

"You're not leavin' this room. Not just yet, anyway."

"Um, that dead guy," McNolte said. "Did you, um—"

"We'll just have to worry about him later, we've got enough on our plate already. I moved him off the stairs, of course. He was a fire hazard."

McNolte's eyes widened as an icy chill passed over his body. P.W.'s words were not only spoken casually, they had a soft chuckle behind them. The response was made even more monstrous by the simple fact that it came from P.W. Meredith, who was McNolte's best friend, a gentle and thoughtful man to whom life was so important that he spent most of his time bettering it for others, not the kind of person who would kill someone and refer to it in such a cursory way—even *joke* about it—only minutes later.

Recognition glinted in P.W.'s eyes and he smiled. He had seen that look before.

"Don't worry, babe," he said reassuringly. "I'm still the same person you know. It's just that now you know a little more about me. You've seen me do a few things my Uncle Sam taught me when I was a kid. But don't worry. It's got nothin' to do with who I am. If it did...well, if it did, I'd enjoy it. And I don't."

He saw in his friend's eyes a long-ignored world of pain trying to break the surface of P.W.'s gaze. McNolte nodded, his chilly, momentary fear of P.W. gone.

Tossing a friendly wink at Emma, P.W. said, "Come with me, McNolte," and left the room.

As they made their way slowly up the stairs, P.W. said, "You know, McNolte, you don't have to do any of this. You could go home if you want."

"So could you."

"I am home. This is what I do. But you have a whole other life."

"Yeah, well...I guess it's like getting a lead on a really hot story. I can't walk away from something like that."

"Is that what this is to you? A story?"

"No. But it'll probably become one if I live long enough."

After P.W. had left and McNolte had locked the door after him, he went back downstairs. He lowered himself onto his bed again and he and Emma looked at each other silently.

Emma's lower lip quivered as she slowly turned to slide her legs over the edge of the bed. "She had a heart attack," she whispered.

McNolte knew immediately what she was thinking and moved over to her bed, sitting beside her. "Hey, come on, those guys really knocked her around. And she got stabbed, for crying out loud. Plus, she weighs over three hundred pounds. I don't think she needed any help from you to have a heart attack."

But McNolte could tell by the distressed look on her face that she had heard none of it. She looked into his eyes fervently, as if searching for something she needed badly but could not define. Her face tensed, eyes narrowing.

"If I killed that poor, sweet woman," she whispered as she leaned on him, sliding her head beneath his chin and between the lapels of his robe, pressing her face to his bare chest.

His arms slowly moved around her as he said into her hair,

"Hey, I don't think you need to worry about Mama Charity, really. The woman's made of iron. Hell, I think she could run this place by herself. She practically does." He paused when he felt Emma's breath hot on his chest. Her hair smelled of carnation-scented shampoo and felt like strands of silk against his cheek. He found himself holding her tighter, caressing her through the rough terrycloth, palms becoming moist against the warmth of her beneath the material.

Her rapid breathing slowed and became uneven as she slid her hand hesitantly over his ribs and around his side to his back, where her fingers pressed hard against him under the robe, digging in just a little.

McNolte realized he was gently brushing his lips over her hair, taking in her scent, savoring it, following the curve of her shoulder blade with his thumb. The pattern of his own breathing changed and his heartbeat increased, but this time it was not reacting to fear. He was reacting to the warmth and weight of her against him, to the touch of her lips to his chest.

It had been a while since McNolte had been with a woman. He'd had a couple of opportunities, but with the pressure of his debt and his constant battle with cocaine cravings, he had been afraid of what might happen—or what might not happen. Deciding his life was already filled with enough complications and humiliations, he had avoided sex. In fact, he had thought about it hardly at all. But he was thinking about it now because his chest was filling with that soft, anxious warmth that never changed, that never seemed to be dampened by experience or age, that rush of excitement at the knowledge that a new intimacy was about to open up.

He pressed those feelings down and started to pull away from her, knowing this was neither the time nor place for that, not while people were trying to kill them and there was a dead man in the next room.

"Don't let go of me, please," Emma whispered, pulling him to her tightly, clinging to his robe, to him. "Please don't let go of me right now."

He did not, but he tried to reverse the emotional shifts going on inside him as he held her, tried to be nothing more than comforting to her. But at some point—he was not exactly sure when because it happened so smoothly, so quietly—it was out of his hands, and they were kissing hungrily.

By the time their robes were off and bare skin as moving against bare skin, McNolte had forgotten where they were.

"I won't turn you over to Trafficante," McNolte whispered afterward as they held each other under the covers of Emma's bed. "I promise."

"But Leo will kill you if you don't."

"And what do you suppose he's going to do to you?"

She frowned. "You know...I don't know. I really don't know *what* he wants. But whatever it is...I don't like it."

The sudden knock on the door at the top of the stairs startled them.

"Hey, it's me, P.W.!"

As if they were teenagers about to be caught by their parents, they scrambled off of one another and the bed, grabbed their robes, and slipped them on, tying the belts. They stopped, looked at each other for a moment, and laughed at their guilty, adolescent behavior. They continued to laugh as McNolte went to the door and opened it.

P.W.'s eyebrows rose as McNolte led him down the stairs, still chuckling. In the other room, he said, "Well, I'm glad to see the mood's changed down here. Or are you guys just gettin' hysterical on me?"

McNolte and Emma looked at one another and laughed, McNolte sheepishly and Emma into her palm.

P.W. looked back and forth between the two of them and his twinkling eyes narrowed a bit as he nodded knowingly.

"Okay, okay," he said with a smirk, "I believe in making good use of your time, I got no problem with that."

"How's Mama Charity?" Emma asked.

"Not sure yet. Still waiting to hear. I sent Irving to the hospital in a cab. Took me fifteen minutes to explain to the driver that when Irving called him a goat-fucking sand-nigger, he didn't really mean it. I'll call the hospital again in a few minutes. I'm not too sure about Margaret, either. One of those assholes hurt her pretty bad. I took her to the clinic, but she may have to go to the hospital, too. But look, right now, we've gotta get you two moving."

"Where are we going?" McNolte said.

"Well, I stumbled on a possibility, but it's up to you. We got a woman in the clinic with a little boy. Dagmar's her name, and the boy's name is Boy. Just Boy. She and her son live under the city, in the subways. What we call down under. She doesn't talk much, but she's agreed to take you down there with her if you want. I'll go down and get you when it's safe."

"Would…would you be able to find us?" McNolte said.

"Oh, yeah. I've spent some time down there, I know my way around. It won't be a stroll in the park, I promise you. It's ugly and dangerous. So it's your call. If you don't want to go down under, we can try to come up with something else, but there's no guarantee we will. You want my advice?"

They did not respond.

"I mean, it's just advice, I'm not trying to tell you what to do. So, do you want it?"

McNolte exchanged a glanced, then nodded.

"If I were in your shoes, I'd go down under right away. I think you'd be okay. It probably won't be for long, and while you're down there, I might be able to divert our friends' attention to other things.

"What are you going to do, P.W.?" Emma said.

"Never mind me, what're *you* guys gonna do?"

McNolte stepped over to Emma's side and said, "Well, what do you think? Still want to get out of the city?"

"Nope, that'd take too long," P.W. said. "Going to any of the airports or bus depots or train stations'd be suicide. We'd have to find you a reliable car, make sure you had gas and plenty of money for more, *and* work out some kind of destination. You don't have that kind of time."

Emma's face darkened.

"Hey, tell you what," P.W. said. "Remember when I told you I wasn't try to tell you what to do?"

They nodded.

"Forget I said that. I'm tellin' you what to do. Dress real

warm. I'll give you some food to take down with you. You can hand out some of it out to the more lucid folks if you need to make a few friends."

"*Lucid?*" Emma said, her eyes widening.

"Are you sure we're going to be safe, P.W.?"

He chuckled. "Oh, no, no, I didn't say that, you didn't hear me say *that*, did you? No, you won't be safe, but you probably won't be lunch. And I promise you *nobody* wants you bad enough to follow you down there. Nobody's that determined. Or that fucking stupid."

McNolte did not like the sound of that; it gave him a sinking feeling of dread.

"Hey, um, look, P.W.," he said, walking slowly over to the man. "I saw a story about that on *60 Minutes* once, and it, uh…it looked pretty scary down there."

"*60 Minutes?*" P.W. laughed. "If *60 Minutes* showed what's really goin' on down there, Andy Rooney'd swallow his tongue and there'd be a-panickin' in the streets. Whatever you saw, it's worse. I'm just being honest with you."

"Jesus Christ, P.W.," McNolte said, "what kind of chances do we have?"

"Well…I lied a little. There *is* a chance you'll be lunch. But if you stay here, we may *all* be lunch. You're just gonna have to be careful."

Outside, Miranda Otter stopped in front of the corner entrance to the South Street Mission. She stared at the glints of light that shot through the black-painted glass.

Opening the door, Miranda went inside. She took a seat on an old wobbly chair, unseen, and slowly, carefully looked around the enormous, crowded, noisy room for some sign of Emma Shaw.

35.

MORE COMPANY

"I told you we should've taken the freeway," Tonya said calmly as she and Parson Higgins waited in backed-up traffic on Delaware Avenue. Half a block ahead of them, the lights of emergency vehicles spun and a crowd gathered. They had been boxed in for the last fifteen minutes, waiting for traffic to start moving again as rain fell on the car in windblown sheets.

"Fuck the freeway," Parson growled. "I mean, shee-zus, you don't wanna drive in the city, then don't *live* in the city, don't *work* in the city. *Move*. But don't build a buncha big fuckin' roads *around* and *over* the city, my *God*, what a waste of concrete." Parson nodded toward the commotion ahead. "They're starting to move. Pull over when you can and go left on Westlake, then get in the right lane."

"Hey, what is this? You're the one who wanted me to drive this boat, I should be able to go the way I want. Hell, long as I'm driving, we should be in my car, not this dinosaur."

Parson slipped his thin, delicate finger beneath the Homburg he wore and gingerly scratched the top of his bald head with his long, manicured nails. He had cut himself shaving earlier and now it was itching.

"You and your fucking kraut car," he said, glancing at the streak of dark moisture on his fingertip. He had scratched the damned scab off and now it was bleeding again.

"Ha, you kiddin'? That Mercedes is a work of art," Tonya said, lowering her voice to a reverent level as she spoke of her car, which she loved.

"Yeah, well, if I get in a wreck with a dump truck, I don't wanna be driving some fucking work of art. If I wanted to die surrounded by art, I could blow my brains out in a museum, it'd be a hell of a lot cheaper. I want some American-made armor like *this*—" He slapped a hand twice on the dashboard, hard. "—between me and the grave."

"American-made," Tonya said, laughing, shaking her head. "No such thing these days, Parson, no such thing. Only American commercials. Everything else is made all over the globe."

No one knew Parson Higgins's real name—he had been working for Mr. Trafficante since before Tonya was born—but it was obvious with one glance why people called him that. He *looked* like a parson, one of those old-fashioned preachers from the Old West, tall, impossibly thin, with a long, razor-sharp nose, and he always wore dark clothes, shirts that looked like they should have clerical collars. He was sixty-seven years old, but he did not tell anyone because he knew everyone clocked him in his fifties, and he liked that. His face was narrow and quite stern, especially with eyebrows shaved off the pronounced ridge above his deep-set eyes. Rumor had it that he had gotten so sick of crabs and lice during a stint in prison that he had taken to shaving all the hair off his body, and the habit had stuck, but nobody bothered to ask him if it was true. Although he looked like one, Parson Higgins did not have the temperament of a man of the cloth, except for the fact that he refused to carry or use a gun. It was not something Parson talked about, just something he refused to do. The reason was as much a mystery to everyone as Parson's real name.

Tonya Cox, on the other hand, was her real name. Men enjoyed making a joke of it. The second she introduced herself, they said, "Tonya *Cox*? That's your real name?" It was tiring, but at the same time she liked it. The way it rolled off the tongue combined with the connotations of her surname made it sounded suggestive, a little dirty, like the name of a porn starlet, or something. She liked the fact that people remembered it, especially men, liked the look they got when she glared at them after they laughingly asked if that was her *real* name, that withering look that said they knew they had made a mistake and were trying hard to figure out how to make up for it. There were a few, of course, who did not react to the look and just kept harping on her name, making vulgar jokes, some even grabbing their crotches to drive the point home. Usually blowhard men with beer guts and dirty shirts. More than once, she had put a stop to their haranguing by punching them hard in the face with her fist. So far, it had worked every time.

Her dark hair was long, but she wore it pinned up beneath a cap with a bill that came down low over her eyes. In her dark, loose clothes, no one would know she was a woman unless they came up close, and that was the way she wanted it tonight.

Tonya had been working for Mr. Trafficante for a little over six years, which was a record for her considering she usually worked freelance. But she would be thirty soon, and it felt good to have a secure job. Maybe she would stick around for as long as Trafficante would have her. The pay was good, and it was steady. She had managed to put away a good chunk of money to live on when the job finally came to an end, enough to be picky about the next job, and the job after that. But for now, working for Mr. Trafficante was good, she had no complaints. Except, maybe, having to drive Parson Higgins's big, lumbering, ancient Lincoln Town Car.

"Hell, women don't know anything about cars, anyway," Parson grumbled.

"Oh? You don't think so? Well, maybe not most women. But I've blown up my share of 'em," she added, giving him a wide grin.

Parson shook his head, making a growling sound in his throat. "Well, jeez, *anybody* can blow up a car. I mean, a *kid* can blow up a car, he's got the right stuff to do it with. What the hell does *that* take, huh? Nothing. What I mean is, women don't know cars like they don't know guns. They weren't *made* to understand them like men were. Simple as that."

Tonya laughed loudly. "Well, at least you're not sexist." Then she laughed again, a nasty, mocking laugh.

Parson glared at her for a moment. "What, you think I gotta be sexist not to like you?" He nodded absently toward the intersection. "Take a right here on Anderson."

Tonya rolled her eyes, but did as she was told.

"Hell, I could list reasons not to like you all night long and never get to the fact that you're a woman."

Tonya just shook her head, smiling.

While Tonya Cox and Parson Higgins bantered, P.W. telephoned his friend Ty, who was so startled by the late-night call that he would not let P.W. finish apologizing for waking him.

"Whatsamatter, P.W.?" he said groggily. "You in trouble? You okay?"

"I thought it could wait till tomorrow, Ty, but I'm afraid I'm gonna need some help right away."

"What can I do? You want me to call the others? I don't know how fast Jess can get into the city, but I know the others'd be willing to help."

"Yeah, call 'em and get over here. I'm at the South Street Mission."

"That big soup kitchen? What're you doing there?"

"I live here."

There was a brief pause with sounds of movement from Ty's end of the line, then he said, "Oh, jeez, P.W., I didn't know you was—"

"Never mind, Ty. Just ask for me in front when you get here."

As P.W. hung up the phone and returned his attention to the task of preparing McNolte and Emma to go under, Landon Shaw's Lamborghini screeched to a halt in his parking space at OdysseyCorp Labs. When he slammed the car door on his way out, the report cracked through the night like a gunshot, muffled somewhat by the sound of the rain. Shaw's hurried footsteps sent echoing clacks across the wet pavement. He unlocked the door, went inside, and took long strides down a half-lit corridor on his way to Jorgan's apartment.

Shaw had been trying to reach Jorgan for the last hour, but the doctor had not answered his phone, pager, or door when a lab tech knocked several times and called his name.

Halfway to the apartment, Shaw was joined by two

dark-suited security men, but he ignored them as they walked a step behind him. He did not even hear their footsteps above the low hum of rage in his head.

He had not heard from Dunne. Shaw had expected it to take no more than half an hour for Dunne and Morrie to get into the mission, find Emma, render her harmless, and get her back out and into the car waiting at the corner entrance to the mission. He had told them not to kill anyone unless absolutely necessary, but to let no one stand in their way and to move fast. He had called Ramie, the driver of the car, three times, but Ramie knew nothing and kept asking if Shaw wanted him to go inside after them. Shaw told him no, just wait there, but at the first sign of trouble at the mission to get the hell out of there and leave Dunne and Morrie behind to fend for themselves.

The fear that something had gone wrong at the mission pounded like a headache behind his eyes, and as if that were not bad enough, now he had to worry about what the hell Jorgan was up to. The security man at the lab had offered to enter Jorgan's apartment and see if the man was unconscious or dead, or just gone, but he did not like the idea; he wanted to go into the apartment first, for some reason. He had a nagging sense that Jorgan was making trouble, or was about to, and that it would not be a good idea for just *anybody* to be snooping around his apartment if he happened to have conveniently left anything incriminating lying around. Shaw had no idea what that might be, but things had been going so incredibly wrong that he did not want to take any chances.

When he reached Jorgan's apartment, he unlocked it, stepped inside, and looked around at the small living room. He had seen it only one other time since Jorgan moved in, and it had been cluttered and messy. Now it was neat and clean, and he knew instantly that Jorgan was gone.

Shaw made a vague sweeping gesture with his hand and said to the security man, "I want every computer disc, every paper, every folder, every notebook, anything with writing on it, typed or handwritten, I don't care if it's a shopping list, I want all of it on my desk in twenty minutes. And I want two men on Jorgan now. Have them check the mission first, see if he turns up there. And check on his assistant Miranda, he might be off fucking her someplace, God knows why. If they find him, they're to bring him back here. If they can't find him, just make sure he doesn't get anywhere near Emma. Or me."

He spun around and left the apartment, grinding his teeth as he made his way to his office.

Alan Jorgan walked away from his car and crossed South Street to the mission's entrance. He wore his lab coat under his overcoat. He had almost taken it off before leaving his apartment, but decided it might lend him a helpful air of authority when he entered the mission.

He had already tried four others, all smaller than South Street. Although South Street had been the first time come to mind, he had decided it was too well-known, too big; it seemed much too obvious a hiding place. But since he had no success with the others, he had decided to give it a try, and as he crossed the street now, he chided himself for not coming to South Street first.

He had decided to handle himself the same way he had at the others, to try nothing sneaky, just walk in, introduce himself, tell them the truth about Emma, find her, and take her with him. He knew things would go smoothly if he just let them know about the situation instead of creeping around the place. There was no reason for the mission's staff to be suspicious of him, as long as Emma did not react negatively when she saw him. A syringe waited at the ready in the right pocket of his overcoat, and he intended to sedate her the instant it looked like she was going to make trouble. Later, once he had her safely out of the city, he could explain to her that he meant her no harm, and in fact was trying to protect her from her husband. But for now, she had every reason to fear him, he realized that, and it could prove to be a problem.

Then again, she might not be here at all. She might not be in *any* of the city's missions. There was always the chance that Emma had not been at any one of the missions he had tried, but that Shaw's people had gotten to her first, and now they were waiting for Jorgan to show up. The thought gave him a chill.

Once inside the mission, he spotted an Asian woman in her fifties, a bit stooped, wearing a name tag that read KIM LEE and identified her as a volunteer. She was unoccupied for the moment, on her way out of a door with a sign on it that read CLINIC.

"Excuse me, ma'am, but could you help me?" Jorgan asked, smiling. He was not accustomed to smiling and pulled it off clumsily, but it was a genuine try.

Kim Lee looked up at him, returned the smile, and said, "What do you need?"

He removed the Polaroid snapshot from beneath his overcoat and handed it to her.

"I'm Dr. Alan Jorgan and I'm looking for this woman. She's a patient of mine, her name is Emma Shaw. She…she, um, participated in a research program at OdysseyCorp Labs, and she's been exposed to a virus that could be harmful to her and might even be contagious. I have reason to believe she came here earlier tonight, or maybe yesterday, I'm not sure. I need to take her back to the facility. She needs treatment immediately. Have you seen her?"

The woman looked up from the picture slowly. Her smile was gone and at first, Jorgan thought she looked suspicious. But it seemed to be nothing more than curiosity when she said, "I know who you need to talk to. Could you wait right here, please?"

"Oh, yes, sure, I'd appreciate any—"

"You won't go away?"

"No, no."

The little woman nodded, then hurried away.

Jorgan looked around the large room for someone who did not belong there, someone with watchful eyes.

He was angry at himself for taking so much time covering his tracks. It had been stupid considering who he was dealing with, but he did it, anyway, hoping to give himself and Emma—if he could find her—as much of a head start as possible.

He had driven from his apartment straight to a used car dealership that stayed open till midnight on the south side of the city to trade in his Buick for another car, something that did not even resemble a Buick. It had taken a lot longer than he had anticipated. He had expected to be the only customer at such a late hour, but the place had been surprisingly busy. Once he had been spotted by a salesman, Jorgan found it difficult to convince the man that he really had no preference in color or make, as long as it was small, economical, and fit to take on a road trip right away. He had driven away, finally, in a blue Toyota Corolla, leaving the salesman with definite suspicions, but free of his Buick.

When his eyes swept past Miranda, alone and seated against a wall, Jorgan did a quick double-take.

"Oh, shit," he muttered. Then he called her name. "Miranda. Hey, *Miranda!*"

She flinched, as if she had been dozing, and she stared at him for a long moment, her puffy, reddened face blank, completely lifeless. Then she tilted her head to one side and looked deeply disappointed, almost as if she were about to start crying.

Angry and fed up with her, Jorgan headed toward her, planning to tell her to go home and mind her own goddamned business. But a hand closed in a steely grip on his neck and something stabbed into his lower back on the right side.

A voice spoke into his ear, slightly accented, Latino: "Do as you're told and don't try anything, or the kidney gets it."

Miranda watched as the tall, muscular Latino boy made Dr. Jorgan turn, and stayed close behind him as they walked away, with his hand clamped on the back of Jorgan's neck.

Something was wrong, and Miranda bolted to her feet as panic swelled in her chest. No one seemed to notice her, but Dr. Jorgan had seen her, and now he was gone, led off so swiftly by that unsavory-looking fellow through a doorway across the room.

Miranda suddenly felt vulnerable, as if she were being watched by hidden eyes. But she knew Dr. Jorgan was in some kind of trouble, all because he had come looking for that pampered bitch. Her thoughts began to buzz and swarm in her head like mad bees.

She turned and quickly left the building, and stood outside

in the rain for a moment to take some deep breaths and calm herself. Then she began to walk around the building again, not daring to leave because Dr. Jorgan and, she was certain, Emma, were both in there, and not daring to go back inside just yet because something was terribly wrong, but she did not know what and did not know how to deal with it.

Miranda turned her face up to the falling rain, hoping it would clear her thoughts.

Miranda kept walking around the building as Jorgan leaned against a warm dryer in the closed laundry room and stared at the black eye of the 9mm pistol being aimed at his face by a large man with a white Santa Claus beard and mustache. Juarez stood beside him, holding his .38 special at his side.

"Who are you?" Santa said.

"Dr. Alan Jorgan." His voice wavered as he spoke and a bead of sweat dribbled down his forehead, over his temple, and down into his beard. "I work for OdysseyCorp Labs and I'm looking for Emma Shaw."

Santa frowned at Jorgan's answer in surprise, as if it was not what he had expected.

"Well, you're honest, I can say that for you," he said. "But who *are* you, why are you looking for Emma?"

Jorgan flinched. "She's here? Where? Where is—"

"What do you *want* with her?" Santa did not raise his voice, but what it lacked in intimidation was compensated for by his face: eyes cold, cheeks tense, lips pulled back to show teeth between the beard and mustache.

It was enough to make Jorgan gulp, clear his throat, and speak with a fearful politeness when he said, "Oh, I'm sorry, I thought I said that I'm, uh, her doctor. Didn't I say that?"

"*You're* the one who did that to Emma?"

"You mean...the operations? Yes, I did. At OdysseyCorp."

"And you're planning to take her back to your lab?"

"Oh, no, absolutely not, that would be too dangerous."

P.W. blinked and frowned again. "Then why did you come here for her?"

"To protect her from her husband."

P.W. cocked his head, suddenly extremely suspicious of this odd, scruffy man. "Well, you're full of surprises, aren't you? Go on, tell me more."

Jorgan frowned and looked at P.W. with genuine puzzlement, and something else: the dawning of the realization that he might have stepped into a deeper puddle than he had thought.

"Has Shaw been here?" Jorgan asked.

"Who?"

"Landon Shaw. Emma's husband, the man who *really* did this to her. Has he been here?"

"What if he has?"

Jorgan sighed with frustration and snapped, "Dammit, will you—who *are* you, anyway?"

"P.W. Meredith." He switched the gun to his left hand, still aiming it at Jorgan as he reached out his right hand to shake. "Pleasure to meet you."

Jorgan's face curled into a slightly wincing look of confusion. After a moment, he shook P.W.'s hand cautiously.

P.W. dropped the hand abruptly and began to pat him down, walking around him slowly. Jorgan absently lifted his arms out of P.W.'s way.

He found a heavy lump and removed a .25 caliber automatic from a pocket of the lab coat. He smiled broadly as he extended the gun to the young man beside him.

"Here, Juarez, go put this in the nursery toybox," P.W. said, then watched Jorgan's eyes widen as he realized what he had just heard. Reaching over to pat him on the shoulder, P.W. said, "Just kiddin' ya, babe. Hell, the kids in this part of town'd probably break in their teeth on a pea-shooter like that."

"Well," Jorgan said, failing to conceal his defensiveness, "I couldn't very well protect Emma unarmed, could I?"

"Oh, you had the right idea, but that's a damn-fool place to keep your gun. People'd be dressin' for your funeral by the time you got it outta that pocket. Now, let me get this straight, Doc. You cut open that girl's head a couple times, played with her brains like she was a fuckin' board game, and now you wanna *protect* her?"

"I-I...I couldn't help her *then*. I was...doing my job. I couldn't—"

"Just doin' your job?" P.W. said. "Hey, Juarez, get some strudel for Herr Eichmann here, maybe get him a chair. He's probably tired from doing his job."

Jorgan's confusion and frustration were replaced by a growing fear. "Now, wait, you don't honestly think I'd just walk in here and *introduce* myself if I wanted to hurt her, do you?" There was note of desperate pleading to his voice.

"Well, until you convince me you *don't* want to hurt her, that story works for me, Doc. So what *really* brings you to this part of town so late on a rainy night? Shouldn't you be at home reading *Scientific American*? Smokin' a pipe, maybe?"

Jorgan sighed again, running fingers through his stringy hair nervously. "I came here to keep her from her husband and get her some treatment."

"Treatment? For what you did to her?"

"No, for what went *wrong* with what I did to her."

P.W.'s face became serious as he stepped closer to Jorgan. "What the hell're you talking about?"

Jorgan took in a deep, steadying breath. "I think she's contagious."

P.W.'s lips parted and his jaw slackened as his mind bombarded him with the possible significance of that statement, and he swayed with its impact.

"Come again?" he whispered.

"Are you familiar with her condition?"

P.W. had *thought* he was, but now he was not so sure. "Why don't you fill me in, Doc."

Jorgan sputtered for a moment as he groped for the simplest explanation, then spoke rapidly, cutting through the information as quickly as possible. He stopped halfway through, took a deep, calming breath, then said, "But something went wrong with that synthetic virus, something early on that slipped right by us. The virus is mutating now. Rapidly. I don't know how it's transmitted, I'm not sure what the reaction of the infected might be, I don't know what symptoms might appear, but I'd rather find out in a laboratory than in the streets." He took another deep breath to calm his frustration and fear.

P.W. nodded slightly. "Tell me, Doc, does your mama know you do this kinda thing for a living?" His voice was flat and low and humorless, distracted by the frantic thoughts tripping over each other in his head.

"Oh, for crying out loud—*look,*" Jorgan barked, "if you're gonna shoot me, then shoot me, but don't *lecture* me. There's a good possibility we might be able to use the same technology to heal without surgery, I just don't happen to work in that department."

"Mm," P.W. grunted. "Kill 'em, *then* cure 'em."

"If she's here, please tell me. I need to get her to a facility with the means to treat her and start the appropriate tests."

P.W. realized he had been buying the whole thing, even starting to feel panicky, until Jorgan said *that.* A "facility"—he was just going to walk into a hospital and admit Emma, hook her up to some machines? That made no sense. Aside from the fact that P.W. doubted such a facility existed outside Jorgan's own laboratory, Shaw would be on them in a heartbeat. *If* Jorgan was indeed trying to protect Emma from him, which P.W. was beginning to doubt.

"Why don't you keep the doc company for a little while, Juarez," P.W. said, turning away from Jorgan. "Maybe get some free medical advice while you got him here. I'll be back."

He unlocked the basement door and closed it behind him before starting down the stairs.

While P.W. went down to the basement to tell McNolte and Emma about their visitor, Tonya Cox drove slowly past the South Street Mission and turned right on Beacham.

"I remember when this was a department store," Parson Higgins said, looking out his window at the building. "My mother used to bring me here every Christmas to see Santa Claus. Then she'd take me down to the basement, which was where they had their toy department, and she'd leave me there while she shopped. I usually ended up breaking something, then she'd take me home and beat the shit out of me with a broomstick. Miserable bitch."

Tonya parked at the curb across the street from an alley that ran behind the mission.

"A man whose own mother hated him," Tonya muttered as she killed the engine. They both got out, Parson carrying a small but bright flashlight, and went to the rear of the car, where he took the keys from Tonya and opened the trunk.

"They don't make department stores like that anymore," Parson said with a wistful nostalgia uncharacteristic of him. "Everything you wanted in one big place. The elevator bells ringing...the sound of cash registers. And it always had a...a *new* smell, like a new car does, only it was the smell of new... *stuff.* Just all kinds of *stuff.* I did my first shoplifting in that store."

"Good times," Tonya deadpanned.

Parson reached into the trunk and opened a bulky black satchel. As Tonya lifted a small, heavy, gray suitcase from the trunk, Parson opened his black bag and shined his light into it, checking its contents. He removed a small, plastic, rectangular device that looked like a beeper and clamped it to the lapel of his overcoat.

"Now all we got," he muttered, "are a bunch of big fuckin' neon-rainbow–colored oversized daycare centers. *Malls,*" he said with a disdainful grunt as he hooked the satchel's strap over his left shoulder and slammed the trunk.

The two of them jogged across the street toward the mission.

While Tonya Cox and Parson Higgins approached the mission, Emma followed P.W. up the basement stairs with McNolte right behind her. The three of them stepped into the unusually quiet laundry room.

"Dr. Jorgan," Emma said coolly and uncertainly when she saw him.

She was about to say more, but Jorgan held both arms out to her and took a broad step toward her, saying, "Emma, thank God, I thought—"

Juarez stepped in front of him and pressed the gun to his chest. "Uh-uh, no, that ain't no good for the health of your ass," he said, pushing him back. "Just stay right there so you don't get yourself killed, man."

Jorgan's attention was only vaguely distracted by the gun against his chest. He tilted his head from left to right to look at

Emma over Juarez's shoulders as he continued to talk in spite of the interruption.

"I thought he might *have* you by now. Look, Emma, I've got to get you out of here, you need treatment, and I can help you hide from—" He cut himself off bluntly and winced with confusion at Emma. "Why is your face—and your *hands*, my God, why are they *black*?"

Emma's and McNolte's hands and faces had been blackened with shoe polish and they wore ragged, dirty clothes. Each carried a cloth bag hanging from their shoulders by a strap and a heavy eighteen-inch Mag-Lite.

"What's this about my condition being contagious?" Emma said curtly.

"I tried to tell you before you left the lab, but you wouldn't let me. The virus is mutating, Emma. I need to see how far it's gone and what it's done to you, if anything. I've got a friend in Boston who has access to a lab in the basement of a university hospital."

As he went on, she remembered how nice Dr. Jorgan had been to her, how well he had treated her in every way, and she felt those good thoughts being sucked down a drain in the back of her mind when it struck her that she was no longer confined and did not have to listen to him or even let him anywhere near her.

"You want me to go to *Boston* with you?" she said, incredulous.

"We'll have to drive to an airport out of town. Shaw's probably covered every—"

"You cut my head open," she said, clenching her black hands into fists. "*Twice!*"

Jorgan paused as he watched the black-faced man beside Emma put his arm around her shoulders protectively. His throat tightened, but he tried to conceal it as he spoke soothingly to her.

"Don't get upset, Emma, please, you know what might happen if you let yourself—"

"You cut my *brain*," she shouted, and the man held her to him, bowing his head to whisper something in her ear.

Jorgan slipped the small, thin syringe from his coat pocket and started to remove the plastic cover from the needle as he said, "I brought this for you, it'll make this easier and safer, and I can—"

"*Hey,* doctor-boy," P.W. barked as Juarez touched the barrel of his gun to Jorgan's left eye and shouted, "Drop it, man, drop it *now.*"

The syringe skittered over the floor.

Tonya Cox and Parson Higgins stepped up on the curb and approached the closed doors of the delivery elevator in the sidewalk that stretched along the west side of the South Street Mission. Tonya stopped at the elevator, but Parson walked on toward a dark, unmarked door in the side of the building.

"I thought we were gonna use the elevator," she said.

"Who the fuck'm I, *Batman?* I'm not jumping into any fuckin' basement from the sidewalk. C'mere." Parson shined the flashlight over the door, tried the knob, made a cursory inspection of the locks. There were two: the one in the knob and a deadbolt. "Hold the light," he said, handing the flashlight to Tonya. Parson opened his satchel, removed a foot-long black leather case and opened it to reveal a row of various-sized drill bits. He chose one, slapped the case shut, and put it back in the satchel. His hands moved fluidly and quickly as he removed a cylindrical, gray and black device. "Put the light on the locks," Parson said, fitting the bit into the end of the device. The drill made hardly any noise as Parson drove the bit into the deadbolt. It was almost inaudible beneath the sound of the pouring rain.

The bit moved through the lock's brass-coated steel as if it were clay, then Parson slid it into the doorknob. He dropped the drill into the satchel, opened another black case, this one smaller, and chose one of several narrow strips of metal with small barbs cut into the edges. He slid the metal strip into each lock and turned it as easily as if he were unlocking his own front door. Parson took the flashlight from Tonya and shined it into the doorway as the door opened. The light fell on a narrow, steep staircase that led downward into blackness.

"Jump into the fuckin' basement from the sidewalk," Parson

muttered, shaking his head. "Where the fuck did Leo *find* you, anyway? Shee-zus."

They passed through the doorway and descended into the dark.

As Tonya Cox and Parson Higgins disappeared through the doorway, Miranda stood at the mission's corner entrance watching them. She had been there for half a minute, having cut another walk around the building short when she saw them huddled at the door.

For a moment, Miranda felt the bitter cold of the night and the aching wetness of her clothes, and she felt completely solid and visible. With that brief feeling of solidity came a high, keening panic, and she knew she should leave immediately because there was going to be trouble.

She was still bothered by the way that young man had ushered Dr. Jorgan away, and she was quite certain now that he had been holding a gun to the doctor's back. And now there were two suspicious men sneaking around inside the mission.

Dr. Jorgan had walked into a trap set for Emma by Mr. Shaw, that *had* to be it. That meant she might never see him again. Shaw's people would not let anyone stand in the way of getting Emma, especially if Shaw knew what Dr. Jorgan was doing there. He might never get out of there alive. And all because of that bitch, because she had posed and strutted and convinced him that she was what he wanted, what he needed, when she was nothing but an empty-headed, overgrown, spoiled brat.

The biting chill went away and Miranda felt an overwhelming calm. She started down the sidewalk, wondering if the two men had left the door unlocked.

In the mission's laundry room, Jorgan raised his arms, palms out, fingers splayed as he stared at Juarez's gun.

"I'm sorry, I'm *sorry*," Jorgan said. "It's a sedative, that's all, I don't want to *hurt* her, I...I'm sorry." His hands trembled.

"I'm not going anywhere with you, Dr. Jorgan," Emma said. "Tell Landon I said he can go fuck himself."

"I won't be seeing him, Emma, because if I did, he'd kill me for doing this. If he gets you back to the lab, you'll never come out again." He lowered his arms slowly, never quite relaxing them.

"He's already tried to kill me," Emma said. "He's still trying. There are two men downstairs, one dead. They're wearing surgical masks," she added.

"Surgical masks, you *see*?" Jorgan said. "I'm not making it up, it's not just me. Landon knows you're contagious, and if he's afraid of it, then you should be, too." He looked at the others. "All of you."

Emma's body stiffened as she leaned against McNolte. Her mind was spinning with the possible consequences if the virus were actually contagious, and the surgical masks on those two men made it seem quite possible. But how could she trust Jorgan?

"What do you want to do about it?" McNolte said.

Jorgan said, "I need to take her to a—"

"What's your second choice?"

"Second choice? I...I don't understand."

"What other options do you have?"

"Options? There *are* no other options. I need to take her to Boston, where I can—"

"You're not taking her anywhere," McNolte said. "What can you do here."

"*Here?*" Jorgan laughed without smiling. "That would be... well, I couldn't do *anything* here, except maybe examine her."

"How long would that take?"

"No," Emma shouted. "He's not touching me."

McNolte turned to her. "What if he's telling the truth?"

"If he were telling the truth, he wouldn't be here." She narrowed her eyes as she glowered at Jorgan. "Why *are* you here if I'm contagious? If it's so dangerous, why are you putting yourself at risk?"

Jorgan's arms became limp at his sides and his shoulders sagged. Deep creases cut into his forehead as he looked directly into Emma's eyes.

"Well, I huh-had to c-come here," he said quietly. "For, um... for you, Emma."

"It's a little late to start being noble, don't you think?" Emma was unconvinced.

"No, no, you don't under—" He stopped and pressed his lips together hard, willing himself to stop stammering. "Emma, please, could I speak with you? Just for a few seconds?"

She was confused for a moment. "You mean…alone?"

He spread his arms. "Look, I'm unarmed and they have guns, I'm not going to hurt you. Just a few seconds is all—"

"Anything you want to say to me will have to be said now," Emma said impatiently.

His face began to perspire as his mouth opened and closed and his lips tried to form words. "I…I came for *you*, Emma. That's the only reason."

P.W. smacked his lips twice and said, "I think the boy's got a crush on you, Emma."

Jorgan winced as if stabbed and lowered his head.

"And," P.W. added, "I think he's wasting our time."

Emma's upper lip curled back slightly as she looked at Jorgan with disgust. "So do I, P.W."

"Juarez, why don't you lock the doc up in the basement for now," P.W. said, tossing Juarez his keys.

Jorgan struggled halfheartedly when Juarez clutched his elbow, but he did not take his eyes from Emma as she left the laundry room with the two men.

In the basement, Tonya Cox and Parson Higgins had quickly and quietly located the furnace room and were working on a heating duct. Standing on a couple of crates, Parson was drilling a hole into the side of the duct with a 3/4" bit in a compact and heavy-duty silver drill. Nearby, Tonya hunkered over the suitcase and opened it. Encased in molded foam padding were two eighteen-inch cylindrical gray tanks with short hoses coming from one end of each, and two small gas masks.

Parson put the drill in his case and reached down as Tonya lifted one of the tanks to him. It had a rectangular black magnet on its side which clanked firmly onto the side of the duct. Parson carefully fitted the hose into the hole he had drilled, produced a roll of duct tape, and wrapped it carefully around the hose, fastening it securely onto the hole. Then he stepped down, moved the crates, and did the same thing on the other side of the duct as Tonya took the masks from the suitcase.

They were vicious-looking insectile pieces of black and red plastic with a round filter over the lower half of each, and had adjustable straps that wrapped around the head. When the masks were fitted snugly into place, Tonya and Parson reached up and each turned a nozzle.

The tanks began to hiss.

Juarez jerked Jorgan's left elbow hard, pulling him toward the basement door, and Jorgan resisted. He wondered where Emma could be going with those two men. He could not let her get away, and he tried to wrest his arm from Juarez's grip.

"I will hurt you *so* fuckin' bad if you don't knock that shit off," Juarez said, dragging him over to the basement door. He handed Jorgan the keys and said, "Unlock it."

The door was swinging open when they heard hurried footsteps coming up the stairs.

"Nobody's supposed to be in there," Juarez muttered as he shoved Jorgan aside and stepped forward, gun raised.

Jorgan stepped back at the sight of the two masked figures halfway up the stairs. One of them immediately drew a gun and the other said in a deep male voice, "Goddammit, no guns, Leo said no guns."

Juarez's gunshot was loud, while the shot from the stairs was a thick spitting sound.

Jorgan hit the floor and began crawling toward the big sink, toward the open doorway through which Emma had disappeared. But he was feeling impossibly heavy.

Juarez took a bullet in the chest and collapsed before he could fire a second shot.

"Leo said no fucking guns," Parson growled as they went the rest of the way up the stairs. "Now we got people shooting at us, a fuckin' corpse on the floor..."

"Hey, did you get shot?" Tonya said. "No. So quit your bitchin'."

"Yeah, but he *said* no fucking guns. It's a homeless shelter, a glorified soup kitchen. Who the hell expects to get shot at in a fuckin' soup kitchen? That's like being raped in church, or something."

"What about that other guy?"

Once in the laundry room, they looked around for him, but he was gone. "Don't worry about him, he won't get far. Pretty soon, he'll be dead to the world. Just like everybody else in the building."

Outside, in the alley behind the mission, P.W. had introduced McNolte and Emma to Dagmar and Boy as they stood in the rain, and a discomforting anxiety hung in the air between them.

It was difficult to tell how old Dagmar was. What little of her face was visible in the wild tangle of dark, matted hair was narrow and long with sunken cheeks and deep lines slashing downward on each side of her mouth. Her eyes were invisible in deep ovals of darkness and she never fully lifted her head. She wore a tattered pair of black pants and two filthy blouses, one atop the other, and a dark, hole-riddled scarf was wrapped around her impossibly thin neck.

At her side, Boy held her hand and fidgeted nervously as he stared at the sidewalk. He looked to be about eight or nine years old. He had his mother's hair, and about as much of it, and there was a clean, white bandage over the bump on his forehead. His clothes were just as dirty as Dagmar's, but they had seen less wear. His shoes did not match, but they were in fairly good shape, and although it looked like the halves of two separate coats stapled together, his coat looked heavy and warm.

"Take 'em straight to your place, Dagmar," P.W. said, speaking loudly to be heard over the rain. "Keep 'em away from trouble and watch for me, I'll be down as soon as I can."

She nodded silently.

"Now, for God's sake, McNolte," P.W. said, "don't lose that gun. And remember everything I told you about it. And Emma," he said, stopping in front of her and putting a hand on her shoulder, "don't hesitate to use that...that thing of yours if there's any trouble. Even if you have to knock McNolte for a loop to do it."

"How long before we see you?" McNolte said.

"I don't know. A day, maybe two."

"*What?*"

"Well, McNolte, what'd you expect? I've gotta do a little prestidigitatin' to get all those nice folks off your endangered ass, and I don't even know *what* I'm gonna do yet. Don't worry, as long as I know you're safe, I can probably come up with something sooner, I don't know."

"You say we're safe," McNolte said, almost too quietly to be heard, "but you sound like you're afraid it's the last thing you'll ever say to us, and it's scaring the shit out of me, P.W."

"Hey, hey, babe, I'm tellin' ya, you're gonna be fine. Just don't make eye contact with anyone, and don't look afraid. That's why your faces are painted black. It's so dark down there, nobody'll see your faces and you can be as scared as you want, just don't show it. Soon as you do, somebody in the dark is gonna take advantage of it."

"Okay, P.W., okay, I didn't want to go down there before, but now that you've told me *that*, I can't wait."

"Get goin'. You're already soaked." P.W. was turning away from them when the door was pulled open and Jorgan fell out onto the sidewalk, splashing face-down in a puddle of water. He tried to get up, gasping for air as if he had been holding his breath, but he fell a second time, all the while sputtering breathlessly, fearfully, "G-guns! Somebody's shooting!" Jorgan got to his feet and tried to run, but P.W. grabbed the collar of his coat and stopped him.

"What the hell're you talking about?" P.W. asked.

"Two men with g-guns. They came from the basement. They shot your friend."

P.W. rushed to the door. It was locked. He groped for his keys, then froze. "Oh, shit. Juarez's got 'em." He turned to McNolte. "You guys get going. *Now!*" Then he grabbed Jorgan's arm and said, "You're coming with me, Doc."

"Where?"

"To the front of the building."

"I'm not going back in there," he said, desperately trying to pull away from P.W. "It's a nightmare in there. They did something. To the people."

P.W. jerked him around until they were facing each other. "What're you talking about?"

"I don't know, I don't know. But it's a nightmare in there and I'm not going back."

"Like it or not, you are, because I'm not lettin' you go. Now, the less trouble you give me, the safer you'll be." P.W. showed him the gun. "Still got this, remember."

As P.W. jerked him around the corner of the building, Jorgan looked over at Emma, who was crossing Beacham with her new friend and a woman and child.

"Wait, wait," Jorgan said, then shouted, "Emma! Emma, where are you going?"

She did not look back.

"Never mind her," P.W. said, pulling him along. "She'll be fine."

"But where are they going?"

P.W. laughed but did not slow his quick pace. "C'mon, now, do I look like I just crawled up outta the sludge this morning? Don't worry, she's going someplace where people like you can't find her."

"Goddammit, I told you, I came here to pro—"

"Yeah, protect her, I know, I know. Give it a rest, Doc, I'm not in a talkin' mood." He slowed a bit. "Just...just tell me one thing, and tell the truth. That was horseshit back there about her being contagious, right?"

"I swear to God it was not."

"Yeah? We'll...we'll talk about that later."

P.W. walked faster, dragging Jorgan along. Jorgan looked back over his shoulder as Emma and the others headed down Beacham. As they moved along the sidewalk, neither P.W. nor Jorgan noticed that they had just walked past Miranda.

She stood in the darkness of the open doorway through which the two men had disappeared only minutes ago. She had ducked in when she heard voices around the corner. They were so close when they passed, she could have reached out and touched them, but she remained still, listening. When they passed, she peeked her head out of the doorway, watching their backs as they neared the corner.

Then, moving faster than she had moved all day, Miranda rushed out of the doorway and into the street, clothes soaked, hair plastered in wet strings to her face. A passing car honked angrily at her, but she did not even blink, just kept walking as she looked down the block at the four people who had nearly gotten to the corner. Once on the sidewalk, Miranda broke into a clumsy jog to keep up with Emma.

When they reached the mission's corner entrance, P.W. used the finger of his gun hand to hook the handle and pull the door open. He was about to push Jorgan in ahead of him, but he was struck with a cold paralysis. His arm went limp and fell away from Jorgan's coat. P.W.'s jaw dropped open and he made a choking sound in his throat.

"Oh, Jesus," Jorgan said with quiet horror. "Oh, my God."

The receiving room was dead silent, and the floor was carpeted with bodies, some stacked three and four high, all of them perfectly still.

36.

DOWN UNDER

The humid air of the subway station reeked of urine, feces, and putrid garbage. To Dagmar, it was the smell of home.

She had gone down shortly after giving birth to Boy in the South Street Mission. She had decided to call him Boy until she came up with the right name, but after a while, Boy stuck. It had been bad enough living on the streets alone, but she did not want Boy to be exposed to the elements all the time, not until he was older. It was just as dangerous down under as on the streets—even more so in some ways—but they stayed dry and did not have to deal with the cold stares and cruel words of passersby, people who accused her of being an unfit mother, who had no idea of the monstrous man her father had been, how he had kicked her out of the house when he found her doing some acid in the nude with her boyfriend, sending her alone into the streets to survive in any way she could. The years since then had taken their toll on her face, and on her mind. Looking at her, no one would guess she was only nineteen.

As bad as street life was, it did not approach the nightmare her life had been back home. Her father's unpredictable cruelty made the dangers of her present life seem minimal, even at their worst. Dagmar supposed that was why she had always turned down the invitations of Willy and Mama Charity; as nice as they were, living at the mission under their rules would feel too much like being a kid at home again, helpless under her father's violent hand, subject to sweeping moods. Having no roof at all was preferable to that black, smothering feeling.

Everything in the subway station, even the rancid air, vibrated with the echoing roar of the intermittent trains. Several street people stood or sat against the tile walls, and a couple were stretched out on the concrete floor.

A cramped newsstand was dark behind its metal security gate, and a fat black man sat at his shoeshine stand, head bent forward, chin on his chest, sound asleep.

A series of large, round mosaics were inlaid in the wall from the stairs all the way to the token booth. Each mosaic depicted an optimistic scene of Americana: a farmer tilling the field, a man fishing at a mountain stream, a majestic cityscape, a school bus full of children, and a faceless family—Mom Dad, Son, and Daughter, plus a dog—standing on their big green lawn in front of their picket-fenced house, an American flag displayed in front.

Dagmar had stopped noticing the mosaics a long time ago, especially the last one. The first time she saw them, she had laughed hysterically until she was racked by sobs that had made her baby wail with fear.

"Hide your flashlights," she said to the others. If any of the subway cops saw the Mag-Lites, they would know where they were headed and probably would give them trouble.

McNolte and Emma tucked the large, heavy flashlights beneath their coats and held each in place with an arm.

Dagmar turned to McNolte and nodded toward the token booth. P.W. had given him some change for tokens because there was no way the four of them would be able to sneak by unnoticed. She and Boy usually made it, but sometimes even they got caught, and then she would have to give head to one of the cops or the guy in the booth, or she and Boy would have to go to another station.

McNolte fished some money from his pocket and went to the window. The grizzled, silver-stubbled man in the booth made change and dropped it and the tokens into the aluminum bowl built into the narrow counter just beneath the glass and steel partition, saying, "There you go, Mr. Jolson."

Once the tokens were passed out, they went through the turnstiles and Dagmar stepped in front of them, leading Boy by the hand.

"Stick close," she said. "Gotta jump soon."

McNolte looked at Emma, telling her with his eyes that he had no idea what Dagmar was talking about. Uncertain and afraid as they were, they kept up with the woman and her child.

She led them all the way to the end of the platform, right up to the edge, turned to them and said, "We gotta wait here. Train's comin'."

Sure enough, a faint glow began to brighten the darkness in the tunnel to their right, and behind it came the rumbling rush of a train.

McNolte swayed as the train's backdraft pulled at him, and Emma gripped his hand. The train screeched to a stop, doors hissed open, and a handful of people got out. The only other person on the platform sat on a bench and did not even look up from the paper he was reading when the train arrived.

McNolte looked down at Dagmar, waiting for a sign from her, a look, a nod, anything. But she simply stood there holding Boy's hand and staring at the train, blank-faced and still.

When the train began to roll away, Dagmar glanced at them and jerked her head to the right, toward the tunnel. As soon as the rear of the train passed them, she let go of Boy's hand and jumped off the edge of the platform. An instant later, Boy followed her.

"Holy shit," McNolte muttered, trying to work up some spit in his sandpapery mouth.

Emma looked at him, shook her head, and said, "Oh, no. You got me into this, McNolte, you're not chickening out now." She stepped away from him and jumped off the platform.

McNolte looked over the edge. It was only five feet, but something about that jump seemed so final.

"Hurry up," Dagmar said, wondering what the man was waiting for.

McNolte jumped.

Dagmar felt a rush of anger and wanted to shout at the man. She had agreed to bring them because P.W. had asked her as a favor, and he and the others at the mission had always been so good to her and Boy that she could not refuse. But she almost changed her mind then and there, because he was slowing them down. She did not want anyone tagging along who might jeopardize Boy's safety. It had not happened yet, but Dagmar was dreading the day when she was caught by one of the subway cops and he was more interested in Boy's favors than hers.

She swallowed her anger and pointed to one of the many rails. "Stay away from that. It's hot." Once she had seen a drunk fall on the rail, and she had covered Boy's eyes with a hand as the drunk's body jittered and thrashed.

McNolte and Emma followed her into the tunnel; the rancid odor became worse, and the darkness grew deeper until McNolte turned on his flashlight. Emma followed suit.

"No, not yet," Dagmar said, turning to face them. "You want the subway cops to see us?"

"No," McNolte said, as they turned off the flashlights.

About fifty yards into the tunnel, Dagmar and Boy took an abrupt right and appeared, for a moment, to pass through the concrete wall like ghosts. Then McNolte and Emma saw the narrow passage they had edged through. There was a rich darkness beyond it, a swirl of black writhing within blackness.

McNolte went through first, tripping on a large chunk of broken concrete and nearly falling, and Emma was right behind him. Once through, neither of them moved because they could not see a thing, not even each other, and they stood only inches apart.

"Okay," Dagmar whispered, "you can turn 'em on now."

McNolte and Emma turned on their flashlights and breathed sighs of relief when the light held back the heavy, oppressive darkness.

Dagmar winced at the light and looked away from it. She had grown accustomed to the darkness down under, so much so that she and boy only went up during the night, and then only when they had to. The glow of the flashlight hurt her eyes, and she knew it would do the same to anyone else down there.

"You're gonna have to put your hands over those lights and shade 'em a little," she said. "Long as they're that bright, they're just gonna bring trouble."

McNolte wondered what kind of trouble might be drawn

by light in such impenetrable darkness, but before he could ask, Dagmar was on her way again, saying over her shoulder, "Stick real close and don't talk to nobody you see. Don't even look at 'em."

They did as they were told

At no time did they look back, because they assumed no one would be foolish enough to follow them.

P.W.'s first thought as he stared in at the bodies all over the floor of the receiving room was that Jorgan had been right, Emma was contagious, and it had spread through the building rapidly. But that possibility dissolved after a moment's thought; it simply did not make sense. That did not change the fact that *everyone was lying still on the floor.*

When he moved to pass through the doorway, Jorgan held out an arm and stopped him, saying, "No, wait. The two men in the basement—the ones who shot your friend—they were wearing gas masks."

P.W. stepped away from the doorway, letting the door swing closed, and turned slowly to Jorgan. "Gas masks?" There was a sharp edge to his voice.

"Yes, and I suspect—"

Before he knew what was happening, Jorgan's back was against the wall, his feet a couple of inches off the ground, and his throat was clamped shut by P.W.'s big hand. The barrel of P.W.'s gun was in his face again.

"What do you know about this?" P.W. roared into Jorgan's face.

Jorgan tried to speak, but he could not even breathe.

"Listen," P.W. said through clenched teeth, "I didn't like you the second I saw you, but I'm gonna do you a favor. I'm gonna let you go and give you five seconds to start talkin' before I rip your fuckin' eyes out and feed 'em to you like grapes. Understand?"

Jorgan's face felt swollen and hot and his ears were beginning to ring.

"Do you understand?" P.W. said again.

He nodded as much as P.W.'s grip would allow.

When he was released, Jorgan collapsed to the wet sidewalk,

his back still against the wall, gagging and heaving for breath. He stroked his burning, aching throat as he tilted his head up, letting the cold, reviving rain fall on his face.

A young couple walked by, but they only glanced at the gun P.W. was pointing at the top of Jorgan's head. They passed by without missing a step.

"Start talkin', goddammit," P.W. said.

"I don't know *anything* about this," Jorgan shouted, his voice ragged. "But I've got a pretty good idea what's going on here, if you'd just let me talk."

"Get up."

Jorgan talked as he got to his feet. "Those two men were wearing gas masks because, I suspect, they've gassed everyone in the building, and I'd bet money they're in there right now looking for Emma. They work for Landon. They must."

"He wouldn't kill a whole building full of people just to find her, would he?"

"No, he's not stupid. He probably used—would you put that gun down, please? I'm not armed and I'm certainly not dangerous."

P.W. lowered the gun.

"The people in there will be out for maybe an hour, hour and a half, and they'll wake up with headaches, but that's all. Landon probably used HC-13. It's potent and disperses quickly. A few minutes after it's been administered, you can move unaffected through the targeted area without a mask."

"And how the hell do you know so much about it?"

Jorgan chuckled. "I helped create the damned stuff."

P.W. looked at Jorgan for a moment, differently than before. He was deciding whether or not to trust the man.

"Okay," P.W. said, "since you're an authority, what do you suggest we do?"

"I suggest you save your bullets for whoever's been prowling around in there. It should be safe for you to go inside by now."

"Let's go, then."

"Oh, no. Do you know what Landon's people will do if they find me here?"

"Probably the same thing I'll do if you try to leave. Let's *go*."

P.W. pushed Jorgan ahead of him and they both went inside.

The door was not even all the way closed behind them when the gunfire began.

The foul, sickening odor in the darkness became almost as tangible as the cobwebs that caressed their cheeks and foreheads as they moved deeper into the city's black belly.

As they followed Dagmar's winding route, McNolte moved his flashlight around now and then, its glow bleeding between his fingers. Fat concrete pillars stood among the rubble, chunks of broken metal and glass littered the ground along with the blackened remains of old fires. There was an occasional oddity: a broken chair, a rusted bucket, old bedsprings, the skeleton of a bicycle. Although he saw no ceiling when he turned the light upward, there were great, filthy pipes and cables intertwined above them.

And there were people, of course. Some of them appeared to have been people at one time, but not any longer. Many of them huddled over small fires, which Dagmar steered them away from, but some just sat or lay in the darkness. The orange flicker of the fires was nearly smothered in the dense blackness, but there was just enough of it to cast dancing shadows over the long, hopeless faces that gaped at them in the dark.

As they went deeper, their path narrowed as the surroundings became more populated, more cluttered. Makeshift shelters became more common, until there were so many they were crowded together in the dark.

Eyes peered out of a cave made up of stacks of cardboard boxes.

A man lying on a pile of rags groaned and turned away from them to curl up in a ball as they passed.

A pale, androgynous face with strings of black hair hanging over the eyes peered up at them from inside a battered cardboard box turned on its side.

A woman with wild, white hair tangled around her head like Medusa's snakes pounced out of the darkness, swinging a broomstick and shouting at them savagely, "You can't have me! You get away from here, you godless fucking spies! You can't have me!" The woman had no nose, just a dark triangular cavity where her nose used to be.

The broomstick whistled through the air, too close for comfort, and Dagmar shouted, "Calm down, Anna, they're with me, calm *down*." She reached into her bag and threw a sandwich at the woman, then a cupcake.

Her attention diverted, Anna hunkered down in the dark and tore at the wrapping as they quickly moved on.

Sitting on an overturned crate, a man gnawed glistening gray meat from a bone, shrinking away from them as they passed.

The darkness was alive with rats. Their guttural squeaks, skittering feet, and frantic chewing sounded from every direction. They stayed away from the light, but McNolte caught a glimpse of a couple of them and his breath caught in his throat. They were the size of cats and their eyes burned in the flashlight's glow.

Sounds emerged from the darkness all around them. Dripping and slithering. Shuffling movements. Gasping breaths. Plaintive wails.

A baby cried somewhere, and a man's hoarse, throaty laughter went on and on, seeming to come from nowhere and everywhere, sometimes sounding close, sometimes far away.

The fires that flickered here and there in the darkness looked like the watchful eyes of predatory beasts, and McNolte did not look at them long because he did not like the chill they gave him.

Dagmar and Boy disappeared abruptly before them. Emma pressed herself to McNolte as her fingers dug into his arm.

"Down here," Dagmar whispered.

Their flashlight beams fell on a small, sagging fortress made of soggy cardboard boxes and the halves of a broken card table top. When they stepped through the small opening at one corner, Dagmar moved an old box the size of a washing machine into the space, closing them in. They all sat Indian-style on the ground around the meager fire in the center of the space.

Within the makeshift walls, a slight figure was curled up on a filthy blanket.

"We're back, Wanda," Dagmar whispered.

The figure slowly sat up. The old woman was almost completely bald except for a few wisps of gray, and her scalp was covered with crusty scabs. She had no teeth and her entire face seemed to be sinking into her mouth as it opened and closed lazily. She had been asleep, and her tiny eyes, nearly lost beneath sagging, white folds of flesh, squinted against the flashlights.

"Turn those off now," Dagmar said as the four of them huddled in the patchwork enclosure, setting down their bags.

McNolte and Emma glanced at one another nervously, reluctant to surrender their only source of light.

"Turn 'em off now, we're here," Dagmar said, voice brittle with frustration.

They turned off their flashlights, leaving the small, weak fire as their only light source.

Somehow, the sounds seemed louder when it became darker, and the unsettling laughter seemed to be drawing closer.

"Uh, I-I...I'm sorry," Dagmar whispered.

"What are you sorry about, Dagmar?" Emma said.

"Um, for talkin' short to you like that. Guess I'm just not used to—"

"Don't worry about it, you weren't rude at all," Emma said. "You know the rules down here. We don't. You go ahead and tell us when we're doing something wrong, okay?"

From a pile in the corner, Dagmar added shards of wood to the fire in the center of a small circle of rocks and chunks of concrete.

"You almost let the fire go out, Wanda," she said without anger. It was a simple, friendly statement.

The light from the growing fire darkened the old woman's sunken cheeks as she smiled, showing her gums.

"Thorry 'bout dat," Wanda said, voice crackling with phlegm. She broke into a bout of loud, wet coughs that racked her frail body and went on far too long. When the coughing finally stopped, she spit a wet, black gob into the fire and it hissed for a few seconds. "Fell atheep," she said. "Not feeling tho good."

"Anything I can do?" Dagmar said.

"Aw, no, honey, nothin' you can do." Wanda turned her gaze to McNolte and Emma and studied them for a moment. Her eyes appeared to have no whites, only glistening, bleary pupils that were much too large.

"Brought some food," Dagmar said.

Wanda's hairless eyebrows seemed to rise, but it was hard to tell. She smiled and webs of spittle stretched between her lips. The corpse-like woman became almost girlish as Dagmar began to empty her bag. She handed Wanda two small bunches of bananas, some grapes, and a few cellophane-wrapped cupcakes.

"Where'd alla thith come from?" Wanda said.

"P.W. sent it," Dagmar said. "And there's more."

Wanda laughed a low, phlegmy laugh and said, "Feelth like my birthday, or thumthin'." She squinted at McNolte, then at Emma. "Who dey?"

"They're gonna be staying with us for a while."

"Hello," McNolte said. "I'm McNolte, this is Emma."

"Emma Shaw," she said, leaning forward and extending a hand to the old woman, smiling.

Wanda closed her white, knobby, blue-veined hand lightly around Emma's four fingers and said, "Nithe t'meetcha."

No one spoke for a while and McNolte and Emma began to relax a bit in spite of the low, ominous laughter that continued outside the walls of cardboard and wood that surrounded them.

McNolte spoke in a sleepy whisper. "That sound, that laughter...what is it?"

"Oh, that's the Laughing Man," Dagmar said, putting a few more sticks on the fire.

"Who is the Laughing Man?" Emma said.

There was no joy in the laughter; it was, instead, cold and cruel.

"Nobody knows, really. He's just down here, y'know? He wanders around laughin' all the time. He's really mean and cruel. But you shouldn't worry, 'cause I don't think he'll bother us. That's why we got the boxes stacked up around us, see. To keep the fire from showin' in the dark. 'Sides, he hardly ever comes over this way, the Laughing Man."

Dagmar's reassurances did not make McNolte feel any better, nor did it make the laughter sound any less disturbing. He reached out and took Emma's hand.

After a while, McNolte's head began to nod forward heavily. He sat up with a jerk a couple of times, fighting his exhaustion, but failing. Finally, Emma put an arm around him and gently pulled his head down to her lap.

Dagmar peeled a banana, broke it in two, and handed half to Boy, who had been sitting beside her so quietly that McNolte and Emma had forgotten he was there. He gobbled the banana up with relish, and when he was done, Dagmar handed him half of a sandwich that had been wrapped in waxed paper. As she ate her portion, she watched Emma, who was staring now at the fire, enjoying the odd peacefulness there beneath the city, ignoring the smells in the damp air and the guffaws of the Laughing Man.

"Your name's Shaw, huh?" Dagmar said.

Emma was mildly startled. "Yes. Why?"

Dagmar shrugged, taking another bite of her sandwich. The fire's glow made her look much older than her years; it deepened the long creases in her face and had a strobe effect on her eyes, making them disappear in their deep, dark sockets for one instant, then glimmer the next among the lines of stress and exhaustion that surrounded them.

"Just know somebody named Shaw, is all," she said, still chewing.

"Somebody down here?"

She shook her head. "He don't live down here. Just comes down sometimes. Takes people."

"I'm sorry? He...*takes* people?"

Taking another bite, Dagmar looked down at Boy, who was devouring his sandwich, and absently ran a hand over his tangled hair. "Sometimes the people he takes don't come back," she said. "The ones who do are always different somehow."

Emma's voice lowered to a whisper and was beginning to tremble. "What do you mean, different?"

"Remember the woman who attacked us on the way in?

She used to have a nose before he took her. When she came back down, it was gone and she was crazy. Still is. Another one couldn't talk anymore, couldn't make a sound. One was just...a vegetable. It was almost like his brain was turned into mush, or somethin'. Couldn't even stand up on his own. They brought him back and just...dumped him here. He died not long after."

"They?"

"He's always got other men with him when he comes to take people. But when they bring 'em back...*if* they bring 'em back... he never comes. Just his men."

"Who is this man?" Emma breathed as McNolte stirred in her lap. He had been dozing but was awakened now by the alarm in Emma's voice.

"I know his name. He must be real important up top 'cause I saw his pitcher on a magazine cover once at the newsstand in the subway station. But down here, everybody calls him Experiment Man. 'Cause that's what he does. Least, that's what we think he does. He experiments on people. Him and his men tried to take Boy once," she said, stroking her son's hair again. "But I fought 'em. We got away. Most folks don't fight, though. Most folks down here don't know how to fight anymore."

McNolte sat up and looked at Emma with a frown.

"Who..." Emma stopped, swallowed, licked her dry lips. "Who is the Experiment Man?"

"His name is Shaw, too," Dagmar said casually, finishing off her half of the sandwich. "Landon Shaw."

When P.W. and Jorgan went through the door, they were so distracted by all the bodies stacked on the floor that they did not notice the two standing figures until the first gunshot was fired.

The first bullet landed in P.W.'s left arm, just above the elbow. He cried out in pain, then raised his gun and fired back without aiming as Jorgan raised his arms protectively over his face.

Tonya Cox and Parson Higgins were no longer wearing their gas masks. Tonya fired a second time as Parson stood behind her looking tense and bitterly annoyed. Her second shot was unsuccessful.

When P.W. fired again, he had better luck. The bullet hit

Tonya in the throat with a small splash of blood and knocked her on her back, kicking and gurgling.

"Oh, shit," Parson said as P.W. took aim at him. He raised both arms and shouted, "Goddammit all to hell, I'm *unarmed!*"

Stepping over and around bodies, P.W. made his way toward Parson, holding the gun on him. He did not look back at Jorgan, who was just beginning to lower his arms uncertainly.

P.W. fired, anyway, aiming low.

The bullet lodged in Parson's left shin and he let out a shrill scream as he hit the floor, crying, "Son of a *bitch*, I said I was unarmed, you fuckin' asshole!"

By the time P.W. reached Parson's side, a pool of blood had spread rapidly around Tonya's head. Her movements had slowed to an occasional twitch, and the bubbling sounds coming from her punctured throat were faint.

P.W. aimed his gun down at Parson's face and said, "Who sent you?"

"What?" Parson said, sitting up and rocking back and forth, wincing.

"I said, who sent you? Landon Shaw?"

"*Who?*"

"Lan—just tell me who sent you."

"Nunna your fuckin' bidness."

P.W. bent over and pressed the end of his gun to the man's philtrum, the narrow dip in the flesh just beneath his nose.

"You wanna die?" P.W. said.

By then, Jorgan had joined him and was fidgeting nervously as he watched.

"Why?" Parson said. "You wanna kill me? What good would that do ya, huh?"

P.W. thought about that a moment, then reached down and clutched the front of Parson's shirt and lifted him to his feet. Parson cried out in pain, but stood with his weight on his right foot and swayed slightly. P.W. pulled him close and said, "Let's go someplace where I can do something really productive, okay? Whatta you say to that, huh?" He looked over his shoulder at Jorgan. "Check some of these folks, Doc, and make sure they're still breathing."

P.W. waited as Jorgan felt for a pulse in some of the nearby bodies.

"They're alive," he said. "They've got healthy pulses and they're breathing."

P.W. looked at Parson and said, "HC-13?"

Parson's eyes widened and he seemed about to speak, but he said nothing.

"Gimme a hand, Doc," P.W. said, and the two of them helped the crippled man over the limp bodies, down a corridor, and around a corner to Willy's office. They had to step over Willy, who was lying in the open doorway. P.W. dropped Parson in a chair and glared down at him.

"Now we can talk," P.W. said pleasantly, smiling. "How come no gun, pardner? Afraid of 'em?"

Parson's tightly closed mouth worked silently, as if he were preparing to spit. Instead, he said, "Religious reasons."

"Look, I need to know what you're doin' here, my friend. That's all. Just tell me what you're doin' here."

"Like I said, *my friend*, that's nunna your fuckin' bidness."

"Oh, now, I don't think you should take that attitude. By the way, I'm P.W. Meredith, nice to meet you." He held out a hand to shake. "And who are you?"

Leaving his hands in his lap, Parson said, "I don't give a flyin' fuck *who* you are, buddy."

"Okay, okay," P.W. said, nodding his head, still smiling as he dropped his hand to his side. "If you won't tell me your name or who sent you, then I can't guarantee you're gonna have a good time, here, know what I mean?"

Parson laughed harshly. "And exactly whatta you gonna do to make me talk? I was tortured in Korea, you fuckin' hillbilly."

P.W.'s eyebrows shot up and his mouth formed a big O. "Really? Well, I was tortured in Vietnam, how about that, huh?" In a smooth, quick movement, P.W. reached down, grabbed the little finger of Parson's left hand and bent it back until it cracked like a firecracker.

Parson's scream filled the room as his face broke out in glistening beads of perspiration.

Jorgan spun around and headed for the door, his shoulders

hunched and his face screwed into a mask of sympathetic pain and disgust.

P.W. went on smiling as he said, "I just don't have time for the kinda complex, long-term bullshit they pulled back there in the jungle, know what I'm sayin'? So we're just gonna focus on your fingers for now."

Clenching his teeth, Parson spit out the words: "What the fuck do you want?"

"I want to know who sent you here. You don't tell me and I'll have to make my way through the other nine and you'll never play the violin again, I promise. Course, it's up to you, my friend."

Parson's little finger remained where P.W. had left it: bent backward at an impossible angle, with a single shard of bone cutting through the bloody flesh at the top of his palm. Tears glistened in his eyes as he glared defiantly up at P.W.

Reaching down to grip the next finger, P.W. said, "I'll break 'em all and kill you in the end if that's what you want."

The man's arm trembled as he closed his eyes and waited.

P.W. jerked the second finger all the way back until it cracked sharply.

Parson screamed again, pounding his right fist on the concrete floor.

P.W. waited for him to calm down, then said, "Ready for another?"

"All right, all right, you asshole," he growled, his whole body trembling. "We were sent here by Leo Trafficante."

P.W.'s eyebrows lifted as he looked at Jorgan, who looked equally surprised.

"Is that a fact?" P.W. said, looking down at the man.

"That's a fact," he said, averting his eyes, ashamed now.

Grinning, P.W. turned to Jorgan. "Boy, this is some party we got here, ain't it? And we didn't even send out invitations." To Parson, he said, "I want a phone number right now."

"What're you talkin' about?"

"A phone number where I can reach Trafficante right away." Over his shoulder, he said to Jorgan, "Get me a pen and paper from the desk, would you please, Doc?"

Jorgan brought him a pencil and a notebook.

P.W. stuffed the gun beneath his belt in the small of his back and poised his hand to write. He winced only slightly at the pain in his arm, refusing to pay it any attention, which, he assumed, was exactly what the bald war horse seated in front of him was doing. "I'm waiting."

"What if I don't know a number to reach him?"

"Then you'd better do all your nose-pickin' right now, 'cause you won't be doin' it anymore in about five minutes."

Parson's eyes closed slowly as he sighed in surrender and gave P.W. the number.

P.W. wrote it down, then pocketed both the pad and the pencil. He removed the gun from beneath his belt and offered it to Jorgan, grip first. "Take this and make sure he stays right where he is. If he moves, shoot him."

"Wait, I-I-I—"

"You-you-you just stay right here and make sure he doesn't move, all right? Otherwise, he might want to kill *you*. You can squeeze the trigger, can't you? Just keep it pointed at him. If you can see the hole in the front of the gun, you're doin' it wrong."

Jorgan snatched the gun from him angrily, saying, "All right."

P.W. went to Willy's desk and got a spare set of keys from the bottom drawer, then left the office and moved quickly down the corridor to the laundry room.

He knew Juarez was dead the second he saw his empty, staring eyes, but he got down on one knee and felt the young man's neck for a pulse to make sure.

"Dammit." He stood and rubbed his eyes rapidly. He felt a surge of palpable anger move through him, and it was directed at McNolte and Emma. A vague thought occurred to him—*Boy, I could sure use a drink right now*—and it felt so natural that he actually found himself entertaining the possibility of having one.

He kicked the side of a washing machine hard as he roared silently at himself, *This is nobody's fault, goddammit, you could've walked away anytime you wanted, but you didn't, and now they're in trouble, and McNolte is your friend, so shut the fuck up.*

As he passed Juarez's body, he whispered, "Sorry, kid."

He went down the stairs to the room where McNolte and Emma had made their beds, found his case, and removed the only remaining gun—a Smith and Wesson 9mm with a silencer, his "hushpuppy" from Vietnam—loaded it, then went back upstairs.

When he stepped out of the laundry room and into the corridor, he heard someone calling his name, and he recognized the voice almost immediately. He jogged down the corridor and into the receiving room, stepping over and around bodies all the way, and he saw Ty and Buddy. They looked pale, horrified. He grinned and waved at them.

"P.W.?" Ty croaked. "What...the fuck...is going on here?"

P.W. felt a nostalgic pang at the sight of the old friends he had not seen in years, and he could not hold back a laugh. "It sure is good to see you guys. Come with me and I'll tell you the whole ugly tale."

They started toward him hesitantly, walking around the bodies with fear and disgust in their faces. Before they were halfway across the receiving room, the entrance door opened and Irving, the shelter's maintenance man, walked in.

"Holy shuh-shuh-*shitballs!*" he cried, looking around the room aghast.

"Don't worry, Irving," P.W. said, "they ain't dead, just out cold."

As Ty drew nearer, he said, "What have you gotten yourself into, P.W.?"

"*That* is the sixty-four billion dollar question, gentlemen."

As he led them to Willy's office, P.W. talked fast, giving them a shorthand version of what was going on.

Ty and Buddy were P.W.'s age. Ty was a solidly built, bullet-shaped black man who stood five feet, eight inches tall, but had no neck to speak of and noticeably large hands and feet. Buddy stood five inches taller and was slender but tight and muscular, with curly red hair shot with gray, and his lean, long face was salted with freckles.

"You're bleeding, P.W.," Buddy said as they went into Willy's office.

"Yeah, but I'll be okay. Just a flesh wound. Dr. Jorgan, I'd like you to meet my friends Ty and Buddy, and this is Irving."

"Hiya," Ty said distractedly before turning back to P.W. "Hey, man, your flesh is pretty much all you got, and yours is bleeding pretty damned bad. Is there a first aid kit anywhere? Maybe some alcohol?"

P.W. nodded. "Yeah, in the clinic. Go back the way we came and go through the door that says 'clinic.' And bring enough for our friend, here."

Ty hurried away.

Jorgan was still holding the gun on the bald man and avoiding his gaze. Parson was silently staring daggers at Jorgan.

"Will you take this, please," Jorgan said with quiet urgency, handing the gun back to P.W. "I'm just not very good at this sort of thing."

P.W. smiled as he took the gun. "I figured being shot at would change that."

"Well, it *didn't*." He stepped close to P.W. and lowered his voice. "I want to talk to you. Privately. Right now."

P.W. eyed him suspiciously.

"I have a suggestion I think you might like. But I want to talk privately."

After thinking it over a moment, P.W. turned to Buddy and offered the gun, saying, "You wanna watch this guy for a minute?"

"The hell you talking about," Buddy said, reaching behind him and beneath his down jacket to produce a Para-Ordinance .45 automatic. "I brought my own."

P.W. chuckled and shoved his gun beneath his belt, then led Jorgan out of the office and into the corridor, where they faced each other.

"I've been thinking," Jorgan said. "How would you like to do something that would eventually rip the lid off of Shaw's little secret? Something he'd have a hard time avoiding and couldn't influence with his money? Well...he might be able to slow it down by handing out a lot of cash, but he wouldn't be able to *stop* it."

"Sounds good to me, Doc. But what's in it for you? I figure

there's gotta be something in it for you, right?"

"Just one thing. I'll tell you how you can utterly ruin Shaw, but it has to be done right away, before all these people come to, and it has to be done right. And you've got to tell me where Emma is."

P.W. laughed. "You had me right up to the Emma part. You kiddin', Doc?"

"I'm not."

"Look, not that I know shit from Shinola, but I think Emma's already found herself a fella, and I don't think—"

"You don't understand. She really is contagious, P.W. She's dangerous. All I want to do is help her and keep her from hurting anyone."

"Yeah, but you've also got the hots for her, Doc, that's obvious to anybody who's awake. I'm not gonna betray her trust 'cause you got a tentpole in your pants."

"They went underground, didn't they?" Jorgan said. "Underneath the city, right? Yes, I think I'm right. I'm not the idiot you seem to think me to be, P.W. She's down there now, and if Shaw finds out, she's dead. He knows his way around down there. That's his hunting ground. And you sent them down there, didn't you?"

"What do you mean, that's his hunting ground?"

"That's where he gets his guinea pigs. He was taking people from the subways before most people knew there was anybody down there."

P.W. took in a deep breath and let it out, rubbing his hand over his face. "All right, Doc, what have you got to tell me?"

"Not until you confirm it. They're down there, aren't they?"

P.W. said nothing.

"Goddammit, don't you see I'm on your side? What do I have to do to convince you?"

"Tell me what I can do to nail Shaw."

"Okay. Get somebody out there at the entrance to keep any bums from wandering inside and seeing all those bodies, because sooner or later, somebody's gonna call the cops, and Shaw owns them. Then, we call the State Department of Emergency Services. I'll talk to them, I speak their language.

If I tell them what's happened, they'll have some hazardous material specialists here faster than you can say 'media circus,' and once they're involved, it'll be nearly impossible to cover it up. But we've gotta do it before these people come to, otherwise they won't believe us. The gas leaves no trace in the air, and traces in the body don't last. But if they see all these people lying on the floor in here, they'll be like dogs on a scent. We don't have much time."

"How will that expose Shaw?"

"They'll test everyone and find traces of HC-13 in their systems. Shaw is the only one in the country who manufactures HC-13. He's the only one who *can* be responsible for it."

P.W. smiled. "Okay, let's do it. I've been thinking, and I've got a few ideas of my own, but that's a good one. I need a number where I can reach Shaw."

Jorgan nodded. "Okay."

"Good, between the two of us we might be able to make a couple of rich, powerful assholes wish they'd stayed in bed this morning."

"Wait. They're under the city, aren't they?"

Finally, P.W. nodded and said, "Yeah, that's where they are, and that's where they stay until I go get 'em. I know exactly where they are. It's my territory, too, Doc. I had a room down there for a while."

Jorgan nodded, satisfied.

P.W. said, "Now let's go to the phone and do some damage."

"I don't understand," McNolte whispered to Emma. "Even if he does get his guinea pigs down here, why would he come for them? Wouldn't someone in his position send other people to do that?"

She shook her head, staring into the fire. "No, not Landon. It makes perfect sense. He's a…a control freak. He wants a hand in every part of his work, even the parts he doesn't understand. And he's cruel, too. Sadistic. Coming down here, taking advantage of these people, hunting them down like—" She paused when she thought of all the stuffed, glass-eyed heads on the walls of Landon's den, of the hollowed-out elephant legs used as umbrella stands, and the tusks over the fireplace. She hugged herself and shivered. "It's exactly the kind of thing he'd do."

McNolte put an arm around her and held her close. "Are you cold?"

"No. Afraid."

"Hey, he doesn't know we're down here. And even if he found out, he'd still have to *find* us. We're going to be fine."

"Even so...just knowing he comes down here makes me feel...sick to my stomach. Like we're not so safe after all."

Boy lay on Dagmar's lap and she had her arms wrapped around him, stroking his forehead as he dozed.

Wanda snored wetly on her blanket, cupcake crumbs clinging to her rubbery lips.

The Laughing Man was closer. His laughter was guttural, almost as if he were gargling something. Soon, he was so close that McNolte could hear his footsteps.

It was McNolte's turn to shiver, and he held Emma close.

37.

MANIPULATIONS

It was twelve minutes after three in the morning, and Leo Trafficante was seated at his desk in his office waiting for the telephone to ring. He had stopped drinking scotch about an hour ago, and now a large ceramic mug of coffee stood on the desktop with a halo of shifting steam floating over it.

A sixty-two-inch television screen, usually tastefully concealed behind an original Jackson Pollock, was on a local news channel, the sound muted, and Trafficante watched the silent images as he sipped his coffee and smoked a cigar.

He had let his Shi Tzu, Augustus, into the office, and the dog lay on the floor beside Trafficante's chair. He occasionally reached down to stroke Augie's luxurious coat, and the dog would raise his head to look up at him for a moment, as if checking to see if he needed anything before going back to his nap.

There had been nothing of interest on the news except for the updates on that fire in the city, a small diner and an old warehouse. Trafficante paid close attention to those reports because he was certain the fire had something to do with Emma. It was only a suspicion until it was learned that someone had shot the place up with an automatic weapon just before the fire had started. First, Shaw spent a year torturing his wife, and now apparently he wanted to kill her before anyone found out, and he obviously did not mind killing others in the process. Apparently, Shaw had become an equal opportunity employer and had taken on some mentally handicapped help, because the attempt in the diner had not worked. Emma was still out there.

The thought made him turn to his telephone. He had expected to hear from Parson half an hour ago, but the sleek, black instrument on the desk remained silent.

Trafficante picked up the receiver and hit the redial button. He had already called twice, but decided to give it one more try before making his next move.

Parson's cell phone, which Trafficante knew would be left in the car when they went to work, still went unanswered.

Trafficante hung up and hit a button on his desk. A moment later, his office door opened and his secretary walked in. He was six feet, four inches tall and Trafficante was convinced the man had muscles under his fingernails, which was one of the reasons he had been hired. His name was Ollie.

"Parson and Tonya haven't even gotten back to the car yet," Trafficante said. "I want three more men on the mission, and get—"

The telephone trilled and he swept up the receiver before the first ring was finished.

"Yeah," he said curtly.

"Mr. Trafficante, please," an unfamiliar male voice said.

"Who the hell is this?"

"Who I am isn't as important as what I know, and if you're thinking of hanging up, I wouldn't. Am I speaking to Leo Trafficante?"

He glanced at Ollie once with puzzled eyes, then looked down at the desktop. "You are."

"Good. Mr. Trafficante, I have a deal to make with you. You let Emma Shaw go, just forget all about her and leave the poor woman alone, and I won't tell General Horner at the Pentagon that you've been buying top secret defense information for nearly fifteen years. How's that sound?"

It was said matter-of-factly, with no malice or threat, and it made Trafficante's eyes blink several times in rapid succession. When he spoke, he, too, sounded casual. But he was not. He was searching some mental files for information. Who would have access to such facts? What could he do to head off the release of such information and weaken any damage that might result?

Was Shaw stupid enough to try something like this?

"Is this a joke?" he said with a chuckle.

"Oh, no. I'm afraid not."

"I'm hanging up."

"Not a good idea. They'll nail Landon Shaw first, but you'll be next. And you know it."

Trafficante did not hang up. He did not even move.

"What makes you think they'd nail anyone at all?" Trafficante said quietly, frowning.

"Hey, look, Mr. Trafficante, I know you've got friends in high places, maybe all the way to the Oval Office, for all I know. But you know as well as I do that if Uncle Sam has to choose between protecting you and looking bad, he'll cover his own ass and cut his losses, and you'll be shit outta luck."

Trafficante's frown narrowed his eyes to coin slots as he took a drag on his cigar.

"You haven't thought this through, friend," he said. "It's real hard for me to take somebody seriously if they haven't thought a thing through." He was just stalling, going over the possibilities in his mind, looking for the worst-case scenario.

"Oh, *I* have, it's just that *you* haven't, and you're probably wrackin' your brain right now to figure out who the hell I am and who put me up to this, but you can stop wasting your time. I'm a civilian, Mr. Trafficante, I don't run in your packs and I got no iron in this fire. I'm nobody. Which makes me a wildcard. Which means you'd better take me *very* seriously."

Another pull on the cigar. "What exactly do you want?"

"I told you. I want you to leave Emma Shaw alone. I think she's been through enough, don't you? I mean, between you handing her over to her sick fuck husband, and her sick fuck husband playing with her brain like it was a Rubik's Cube, I think she deserves some peace."

Emma, Trafficante thought with a twitch of a smile playing at one corner of his mouth. *Could she be pulling this?*

It seemed unlikely, but it was not out of the question. She was smart enough to do it, but would she have the guts? After so many years of being cowed by Landon Shaw, would she muster the courage for this?

"You just want me to make you a promise that I'll leave her alone?" Trafficante said. "We're working on the honor system, huh? Is that it?"

"Not exactly. I want you to understand that if another attempt is made to kill or kidnap Emma Shaw, I will see that General Horner gets hold of some pretty upsetting information. Understand?"

"Whoever you are, you're a fucking idiot. You tell me you want me to make you a promise? And you expect me to take you seriously? Is it April Fool's Day, is that what this is? Go fuck yourself, pal." He hung up.

Trafficante stood there behind his desk a moment, chewing on his cigar.

"Something wrong?" Ollie said.

He did not respond. He reached down and stroked Augustus. The dog stood and stretched, walked in a circle a couple of times, then curled up again. Trafficante picked up his coffee mug and was stepping away from the desk when the phone rang again.

"*What?*" he shouted into the receiver.

"I meant what I said about that information," the caller said. "But I guess that doesn't matter much now, does it?"

Trafficante waited for the man to continue, and when the line remained silent, he said, "What the hell's that supposed to mean?"

"Well, it seems your two goons fucked up at the mission. One of them's dead. I'd say those tanks of HC-13 are being looked at by some kind of hazardous materials specialists wearing spacesuits by now. Lots TV cameras and reporters, of course, because this is gonna be a *big* story. And those reporters'll have lots and *lots* of questions. You'd better hope I'm in a good mood if they ask *me* any of 'em."

He hung up.

Trafficante's white-knuckled hand clutched the receiver tightly as he lowered it to the cradle.

After a long silence, Ollie said, "Trouble?"

Trafficante nodded slowly, his shock bright on his face. "Yeah, maybe so," he said, rounding the desk and swiping his coat from the narrow closet. "Get the car, Ollie."

Landon Shaw's cell phone chirped in his suit coat pocket as he paced his office. He removed the phone, flipped it open, and said, "Shaw."

"Mr. Shaw, I'm going to make you a deal, and I suggest you listen unless you want me to go to General Horner and tell him you've been selling national secrets."

Shaw coughed and stammered a moment, then said, "Who *is* this?"

"No, no, Mr. Shaw, this isn't a conversation. Just listen. If you don't call your dogs off of Emma right now and stay away from her *permanently*, then General Horner finds out about your little auctions, and you take a long vacation to a place where the men are men and the *women* are men, too, if you get my meanin'."

Shaw's back stiffened and he spoke rapidly. "Do you know where Emma is? Is she with you? Listen to me, whoever you are, she's *dangerous*. Do you understand me? You've got to let us help her because her condition is—"

"What do you plan to do with the cigar *this* time when you get your hands on her, Mr. Shaw? Stuff it up her ass?"

Shaw flinched and was about to respond when the caller continued.

"Save your breath, Shaw. There's nothing you can say that'll do you any good. Besides, you're gonna have other things on your mind for a while."

"I don't under—I'm not—what do you mean?"

"Seems Mr. Trafficante sent a couple of his men to the South Street Mission to find Emma. They gassed everybody in the building with HC-13. I understand that's your baby, ain't that right?"

"Are...are you serious?"

"Things didn't turn out the way Mr. Trafficante had hoped and his two operatives were discovered. Not to mention the two tanks of HC-13 they used. You can get all the details on the news. It's gonna be a real big story, I suspect. They're gonna have a lot of questions, you know. Especially considering the fact that you're the only person on the planet who manufactures HC-13. Can you imagine the scandal if they found out you'd sold a gas that you made for our government to a lousy goombah like Leo Trafficante? And even worse, that you've been selling their secrets to everybody from camel-jockeys to fuckin' Eskimos for the last fifteen years?"

Shaw's mouth hung open and he made small clucking sounds in his throat, but no words came out.

"If you don't want that to happen, Mr. Shaw, then remember what I said about Emma. Stay away from her and hope nothing accidental happens to her, because if it does, you're gonna be blamed for it. If that happens, I shoot my wad. Right on General Horner's desk."

The connection was severed with a gentle click.

Shaw's hand slapped the phone together and he leaned his hips against the edge of his desk as he exhaled the words, "Oh, God, oh, my God." He stormed out of his office, past his secretary's unoccupied desk, and out the door and down a narrow passageway to a main corridor. The phone chirped again and he nearly dropped it trying to get it open.

His voice was dry and hoarse when he said, "Shaw."

"Where are you?" Trafficante said.

He pounded a fist on the wall angrily as he shouted, "Goddammit, Leo, what the fuck have you done?"

"Cool your jets, flyboy," Trafficante said in his moist and quietly menacing way. "We've got ourselves a problem."

"What do you mean *we*?"

"I mean that whatever the hell's going on, it's a problem for both of us."

"And what the hell is going on?"

"I sent a couple of my people over to the mission to get Emma. They were gonna fill the place with your fancy gas, look around until they found her, and get out before anybody woke up."

"But they got caught and now there's a big scene over there and the specialists are looking at my tanks, I *know*, Leo, somebody already called and told me how you fucked up. My God, how could you be so—"

"Shut your hole, Shaw, we don't have time for that shit now. I got a call, too, and I don't know if there's any truth to it. I don't suppose *you* have any idea who our mysterious caller is, do you?"

"I've got an idea. And even if it isn't who I think it is and there's any truth to it, I'll blame the son of a bitch I'm thinking of, anyway."

"Who are you babbling about, Shaw?"

"Jorgan. Dr. Alan Jorgan. He was working on Biofire, and he's got a hard-on for my wife. He's a lot like you, Leo. He's sure got the same shitty taste in women."

Trafficante was silent for several seconds, then: "It's in my best interest to work with you for the time being, Shaw, because this affects both of us. I think we should meet at the mission, see if anything's going on, and if it is, I'll do everything I can to help you clean it up. But when this is over, Shaw, I promise you're gonna curse your mama's cunt for ever letting you go. I'll meet you half a block east of the mission in fifteen minutes."

Trafficante hung up and Shaw put his phone back in his pocket as he stalked down the corridor and around a corner, then went through the first open door he reached. It was a small employee lounge, and three techs and a janitor looked up at him when he entered. He pointed to a small East Indian woman standing beside a candy vending machine and said, "What kind of car do you drive?"

She blinked, startled, then said, "A Honda Civic."

Shaw shook his head violently, muttering, "Fucking slope-head deathboxes. *You!*" He pointed to a young man with glasses seated at a table with a half-eaten sandwich in front of him. "What kind of car?"

"A 1989 Buick Skylark."

Shaw stormed toward him, snapping his fingers. "Give me your keys. C'mon. Now."

The man fumbled in his pocket nervously, handed the keys over, and Shaw spun away, hurrying for the door. "I'll take good care of it," he said, on his way out of the lounge.

Any reporters hanging around the mission would recognize him immediately in one of his trademark cars, but certainly not in a Buick. Of course, he probably would not get there as fast, and if he went too far over the speed limit, the cops would not recognize him in the Buick and he might get pulled over, but he would deal with that problem if it came up.

He got in the elevator and started up to the next floor. He needed one more thing.

A squirt gun.

By the time Landon Shaw was speeding along the freeway in his borrowed Buick, a bespectacled Japanese man with a pocket protector filled with pens in the pocket of his orange jumpsuit was talking on the telephone in Willy's study while P.W. and Jorgan watched and listened. Parson sat quietly, his finger splinted and bandaged.

The man's name was Mr. Kanagi and he was from the County Department of Emergency Services. While he knew nothing about a gas called HC-13—he had never even heard of it, which he found unsettling—and could not say exactly what had happened at the mission, he knew an emergency situation when he saw one, and he was telling someone at the other end of the line to send specialists from the state level immediately and call for ambulances and the police. Four other men, all in orange jumpsuits, were busy cordoning off the block outside and closing intersections to traffic with bright orange cones and red flares.

"You were right, Doc," P.W. whispered with a smile, "this worked real nice."

"I hope *you* were right," Jorgan whispered back.

"About what?"

"About calling Trafficante and Shaw."

"Oh, hell, I don't know *what'll* happen because of that. But I know that whatever happens, it'll take their minds off McNolte and Emma for a while. It'll confuse the shit out of 'em, I'm pretty sure of that. Hell, they might even come *here*," he added with a laugh. "They sounded panicky enough."

"You're laughing. Why are you laughing? I've got no personal experience with Trafficante, but you have no idea what Shaw is like, you don't know what he's capable of—"

"Doc," P.W. said, putting a hand on Jorgan's shoulder, "human beings are never more vulnerable and never more stupid than when they're pissin' themselves with fear tryin' to cover their own asses. I'm not worried about a thing, and that's what gives me an edge over them. Right now, they're scared shitless." He clapped the shoulder once, then turned to Kanagi as he hung up the telephone.

"I expect them to move quickly," Kanagi said to P.W. "This place will be swarming with police and ambulances soon. And probably the press. I hope the publicity doesn't bother you because there's not much I can do about that."

P.W. grinned and shook Kanagi's hand. "Bother me? That's music to my ears, Mr. Kanagi."

"Who is this?" Kanagi asked, looking at Parson.

"Oh, he came in from outside," P.W. said. "Hurt himself in a fight. I was just helpin' him out."

Kanagi nodded.

Jorgan sighed and said, "I'm illegally parked. If it's going to be that busy, I'd better move my car."

"Don't be long, Doctor," Mr. Kanagi said. "The state people will want to talk to you about that gas as soon as they get here."

"I'll only be a minute." He looked at P.W. and jerked his head toward the door. P.W. joined him at the doorway, his back to Kanagi. "Why did you do that?"

"What, lie about our friend? Because if the cops get to him, we lose what little leverage we've got. If Shaw owns the cops like you say, I figure they'll just kill this guy for the boss. I want to keep him to ourselves for now."

Down the corridor, Jorgan made his way over and around the bodies until he was outside on the sidewalk.

The rain had slowed a bit, but it was still enough to soak Jorgan's long, unruly hair before he was all the way across the street. As he neared his car, he looked over his shoulder and down Beacham, in the direction he had seen Emma go with the others. There was no sign of them now, of course.

As Jorgan got into his car, one of the orange jumpsuited men jogged over to him. "You're gonna have to move your car out of here, sir, we've got a—"

"I'm Dr. Jorgan, the one who *called* you," he said impatiently. "I'm moving my car now, then I'm going right back inside."

The man nodded, then hurried back toward a white van that bore the county seal parked near the corner entrance.

Jorgan started the car and made a U-turn, passed the van, and turned right on Beacham. He crept by a large black Lincoln Town Car, wondering if it belonged to the two with the gas masks.

He parked on Beacham and got out of the car. His curiosity about Emma made him decide to take a short detour around the corner and onto Van Dolen before going back inside, just in case she had not gone down under yet, for whatever reason. If he could find her—and he prayed that he would—they could leave together immediately. With both Shaw and Trafficante preoccupied with the screw-up at the mission, he and Emma might be able to catch a plane out of town undetected in the chaos. If he could just talk to her long enough to convince her of the danger she was in, he could have her in Boston by daylight, and everybody else involved in this deadly farce could go fuck themselves.

But that was only if she had not gone down under yet, which seemed unlikely. Jorgan was more than willing to go down after her, but it would be foolish. He did not know his way around, and he knew how dangerous it was; getting himself hurt or killed was not going to help Emma. It would be much wiser to stick with P.W., who claimed to know exactly where Emma was, and who intended to get her out himself when the time was right.

Walking quickly, he rounded the corner onto Van Dolen and stopped at the edge of the stairway that led down to the subway station. A smelly little man mumbled to himself as he shuffled by slowly, holding a brown paper back with the neck of a bottle sticking out of the top; Jorgan smelled a robust melange of body odor, alcohol, and feces as the man passed.

He saw no sign of Emma as he looked all around him, and he had not expected to; it had been an act of desperation to come looking for her. Glancing at his watch, he decided he could spare a few more minutes, and he hurried down the subway stairs.

They were nowhere in sight, of course. Jorgan asked the man in the token booth if he had seen a man and woman with their faces painted black.

Giving him a tired, bored look, the man said, "Mr. and Mrs. Jolson have left the station."

Jorgan's mouth dropped open. "What? *What?*" He frantically looked all around him again. "They're here?"

"They were. They ain't here no more."

Of course not. They were long gone, hiding somewhere in the foul gloom of the city's lower intestine.

A wave of disappointment seemed to double his body weight and make him feel like a giant brick. He tried to keep his feet from dragging and tripping him up as he went back up the stairs and around the corner to the mission's entrance.

He was passing his car again and about to cross Beacham when he heard running footsteps splashing through puddles. He turned toward a dark figure rushing toward him from the sidewalk and almost spoke to ask who it was when the face became visible in the misty glow of a streetlight.

While he was still walking, without missing a step, Landon Shaw threw a punch with his left hand and drew his gun with his right.

The bridge of Jorgan's nose crunched beneath Shaw's fist and pain shattered through his face and head. Blood began to flow into his mouth and down his throat as he stumbled, flailing his arms to avoid falling. He slammed into the side of his car, grunting in pain. "Son of a bitch," he said, fumbling his car keys from his pocket as he pushed away from the car.

Shaw stabbed his gun into Jorgan's gut and pressed him hard against the car with his body. "What have you done?"

The keys dropped from Jorgan's hand and jangled on the pavement. "Whuh-what're you—"

"Tell me what's going on or I'll kill you right here and now."

"I-I-I—"

Shaw bent his knees, reached down, and picked up the car keys. "Is this your car?"

Jorgan nodded, wiping the back of his hand over his bloody mouth.

Shaw pointed at the car and said, "Inside. Now." He unlocked the door.

Still reeling from the punch and soaked to the skin, Jorgan got into the car awkwardly.

Shaw leaned into the car and shoved Jorgan over into the driver's seat, then got in and slammed the door, his gun on Jorgan all the while.

"Two things," Shaw said. "One: What's going on here? And two: Where is Emma?"

Jorgan squinted as his nose throbbed and continued to bleed.

"Exactly what the man on the phone said, Landon, that's what's going on here. We called the county people, they came out, looked around, and called the feds, who are on their way. They've got two tanks."

"So what? Those tanks are unmarked and—"

"I told them what it was," Jorgan said quietly. The words seemed to empty him as they were spoken. A wave of relief, of freedom, rushed in to fill that emptiness. It was an exquisite feeling, and he closed his eyes and leaned heavily against the door to savor it for a moment. Then he surprised himself by laughing. It was a sharp, piercing laugh, which he cut off with a gulp. But it had been genuine, that laugh, real and honest—not the kind of sound he was accustomed to hearing from himself.

Shaw glared at him. His face was absolutely calm and still— except for a twitch in the left corner of his mouth, and another in his cheek just below his right eye. His eyes were hidden in black ovals of shadow, but Jorgan knew they were burning with rage, he could feel it; he had felt it plenty of times before.

But Jorgan still felt like laughing, and he knew there was nothing Shaw could do to change his sudden, unexpected giddiness. Shaw no longer mattered. The only thing that meant anything to him was Emma, he felt that much more clearly now, with yet another gun pointed at him. If he never saw Emma again, Jorgan knew he had done his best to help her escape this prick. Even if he could not have her, at least he had gotten her away from this twisted, evil son of a bitch. That, along with the fact that everything that had happened and would happen there that night was going to ruin Shaw's life, made Jorgan feel deliriously happy.

"That was a big mistake," Shaw said.

Jorgan was startled from his thoughts and realized he had lost track of the conversation. "I'm sorry?" he said, looking at Shaw's gun.

"I said, that was a mistake. You've only hurt yourself."

"Oh, I don't think so. Whatever happens to me, it's worth it. You know why? Two things: One, you can't have her anymore. And two: Your ass is in the wringer, Landon." He continued to stare at the gun, his brow creased with a frown in spite of his smile.

Something was not right about Shaw's gun.

If you can see the hole in the front of the gun, you're doin' it wrong, P.W. had said.

There was no round, black hole at the end of the short barrel. Instead, there was a small, round piece of gray plastic with a tiny hole in the center.

Jorgan laughed again, and he kept laughing, even as he said, "It's a *squirt* gun." Still smiling, he curled his right hand into a fist as he drew his arm back, ready to return Shaw's punch.

"Remember Bloodburner?" Shaw said.

Jorgan's fist remained where it was, cocked and ready to fire, as his smile disappeared and the mirth left his eyes.

He remembered Project Bloodburner well. It had yielded a clear, water-like fluid that, when brought into contact with human skin, was absorbed into the bloodstream almost instantly, where it caused three separate chemical reactions, which resulted in the rare and bizarre occurrence known as spontaneous human combustion. It was still rare, but it was not necessarily spontaneous anymore. The fluid left no traces. Neither did the victim, because the fire started inside and worked its way out, burning unstoppably at extremely high temperatures. Water from a hose could not stop it once it started, and it left behind nothing but a pile of greasy ashes, maybe a few chunks of bone.

If you poured a bucket of the stuff into a swimming pool full of people, everyone in the water would be burned alive within minutes.

And if you put some in a squirt gun, you would have one hell of weapon.

Jorgan noticed for the first time that Shaw wore tight leather gloves. It was sensible. It took only a drop or two on bare skin, and...

Jorgan had seen what Bloodburner could do. He had watched flames belch from inside a man so quickly that he had time to do no more than release a mule-like honk before he was engulfed and dead. But before those flames became visible, there had been a moment of abominable pain for that man, a moment in which every muscle tensed and his arms and legs stiffened, as if he were being electrocuted, and his face turned a violent red as his eyes melted from their sockets and ran down his face like bloody milk. It was a moment that Jorgan was certain had lasted an agonizing eternity for that man.

Alan Jorgan was the first to admit he was a coward. He did not want to experience that moment or feel those flames inside of him. He was willing to die for Emma's safety—after all, there was very little in his life that had not ended years ago, anyway—but not that way. Not that way.

"I don't want to kill you, Jorgan," Shaw said quietly, almost soothingly. "I'd *like* to, don't get me wrong. I sure as hell don't need you for Biofire, I've already replaced you on that project. Ben Mason. I should've given it to him in the first place, but... it's too late for that now. However, I need somebody to blame for Leo's fuck-up, and I think you're the best man for the job. Just another crazy, disgruntled employee who snaps and tries to do some damage. And when it gets out that you used to work in the human organ trade—and it will—everyone will nod and say, well, he was just a breakdown waiting to happen, somebody *that* twisted, a guy who'd steal organs from people's bodies, why, he was a fucking *mess*." He raised the gun slightly, aiming at Jorgan's face. "But I *will* kill you if you don't tell me where Emma is right now. I mean it, Jorgan."

Jorgan believed him.

Reaching up to wipe blood from his face with the sleeve of his coat, Jorgan stammered, trying to come up with a convincing lie, something Shaw would believe, something that would sound just unlikely enough to be true, but he turned up nothing. In his head, he heard a steady ticking, like a clock, a mental clock that ticked the seconds away as he stared at the squirt gun.

The only thing that came out of his mouth was insipid, and he was certain Shaw knew it was a lie before he was finished uttering the words: "They went to Rockhurst Station to catch a train."

"Don't lie to me, Jorgan. It's no different than not answering. It'll just get you killed. If they don't want to be found, they would know better than to go to a train station. Now, try again, and this time tell the truth."

Sweat mixed with blood on his face. He held up a hand and made a gentle, reassuring gesture as he said, "I-I swear to Guh-God I d-don't know where she is. Thuh-they'd gotten her out of the mission buh-before I got here, and the guy in there, the one who called you, he won't tell me where she is." His eyes did not leave the squirt gun, or Shaw's finger curled behind the trigger guard.

As Shaw began to squeeze the plastic trigger, Jorgan screamed and held his arms up protectively over his face.

Shaw intentionally turned the gun, and the clear stream hit the windshield, dripping down onto the dashboard. Still screaming, Jorgan nearly climbed over the back of the seat, and his scream formed words: "Down under down under they went down under, goddammit!"

Jorgan sobbed quietly, his legs pulled up beneath him and his back pressed hard against the back of the seat as Shaw smiled and slowly lowered the gun.

"Now, *that*," Shaw said, "sounds more like the truth. When did they go?"

"Half an hour ago. Maybe forty-five minutes."

"Idiots," Shaw whispered, shaking his head. "*Idiots.*"

"They went with some woman who lives down there."

"Won't make any difference. They don't have any idea what they're getting themselves into." Shaw took in a deep breath as he opened the door and eased out of the car. "Looks like I'll just have to go down there and get them. Like they say, if you want something done right...et cetera, et cetera." He stood and turned, bent down a little to look into the car at Jorgan, smiling. "Thank you, Jorgan."

He knew it was coming only a second before it splashed over his face.

Shaw slammed the car door.

Jorgan felt the fire inside him.

When the fire flared, the heat cracked the passenger-side window. The flames burned powerfully, but died down not long after they had appeared, leaving a few stray flames to burn flutteringly on the charred seat and half-melted dashboard as smoke quickly filled the car's interior.

Walking away from the burning car at a good pace, Shaw put the squirt gun in his coat pocket and started to remove his cell phone from another pocket to call Kriezler, chief of security at the lab, and have him bring Woods and Bee-Bop, as well as all the necessary equipment, and meet him so they could go down under together. But he decided against it.

For one thing, it would take them too long to get to the city; Shaw wanted to move immediately. And for another...what did he need them for, anyway? He had a gun, and he kept a pair of infrared goggles in his downtown office. He could go down under on his own.

He pulled the collar of his coat up around his ears against the rain as he walked back to his borrowed car parked half a block away on Van Doren.

38.

THE LAUGHING MAN

Emma's head rested on McNolte's chest and he absently stroked her back. Her breathing was slow and regular and he hoped she was asleep; she needed it. He was slumped against a large makeshift cushion of smelly old rags and large balls of wadded newspaper. Despite the odor, it was not uncomfortable.

Boy was asleep in Dagmar's lap and Wanda was curled up in the corner. Dagmar was staring into the fire, lost in thought, her eyes filled with the kind of bone-deep sadness that settles in once the tears have dried up.

McNolte was surprised to notice that he was almost actually relaxed. Most of the tension that had been humming through his body had calmed and his heartbeat had slowed to a normal rate. There was still a nervous edge, but it was not enough to keep him from falling into a comfortable, soothed, near-dozing state.

With all the sounds around him, he could imagine himself reclining on the patio of some lower middle-class apartment complex on a quiet afternoon, because they were the sounds of people going about their lives. There were footsteps and occasional voices, the crying of a baby, the scuttling of the rats, and, of course, the Laughing Man guffawing somewhere deep in the dark. In a way, it *was* an apartment complex, but without apartments, and it was far beneath lower middle-class. The only problem was that people were not living there, they were barely existing, and in some cases dying there.

And some were being taken someplace else to die, but they could not die until they had been cut and mutilated and defiled in ways McNolte could not even imagine, all in a nice, clean, comfortable laboratory setting, where he hoped they were at least given a decent last meal. It seemed even worse that some people were allowed to live and were brought back to their filthy, dangerous home beneath the city.

McNolte was dragged from his peaceful ruminations by the sound of the Laughing Man. His laughter had been so constant that it had become a kind of white noise that he barely heard, and by the time McNolte noticed that the sound had grown louder and closer, it was *too* close. McNolte gently pushed Emma off of him and onto the piled rags and paper and hustled to his feet. He turned and gasped when he saw the Laughing Man a mere two feet away, peering over the stacked boxes at Emma, who was getting to her feet beside McNolte.

He was enormous, six and a half feet tall, maybe taller, with huge shoulders, long, fleshy arms that had muscles beneath the fat. Spittle and bits of ugly matter clung to his long, bushy, black beard and his mouth hung open loosely, showing long, gray, rotting teeth. His hair was just as wild and filthy as his beard, except on the left side of his scalp, where a large patch of the hair was gone and an inflamed, moist rash glistened in the firelight. He wore a tattered brown corduroy coat buttoned to his neck, the sleeves missing.

When McNolte popped up from behind the stacked boxes, the Laughing Man was startled. He rolled his big, milky eyes in alarm and lifted his right arm. His hairy fist was wrapped around the handle of a baseball bat that had several long, rusty nails sticking out around the splintered, rounded end.

He sliced the bat through the air, aiming it directly at McNolte's head. McNolte tried to throw himself backward as he raised his arms protectively, but the bat moved faster than he could and drove half a dozen nails into the flesh of his left upper arm. The Laughing Man used the painfully embedded nails as a hook to pull McNolte toward him with a rough jerk.

McNolte tumbled through the stacked cardboard boxes that made up the wall of Dagmar's home. He cried out when he felt the nails rip from his arm as he fell forward and hit the ground hard.

The Laughing Man grabbed a handful of McNolte's hair and dragged him away from the fallen boxes, then dropped his bat to pick him up off the ground with both hands. Emma screamed as he lifted McNolte up over his head.

Struggling uselessly, McNolte took flight as the Laughing Man heaved him into the darkness. He hit the ground and rolled over chunks of concrete and bits of metal and broken glass, and he felt something sharp cut into his back and lodge itself just beneath his right shoulder blade. The pain in his arm and back was so intense that he vomited as he lifted himself up with his right arm. When he tried to stand, dizziness slapped him back down to the ground.

The South Street Mission was filled with a different kind of chaos than usual, and it made P.W. nervous. Paramedics and EMTs were everywhere, working with the bodies all over the floor. The unconscious people had begun to stir at about the time the first ambulance arrived, and as Jorgan had said, they all had miserable headaches.

With a paper cup of water, P.W. made his way back to a frail old man who was out of breath and looked extremely unwell. He had almost reached the old fellow when a young man with shaggy red hair came in wearing a soaked orange jumpsuit under a raincoat.

"Hey," the young county man said, "where's Dr. Jorgan?"

"I'm not sure," P.W. said. "He went out to move his car a few minutes ago." He saw the troubled look on the young man's face, and checked his watch. Jorgan had been gone for twenty minutes—too long. "What's the problem?"

"His car's on fire down the street."

"How do you know it's his car?"

"I saw him move it."

P.W. took the cup of water to the old man, then hurried outside with the young man without bothering to put on his coat.

"Over there," the county man said, pointing.

It was not much a fire, but there flames in the cab and smoke was pouring out the driver's side door, which was open a few inches. Four of the orange jumpsuited men were standing close by, watching the fire.

"What the hell," P.W. muttered as he hurried toward the car.

People were the same in so many ways. NASA scientists would drop what they were doing to join plumbers and gynecologists and convenience store clerks to watch a car burn. Along with monster truck rallies and reality TV, it brought out the redneck in everyone.

"How the hell did this happen?" P.W. said.

They all spoke at once to say they did not know.

"I don't suppose anyone thought to call the fire department," P.W. said.

None of them spoke as they exchanged embarrassed looks for a moment. Finally, one of them said, "Uh, I guess I could go call 'em on my radio."

When he spoke, P.W. was not smiling and his voice dripped with sarcasm. "Yeah, why don't you do that when you get a chance."

The man started back toward the van.

"And while you're at it," P.W. added, looking at all of them, "why don't you use some of my tax dollars to buy yourself a book or two and expand your fucking horizons."

"Hey, buddy," one of the men said, "just chill out, okay? It's not like there were people in the car."

"Thank God for *that*," P.W. said, walking past the man to the car. "You probably would've sent somebody out for snacks."

P.W. used his foot to push the door open all the way, and he stepped back when clouds of dark smoke streamed out of the cab and rose toward the raining sky. As it cleared, he looked into the front seat and saw something odd. There was something black and glistening in the passenger seat with an awkward, sprawled shape to it. When he leaned down toward the car's blackening, smoking cab, he was assaulted by an odor he had first encountered in Vietnam, a smell like burning pork. His insides seized up.

"Oh, Jesus," one of the men behind him said.

P.W. backed away quickly, taking deep, rapid breaths, pressing his lips together tightly and holding one hand to his stomach. He walked unsteadily away from the car, plumes of vapor bursting from his mouth into the cold, rainy night.

The county men converged on the car, exclaiming their shock and horror, but P.W. did not hear them. He was too busy thinking, *Who would want Dr. Jorgan dead? Who would do such a thing?* The answer came quickly and he had no doubt he was right. He knew in his gut it was Landon Shaw, but that was not what occupied his thoughts.

P.W. remembered what Jorgan had told him about Shaw, what he did down under, that he knew his way around, that it was "his territory." As he headed back to the mission, P.W. asked himself one question over and over: *Did Jorgan tell Shaw where McNolte and Emma had gone?* There was no way to know, of course, but could he afford to assume otherwise?

P.W. did not think so.

That was why he ignored Mr. Kanagi's questions as he stalked through the mission toward Willy's office, where he planned to give Ty and Buddy a few instructions, then prepare himself to go down under.

Emma screamed again as she tried to stand, but she felt a hand on her shoulder pushing her down.

"Shh!"

Emma's head jerked around to see Dagmar leaning close as Boy awoke and huddled down at his mother's side.

"Just be quiet and don't act scared," Dagmar whispered as she reached for one of the bags of food. She removed some pieces of fried chicken individually wrapped in aluminum foil and stood, turning toward the enormous cackling lunatic. She took a couple of steps toward him as she held out one of the clumps of foil. "Here," she said, "it's chicken. Take it. You can have all of it, just leave us alone. Please." Her words were stiff, as if she were reading cue cards, but she succeeded in covering her fear.

The Laughing Man stared down at her for a moment, then looked at Emma. A crooked, wet grin opened up on his face and he laughed, pointing at Emma's shoe-polished face; his laughter tumbled out of him, a thick, gurgling sound. He looked at Dagmar's offering again.

"Go ahead," she said, "it's chicken." She cautiously moved forward a little more, leaning toward him. Her movements were those of a child feeding a fawn at a petting zoo. She caught only a glimpse of McNolte shooting out of the darkness, hunched forward, and she cried, "No, please don't!"

McNolte plowed with a grunt into the Laughing Man's left side, and the giant careened a few steps but did not go down. McNolte did, however, and slid over the ground face-down and with a shout of pain as the Laughing Man caught his balance, turned around, and delivered a hard kick to McNolte's side. The boots he wore were old and weathered, but they were still heavy enough to send violent waves of pain through McNolte's chest and abdomen.

"No, please!" Dagmar shouted at the Laughing Man with a tremor in her voice. "Please don't hurt him. Just take this and go, okay?"

The Laughing Man kicked McNolte one more time, then turned to Dagmar again and moved toward her quickly, menacingly. Emma watched him, assuming he was simply in a hurry to get the chicken and return to whatever dark corner he inhabited. He swung the bat so suddenly, so fast, that it did not register in Emma's mind until the nails had already torn into the flesh of Dagmar's forearm. Dagmar fell backward as the foil-wrapped pieces of chicken scattered over the ground.

Emma stood and lifted her long, heavy Mag-Lite, ready to use it as a weapon, but knowing all the while that she would have to flame him, and in the process flame the others. But before she could consider doing that, a figure came out of nowhere and jumped onto the Laughing Man's back.

It was a short figure, and at first, Emma thought it was Boy, but he was standing in front of her, right beside Dagmar.

The Laughing Man let out a long, pathetic wail as the figure began to lift its arm up and down repeatedly, pounding the Laughing Man's chest.

Emma glimpsed the knife. The person on the Laughing Man's back was stabbing him in the chest repeatedly with a knife. Three times, four times, the blade made an ugly, thick sound each time it entered him, and he dropped to his knees with a heaving sound, then flopped face-down on the ground, groaning as his arms flopped uselessly.

When McNolte saw the Laughing Man topple, he wondered who had managed it—Emma or Dagmar.

Sharp, breathtaking pain clutched his chest as McNolte propped himself up on one elbow, pain so excruciating that it made tears spring to his eyes and sent chills across his back. He was certain the Laughing Man had cracked one of his ribs, maybe more, but he was determined to get to his feet, because someone had appeared from nowhere to dispatch the lumbering beast, and he wanted to know who it was.

He was on his knees, breathing shallow, wheezing breaths, when the figure got to its feet and, still clutching the knife in a fist, started toward the cardboard shelter, moving with purpose.

Emma gasped and said, "Miranda!"

The second the short, squat woman stepped into the firelight, her face became visible. It was a dead face, utterly lifeless.

Miranda stuffed her left hand into her coat pocket and removed something small and dark and heavy-looking, and without missing a step she lifted her hand almost casually and swept it toward Dagmar's head. There was a thick *pop* sound and Dagmar dropped to the ground. Then she swept her hand in a backhand motion toward Emma.

Emma felt the blackjack knock against her skull and was conscious only long enough to see the black ground coming toward her with the speed of a train.

McNolte was on his feet by the time Miranda had knocked Emma to the ground. He groped through the layers of clothing for the gun P.W. had given him. He remembered that P.W. had stuffed it beneath his belt in the small of his back, but he could not feel it because his whole body had become numb. Reaching back for the gun sent through him a blade of pain so strangling that he could not cry out; he could do no more than whimper as he removed the gun and staggered forward with no idea what awaited him.

While McNolte fought his pain, Miranda reached down and grabbed Emma's flashlight, then turned Emma onto her back, reached beneath her head, grabbed a fistful of her clothes and dragged her out of the partially collapsed cardboard shelter. Emma was dead weight and Miranda struggled with her at first, but once she found her stride, she started moving steadily in the darkness back the way she had come, the flashlight's beam bobbing ahead of her to guide the way.

Until someone jumped on her back and wrapped small arms around her neck, squeezing her throat.

She knew right away that it was the little boy. She had considered hitting him with the blackjack as well, but saw no point because he was just a little kid and she had not expected him to be a problem.

Miranda let go of Emma and was swinging the flashlight back to knock the boy into next week when she saw his small fist slice out of the darkness holding a shard of broken glass, which he drove into her right cheek. She felt no pain at first, just the sharp edge of glass cutting all the way through her flesh and crunching grittily against her teeth, then pulling out again. A wet exhalation gushed through the hole in her cheek and she staggered to one side, dropping the flashlight and nearly losing her balance as she reached back over her shoulder and found the boy's neck.

Before she could get him off of her, he brought the piece of glass down again and it tore into the right side of her nose, slicing down through her nostril. Then again, into the flesh above her upper lip, where the glass was chipped against her front teeth. And again, into her chin, digging into the bone. He did not make a sound as he tore up her face.

All the while, her arms flailed, first behind her in an attempt to grab him, then in front of her to stop the movement of his right arm. She could taste blood in her mouth and felt it running down her face, but she still felt little more than a harsh stinging where she had been cut.

Before he could stab the shard of glass into her face again, Miranda clutched his arm with both hands, bent forward and flung him off her back, slamming him to the ground hard. He was already starting to get up when she kicked him in the stomach hard enough to drop him again. He lay before her retching as she removed the blackjack from her coat pocket and swept it down hard against his head twice.

When she was certain the boy was unconscious, Miranda picked up the flashlight, grabbed a handful of Emma's clothes again, and continued to drag her into the darkness as McNolte closed in on her. He had watched her dragging Emma away, had seen Boy try to stop her, and he had tried to cry out, but could not because of his pain. Whoever she was, he knew her name was Miranda because he had heard Emma call the name moments ago. And he had heard the fear in her voice, too.

McNolte wanted to take advantage of his close proximity to the woman because he knew he would lose it soon, and he raised the gun. It slipped from his trembling, sweaty-palmed hand, skittered over the ground, and he got on his knees, groped over the gravel and dirt and debris until he found it, then stood again, and took a few stumbling steps forward to close the distance between himself and Miranda. He was still taking shallow, rapid breaths to avoid pain, and he knew he would hyperventilate soon; his head already had a dizzy, shrinking sensation that was only growing worse. He staggered forward some more, then clutched the gun between both hands. His vision was blurred by tears of pain and the glow of the flashlight Miranda carried was little more than a pale smear in the darkness, but he aimed the gun in that direction.

From behind him, McNolte heard a low, wet grunt an instant before a large hand closed on his hair, lifted him from the ground, and threw him on his back like a sack of potatoes. He squeezed the gun, firing it wildly into the darkness as a knee slammed down on his stomach and two hands closed around his throat, squeezing so hard that McNolte could hear his own cartilage grinding. Warm blood spattered down from the Laughing Man onto McNolte's face.

He could not breathe and tears flooded his eyes, but he could still move his arms and he flailed them blindly in spite of the daggers of pain that cut into his ribs. He hit the Laughing Man again and again. The sharp smell of Laughing Man's body odor was overwhelming and his hulking body was hunched too low and close for McNolte to get the gun beneath him. As his eyes threatened to pop from their sockets and his face swelled to the point of bursting, McNolte lifted the gun and tried to place the barrel beside the Laughing Man's head, but the tremble in his hand became a convulsion and his grip on the gun weakened as consciousness left him in a gush, as his lungs burned for breath and his throat exploded with pain.

The gun slipped from McNolte's hand as the Laughing Man laughed.

Miranda dragged Emma through the darkness, the flashlight beam leading the way. But the bar of light did not reach far. From behind her, she heard the gunshot and the sound of McNolte's struggle, but she ignored it and moved forward, swallowing the blood that gushed into her mouth from her wounds.

It was Miranda's intention to get out of the city's dark, ugly cellar with Emma and confront Dr. Jorgan. He was up there somewhere, she knew, and she wanted to drop Emma's limp form before him and let him know that she was not the superwoman he had thought her to be, that she was a failure to the project and a failure to him, just another pretty face and nothing more. And then she would kill Emma Shaw right there in front of Dr. Jorgan and make him see the error of his ways. So determined was Miranda to accomplish this that the possibility that she might not make did not occur to her. She ignored her weakening state and growing pain to focus instead on the fact that she was lost.

Miranda realized she was lost when she came upon someone she had not seen on her way in: a bulbous, bald, sexless creature that hunkered in the darkness with just a few rags dangling from its white rolls of fat, which were covered with open sores. When the flashlight's beam landed on the huge figure, it leaned forward, opened its mouth, and released a sound that fell somewhere between a guttural hiss and a growl, revealing wet gums that held three teeth on top and two on the bottom.

Not wanting to make trouble, Miranda took several quick steps away from the creature, then turned around and swept the flashlight's beam back and forth, trying to figure out where she had gone wrong. After a moment of frantic thought, Miranda decided to go back the way she had come and find the little fortress of cardboard boxes in which Emma had been hiding.

But she could not find the boxes. It was as if the small, damaged shelter had never existed.

Blood ran into Miranda's mouth from the holes that had been torn in her face. She bent forward to spit blood to the ground, then wiped her mouth on her sleeve.

Miranda had no idea what direction would lead her to the streets above, to the mission where Dr. Jorgan was still stupidly trying to save the life that Miranda now held in her hands.

Tightening her grip on Emma's clothes, Miranda decided to wing it. She forged ahead as blood ran down her face and into her mouth. Emma's limp and unconscious body crunched over the ground as Miranda dragged her through the darkness, moving the flashlight back and forth slowly, searchingly.

Miranda was certain there was a way out somewhere nearby, even if it was not the one through which she had come, but she could not find it.

Somewhere in the darkness ahead, she saw another flashlight beam sweeping back and forth. Miranda steered herself and Emma toward that light, hoping it was someone friendly. When she was close enough, Miranda turned her flashlight on the figure. It was a man wearing a white surgical mask over his nose and mouth. He held the light in his right hand and something else in his left, which was swallowed by the darkness. His eyes were familiar...extremely familiar.

He shone his flashlight in her face and made her recoil from the brightness.

"Miranda," the man said in a friendly tone.

His voice pierced her with an icy chill.

"Mr. Shaw?" she said.

"Yes, that's right. Jesus, Miranda, you've been hurt. You're bleeding. What, uh...what are you dragging behind you, there?"

Miranda could not speak for a moment. She was so startled to see Mr. Shaw there under the city in that hellhole that her voice had momentarily left her.

Shaw's flashlight beam moved down Miranda's body and to the side, shining on Emma's legs.

"That's a person, isn't it?" he said, coming closer. Then he smiled warmly at her and the incongruity of it made her feel woozy. "That's...that's my wife, isn't it, Miranda?"

She coughed, then said, "Uh, Mr. Shaw, uh...I just want you to know—"

Before she finished, he raised his left hand and she saw the gun.

It fired.

The cloying humidity and rank odors down under brought a rush of memories back to P.W., memories of the time he had spent beneath the city during the winter before he was taken in at South Street. The memories were vivid enough to evoke the unmistakable taste of alcohol in his mouth and throat, the taste that had been with him day and night back then. Specifically Jack Daniel's, his whiskey of choice, which he could scarcely afford by then. He smacked his lips, the taste so strong that he thought for a moment he could smell liquor on his own breath. But he let his memories disperse like smoke as he focused on finding McNolte and Emma, and avoiding trouble in the process.

Nothing had changed down under—not for the better, anyway. The rats were bigger than ever and the darkness seemed more crowded with people seeking shelter from the hostile streets above. P.W. had not been down there in over three years, and then only briefly with Dagmar to take some medicine to Boy, who had been too sick with the flu to come up top.

He held his gun in his right hand, and under his right arm he held one of the Mag-Lites from the mission. He was familiar enough with the layout that he knew he probably could find Dagmar's cardboard shelter without the light once his eyes had adjusted to the darkness, but he was not about to try.

The moment his light fell on what was left of Dagmar's shelter, P.W. knew things had gone terribly wrong. One wall had been toppled, the damp cardboard boxes scattered over the ground, most of them crushed. It was not like Dagmar to ignore such disorder; she lived in filth, but she took as much pride in her meager home as she could under the circumstances.

"Dagmar?" he said softly as he neared the shelter. When he saw her lying on the ground, he dropped to one knee beside her. She did not move when he placed a hand on her shoulder, and for a moment, he was sure she was dead.

"Thomebody hit 'em both over the head," Wanda said, her voice a fearful whimper.

P.W. looked over at the old woman lying in the corner and was about to ask her who had hit them, when Dagmar moved.

"Dagmar, honey," he said, "what happened? Are you hurt bad?"

She frowned as her head turned slowly back and forth. "No, no, not bad, but…" She gingerly touched the top of her head and winced. "…I got a bad headache."

"Who did this?"

"Some woman. Her name…your friend, Emma…she called her Miranda."

P.W. remembered the name from Emma's account of everything that had happened to her. "Where's Emma now?" he said.

"I…don't know. She…she's not here?"

"How about McNolte?"

"He…fought with…the Laughing Man." Her voice was thick and she kept rubbing her head, eyes narrowing to slits.

"Are you hurt, Dagmar? You gonna be okay if I leave you here for a bit?"

Her eyes widened suddenly and she lifted her head with a gasp. "Where's Boy? Oh, God, where'd Boy go?"

"I don't know. I haven't seen him."

She struggled to her hands and knees, then got to her feet. Once standing, she swayed a bit but seemed to ignore her dizziness, moving around P.W. and out of the small shelter.

P.W. got up and followed her, saying, "Hold up a sec, there, Dagmar, I've got light here."

As they walked away from the shelter, P.W. swept the light over the filthy ground ahead of them, over the rubble and litter and black clumps of human feces.

"Why would he go off like that?" she said, panic quavering in her voice. "Unless he was taken, oh, Jesus, if he was taken—"

"Hey, don't worry just yet, okay?" he said.

They found him curled up in a ball, his shoulders hitching with silent sobs. Dagmar knelt beside him and wrapped her arms around him, murmuring words of reassurance as she held him tightly.

P.W. leaned down and spoke quietly to Dagmar. "I'm gonna go look for McNolte, okay? Don't wander far from here, and I'll be back."

She glanced up at him and nodded once, holding her injured son close and whispering into his ear.

Moving away from them, P.W. continued to sweep the beam of the flashlight back and forth to cut through the darkness, like a jungle explorer slicing through the brush with a machete. And it was not long before he found what he was looking for.

McNolte. Lying motionless on his back. Arms splayed. Mouth open. Eyes closed. A large bruise discoloring his throat and neck.

"Oh, God, kid," P.W. said, his voice as small as a child's. "Oh, Jesus, God, McNolte. Kid."

P.W. reached down and touched McNolte's hand and found the flesh cold. He growled—actually released an animal-like growl—because of what McNolte had done to save Emma, because of what he had done to subvert the rich and powerful people who had wanted Emma dead, or at least captured and incapacitated.

"Jesus, kid," he said, "I'm so sorry."

39.

LOSING CONTROL

The orange light of dawn was creeping into the sky behind onyx clouds, bleeding through fissures here and there by the time Shaw got to the OdysseyCorp building. Emma was slumped beside him in the passenger seat, unconscious.

The black-and-white–striped security arm was not raised for him as usual because he was still driving the borrowed Buick, and as he approached the gate, he shoved Emma down so her face was not visible; he did not want any of the guards to recognize her.

"Oh, it's you, Mr. Shaw," the guard said, quickly throwing the switch that made the arm swing up.

"Don't let anyone in here until I say otherwise," Shaw said, rolling down his window.

"No one?" the guard said, tossing a single glance at the limp body in the seat beside Shaw.

"*No one*, unless you get word from me. And I want more men on the gate. Anybody gives you any trouble, shoot them." He powered the window up as he zipped into the parking lot.

On his way back to the lab, Shaw had called ahead and talked to Dr. Benjamin Mason, who had replaced Jorgan on Project Biofire. He had told Mason to prepare one of the isolation chambers and to have a gurney ready and waiting at the back entrance. He had also given the order to double security in and around the building, just in case Leo and his goons showed up before he did; he wanted to hold that particular problem off as long as possible.

As he pulled around the corner of the building and into his parking space, the door opened and two tech assistants came out, one of them pushing the gurney.

Shaw did not speak to them as he hurried from his car and into the building, leaving Emma for them to handle. Just inside, Dr. Mason stood with his hands in his lab coat pockets. He looked tired, and Shaw liked that; it meant he had been working hard. Dr. Mason opened his mouth to speak, but Shaw did not give him a chance.

"She's all yours, Ben," he said, patting the doctor's shoulder once as he sidled past him, heading for the nearest elevator in a rush.

Shaw's clothes were soaked and filthy, his hair a wild mess, and he drew more than a few curious stares in the corridor. At the elevator, Shaw punched his code into the keypad on the wall, then placed his palm over the glossy rectangular scanner, ignoring the guard seated nearby who said, "Good morning, Mr. Shaw." He stepped inside the elevator and hit the top button, then the button to quickly close the doors.

Shaw had made good use of the time it had taken to drive back to the lab. First, he had called his chief publicist, awakened him out of a deep sleep, and told him the story they would be using to explain the events of the past several hours.

An unbalanced and disgruntled employee of OdysseyCorp Labs, Dr. Alan Jorgan, after being dismissed due to erratic behavior brought on by growing mental illness for which he had refused to seek treatment, had stolen two canisters of an experimental gas and released that gas in the South Street Mission, hoping the blame would be placed on OdysseyCorp and Landon Shaw, thus casting them in a bad light in the media. Any resulting damage or necessary medical bills would be covered by OdysseyCorp, though it was unlikely that the gas had caused any harm to those exposed to it.

Then he had given the publicist a personal statement in which he had expressed regret about the unfortunate condition of Dr. Jorgan, who had disappeared, along with assurances that OdysseyCorp would cooperate in every way with the police to apprehend him.

Then he had called the chief of police and told him the same story. Shaw did not expect the chief to believe it; he did not pay the man to believe anything, he only paid him to cooperate, and that was what Shaw expected him to do.

The elevator stopped and the doors slid open with a whisper. Shaw hurried down the corridor, absently fumbling with the change and keys in his pocket.

He was eager to get into his office, lock the door behind him, put on some soothing music, and sit alone for a while with a brandy. He craved relaxation, solitude. He had to give some thought to his problem with Leo Trafficante.

He also needed to call a number that had been busy every time he had tried it from the car. He had an acquaintance in the EPA whose services were easily bought, and Shaw had planned to get the guy out of bed and use him to hold off the county and state people who had been sniffing around the mission earlier. Apparently, the son of a bitch was already awake, but not in step with the times enough to have Call Waiting. Shaw's connection in the EPA would be able to help only so much, and more would have to be done to keep Leo's botched job from turning into a major disaster for both Leo and himself. That would require a great deal of thought and planning, which was what Shaw hoped to accomplish in the privacy of his office with that calming music and brandy.

Given enough time, Leo might cool off on his own and forget the whole thing, then they could go on with their deal and the status quo would be restored. Then again, he might not.

Shaw turned down a short, narrow corridor which had only one door down at the end. He opened it and entered the outer office, passed his secretary's unoccupied desk, and stopped at his office door. He punched his code into the keypad and placed his hand on the screen. There was a soft, muted beep, and the door's lock made a chunking sound. Shaw opened it and stepped inside.

"Hello, Landon."

Shaw froze. His already weary knees weakened for a moment, almost to the point of collapsing beneath him, and he clutched the doorknob, leaning on it heavily as he stared slack-jawed at Leo Trafficante, who was leaning back in the chair behind Shaw's desk, smiling around the cigar clenched between his teeth.

The leather-upholstered chair in front of Shaw's desk had been turned so that it was facing the south wall, and sitting in it with his legs crossed and his large hands dangling loosely over the ends of the armrests was Leo's secretary and shadow, Ollie.

Anger moved like mercury through Shaw and he squeezed the doorknob until his white knuckles cracked loudly.

"You son of a bitch," he whispered, because his shock, mixed with his fatigue, prevented him from mustering his full voice. He glared at Leo. "What the fuck are you doing here?"

"Waiting for you," Leo said, plucking the cigar from his mouth between the knuckles of his first two fingers. He looked away from Shaw and said, "Tubo. Clean him."

Another man—as big as Ollie, maybe bigger, with a small, balding head atop enormous shoulders, and eyes that would have met if it were not for his nose—emerged from around the open door and grabbed Shaw's arms, lifting them roughly. Once Shaw's arms were outstretched, Tubo frisked him, slapping his body harder than necessary as he worked his way down, then up again, groping his legs from his crotch to his ankles and back. Then he checked Shaw's overcoat. He removed the squirt gun, holding it up and firing a few spurts of water into the air before saying, "Good thing we checked. He coulda killed us all."

Trafficante laughed heartily. "Tubo's a card. Cracks me up."

Tubo tossed the squirt gun onto the desk, followed by Shaw's cell phone. He turned to Trafficante, dangling Shaw's .380 caliber SIG 320 by the trigger guard between thumb and forefinger, and said, "He's clean now." Then he stepped away quickly, as if he did not want to obstruct Leo's view of Shaw, keeping the gun.

Leo was still smiling when he said, "Ollie, get up and give the man a seat."

Ollie rose and stepped aside.

Shaw did not move, just continued to stare at Leo. He was so angry that he thought he might throw up. But he fought to control his anger because he knew it would get him nowhere with Leo right now, not with two of his gorillas standing at the ready. But Shaw knew there was a chance something positive might come out of the situation, as ugly as it appeared to be at the moment, so he was not about to show his anger, or any other feelings, for that matter. Once he had closed his mouth and recovered from the initial shock of finding Leo in his office, his face became, and remained, stonily expressionless, his posture relaxed and casual.

"What, you don't want to sit down?" Leo said.

"Sure," Shaw said, "sure, I'll sit down."

He moved forward and eased himself in the chair slowly, never taking his eyes from Leo. Ollie stood to his right, Tubo to his left, both of them slightly behind him.

Leo leaned forward, put his elbows on the desktop, and rolled his cigar between the thumb and forefinger of his right hand. "So, Landon," he said. "Where is she?"

"I told you before, Leo, I don't know." Even as he said the words, he knew that Leo knew they were not true.

Leo grinned, chuckled. "I know that's bullshit, Landon. When I asked you where she is, I meant...where in this *building*. Because I know she's here."

"Okay," Shaw said. "But I'd like you to answer a question of mine first. Just because I'm curious. Okay, Leo?"

"Sure," Leo said. "Ask away."

"How did you get in here? Into this building? Into my office?"

Leo loose a big laugh then, as if someone had just told him a hilarious joke. "Landon, you poor, naive son of a bitch. You just haven't been able to see the big picture, have you? We've been working together all these years and you're still blind as a bat."

Leo's condescending tone made Shaw's insides boil, but he held it in, did not let it show. He glanced at the squirt gun on the desk, then his eyes returned to Leo. "Blind to what?" he said.

"Landon, your entire security force was working for me long before you even hired them."

Shaw's teeth clenched behind his expressionless face, but he said nothing.

Leo said, "Do you really think that I would do the kind of business with you that we've been doing without keeping an extremely close eye on you, Landon? I hope you know me better than that. I really do."

Shaw's anger remained coiled tightly inside him like a tense snake, but he showed nothing. He believed Leo's claim—it was the only way he could think of that Leo could have gotten into his office. It enraged him, made him realize that a great deal of the control he had *thought* he'd had over his business was nothing more than an illusion. He wanted to scream at Leo, throw things, break glass—but he was intensely conscious of Ollie and Tubo, whose eyes had not left him. Shaw could feel their threatening glares burning into him.

"Where is she, Landon?" Leo said. "What have you done with your wife now?"

"She's in isolation. She's quarantined. I told you before, she's contagious, Leo. I know you don't believe me, but that doesn't change the facts. She's comfortable and safe right now, Leo, so you don't have to worry about her."

"As long as she's in your care," Leo said, mouth curling into a sneer around his small teeth, "then I'm worried about her. But she's not really in your hands, that's why I'm so calm right now. My people are taking care of it. I'll have her out of here in no time."

"That would be an extraordinarily big mistake, Leo. Look, you don't have to believe me. I put a new doctor on the project and he's been going over all the records for the last couple of days. Talk to him. He'll tell you."

Leo said nothing. His eyes narrowed as he puffed on his cigar.

Shaw's gaze wandered once again to the squirt gun on Leo's desk but lingered only for a moment.

"Well, I'm just wasting my time here," Leo said, standing behind the desk. "Tubo, why don't you take care of Mr. Shaw so we can be on our way."

Tubo slipped his hand beneath his coat and produced a silencer-equipped Beretta 9mm. Fear burned in Shaw's throat. Tensing in the chair, he turned to Leo again, mouth dry, heart pounding now like jungle drums.

"Leo, this is a mistake," he said. "You need me. I'm the only one who can clean up the mess your idiots made at that mission. I was just coming in here to call a friend of mine, a guy at the EPA who can—"

"Think about it, Landon. If you're dead, what do I have to worry about?"

"You have to worry about the guy who called and threatened to tell General Horner that you've been buying the Pentagon's goods from me, *that's* what."

"What, you don't think I can take care of him?"

"Are you sure you can?"

Leo gave a look of utter contempt and shook his head slowly, as if amazed by Shaw's tenacity. Then he looked at Tubo and said, "Kill this sick fuck."

Shaw knew he did not have a fraction of a second to spare, so he took no time to think, did not even entertain the most vaporous of thoughts, he simply threw himself out of the chair at the desk, grabbed the squirt gun, spun to his left, and shot it into Tubo's face before the man could even raise his gun.

Tubo sputtered wetly as he stumbled backward, his small eyes wide with surprise as he gawked at Shaw. Those small eyes darted from Shaw to Ollie to Leo, then back to Shaw again, and he smiled. Then he laughed.

Then Ollie laughed, too.

Even Leo smiled as he looked at Shaw with an odd expression; it took Shaw a moment to recognize it as one of pity.

"I'm afraid you've really broken under the pressure, Landon," Leo said quietly, even a little sadly. "Using a squirt gun when you know—"

Tubo made a horrible vomiting sound and startled the others, who turned as his eyes grew wider. He dropped his gun and slapped one hand to his abdomen and the other to his throat, mouth open, lips working, tongue wriggling as it jutted from the center of his mouth. He coughed once and spittle flew; when he coughed again, a dull orange flash came from between his lips with a puff of smoke, and he fell backward onto a glass-topped coffee table. Glass shattered and the wood frame splintered, and Tubo was a raging fire, flames roaring with the fury of a gasoline fire, or worse, as if gas jets were powering the flames. Black smoke billowed from the fire, and a moment later, the alarm bell began to ring shrilly and discreetly concealed sprinklers rained water down on Shaw, Leo, and Ollie with a snake-like hiss.

"What the *fuck!*" Leo bellowed as he reached into his coat and removed his gun.

Shaw turned the squirt gun on Ollie as Ollie fumbled for his own gun and muttered, "Oh, Jesus, oh, Juh-*Jesus*," while Shaw pumped the trigger and splattered his face.

Ollie dropped the gun and began crying out like a small boy in terror as he backed away, slammed into the wall and began slapping at his face, trying to wipe off the clear fluid that had splashed into his eyes.

Shaw turned the squirt gun on Leo as Leo lifted his own gun and aimed at Shaw. Instead of firing, Leo opted to take cover and dropped behind the desk an instant before Shaw sent a stream of clear liquid in his direction.

Walking backward, Shaw groped for the doorknob as Ollie whimpered one last time before being consumed by an oxygen-sucking rush of flames.

The fire that a moment ago had been Tubo had caught on the sofa next to him, and the cushions were producing even more black smoke.

"You goddamned son of a bitch!" Leo bellowed from beneath the desk. He fired his gun once and a bullet hole appeared in the front of the desk.

Shaw tensed, stopped breathing for a couple of heartbeats, then, when he knew he had not been shot, he spun around, opened the door, stumbled out of the office, and ran squarely into a large man with a bushy white beard who stood just outside the office, ran into him hard. Shaw fell backward and when his ass hit the floor, the squirt gun tumbled from his hand and bounced over the floor. Shaw scrambled to his feet, hoping to get the squirt gun, but once he was standing, he did not move. The white-bearded man pressed the barrel of the gun to Shaw's forehead so hard that it bent Shaw's head back.

"Landon Shaw," the man said with a weary smile.

Shaw was so surprised, he could not move.

The man stepped over to the gun and picked it up. He did not seem to notice it was a squirt gun, did not even look at it, just dropped it into the pocket of his down jacket.

Smoke poured from the open door and began to fill the outer office. It made Shaw cough, made his eyes burn and tear up.

"You been playin' with matches?" the man said quietly, smirking.

"Who the hell are you?" Shaw said. "How did you get in here? The security guards should—"

"Your security guards ain't in any shape to do *nothin'*, my friend."

Shaw gawked at him, wondering how so much could go so wrong so fast.

Something about the man's voice was just familiar enough to break through Shaw's pounding rush of adrenaline, but not enough for him to identify it. The man's face was filthy and dripping sweat, and there was blood on his down jacket. When he coughed from the smoke, his wincing face registered pain. He was hurt. And fatigued. But he still had a gun to Shaw's forehead.

The relentless wail of the smoke alarm and the pealing of the fire alarm in the corridors outside bored into Shaw's head like drills...but he heard no voices, no running footsteps. No one was reacting to the fire.

Behind him, in the burning office, Shaw could hear Leo coughing and retching. The sound was getting closer. Leo was coming out.

Shrill panic began to rise in Shaw. Leo with a gun behind him, and this Neanderthal shoving one in his face.

"How many people in there?" the man asked.

Shaw's chin jittered but he said nothing.

The man slapped his big left hand to Shaw's chest and closed his fist around a clump of shirt and coat, pulling Shaw close to him. The movement made the man wince in pain and it forced him to pull the gun away from Shaw's forehead for a moment as he opened his mouth to repeat the question.

Shaw took advantage of that moment and shot his knee up swiftly, savagely. He hit his target.

The man grunted and staggered backward, doubling over in pain, mouth hanging open, left hand falling to his wounded groin.

Shaw ran out of the inner office, past the bearded man, down the short, narrow corridor, but he seemed unable to run fast enough. Everything seemed to slow down for him and he was consumed by a feeling of utter hopelessness. Ahead of him, he saw no one passing in the main corridor, heard no sounds of movement. Between coughs, he shouted, "Fire! Fire!" He hoped to cause a panic and fill the corridors so he could get lost in the shuffle, but he was suddenly struck with the fear that the whole floor was empty except for himself and the two armed men behind him.

P.W. fought to shut out the pain rocketing upward through his abdomen from his groin, but it was getting harder to do because the pain grew steadily, slowly worse, and the bullet wound in his shoulder was hurting worse than ever. On top of that, he was exhausted. And, worst of all, he simply was not as young as he used to be.

P.W. stood up straight as a beefy man staggered out of the smoky room, wet, hacking, and covering his eyes with one hand while holding a gun with the other.

"Shaw!" the man called, hoarse and gasping. "You fucking son of a bitch, I'm gonna rip your head off and shit down your goddamned—"

The man's words were interrupted by more coughing, and as he was doubled over hacking, P.W. simply plucked the gun from his hand. The man stood up, bleary eyes blinking, but before he could focus on anything, P.W. brought the butt of the gun down hard on the man's temple. He hit the floor without making another sound.

P.W. peered into the doorway, through the smoke, which was not as thick as it first appeared, but he could not see any flames. The sprinklers, which were still spraying water down from the ceiling, seemed to have taken care of the fire, so there was no danger of it spreading. P.W. was relieved; he did not like the idea of going through all of this only to die in a burning building.

A cloying odor filled his nostrils. It was the same smell that had come from the burnt cab of Dr. Jorgan's car. Cooked flesh.

Squinting his eyes against the smoke and coughing a few times, he stepped inside and looked around.

To his right, a charred body lay on the floor. At least, it had been a body at one time. Now it was little more than blackened sticks of bone in a pile of ashes.

There was another to his left, lying on the broken remains of a coffee table and beside a smoldering sofa.

Somehow, the same thing that had been done to Dr. Jorgan had been done to the two crispy piles of remains on the office floor.

P.W. stuffed the fat man's gun under his belt and reached into his coat pocket for the gun he had taken from Shaw.

"Son of a bitch," he muttered when he realized it was a squirt gun. But he doubted it was filled with water.

While P.W. stared at the two piles of blackened remains, Shaw was staring at some bodies, as well. He had discovered them when he bolted out of the narrow corridor that led to his office.

The first, sprawled just a few feet away from him, was a middle-aged woman in a lab coat. He could not remember her name—that sort of thing was irrelevant to Shaw—but he had seen her around. Her eyes were open and there was blood on her face. It had come from her nostrils and dribbled over her cheeks to her ears and throat.

Another was curled up around the base of a drinking fountain. Two more were in the middle of the floor farther down the corridor.

The alarm bell rang on and on. None of the bodies moved.

The sound of his own rapid, thundering heartbeat overwhelmed the shrieking fire alarm in Shaw's ears as fear rose in him like mercury in a thermometer. His knees weakened as he stared at the bodies and he tremulously breathed a single word over and over.

"Emma...Emma...Emma..."

He did not take time to wonder how she had come around so quickly or how she had managed to do so much damage in such a short time. He had to get out.

He gulped repeatedly, although his mouth was bone dry and he had nothing to swallow. Moving away from the wall, he started running again.

Everything was out of control, out of *his* control. Emma was loose, Leo was trying to kill him, there was a shaggy-faced maniac with a gun behind him, and his security staff did not even *work* for him, they had *never* worked for him. Even his thoughts no longer seemed to be his own; they whipped around in his head like rubble being thrown around by a tornado. Panic was cutting off his airway like two strangling hands on his throat as he rounded a corner on his way to the stairs; he did not have time to bother with the elevator.

Shaw blurted a sound of surprise and jerked to a stop when he saw a man several feet away, between him and the door that led to the stairwell, leaning wearily against a wall. His clothes were soaked, his swollen face was covered with blood and his hair dangled in matted strands over his eyes. Behind him, more bodies lay in the corridor.

Shaw watched, mesmerized, as the man moved forward painfully, wheezing with each breath. He lifted his sagging head slowly, until his eyes—nearly swollen shut and glistening like two fresh cuts—met Shaw's.

"Who the hell are you?" Shaw said, voice low and breathy. "What're you doing here? You don't belong here." He was not speaking to the stranger so much as he was thinking out loud. The man looked like a street bum, like someone from a soup kitchen or...a mission. "Who *are* you?" Shaw said again, louder this time, voice stronger.

The stranger's mouth twitched, then curled up into a stiff, bloody aberration of a smile. His lips were so swollen that they completely covered his teeth; perhaps he had no teeth at all. When he spoke, the man's voice was thick and his words came slowly.

"I...been...looking f'you...Mr. Shaw."

Shaw's eyebrows rose above widened eyes. That was two

total strangers who knew his name in the last few minutes. One had a gun, and this one...this one was simply pathetic.

It occurred to Shaw that he did not have time for this. He did not *care* who this bloody stranger was, he had to get *out*.

Shaw rushed forward toward the stairs, keeping his distance from the man, who made no move to stop him.

A moment before Shaw reached the door, even as he was reaching for the knob, his knees buckled beneath him and he fell forward, slamming into the steel and dropping to the floor with a grunt. He scrambled onto his knees and slapped his right hand onto the doorknob. His palm was slick with sweat and his hand fell away as if the knob had been greased. When he reached for it again, he realized how heavy his arm felt. Like lead. Sweaty lead. Impossible to lift up to that doorknob. Impossible. He had no choice but to let his arm drop.

His whole body felt heavy, and now he was sweating profusely, much worse than before, rivulets of it running down his face and back, dribbling over his ribs. And yet he felt cold, as if he were in a meat locker, and a shiver passed through him, so severe that he made a quavering sound in his throat. The shivering stayed with him, uncontrollable and disabling.

The steel door before him blurred into soft focus, then became clear, then blurred again.

In his ears, deep inside his head, another sound joined the beating of his heart and the cry of the fire alarm. It was the high, keening ring that sounded after a head injury or accompanied by a high fever.

His stomach began to churn. It was not the usual burning sensation that he felt so often; it was a nauseating roiling.

Shaw fell over on the floor, landing on his right side. Something was terribly wrong and he was afraid now, filled with genuine fear because something he did not understand was happening to him.

He lifted his head and looked around. His watery eyes could not see much, but he saw well enough to know that Emma was nowhere near him. The only movement he saw was that of the bloody-faced stranger, who had turned around and was now facing him.

The man dropped to one knee, leaning his shoulder against the wall.

Shaw blinked a few times until his vision was clear enough to see that the man was still smiling through all that blood.

"Not feeling...so good...are you...Mr. Shaw?" the man rasped through his swollen smile.

Shaw tried to speak, even though he was not sure what he was going to say, but instead, he vomited on the floor. Powerful convulsions worked through his body as a great wave of vomitus spewed up and out of his throat and splattered onto the carpet, splashing droplets back up in his face.

"Think maybe...you got...a flu bug...Mr. Shaw?"

Shaw coughed and spat and tried to crawl crab-like away from the puddle, but collapsed beside it, groaning miserably, weakly. He looked up at the stranger, who was skewed sideways because of the way Shaw was lying, and tried once again to speak. But he could not. Not just yet. The weakness was overpowering and his throat was burning and he was too busy worrying that he would vomit again, because there was more activity going on in his stomach.

The stranger laughed. It was a coarse sound, and it was accompanied by a cry of pain. Then he fell silent, his wheezy breathing quick and shallow.

Shaw's nausea began to pass rather suddenly. The shivering calmed and the ringing in his ears began to fade. Shaw breathed a quiet sigh of relief, certain that, in a moment, he would be able to get up and go on his way.

"Where's Emma?" the bloody stranger said.

"Whuh-what?" Shaw croaked.

"Where's Emma?"

The chill passed; instead of feeling unbearably cold, Shaw felt hot and clammy and uncomfortable in his clothes, which were clinging to his moist body. He let go another sigh, smiling a little, indulging himself in his hasty and unexpected recovering. He ignored the stranger.

Shaw got on his hands and knees and prepared to stand, still weak from his sickness but eager to keep moving. He hefted himself up on one knee, grabbed the doorknob, and was about to get on his feet when the stranger spoke again.

"I said...where...is Emma?"

Lifting his head slowly, Shaw turned to the man and said, "Fuck you, okay?"

"No. No. Not okay."

Shaw's limbs collapsed and he vomited explosively again, both at the same time. He vomited on his left arm as his body slapped to the floor. He wondered vaguely how he could possibly throw up so *much*. He tasted blood this time, and an instant later, he felt a warm, wet dribbling sensation in his nostrils. His nose was bleeding. And his heart jittered around in his chest, pounding irregularly in his ears.

"Oh, God," he whimpered, his body shivering again as sweat poured off of him once more. "Oh, my God."

"Thass no...flu bug you've got...Mr. Shaw," the stranger said. "Juss a...touch of...Biofire. Thass all."

"Oh, Jesus Christ, how...how can you...how..."

"Tell me...where is she?"

"Who *are* you? How...can you..."

"Tell me...or I'll kill you now...and find her myself. Or maybe...you'd like...to be a vegetable. How about a stroke, Mr. Shaw? A massive...stroke."

Shaw's mind was becoming more of a jumble with every second that ticked by, and that frightened him, because even though he did not know who the man was, it was obvious that he possessed the same ability as Emma, and if Shaw waited too long, he might not be able to answer the man's question at all. He might be dead. Or worse.

"Fourth floor," Shaw said, coughing. "An isolation chamber. I-I...I don't know...which one. Fourth...floor."

From down the corridor, a voice called, "Hey, McNolte, how you doin'?"

"Back off, P.W.," the man replied as loudly as he could, which was not very loud at all. "I don't...want...to hurt you."

"Yeah, yeah, I know, I'm keepin' my distance, but...you're on the *floor*, babe, so I'm worried. It doesn't look good."

"Fourth floor, P.W., she's...on the fourth floor...in an... isolation chamber."

"I got Ty with me here, McNolte, and Buddy's on the fourth floor right now. You sure she's up there?"

"According to…Mr. Shaw, yes…she's there. Go get her, P.W. Please."

"Okay, listen, McNolte, I'm leaving Ty here with you. I'm on my way up right now."

"Stay…away…Ty," McNolte said, his voice weak.

"Hey, I'm stayin' away, but…I'm right here, Mr. McNolte, don't you worry, I'm right here."

In the blurry distance, Shaw saw a figure hurry away while another stayed. He fought to get up off the floor, battled to lift himself to his knees. After years of countless push-ups and crunches and endless hours in the gym on the best equipment money could buy, he could not make his limbs lift him up from the floor because they were now beyond his control. When he tried to push himself up, his arms and legs quaked with weakness and shivered from the chill of his fever, and he dropped back onto the floor, helpless.

"Don't worry, Mr. Shaw," the man called McNolte said, his voice like gravel being ground together. "I'm not going…to kill you. I don't have…the energy. I'm kinda…flamed out."

Shaw felt a wave of relief pass through him, and he closed his eyes, listening to his heart pound and his breath rush in and out.

"Besides," McNolte went on, "you're no good…dead. We've got…so much on you…on what you've…been doing…you'll be in…so much trouble…for so long…" He laughed, and it was followed by a cry of pain.

Shaw felt relief coming again. The nausea, the chills, the bone-deep weakness all began to fade.

"I'm not…gonna…kill you…Mr. Shaw," McNolte said.

Shaw managed to get to his knees. He grabbed the doorknob again.

"I'm just…"

Shaw's first attempt to turn the knob failed because his palm was so sweaty, but he was able to plant one foot on the floor. He got a grip on the doorknob as he started to lift himself to his feet.

"...gonna make you..."

Clutching the doorknob with both hands, he lifted himself up, up, up, until he was standing on both feet.

"...wish you were dead."

Shaw's limbs betrayed him. He dropped to the floor again. His stomach erupted and he turned on his side and retched, but nothing came up. Just dry heaves. Again and again and again.

His bowels released with a farting sound and he filled his pants with liquidy feces, again and again, as his stomach continued to convulse, throwing up nothing, again and again.

"Don't worry...Mr. Shaw," McNolte croaked. "Iss juss...a touch...of Biofire. You'll...get over it."

40.
COLONEL LELAND TRAVIS

From the *Searchlight*:

OUTBREAK AT ODYSSEYCORP!
27 FOUND DEAD!
3 COMATOSE!
DOZENS INJURED!

Twenty-seven employees were found dead of undetermined causes in a building containing the deadliest virus known to man! Emergency Services workers refused to comment after setting up roadblocks for a twenty mile radius around OdysseyCorp Labs yesterday morning.

Among the injured were Landon Shaw, founder and CEO of the research and development laboratory that strives to end the suffering of millions by finding cures to the world's most dangerous incurable diseases. Shaw was unavailable to comment; sources close to him say he is very ill.

Along with hazardous viruses and diseases, OdysseyCorp is said by experts to be a center for secret UFO research. Many have speculated that the employees were affected by a dangerous alien plague brought to earth by a UFO....

From the *Journal*:

Landon Shaw, CEO of OdysseyCorp Labs, has been arrested for the murder of an unidentified woman whose body he allegedly used to fake the death of his wife, Emma Shaw.

A *Mercedes-Benz registered to Shaw was fished out of the Thunderhead River one week ago with a woman's body strapped into the driver's seat nearly a year after Mrs. Shaw's sudden disappearance. The body was identified as Mrs. Shaw's and was cremated the next day.*

A woman identifying herself as Emma Shaw was admitted to Price-Deighton Hospital two days ago with severe head injuries. She was accompanied by two men, both of whom were also seriously injured, one of whom had suffered a gunshot wound.

Police were notified, and a positive identification was made of Mrs. Shaw, who claimed her husband had been holding her for months in OdysseyCorp Labs.

Shaw was hospitalized shortly after his wife, having been struck ill along with dozens of others in OdysseyCorp Labs after an undisclosed incident that left 27 dead. He was well enough, however, to be placed under arrest. A police officer has been posted outside Shaw's hospital room.

"We will investigate this thoroughly until we learn who was in that car," said Police Chief William Bingham. "But right now, all we can do is speculate, and this department is not in the business of speculation."

Mrs. Shaw was accompanied to Price-Deighton by writer Neil McNolte, who was badly beaten, and P.W. Meredith, a volunteer worker and resident at South Street Mission.

Two days ago, what was thought to be a gas leak in the mission rendered everyone in the building unconscious for about an hour. At the same time, an as yet unidentified man was burned to death in a car outside the building. Although the car in which the burn victim was found was registered to Dr. Alan Jorgan, an employee of OdysseyCorp Labs, and there was speculation that the gas released in the mission had been manufactured at OdysseyCorp Labs, no firm connection has yet been established between those incidents and Mrs. Shaw's falsified death.

A full investigation is underway and Chief Bingham has promised regular updates to keep the public apprised of the situation.

Low, throbbing waves of pain passed through P.W.'s shoulder, just far enough beneath the surface of his awareness to be negligible thanks to the pain medication, but irritating nonetheless. He sat on the edge of his hospital bed facing the narrow table on which his breakfast tray rested. Dr. Langley had ordered his breakfast, which was why it had been so damned boring.

"You need to change your diet," Dr. Langley had said during his visit just before breakfast arrived. "I'm letting you go today, but I want you to know that your cholesterol level is nearly equal to your weight. You're not a young man anymore and you can't afford numbers like that. I don't want you dropping dead of a heart attack, understand? Lots of vegetables and fruits. Cut out the red meat. No more rich foods, P.W., I mean it. I've ordered you a good, healthy breakfast, and I want you to pay attention to what's on your plate, because that's what you'd better start eating for breakfast every day from now on unless you want to go belly up."

Hot oatmeal, an apple, a banana, and a glass of orange juice. No eggs, no bacon, no sausage. No pancakes or hash browns. It was depressing.

P.W. shook his head as he pushed the wheeled table away, having eaten most of the breakfast.

"Not a young man anymore," he whispered to himself. He was more aware of that fact than Dr. Langley or anyone else. Nothing anyone said or did could prove more conclusively to P.W. that he was no longer a young man than what he had been through in the last few days.

Every muscle in his body groaned silently with pain. Muscles he had forgotten he possessed had been awakened and were protesting with twitches and cramps.

He knew that if he'd had some way of knowing what he was getting into before he had agreed to help McNolte, he would have done it, anyway. It would have been just as unwise as going into it blindly, of course, but he would have done it, anyway.

Then again, things had turned out pretty well, considering how disastrous things *could* have been. He and McNolte and

Emma were still alive, though worse for wear. And they were all in the same hospital, along with Mama Charity, with whom he had spoken earlier that morning. She was weak but doing well, and she had to change a lot of things in her life, too, including her diet, just like P.W. Maybe they could do that together. Maybe eating rice cakes and dry bran muffins would not be so bad if he had somebody to do it with, especially if that somebody was Mama Charity. It was her nature to approach every situation, every problem, with the same enthusiasm, determination, and positive outlook. Maybe some of those qualities would prove to be contagious. He hoped.

As the word "contagious" passed through his mind, P.W. thought of Emma and McNolte, as he had again and again ever since he had been brought to this sterile, lime-green room.

The doctor in charge of Emma at OdysseyCorp, a Dr. Mason, had fought P.W. at first, physically, punching him, kicking him. P.W. had driven two stiff fingers into the doctor's throat with a swift movement of his hand, sending him to the floor gagging and choking. When he was finally able to talk, he was little more help than he had been before.

"What were you going to do to her?" P.W. asked.

"Operate."

"Why? For what purpose?"

"To implant a chip in her brain that would enable us to control her ability so she couldn't flame us. It was going to intensify electronic interference in her brain to enable us to—"

"Okay, okay, that's enough of that shit. What would you have to do to stop it?"

The doctor looked at him with a puzzled squint. "Stop it? Stop what?"

"To *cure* her. To get rid of that...that *thing* in her head."

"*Cure* her?" the doctor said with a pained smirk. "You must be joking."

"Do I look like I'm joking?"

"No, no. Of course not. But there is no cure. What has been done to her is irreversible. She will be the way she is now for the rest of her life."

Dr. Mason had fled not long after that, and P.W. had been

unable to stop him. He had lost too much blood and was simply too weak to chase anyone.

The conversation with the doctor had been haunting P.W. ever since. If what he had said was true, then what *would* become of Emma and McNolte? Would they have to live the rest of their lives with such an odd and dangerous condition? Would they be *allowed* to live their lives by the authorities?

P.W. sighed as he stood and walked slowly away from the bed toward the closet. Willy had brought him some clean clothes, and P.W. wanted to get into them because he would be released soon, and he could not wait to get out. He despised hospitals. He had spent time in hospitals before, all of it nightmarish. Most of it in Vietnam. He could not get out soon enough. Besides, he wanted to be in some halfway decent clothes if the press caught him on the way out. They had attached themselves to the hospital like a giant, sucking parasite. He hoped to avoid them, but if he failed, he did not want to look like a weak and shaky hospital patient when he left. Even though that was exactly what he happened to be.

Dr. Langley also had told him that McNolte and Emma would be released today, as well, and P.W. had called Willy to let him know they would need a ride. He did not know where McNolte or Emma planned to go after leaving the hospital, but he wanted to make sure they all left together. Somehow, P.W. felt a need to keep an eye on them all, to take care of them.

He was opening his closet when the door of his room opened and a tall man stepped inside. His silver hair was close-cropped and he wore an overcoat open to reveal a dark blue suit. He held a black cane in his left hand and leaned on it with each step.

"P.W.?" the man said, smiling.

P.W. closed the closet door and grinned. "Travis?"

"Yours truly."

"Son of a bitch." P.W. laughed the words as he stepped forward and hugged the man cautiously, being mindful of his injured shoulder. "How you doin', man?" he said, taking a step back.

"Looks like I should be asking *you* that question. What're you doing in here, anyway?"

"Oh, hell, I'll be okay, don't worry 'bout me. I can't believe it. You came all this way to see me?"

"Yes. But I can't stay long."

"You're not in uniform."

"That's right. And officially—" Travis's smile melted away. "—I'm not here, either."

"Oh?"

"That's right. We haven't spoken. After I leave this room, you *still* haven't seen me since 1972."

"So, why are you...*not* here?"

"Mind if I sit?" he said, moving to the chair beside P.W.'s bed.

"Not at all." P.W. sat on the edge of the bed and faced Travis in the chair, his hands wrapped around the handle of the cane between his knees.

"I've got my ass on the line here, P.W.," Travis said quietly. "I'm not complaining, don't get me wrong, I owed you a favor and I've done everything I can to come through on it. I just want you to understand the situation."

"What's the situation?"

Travis took in a deep breath and let it out through pursed lips and puffed cheeks. "I've gone over this with General Horner. And over it and over it, if you know what I mean. We finally came to an agreement. But it was on my word. The agreement we reached goes like this: everything that you've been through never happened. Just like I'm not here now and we never spoke." He waited silently for P.W.'s response.

"Hey, look," P.W. said. "I'm happy to cooperate, you know that, but...I'm not sure I understand you."

"Have you seen this morning's paper?"

"The *Journal*? Oh, yeah, I saw it."

"The press is groping for answers. They won't find them. The answers don't exist. At least...they won't. Soon. What has happened is nothing more than a string of apparently connected incidents, admittedly strange incidents, which are, in fact, not connected at all. Just coincidence, nothing more."

P.W. nodded slowly. "Okay. But...do you think people will buy that?"

"They'll have no choice. They won't be able to find anything else when this is all done."

P.W. nodded even more slowly. He understood Travis's position, but he also understood Emma's, and he was sure she would not like this arrangement.

"I need you to understand this, P.W." Travis leaned forward over his cane, face stern. "I arranged this with General Horner on my word that you and your friends will simply walk away from everything that's happened. No interviews with the press about your ordeal, no exposés about OdysseyCorp, no lawsuits. Nothing. Do you understand me? *Nothing.*"

"Sure, Travis, I understand. But I can only speak for myself. My friends...well, Landon Shaw put them through hell, especially Emma. I can't promise that they won't try to—"

"*Listen* to me, P.W.," Travis said, his voice a thick whisper. "Horner's going to take care of Shaw. There won't be anyone for your friends to take revenge on, do you understand? No one. All you and your friends have to do is put this behind you. Forget it. Understand? Because if you don't...well, think about it, P.W."

Travis stood, leaning both hands on the cane in front of him. P.W. remained on the edge of the bed, but his eyes followed Travis's, which were dark and stern.

"Do you think the Pentagon is going to ignore the fact that Shaw was selling their secrets to his friends for big money under the table?" Travis said. "No, they won't. They want to wipe out every last trace of their relationship with OdysseyCorp. And can you blame them?"

P.W. shook his head slowly.

"The only problem is...*you.* And your friends. You are all a trace of the Pentagon's relationship with OdysseyCorp. Do you understand? And it's on my word alone that you're not going to be wiped out with all the other traces. Are you hearing me, P.W.?"

"I hear ya."

"I...I wanted to do you a favor, P.W. I wanted to pay you back for what you did for me, which was to save my life. I wouldn't be here if it weren't for you, and I want you to know that a day does not pass when I don't think of that, remember it, and feel grateful for it. So I wanted to do you a favor. But now, as it turns out...I'm saving *your* life. And the lives of your friends. I've done everything I can. You're all gonna be safe. As long as you can keep your mouths shut. Beyond that, I can't help you. If any of you breathe a word to anyone...if it gets back to the press...if something resembling this story so much as hits a lowlife *tabloid* in any form...you're all dead. All of you." He bowed his head a moment, then looked at P.W. with sad eyes. "I'm sorry to have to tell you this, P.W., but I've done all I can."

"You've done more than that, Travis," P.W. whispered. "I never felt I needed to be paid back for what happened back in 'seventy-two, but this...Travis, you've done more than pay me back, man. I mean it. And you have my word. None of this happened."

Travis smiled, but it was a weary, guilty smile. "I'm glad to hear it, P.W. And I believe you. I'm sorry that my favor had to work out this way, but—"

P.W. stood. "Hey, hey, you're talkin' like you dropped a snake in my shorts, or something. You saved my ass, man, mine and my friends'. Not another word from you, now, okay?"

"One more thing."

"What's that?"

Travis seemed to wince as he said it. "Don't call me. Or write. No communication. We can't afford it. We...don't know...each other, P.W. Not anymore. Understand?"

P.W. pursed his lips and nodded jerkily.

"I've got to go," Travis said, turning to the door. "There's a plane waiting for me, and I've already been delayed by traffic. I'm behind schedule."

When Travis turned back to face him, P.W. moved forward with his arms spread to hug him again.

Travis stiffened and stepped back, then held out his right hand to shake.

P.W.'s arms sagged and returned to his sides as he nodded slightly. He shook Travis's hand.

"You take care of yourself, P.W."

He shrugged and smirked. "Ain't takin' care of anybody else."

Travis left the room, and the door slowly swung closed behind him.

41.

COVERING THE TRACES

L eo Trafficante stepped into the elevator in his penthouse to go down to the ground floor of the Olympus Towers accompanied by a giant of a man named Anthony, who carried a large suitcase. They were on their way down to the car.

It was natural for those around Anthony to call him Tony, but he angrily insisted on Anthony. And no one argued with him. He stood six feet, nine and a half inches tall, and had hands so big that he could crush a human skull using only one of them, and with surprisingly little effort. Fortunately, there was little call for that sort of thing.

Anthony had been working for Leo for nearly a year, but only on odd jobs. After the deaths of Ollie and Tubo, Leo had immediately promoted Anthony and decided to keep him at his side at all times. In fact, he would be taking Anthony to the bathroom with him for a while.

They were on their way down to the car. Leo's new driver was a man who called himself Groucho, and he was a pretty big guy himself. He was not as big as Anthony, but who was? Anthony sat in the back seat with Leo.

The whole thing probably would blow over, Leo had little doubt of that. It was just a matter of time, waiting it out. But he had no idea how long that would take. In the meantime, he was determined to keep himself as well-protected as possible, just in case. There was no reason for anyone to believe, however, that he was connected to Shaw or OdysseyCorp. He knew Shaw kept no incriminating records of their transactions; he had made damned sure of that. There was no danger of anyone finding anything with Leo's name on it in Shaw's files. But that was not what worried him.

Leo was concerned about the man who had phoned both him and Shaw. He was worried about what that man knew, whoever he was. And he had been trying to find out who the son of a bitch was, but with no success. It was not the man who made the phone calls that Leo had to worry about. It was Uncle Sam. If the Pentagon learned that Shaw had been selling the lab's government work to him, then merely taking a breath would become a dangerous proposition for Leo. That was why he had doubled his security on everything from his apartment to his car.

And that was why he was on his way to Miami. Some sun would do him good. He was sick of the constant rain in this city, especially now, while he was in such a dark mood.

His jet was waiting at Jennick Airport. It had been gone over with the finest of fine-tooth combs, and he had received a call a few minutes ago, just before leaving the apartment, informing him that it was perfectly safe. His car had been inspected as well, with the same care and attention to detail, and also had been declared safe. Leo had been careful over the last few days to make sure he was not in the car when the engine was started; only after it had been closely inspected and was already running would he get inside. The life he had chosen for himself required a certain amount of paranoia at all times, but that paranoia had been amped up to full volume lately. He did not mind because he knew it would pass.

The elevator gave a gentle jolt as it began its descent. Leo reached over and hit a button on the panel and Dean Martin's velvety, boozy voice oozed like honey from the speakers in the wall of the elevator. Leo smiled as he seated himself on the cushioned bench jutting from the rear wall of the elevator.

He had honestly believed that he was going to die in Shaw's office. The smoke nearly had strangled him as he made his way out. He had thought he was home free when he reached the open doorway, but Santa Claus had stopped him. When he had regained consciousness, though, the man with the white beard had been gone.

Leo had gotten to his feet and rushed unsteadily to find an elevator. On the way, he found Shaw lying unconscious on the floor in a puddle of his own urine and vomit, stinking of shit. A few feet away lay another unconscious man, horribly beaten. And there were others lying everywhere, mostly unconscious, some dead, a few just regaining consciousness. The whole thing had given Leo the creeps. When he found an elevator, he used the key given to him by his man who served as head of security at OdysseyCorp to get downstairs and out of the building. He had driven himself back to the city, his face smudged with blackness from the smoke, tense and a little shaky after what he had just seen—two men bursting into flames. Shaw had simply squirted them with a squirt gun, and then, a moment later, they were on fire, burning as intensely as if they were full of jet fuel. They had died horrible deaths, Ollie and Tubo, and Leo was chilled to the bone by how close he had come to meeting the same fate.

But he was not going to let anything like that happen to him. He was not about to let Shaw or his people use any of the lab's bizarre concoctions on him. And he was not going to let Uncle Sam's foot soldiers catch up with him, either.

Leo owned three hotels in Miami, but he was not headed for any of them. Under the name Mortimer Lockman, he would be checking into the Beach Star Hotel, an establishment that targeted tourists on tight budgets, but who wanted a hotel with room service that was on the beach. Sure, the carpet was tacky, the mattresses were like old sponges, and the ice machines were noisy. But it would be safe for him. For a while.

Dean Martin crooned on as the elevator came to a cushioned stop. Leo stood and hit the button again, stopping the music as the doors slid open

Anthony stepped out first into the dark, unoccupied corridor that passed the entrance to the kitchen. Only employees used this corridor, and they knew better than to notice anything, including their boss walking out of an elevator.

Leo and Anthony walked past the kitchen entrance and down to the end of the corridor, to a door with a bright red and white sign on it that read, EMERGENCY EXIT ONLY—ALARM

SOUNDS WHEN OPENED, and Anthony pushed the door open. No alarm sounded. They walked outside into the gray, rainy morning to the car, which waited with engine idling. Anthony opened the door and stepped back to let Leo slide in. After closing the door, he walked around the rear of the car and got behind the wheel on the other side.

The rectangle of tinted glass was raised between the front and back seats, so Leo punched the intercom's button with his thumb.

" Jennick Airport, Groucho," Leo said, although Groucho already knew where they were going.

Leo hit another button and Mel Torme began to sing. The Velvet Fog filled the space around Leo and he leaned back, tilting his head backward and joining his hands over his belly, smiling slightly at the thought of Miami's warm sun on his body.

The explosion was enormous, loud, and fiery. The car's four doors shot outward like huge bullets fired from guns, and the hood and trunk rose high into the air, where they levitated for just a moment before hurtling back down toward the flames that belched upward.

There was no sound from anyone in the car. They had no time to cry out. They were dismembered instantly, limbs and heads blown in every direction in ragged, blackened, bloody pieces. Whatever was left over was burned in the fire.

"Special Agent Brandon, FBI," the tall man in the dark suit said as he entered Shaw's hospital room. His dark hair was cut short, face angular with nondescript features, like a department store mannequin, beige trench coat wet from the rain outside. He carried a Styrofoam cup of coffee in each hand. "How are you feeling , Mr. Shaw?"

He was feeling better, but still not well, not at all. But he was not about to show any weakness to this government goon, so he nodded once and said, "I'm not saying anything until my attorney is present." His voice was dry and raspy.

"That's fine." Brandon set one cup of coffee on Shaw's bedside table, then wheeled the tabletop over the bed so he could reach it. "Feel up to some coffee, Mr. Shaw? You look like you could use it. I asked the nurse and she said it was okay. Hope you don't mind cream and sugar. I didn't know how you liked it." He began to pace slowly at the foot of the bed, never meeting Shaw's eyes.

Shaw was terribly weak and shaky, but he had stopped throwing up, and his stomach and bowels had settled. The aroma coming from the steaming cup was enticing. Besides, he was cold. Why did they always keep hospital thermostats so damned low? His hands trembled as he reached out for the coffee, lifted it with both hands to his lips, and sipped it cautiously. It was hot and delicious.

"Whose body was in that car, Mr. Shaw?" Brandon asked.

Shaw's brow creased as he took another sip of coffee. The warm cup felt good between both palms. "I told you, I'm not answering any questions without my lawyer present. Why the hell is the FBI involved with this, anyway? Where's the police detective I talked to yesterday?"

"This isn't just a homicide case, Mr. Shaw. I think you know that." Brandon took a drink of his coffee and licked his lips. "Your troubles go far deeper than that, I'm afraid."

"What are you talking about?"

Brandon did not respond, just continue to slowly pace and sip his coffee.

"Show me some ID," Shaw said, trying to sound firm and in control as he sat up straighter in bed.

Brandon ignored the demand. "A lot of people want to know about that body in the river, Mr. Shaw. They feel betrayed. Maybe *cheated* is a better word."

Shaw felt his breaths coming more rapidly, felt his chest tighten. He willed himself to calm down, took a couple of slow, deep breaths. He took a couple of swallows of the coffee. Although it was beginning to cool, but it burned all the way down when he swallowed it this time, and he felt the first hints of churning low in his gut, which was never a good sign.

Brandon stopped pacing and faced him. "A man like you can get away with a whole lot of things, Mr. Shaw," he said, so softly that Shaw had difficulty hearing him. "But cheating your country is not one of them. No one ever gets away with that in the end." He finished his coffee, crushed the Styrofoam in his fist, and threw it in the waste can beside the bed.

Shaw realized that Brandon had not been speaking softly; it was the growing ringing in his own ears that made the man's words difficult to hear.

Brandon came over to the bedside as Shaw began to feel a liquidy weakness moving through his body, sinking into his bones.

Leaning close, Brandon said, "I have a message for you from General Horner."

Shaw's vision blurred and it became difficult to breathe. He looked down at the cup of half-drunk coffee in his hand, which he knew he would not be able to hold onto much longer. He wondered what they had used...if it was something that had come from his own lab.

Brandon took the cup from Shaw's hand as he whispered, "Get well soon."

Shaw was dead by the time the man left the room, taking the cup of poisoned coffee with him.

From the *Journal:*

EXPLOSION DESTROYS ODYSSEYCORP
Investigation of Lab Halted by Fire

An explosion started a fire in OdysseyCorp Labs that firefighters could not contain. The explosion occurred at approximately four a.m. The lab had been shut down and no one was inside at the time. One firefighter sustained injuries while trying to battle the blaze. The building was burned to the ground.

The explosion came less than 12 hours after the death of founder and CEO Landon Shaw, who was under investigation for murder. Shaw died of complications brought on by an illness that broke out inside OdysseyCorp and killed 27 other people.

Police are investigating the possibility that the explosion was terrorist-related, although OdysseyCorp had no known government ties....

42.

MCNOLTE AND EMMA

When a popular movie star—a man who was, in fact, the number one box office draw in the world—was involved in a drug-related murder and arrested in a posh Hollywood brothel, stories of the continuing investigation into what had killed twenty-seven people—twenty-eight including Landon Shaw—at OdysseyCorp Labs, as well as the investigation into the orchestrated "death" and subsequent reappearance of Emma Shaw, became less frequent and steadily appeared farther away from page one. Everyone was too busy following the sordid story of the fallen movie star to keep up with something so mundane. Soon, the Hollywood scandal was competing with coverage of a school shooting in Michigan, shoving the OdysseyCorp story even further into the busy background of news stories from around the world.

It was not long before the media left Emma alone and no longer showed up at South Street in search of some connection between the incident there and the deaths at the research lab. Life went on at South Street as it always had.

Mama Charity recovered from her heart attack. It had not been a severe one, but Dr. Langley assured her that if she did not make some changes in her life, the next one would be. She began dieting, exercising at a nearby gym, and working easier hours, and she did it all with just as much enthusiasm as she did everything else. P.W. was inspired to join her. Dr. Langley monitored their weight, cholesterol and blood pressure levels, and saw positive results in the first month, and Irving built them an exercise bike, which they took turns using down in the basement.

Emma stayed in the basement for a few months to let everything cool down. The press did not know she was there, and she kept a low profile as she worked at the mission.

McNolte let his apartment go and moved into the South Street basement with Emma. It made Willy a bit uncomfortable, but Mama just told him to hush, and he always did.

McNolte still had some questions for P.W., but none of them spoke of what had happened to them, what they had been through, so he did not ask them for a long time. He did not know it, but P.W. had a lot of questions for him, too. One day, while they were hauling some garbage to the dumpster in the alley behind the building, P.W. spoke up first.

"Hey, babe, how's your health?"

"My health?"

"Yeah, you know, your...*health*."

McNolte smiled. "You're asking about the Biofire effects."

"Biofire effects? Why, Mr. McNolte, I haven't a clue what you're talking about."

"Smartass. Don't worry about us, P.W. We've learned to control it. We're working toward making it completely dormant. We can't see anyone about it because we're afraid it would get out, the government would find out, and they'd be all over us as soon as they knew we'd been subjects in that project and found out we have the abilities we have. So we're doing our best to put those abilities away. To make them hibernate."

"Emma's doing okay?"

"Oh, yeah, she's doing very well. She talked to her attorney, you know. She's selling their...well, *her* estate. She wants to start looking for another house. We haven't decided where yet."

"We?"

McNolte smiled. "We're getting married."

P.W. grinned and wrapped an arm around McNolte's shoulders, pulling him close. "Well, hot *damn*, boy, you been holdin' out on me? Why didn't you say somethin' sooner?"

"We didn't even know until last night."

"That's some great news, McNolte, really great. You'll name the first bambino after me if it's a boy, of course. Won'tcha?"

"We can think about it. I don't know how Emma feels about initials for names."

P.W. took a step back, and held out his hand to shake. "Paul William Meredith. Pleasure to make your acquaintance."

"Paul William, huh?

"Yeah. Hell, I ain't told anybody that since Christ was a corporal. Everybody's always called me P.W. since I was in diapers."

"Okay, Paul William, can I ask you a question?"

"You know you can ask me anything you want."

"Those guys you told me about, the ones who worked for Trafficante and the ones who worked for Shaw—you never told me what happened to them when they came to the mission. What did you do with them?"

P.W. kept smiling, but something passed behind his eyes, something dark and quiet. "You can ask me anything but that, McNolte," P.W. said quietly. "You don't wanna know."

McNolte never asked again.

At night, in the basement, McNolte and Emma pushed their beds together and wove fantasies about where they would live and what their new house would be like. They could go anywhere they wanted and buy, or even build, the house of their dreams. They could afford it.

Emma said she wanted to buy an iguana and name it Rupert and let it roam the house as it pleased. McNolte wanted a roomy office in which to write, with plenty of windows to let in the sunlight.

Soon, their voices would lower to murmurs, and their murmurs would become sighs as they kissed and caressed one another. And then, as the radio played and the sounds of the mission's life drifted down now and then from upstairs, they would do things to one another's bodies...inside one another's bodies.

They would do things to each other that no one else in the world could do.

ABOUT THE AUTHOR

Ray Garton has been writing novels, novellas, short stories, and essays for more than 30 years. His work spans the genres of horror, crime, suspense, and even comedy. Live Girls was nominated for the Bram Stoker Award in 1988, and Garton received the Grand Master of Horror Award at the 2006 World Horror Convention. He lives in northern California with his wife Dawn, where he is at work on a new novel.

Curious about other Crossroad Press books?
Stop by our site:
http://store.crossroadpress.com
We offer quality writing
in digital, audio, and print formats.

www.ingramcontent.com/pod-product-compliance
Lightning Source LLC
Chambersburg PA
CBHW030756260626
47169CB00001B/78